CHOOSE
THE SKY

ALSO BY ELIZABETH COLE

CHOOSE THE SKY

ELIZABETH COLE

SKYSPARK BOOKS

PHILADELPHIA, PENNSYLVANIA

SkySpark Books
Philadelphia, Pennsylvania
skysparkbooks.com
inquiry@skysparkbooks.com

Publisher's Note: This is a work of fiction. Names, characters,
places, and incidents are a product of the author's imagination.
Locales and public names are sometimes used for atmospheric
purposes. Any resemblance to actual people, living or dead, or to
businesses, companies, events, institutions, or locales is completely coincidental.

Ordering Information:
Quantity sales. Special discounts are available on quantity purchases by corporations, associations, and others. For details,
contact the "Special Sales Department" at the address above.

CHOOSE THE SKY / Cole, Elizabeth. – 1st ed.
ISBN-10: 1-942316-18-6
ISBN-13: 978-1-942316-18-3

Chapter 1

THE GREY DARKENED TO A dull twilight, with only a red stain in the west to show where the sun was hiding. The lady Domina de Warewic pulled her cloak tighter, trying to bury her chin in the soft white fur of the collar. Then a gust pushed one red curl of hair across her face, and she braved the cold to tuck the lock back into her braid with bare fingers.

Despite the wet, biting wind, she kept watching the sky. From her vantage point at the top of the tallest tower of Trumwell Castle, she could see for miles in every direction. The view was not inspiring at the moment, considering the grim weather and the lack of any color in the late autumn landscape. Trees, now stripped of their leaves, stood silent and resolute, a forest waiting for winter.

The waters of the river to the west barely glimmered now, reflecting only a steel grey sky. Aside from the wind that tangled the smallest branches, nothing moved.

Domina exhaled a puff of steamy breath when something caught her eye down below. A single rider approached the castle, the horse's hooves pounding the track on the road from the east.

A messenger from one of the neighboring manors, she guessed, or perhaps one of the larger towns in Shropshire where the de Warewic family did a little business. She didn't leave her post yet. Any message would be brought to her, for she was the lady of the castle now. Indeed, within a quarter of an hour, one of the castle's footmen found her.

"My lady," said the footman, with a bow. "This just came for Lord Godfrey."

She took the slender, cylindrical case he offered. With surprise, she saw the sigil of King Stephen on the outside. Uneasiness filled her, but she kept a calm face. "See that the messenger is fed well and shown quarters for the night. Let the king's servant report that our hospitality was not lacking."

"Yes, my lady."

Domina expected no less, of course, but it never hurt to remind people of their duties. Her estate was far from the civilized centers of the world, but that was no reason to forgo chivalry.

"Go then," she said.

"My lady," the servant said hesitantly, "I believe the messenger expects to bring an answer back."

"He's not going anywhere tonight," Domina replied. "He can wait. Tell him I will bring this letter to my father personally. You may say exactly that, and no more."

"I understand, my lady." The footman bowed again, and then dashed off.

She was left alone, staring at the sealed container holding news from the king himself. It felt uncommonly heavy in her hands. There were penalties for betraying the king's confidence, and breaking a sealed letter addressed to anyone but her was surely a violation. The letter was intended only for her father, Godfrey de Warewic.

"If I read it aloud to him, it will be just as if he read the paper himself," she said to reassure herself. She was performing a filial duty—assisting her father in every way she could, just as she'd done for years.

She descended the steps of the tower, eventually emerging into the castle courtyard. Unlike many such spaces, this one was partially paved in stone—broad, flat rocks hewn from the hills nearby, along the border between England and Wales. The pavers were an extravagance from the castle's first construction, but one she appreciated every day, for it kept the ground from turning to mud in the wet months, or stirring up dust clouds in the dry summer.

Her leather-shod feet moved silently over the stone, but even so, she felt as if she was being watched. She knew that it was only because a stranger was within the walls. The message was harmless, but over the past few years, she'd grown reclusive. As soon as this messenger left the next day, she'd feel better.

Domina turned sharply, walking to a doorway of a two-story building in the far corner of the grounds. Most people would expect the lord of the castle to be within the keep itself, but she went to the more modest structure built of heavy, dark wooden beams, and covered in white plaster. The ground floor was given over to storage of wine and spirits. Above that, however, was a residence. Domina climbed the steps slowly. At the top, a servant was waiting.

"My lady," the maid said, with a curtsey. She was around fifty years of age and carried herself with the confidence of long practice and familiarity. No one had to be told that this woman served in Trumwell Castle her whole life. "He's awake."

"Good. Leave us, Beatrice. I wish to spend some time alone with him."

The maid nodded and allowed Domina to pass, then drew the door shut.

Domina peered into a room lit only by the fireplace and a few candles. The scent of beeswax sweetened the air, but no candle could brighten the mood.

A man lay in the center of a large four poster bed. Curtains covered three sides, but the left hand side, which faced the fire, remained drawn aside, exposing the space within.

The man's eyes were open, and he turned at the sound of her feet.

"Father," Domina said, as she perched on the side of the bed. "It's me, Mina. I'm glad to see you."

He smiled at her, but there was no recognition in his deep brown eyes, the same eyes she'd inherited. Domina's heart sank. So often, this was the expression he greeted her with. Her own father forgot who she was.

"Is it night?" he asked.

"Almost. Has Beatrice given you supper yet?" She saw a tray by the window, with the dishes empty. "Ah, yes. Beef stew, I think. Did you enjoy it?"

He nodded, but said, "Was there no partridge? I like partridge."

"Yes!" She was unreasonably happy he remembered this detail. "You do like partridge, Father. I'll ask the cooks to prepare you some, once we have more in the kitchens."

"The ones you hunt, Mina," he added. "I like those best, for they're the freshest."

"Of course," she said, beaming at him. Ah, he remembered something! He remembered how she always went hunting with her falcons. It was one of her favorite pastimes.

"Have you come to sing to me?" he asked then.

"If you like, Father. But first, I must read you a letter that's come from the king."

"Whatever our king asks, we give," her father said, his voice suddenly much more forceful, as it had been before his collapse.

"Be easy," she murmured. "Let me read."

She broke the heavy wax seal and scanned the words. It was written in French, of course, the language of the court. Domina read French, a little Latin, and even the rough English used by many in the countryside. She'd been well-educated for a lady. She frowned as she finished the brief missive.

"What is it?" her father asked.

"The king sends his greetings, and prays for your good health," Domina said, which was true enough, since that was how the letter began. The words were formulaic, written down by some scribe who wrote a dozen letters like this in a day. The second half of the letter was what made her worried, but she would never distress her already burdened father with news he could do nothing about—if he even understood what she told him.

"King Henry passed away," her father said, in an irritated, querulous tone.

"Yes," Mina agreed. "This comes from his successor,

King Stephen. You met him at his coronation."

"Did I?"

"When you swore fealty," she reminded him. "Remember? You said Trumwell Castle would always be held in his name."

Her father closed his eyes and settled back against the pillow. "I don't remember. Sing to me."

"Just one song." Her mind was racing, and she had little time to linger, much as she would like to.

"Two."

Mina smiled. Some things never changed. "Two, then."

She began to sing a lilting tune in French, one that her mother sang to her and one her father loved. He was asleep before she reached the third verse, so Mina dropped her voice as she eased her way out of the room. At least one member of the family should be able to sleep in peace.

* * * *

Leaving her father's small apartment in the separate building, Domina crossed the courtyard and swept into the main hall of the keep where a number of the castle residents were gathered, enjoying the warmth of the massive fireplace. Her maid Constance, who had been sipping a cup of ale near the fire, rose to her feet at once.

"My lady," she said. "What do you require?"

Domina waved one hand to silence her. "I have a task for you, Constance. Pack a trunk for me, and include my newest gown. Pack for yourself as well. We go to London tomorrow, and may remain up to a week."

Constance nodded and left immediately.

Domina turned to a man who was also sitting by the fire. Haldan was in charge of the castle's garrison, and in her father's practical absence, he was the highest-ranking military man at Trumwell.

He certainly looked like a soldier, with a big and rangy build and a smattering of little scars testifying to his experience in combat. He seemed to not take life too seriously, however, for he was more often found with a mug of ale in his hand than a sword. He had light blond hair and blue eyes that often attracted attention from local women, sometimes to their sorrow.

Mina told Haldan, "Arrange for a suitable escort for me and Constance for tomorrow morning. I want no delays."

He didn't even rise from his bench. "Winter is nearly upon us! Such a journey there and back will take weeks. Are you certain you wish to go?"

"What I wish or not is no concern of yours," she said. "Three men-at-arms should be sufficient, and two squires as well. Giles can lead them. Go now and choose, as well as the horses. Tomorrow we ride out."

He smiled and drained his ale, slowly, before putting the mug back on the table and rising lazily to his feet. "Yes, my lady."

"Present yourself to me when you are done. I'll have instructions regarding the protection of Trumwell while I'm gone."

His eyes lit up. "Yes, my lady!"

He left quickly, likely due to the notion of getting to play lord during her absence, even though Ancel the steward was the one who would ensure that order was maintained.

Domina sighed. If only her cousin Joscelin were still

living at Trumwell. She sorely missed the support of a male relative. Joscelin tried to return to visit whenever he could, but his commitment to the church—not to mention the difficulty of travel—meant that he was gone for long stretches at a time.

Even though Joscelin was as slight and frail as Haldan was strong, Mina had faith that her cousin would have no trouble with Haldan. Men didn't question an order when it came from another man. She prayed for her father's return to health. So many problems would be solved!

Up in her chamber, Domina faced more questions from Constance. The maid had served Domina for years, having grown up in the village nearby. She was a rather plain woman, by most accounts, with stick-straight, dark blond hair she wore in a braid. She had a broad face, thin lips, and eyes she herself described as muddy. Yet Constance possessed a quiet grace of her own, and Domina sometimes wondered if any man was going to seek her out as a wife. On the other hand, Constance never cast her eye at anyone, as far as Mina could tell. Perhaps she was happy as she was.

"What is the news, my lady?" Constance asked.

"According to the message I received today, the king requests the presence of Godfrey de Warewic at court," Mina explained, showing Constance the letter, though her maid could not read.

Constance touched the image of the king's royal coat of arms with reverence, impressed by the missive. "He requests your father's presence. How exciting! But the lord cannot travel."

"Certainly not," Mina agreed. "Yet I'd not dare invite curiosity by saying so, or mentioning any weakness at all. Thus, I'll go in his stead."

"Is that wise, my lady? Your father needs you. The whole castle needs you."

"What other choice do I have?" Domina said. "The steward will take charge in my absence, which I pray will not be long. Likely it is some bureaucratic matter, and I can answer those questions as well as my father could anyway. While I'm in London, I can meet with Joscelin and let him know how everyone at Trumwell is faring."

"It will be good to speak with your cousin," Constance said approvingly. "Perhaps he'll come back with you."

Donna shook her head. "I think that at this stage of his studies, he must remain in London unless there is a crisis. I can protect Trumwell as well. Above all, the family of de Warewic must appear strong. We must let no one suspect that my father is indisposed. If they do…"

She didn't have to finish. The military reputation of Godfrey de Warewic, and of his father before him, was so well-known that people assumed the castle was undefeatable, with a large garrison of soldiers ready to rush out at any moment. Domina had heard so many stories about her father's exploits in the Holy Land, of the battles he'd fought in and the prizes he'd taken. His past alone was formidable protection…as long as people thought he was still hale.

In truth, since her father's sudden, unexplained collapse, Domina had to take control of all their family's lands, and she was not nearly so astute when it came to defense. She studied as much as she could, and she knew enough to present a strong front. But two thin harvests in a row meant that she could ill afford a large garrison. She spent what little money she had very carefully, and prayed for her father's health to return.

Until then, only the ignorance of others protected her.

If the Welsh heard of her father's weakness, they might attack. If any nobles heard of it, they'd work to take her lands. If the king heard of it...Domina didn't want to think of it. As a woman, she'd be given no say in her future, or the future of all her people. At best, she'd be packed off to a nunnery while some oaf was given her title and lands. At worst, she'd be married to one of the king's allies simply so he could maintain the castle in the king's name. He'd be a mindless brute chosen for his skill in battle, and nothing else. She knew what sort of men populated the king's army, and they were nothing like the noble warriors of her father's ilk. Many of those who called themselves knights were often just brigands.

She'd never allow such a man to pass through her castle gates.

But first, she had to endure a trip to London and back, while pretending all was well and concealing the truth.

Chapter 2

JUST OUTSIDE THE DOORWAY OF the building where they'd been cooped up that day, Luc of Breacon stretched his entire body, all six feet of it, and pushed his hands into the air as high as they would go. "At last! I thought the mindless chatter would never end," Luc said to his friend Octavian.

The other knight said slyly, "I thought you thrived on politics. What's the saying? 'You can't master the game if you don't play.'"

Luc made a face. "Don't quote my father's words to me. I've heard them often enough."

And now he was following in his father's footsteps, advancing the Braecon family fortune by maneuvering through the court of King Stephen. It wasn't always as exciting as he'd imagined it to be. "Never would I have guessed that sitting on a padded bench could be painful. But after eight hours, I'd rather fight a battle!"

"At least on a battlefield, you know who wants to stab you. These meetings of all the barons and such...I'm not sure who's friend or foe." Octavian spoke simple truth, for he'd been born far away in the Holy Land. He had only been in England for a few years, and he had much to learn about the politics of the country, which were currently far more turbulent than usual.

"You're doing well, Tav," Luc told him, quite honestly.

"It helps that no one expects me to know anything," Tav replied, a smile crossing his brown-skinned face. "I just listen, so I can report back to my liege lord...not that he troubles himself much about the matters at hand."

Octavian served a lord who owned lands in England, France, and the Holy Land. As a result, his attention was rather divided, and Octavian had considerable leeway to do as he liked, so long as his work served the king.

In contrast, the lords of Braecon had always been close to the royal family, ever since the Conqueror first came to the shores of England and began his reign. Luc was trained as a knight, but he was raised as a noble who would eventually inherit his father's title. As such, he lived and breathed politics. That was his father's desire, and Luc never saw a reason to doubt his path. He would carry on his family's legacy by making himself truly indispensable to King Stephen. During much of this year, his help was needed, for the king had been captured in battle and imprisoned for months by his rival the Empress Maud. Luc's family helped Stephen's queen keep control until Stephen was free again.

The king used his newfound freedom to convene council after council of his supporters. He wanted a resolution to the war, and he wanted to know who he could rely on. Luc was determined that the name of Braecon would be on that list.

He'd already proved his loyalty, in fact. Since being wounded in battle last year, Luc spent months recuperating. He knew he was lucky to be alive, and yet he chafed at the long period of forced inactivity. He was recovered now, praise God, but he hadn't yet returned to the battlefield. Instead, he fought other battles. He was glad his friend Octavian was at his side for many of them. Though they had only met a few years ago and came from wildly different backgrounds, Luc trusted Tav implicitly. They'd fought side by side, and that created a unique bond.

"Shall we find our lodgings?" Tav asked then, looking around.

It was night, and the streets of London were mostly shadows, lit only by occasional torches on a building wall. The two men started to walk to the house of Luc's relative, who graciously hosted them both. Despite the late hour, neither showed much concern about their surroundings. This was not surprising, since both were armed, like the knights they were.

At several points, people who crossed their path looked at them and quickly changed direction, or looked away. Octavian's face pulled into a frown. He'd been born in the crusader kingdom of Edessa, of African blood, so his appearance was unusual in London. Not unique—a handful of people of similar background had made their way from the warmer Southern world to the isle of Britain, one way or another. But Octavian was also a knight, and that made him truly stand out, attracting looks whenever he went out among the general populace. Unfortunately, not all the attention was friendly.

"Sometimes I wonder why I came all this way," he confided to Luc. "It wasn't to sit and listen to old men argue about who's changing sides this month. Or changing back, depending on who's winning at the moment."

"Don't get discouraged," Luc said, his good humor already returning now that they were free of the stuffy chambers of the palace. "Bickering is part of the process. The longer the parties talk, the longer before we have to fight again."

"So which is it you want, Luc?" his friend asked. "Battle or no battle?"

Luc said, "Peace is always better than war. The king doesn't want to prolong this conflict. It's costly, both in coin and lives. Though there's opportunity too, for those who are clever enough to see it."

"You should be ashamed to think that," Octavian said. "War hurts all people, the innocent most of all. As a knight, you swore to protect the innocent."

"So I do!" Luc protested. "But I'm not naive, either. I have to live in this world. Why shouldn't I advance myself?"

Tav shook his head, and Luc sighed, saying, "We simply need to find a way to attain peace."

"I heard nothing in the past fortnight to make me think the cousins will come to an agreement." Tav looked downcast.

"No war lasts forever. Besides, what will you do once it does end? Return to the Holy Land?"

"I don't know." Tav said the words thoughtfully. He said everything thoughtfully. He was one of the most deliberate people Luc knew.

"Well, when the time comes, you'll—"

The sound of a woman's scream interrupted him. Both men fell silent for a moment, instinctively judging direction and distance.

"Around that corner?" Luc asked, pointing to the

north.

Octavian nodded, his hand on the poniard at his waist. "Ready?"

"To protect the innocent? Always."

Then the men both ran toward the sound.

* * * *

Domina flinched when Constance screamed again, the sound echoing through the narrow alleyway. She was as frightened as her maid was, though she tried to tamp down her panic.

The small group of rough looking men who had trapped them in the alley didn't help her fight the fear. The poor light made it hard to see faces or even count the number of people in the blind alley. But at least four or five men blocked the way out.

Domina and Constance stood against the short brick wall that so abruptly ended the way forward. Between the women and the attackers, Giles and the two other men-at-arms stood with swords drawn, ready to engage.

"Stay well back, my lady," Giles ordered. A nervous quaver broke through his warning. He was over twenty and trained to fight. However, the soldier had never been asked to defend his mistress from a direct attack before.

Still, the men-at-arms carried swords. The men who obviously intended to rob them held only knives. In fact, the big man at the back didn't even have a weapon, though his size meant his fists would be punishing all on their own.

When the fight began, Domina put her arms around a terrified Constance. She watched the scene as well as she could, but the near-darkness and the chaotic movements of all the men made it nearly impossible to tell what was going on.

Giles cursed out loud when one of his companions stumbled to the ground. The thieves jeered, and one even tried to rush toward the women. Domina slid one hand down to grip the hilt of her dagger. If only she knew how to use it in a fight! She doubted these men would respect her gender or her status enough to not harm her.

"What's happening?" Constance moaned, her head buried in Mina's shoulder.

Mina was about to lie and tell her that all would be well when something new happened.

The attackers, who had been almost jovial, suddenly began to shift their positions, yelling commands to each other.

"Someone's come," Mina whispered, hope rising in her. A city watch, perhaps?

Whoever arrived on the scene was certainly *not* on the side of the thieves. Mina strained her eyes, catching the glint of blades as they swept through the alley and briefly shone in the meager light.

The thieves didn't know what to do, and being attacked on two sides destroyed their confidence. One of them abandoned his fellows and dashed away. Another tried the same thing, only to be knocked to the ground by one of the newcomers. Two more finally coordinated an attack on the nearest stranger.

Mina gasped when she saw the initial rush. The man would be killed, all for trying to stop a robbery. She closed her eyes, unable to watch a slaughter.

She heard men yell just as metal scraped on metal. A cry of pain burst through the darkness. Mina bit her lip, and peeked.

The stranger stood over one of the thieves, who was on the ground, holding his arm tight to his chest. Another had lost his knife and did his best to scramble toward where it lay...which happened to be right at Domina's feet.

The thief saw the knife, next to the hem of a lady's skirts. His plan could be read in his eyes: seize the knife and hold the lady hostage. Mina narrowed her eyes and took one step, putting her foot down firmly on the blade of the knife.

"How dare you even think it," she hissed at the young thief.

His surprise at her reaction made him stop for a full second, which was all the stranger required. He swept forward, in a move that must be a killing stroke.

Mina looked away to avoid what she knew would be a bloody end to the thief.

She heard a grunt, and then nothing.

"All done," a new voice said. "You may look. I only knocked him out—there's nothing to be afraid of."

"I'm not afraid," Mina countered instantly, though the shaking of her limbs told a different story.

"No, not much, are you?" the man replied, a certain amount of approval in his voice. "And your companion?"

"Constance," Domina said softly. "It seems to be over."

"Oh, praise Him we're still breathing," Constance said fervently as she stepped away from Domina. "Are you all right, my lady?"

"Yes," she said. "Thanks to..."

She hesitated as the man took a step forward, into a little pool of light. He was dressed in well-made but otherwise ordinary clothing, nothing more than a linen tunic and hose. Yet the lack of armor hadn't stopped him from rushing into the fray. He had to be a knight, for he did carry a sword. He was also built like a man who fought for a living, and the simple clothing didn't do much to conceal a well-muscled, trim figure. He was a little taller than she was, with thick brown hair but surprisingly blue eyes, set into a narrow, clean-shaven face.

With a jolt, she realized he was smiling at her, and she was compelled to smile back. *Am I completely out of my mind?* she wondered. *He could be another thief!*

But he said only, "If you don't mind standing a moment more, my lady?"

Without waiting for her reply, he turned back to the remains of the short, ugly fight. He joined his companion, who was several feet further back, and completely in shadow. Mina couldn't tell a thing about the man except that he was also a knight—to judge by the fineness of the sword he carried—and that he was both taller and broader than the blue-eyed stranger.

"My lady," Giles said, rushing up to her. "Are you well?"

"No injuries," she assured him. "The others?"

"We're all safe, my lady. Some cuts and bruises is all."

Mina breathed a sigh of relief. "And those men who attacked?"

"They'll be hauled off to the proper authorities," the stranger replied, as he returned to Mina.

Giles put out his sword, still tense from the fight. "Hold. Who are you?"

"Giles," said Mina. "These two men mean us no harm."

Her order was enough to make Giles lower his sword, though the stranger added, "She's right. We heard the scuffle, and sought to end it. That's all."

"How do we know that?" Giles asked.

"Because my friend has already volunteered to escort the thieves to the nearest dungeon," the other said. "By all means, have one of your men assist, if that will convince you."

"I can go, my lady," said Roger, the oldest of the men-at-arms.

"Then do so," Mina said. With a nod, Roger moved to help take the attackers away. He and the still-shadowed knight dragged the remaining miscreants off.

"You can put that away now," the blue-eyed knight told her, his gaze sweeping over her.

"What?" Mina was fully cloaked, and the only thing the stranger could see of her was her face and her hand... oh. She looked down at the dagger in her grip. She hadn't realized she'd drawn it. She slid it carefully into the slender sheath tied to her girdle, then pulled her cloak to cover her gown again. She reached up to check that her hood was still on, hoping that her distinctive hair was concealed.

She noticed his eyes tracking her movements. "Only an uncouth man stares at a lady," she warned him. Just because he saved her from footpads didn't mean he could look her over like a lamb at market.

"I only wanted to ensure that you suffered no injury," he said smoothly. "I see no damage, for which I am grateful."

"I am unhurt," she confirmed, now feeling terribly awkward. "I thank you."

"You've just come to London," he guessed. "Or you would have known better than to be on this street at this hour."

"We had no choice," she began to protest. "We have been on the road since dawn—"

"My lady, I meant no insult," he said. "Merely making an observation. Let me escort you to your destination. I would not see you molested again."

"We don't know where to *go*," she said, frustration cracking her attempt to remain calm. "We were looking for rooms, but the hour and the darkness conspired to make us lose our way."

"These streets can confuse anyone," he said. "I remember how lost I felt the first time I saw London. There's an inn not too far that would suit a lady of your standing. Can you walk?"

"Yes!" she said. The promise of an inn, with a place to sleep and a meal to eat, was enough to revive her.

"Luc of Braecon, at your service," he said, with a slight bow.

"Braecon," Mina repeated slowly. "That name I've heard. Shropshire?"

"Yes, that is where my father, who is baron now, holds his estates."

After a moment, she said, "I am called Domina. As you guessed, this is my first time in London. You are kind to assist us."

"My pleasure." He offered an arm to her, and after a slight hesitation, she accepted it. Her entourage fell into step behind them.

Her new protector said very little as they walked, and he must have sensed her trembling. He glanced at her.

"It's not far," he said again, in encouragement.

"Good," she replied shortly. Then she added, as if it were shameful to admit, "I'm so tired."

"You traveled all day?" he asked.

"It seemed foolish to stop so close to the city," she said. "But then the gates were busy and crowded, and it took longer than we thought…" She unconsciously tightened her grip on his arm. He seemed so solid, as if he really could protect her from anything the night could throw at her. For an instant, Domina wondered how it would feel to lean against him, to take a deep breath while he held her. Her exhaustion gave way to tingling awareness, and Mina quickly told herself to stop imagining such odd things.

"Very brave, for a woman alone," he commented, his voice warm.

"I'm not alone," she said.

"No husband, I meant." He phrased it almost as a question, as if it mattered to him.

"The distance is no shorter for married people."

"It might seem shorter to them, at least at night," he said, offhandedly.

She halted in surprise. Did he really just *say* that?

He seemed to realize the effect his statement had. "Ah, I apologize. I haven't been in the company of ladies lately."

Domina wasn't particularly assuaged. She only said, "I hope the inn is close by."

"Touché," he said. "I'm afraid that it is."

Only a few moments later, he led Domina and her little entourage to the doorway of the inn. Above the door, the sign showed a picture of a goshawk.

"Giles," Domina said. "See if the innkeeper has adequate space for us all."

"Yes, my lady." The man-at-arms gave Luc a suspicious sidelong glance, to which Luc reacted with exaggerated innocence. "I won't be long, my lady," Giles said before he went in.

Domina took her hand from Luc's arm and stepped away from him, in the guise of offering a curtsey. When she dipped her head, the heavy braid of thick, dark red hair slipped over her shoulder.

Luc's eyes widened, but he said nothing as she quickly tucked the braid back under her hood.

"I thank you for seeing me and my people to safety, sir," Domina said with intense formality. "I bid you good evening."

Luc smiled invitingly. "That's all? What if I asked to see you again? You're in London for the first time in your life—I would be delighted to show you the city. Tomorrow, perhaps."

"I am not here to sightsee," she said coldly. "I have come on a matter of business. Once that is concluded, I will return to my home."

"Then you would deprive the world of your beauty."

She outright glared at him. "What did you say?"

"It was a compliment," he said. "Most women enjoy receiving them."

"Then you should go find the company of such a woman. I do not wish to detain you any longer."

"Oh, I wouldn't say you're detaining me."

"Sir—"

"Luc."

At that moment, Giles returned. "My lady, if you'll come this way, the innkeeper says a suitable room is available for you and Constance, and space in the common room for the rest of us. I asked about food—there's still beef from the evening meal. He'll have it served shortly."

"Excellent, Giles," she said. "I knew I could rely on

you to see to everything."

She gestured for the others to proceed into the inn before her. Then she turned back to Luc.

"Sir—"

"Luc," he repeated. "Luc of Braecon."

"I didn't forget your name," she said.

"Nor will I forget yours."

"Regardless, I do not expect we shall ever see each other again." She paused. Though the man's presence set her nerves jangling, her manners wouldn't let her simply turn away. "Thank you for what you did back there…you and your companion. Good night."

She whirled around and hurried inside before he could stop her. But really, what could he say? She was likely correct—the chances of crossing her path again in London, or anywhere else, were remote.

Yet, even as she stepped inside, part of her hoped he'd object, or even reach out to detain her, to persuade her that perhaps a day in his company would be something she dared to do. If things were different, she'd like to see him again…however fate chose to bring it about.

* * * *

The next day, Luc sat at court among the many onlookers and courtiers, watching the king receive various nobles and others on matters of business. Luc didn't necessarily enjoy such activities, but he had long dreamed of rising in station beyond what he would inherit from his father's title. In truth, Luc would settle for nothing less than being named an earl and earning a seat on the king's council. The privy council consisted of the men who were a king's most valued advisors, loyal and able to offer aid to the king. Luc had no doubt the king knew his loyalty.

After all, his family shared blood with Stephen's, and his father was one of the first men to publicly declare for Stephen when he announced his intention to take the crown of England. Luc fought for the king, and took a wound in battle for the king. He'd sit through as many dull days of court as necessary.

In return, Stephen would one day grant Luc more honor. He'd name him earl, choose a suitable wife to build an even stronger alliance, and offer lands worthy of his new title. Then Luc would serve as one of the privy councillors, helping the king shape the very future of the realm. Assuming, of course, that the empress didn't manage to seize the crown for herself by then. Stephen's future was far from certain, and that meant Luc's future also held some doubt. Still, he believed he'd rise. He wasn't born with ambition for nothing. He could almost taste the triumph that lay ahead.

Still, today was the sort of day when that dream seemed far away compared to the dull details of days at court. Luc was distracted, barely paying attention to the many people coming in and out of the king's presence. Most of the matters had no bearing on him, so his wandering mind didn't pose a difficulty.

Just when he was about to excuse himself, though, another person entered the room.

Luc had been staring at the floor, so he noticed the rich blue cloth of a lady's gown first, because of the way it whispered over the polished wood of the chamber's floor, the toes of the lady's leather slippers peeping out only when she took each step.

Something in the way she moved pulled his gaze upward, following the line of her outfit to where the waist narrowed and the bodice of the gown perfectly echoed her form. The tight bodice rose higher, concealing her cleavage but revealing the bare top of her shoulders, while the tight, laced sleeves hid her arms. The fact that she was almost entirely covered didn't stop Luc from appreciating what he couldn't see. She was fairly tall, with wide shoulders and a long, graceful neck that seemed made to be kissed. Even better, she avoided the sin of wearing too much gaudy jewelry. She wore only one necklace, a small silver cross hanging from a thin silver chain. It left nearly all of her revealed skin to be admired, which he did.

The lady was well worth a second look, and a third, if a man could get away with it. Her long dark red hair was woven into a single, thick braid down her back, leaving her face clear…a jolt ran through him.

"The lady Domina de Warewic," the herald announced at exactly the moment Luc recognized her face.

King Stephen shifted very slightly in his chair. His glance flickered to Luc for a moment. Luc understood the wordless order. *Listen carefully. This is important.*

All distraction was forgotten. He focused on the newcomer, the proud beauty he'd rescued the previous night.

What did the king want from *her*?

Chapter 3

AT THE HERALD'S ANNOUNCEMENT OF her name, Domina advanced down the aisle with Constance trailing along behind to watch that Domina's skirts didn't tangle and trip her. As if she needed something else to worry about! She'd never before been in the presence of a king, and she prayed she wouldn't embarrass herself.

He's a man like any other, she reminded herself. She should speak to him as she would any noble. This was the business of the court, and she must keep her head.

On reaching the space in front of the king's chair, Domina sank into a low curtsey. She was glad she'd had a new gown made up earlier in the year. A quick glance at the gathered courtiers gave her confidence. She was dressed as well as most of them. Perhaps she didn't have the sparkling jewels or elaborate headdresses the ladies here could afford. But she looked like a lady, and that was what mattered. She touched the silver cross she wore at her throat, a wordless prayer for strength.

"Your grace," she murmured. She rose again, keeping her eyes modestly downcast. The king would address her at his leisure.

He was in no hurry. Domina felt the eyes of the king,

and indeed the whole court, on her, surveying, assessing. Was her gown wrong somehow? Had she miscalculated, and now be laughed at? Did people actually *want* to be at court all the time? Domina never would—her nerves were already strained, and the king hadn't even spoken to her yet.

"Lady Domina de Warewic," the king said at last. "Where is Godfrey de Warewic? Does he not accompany you?"

She swallowed nervously, then replied, "He has sent me in his stead." She'd spoken too quietly. The king had to lean forward in his seat to hear her at all.

"It was Godfrey I summoned," he said, a frown crossing his face. "For he is the lord and castellan of Trumwell."

"Indeed, your grace," she said, willing her voice to be louder. "He is unwell at the moment. Just a passing illness," she added in as reassuring a manner as she could. "Because he wished to recognize the seriousness of the summons, he sent me to fulfill the obligation, especially as winter is approaching."

"Lovely as you are to look at, my lady, you cannot aid me. My questions are for your father, because they pertain to the management of your lands and the alliances I wish to reinforce."

Domina curtsied again, saying, "I do believe I can tender such aid then, your grace. My father trusts me with much of the business of his estate. There is rarely a document to pass his desk that I do not read. Many of the day to day tasks are left to me. Please ask me what you wish to know."

"He trusts you so far?" Stephen inquired, a new light in his eyes.

"He does," Domina said, raising her chin. "Nor have I given him any reason to doubt that trust." She meant every word. Their lands would be in complete disarray if not for Domina's careful management.

"Do you know anything of the castle's defenses? The strength of the garrison?"

"Your grace, as you doubtless know, my father has much experience of war. He took care to reinforce the castle's defenses and he developed a training schedule specifically for this garrison. I can give precise numbers of men, horses, weapons, and siege supplies to a clerk, if you like."

He nodded slowly, as if provisionally satisfied with her answers. Domina took a careful breath. This would end well enough. All he wanted was reassurance of the castle's strengths. But why? Did he think an attack was imminent?

"If you please, your grace..." Domina broke off, realizing that the king had not given her leave to speak.

But he waved a hand, inviting her to finish.

"Your grace," she continued. "Has there been any word to cause concern? I—we—have not had any reports of an army moving. If the empress..."

"Her army remains where it was last month," he said shortly.

Domina gave a sigh of relief. She was certain Trumwell Castle could withstand a siege, but she never wanted to put her faith to the test.

King Stephen was still looking at her, his expression speculative. "Tell me, Lady Domina. You must be over twenty, and yet you are not married?"

"I am two and twenty, your Grace. And you are quite correct, I am not yet married. I was betrothed twice, but both times, other events intervened so no marriage occurred." The first time, the neighbor she'd been betrothed to had died of a fever years before the marriage was expected to take place. Domina only met him a few times. The second contract had been declared void when the suitor ran off with the wife of his own liege—Domina counted herself lucky to have been spared.

She added hastily, "I am quite content to wait, your Grace. When my father is well again, he can attend to the matter."

"He need not be concerned," the king said.

Mina nodded, first thinking that the king was merely offering a pretty phrase to the effect that she would not have difficulty finding a suitor, even at her age. But when he gestured to someone among the courtiers, she felt a nervous flutter in her belly. It was the same arrogant knight she had met outside the market yesterday!

"This is Sir Luc, son of Lord Laurence of Braecon, Lady Domina. I think you should know who he is."

"Why is that, your grace?"

The king smiled. "Because if your father sends such a fair lady to court all on her own, he must want her to be well matched."

Domina stood in shock. A marriage contract was precisely what she had hoped to avoid! But she could not oppose the king himself...

Unable to look at the king, she instead cast her gaze on the man he proposed to be her husband. He was handsome enough, she admitted grudgingly. Certainly nothing like the brutish knight she'd always pictured in her nightmares. His whole expression was alert, lively.

In return, he was looking her over carefully—just as he had the last evening—but he didn't smile this time.

Perhaps he was less impressed with her by the bright light of day. Domina was perversely annoyed by the idea.

"Lady Domina, you have nothing to say?" Was the king amused by her reaction? Well, why not?

She cast her eyes downward once more, not trusting herself to look at the king and have him see her true emotions.

"I am honored by your kindness in thinking of me, your grace," she said, speaking slowly, as if she could deny the inevitable. "Yet I wonder how Sir Luc feels about this union." She kept her voice soft, hoping the shaking would not be detected.

The knight glanced at the king and received a nod before replying. "My role is to serve the king in every way I can," Luc said, sounding as if he were discussing the sale of a ship instead of a marriage. "Whatever he commands, I'll carry out."

Domina swallowed. Her mouth was painfully dry all of a sudden. So the man wasn't going to raise any objections to the alliance. She couldn't look to him for common sense. "If he does not oppose the idea, I do not see how I can."

"Then you consent," the king pressed.

Mary, Queen of Heaven, help me deal with this all too earthly king! Inspiration struck her. She said, in a rush, "I am your grace's servant, but first my father's daughter. Please understand that I could never agree to such an important contract without his advice and blessing."

The king raised his eyebrow, but said only, "If all fathers had daughters as dutiful as this one, the world would be much closer to paradise!"

Domina said nothing, terrified she'd angered the king. Instead, she heard Stephen begin to chuckle, then laugh out loud. Other voices joined in, as the courtiers decided to echo the king's amusement.

A hot blush rose in her cheeks. She'd done something horribly wrong, and now everyone was laughing at her. Her first appearance at court would be her last.

The king rose from his chair and stepped toward her. Domina gasped, but didn't dare move.

Stephen stopped a foot away from her, and reached out to chuck a finger under her chin, raising her face to his.

"Well, this lady will make someone a blushing bride!" He smiled at her. "Did you think me serious, dear girl?"

"I…I don't know what to think, your grace," she whispered. Only he could hear her.

Stephen's expression softened. "I may have got carried away with my jest. Your first time at court—I couldn't resist."

"A joke, your grace?" she asked, her voice quavering.

"Just a little joke," he said.

He turned to indicate Luc, who remained standing where he was. "But I do say that Sir Luc will come to Trumwell Castle in order to discuss defenses with Godfrey, and see that the castle is properly fortified. As a knight, he's served me with honor, and I need to know that your castle can hold the territory it overlooks. Luc of Braecon will be my eyes."

Domina glanced between the king and Luc and back again, barely keeping up with this rapid shift in topic.

"Certainly, your grace," she said, falling back on the courtesy she'd been taught. "Whenever an emissary of the king arrives, he is most welcome."

"Excellent. That is exactly what I wish to hear, my dear." The king looked her over once more, and Domina didn't know what thoughts flew behind the royal eyes. "You are excused now. My chamberlain will speak with you further."

She curtsied again, very low. "God keep you, your grace."

Domina backed away from the king and then turned to leave. She forced herself to walk slowly, even though she wanted to dash away.

She conquered one challenge, only to find herself saddled with another. How would she keep her secret if this knight Luc of Braecon came to her home? And what would happen if her deception was exposed?

* * * *

As soon as Domina escaped the royal residence, she breathed a sigh of relief. "Praise Him that's over."

"You did very well, my lady," Constance said proudly. "I would have been in tears. To play a trick like that…"

"The king may play whatever tricks he likes, for that is the privilege of a king." Domina looked up and down the street. "Come, Constance. Now that I have completed my main task here, I will see Joscelin. We must cross the river."

The women soon reached the church and its attendant buildings, where her cousin Joscelin pursued his studies to attain the rank of priest.

Domina hadn't sent word ahead, but she was confident that the mention of the de Warewic name would grant her entrance. The servant who received her looked rather like a churchman himself, and he cast a suspicious eye over the two women, as if they would at any moment turn into serpents.

Nevertheless, he went to announce her to Joscelin. Domina moved to a side room to wait, and Constance stood near her, staring at the gracious lines of the building with awe.

An older man entered after a few moments, clearly the highest-ranking churchman in residence. He greeted her civilly. "You say you are Joscelin's cousin?" he asked.

"Yes, Domina de Warewic. My father Godfrey is his uncle. Joscelin lived with us at Trumwell Castle."

"Ah, yes. He did speak of his life then. A happy time for him, after so much sadness. He mentioned a cousin whom he still prays for."

Domina smiled. "We pray for him, too, though it seems God is already pleased with his work."

"You are grateful, I trust, that such a devout man shares your blood."

Domina nodded, saying, "My father was so proud of him when he chose to pursue the path of a priest."

"He will excel," the older man said. "I would not be surprised if he becomes one of the youngest bishops ever. His speech comes directly from the angels." At a sound, he turned to see someone approaching. "Ah, he has arrived. I will leave you to speak alone," he said, apparently deciding that Domina was no threat to Joscelin's sanctity.

"Thank you," she said.

"Cousin!"

Domina broke into a smile at hearing Joscelin's voice.

Joscelin was about three years younger than her, but even at nineteen, he inspired a certain regard. He had gentle brown eyes that often seemed to look past the world into heaven.

She'd first met him when he came to live at Trumwell, after the death of his parents and sister from a plague.

Though a skinny young child burdened with grief, he had an air of calm and purpose. As far as Domina was concerned, her cousin Joscelin was like a brother.

"I had no idea you were here in London!" he said, embracing her. He stepped back and gazed at her. "What business brings you so far from home?"

"A routine matter," she said, not wishing to worry him. "I had to present myself at court and confirm the strength of our castle and garrison. It is done now, so I'll return home as soon as I can. But I wanted to see you first!"

"I am glad to look on your face, cos," he said. His voice dropped to a more confidential tone. "When they told me you were here, I feared the worst news. How is your father?"

"The same," she said. "No worse, but no better."

Joscelin sighed, and put one hand on her arm. "Dearest Mina, you're doing all you can."

"I only wish I could do more. Or do something else. The right thing."

"Sometimes it is not given to us to know," Joscelin said. "You are an ideal daughter, and you must continue to care for him just as you are. The Lord in his mercy and wisdom will guide you."

Joscelin's voice soothed Mina, and the words that once might have irked her now bolstered her instead.

"I hope you are doing well here," she said, striving for a happier topic. "Both in your vocation and in this city! It's nothing like what I expected—the city, I mean."

"What did you expect?"

"I don't know. Something divine, with gleaming spires and broad streets and marvels from strange lands. The city has spires, but they're half hidden by smoke. As for marvels…well, I can't forget half of what I've seen, though I'd not call it marvelous. There are beggars everywhere, and the smells alone…"

He nodded. "It shocked me as well. There is much to be wary of."

"So I learned. We were set upon by footpads the very evening we arrived."

"God have mercy, Mina!" Joscelin looked incredibly upset. "What happened?"

"Be at ease—it was not as horrible as it might have been. Only moments after the footpads cornered us, two knights appeared and rescued us. God was watching out for me at that moment." Though then God played the trick of making the knight an arrogant man who set her teeth on edge. But she didn't mention that to Joscelin, nor the fact that she saw the very same knight again in the king's court.

"In any case," she continued, "the footpads would have been disappointed even if they'd completed their theft. I must look far richer than I am."

"Do you need money?" Joscelin asked. "I have a little saved."

"Oh, I couldn't take your money!"

"Mina, you need it more than I do," Joscelin argued. "I can work as a clerk, and I can always avail myself of the church's generosity."

Mina looked down, feeling unworthy. "It would help," she admitted. "I feel so ashamed, though, to ask it of you."

"You have not asked, I have offered." Joscelin patted her arm. "I'll fetch it now."

He left and returned a few moments later. He pressed a small leather pouch into her hands. "Not much, just a bit of silver I've saved. It should defray the expense of this trip, at least."

"You are far too good to me."

"What is family for?" he asked. Then he added, "Never go round these streets alone, and not even with Giles after dark. The sooner you're back safe behind the walls of Trumwell, the happier I'll be. You must not risk yourself, a gentle lady like you!"

She laughed, wondering if Joscelin had any idea of how much she'd had to put aside the role of a "gentle lady" in order to run the estate in her father's absence.

However, she promised to be careful. "And as I said, I intend to return home at the first possible moment. London is not for me!"

"You have discovered a truth about the world, dear cos," Joscelin said, with a sad little chuckle. "Wherever people gather, there is much tendency toward vice and evil."

"Just a few moments at the court showed me that," she said. "I was lost among those who lived for politics and personal gain."

He reached for her hand. "Be not forlorn. There is also much potential for good here, even among the worldly court of the king. Those knights you mentioned, for instance. They did their duty to protect an innocent, and they did not even know you."

"That's true. You never lose hope, do you?" She smiled at her cousin, reminded of the arrogant, blue-eyed knight. He *had* rushed in to save a stranger, after all, and he did escort her to safety afterwards. Perhaps she was judging him too harshly.

"Lose hope? Never," Joscelin vowed. "I know how powerful hope is."

"I will try to remember," she said. "Will you pray for me?"

"Every day," he promised. "And you must keep me informed, whether the news is good or ill."

"I don't like to distract you—"

He made a face. "Blood is not a distraction. It is who we are."

Domina kissed her cousin goodbye and left. She and Constance made their way back to the inn, a man-at-arms following close behind. One thing was certain...Mina would not let her guard down again.

Chapter 4

LUC WATCHED AS THE INTRIGUING Domina de Warewic left the audience chamber, her back stiff and straight beneath that incredibly thick braid of red hair. The lady's attendant followed her like a shadow.

After that, there were a few more exchanges with other postulants, none of which Luc heard. His mind was still locked on Domina. Why had she not announced her title the previous evening? Was she hiding something? Was her business in London simply an audience with the king, or did she have another reason to be in town? Why was she in the streets at such a late hour?

Luc came out of his daze when the king's voice rang out, declaring an end to the audience of the day. He'd barely left the chamber when a page approached with a message. The king wished to see him. He followed the boy into another wing of the building where the king had his private quarters.

He was shown into a small chamber, decorated lavishly for its size. The walls were paneled in oak, a fire burned in the fireplace along one wall, and several candles were lit, lending a sense of warmth and luxury to the space.

Luc bowed when he saw the king seated at the table in the center of the room. At his right hand, another man sat.

Stephen motioned Luc forward. The page backed out and shut the door firmly.

"Have a seat. Take some wine," Stephen said. "Have you met Drugo?"

Luc eyed the other man, and shook his head. "Not yet, your grace."

"You've seen him, no doubt." Stephen took a sip of wine, then continued, "Drugo serves as my eyes and ears, even in places where I am presumed to have no such senses. He is one of the reasons I had a court to return to after I was released from my imprisonment in Bristol."

A spy. Luc didn't need the word spoken out loud. He gave Drugo a closer look. The man was at least forty, more likely closer to fifty years of age. He had an ascetic look, as if he were a monk rather than a courtier. His tunic and hose were well made, but so plain as to be utterly forgettable. He wore no rings. Above the cowl of his tunic, his face was thin, with hollow cheeks and an angular jaw. He wore a short, sharply-pointed beard. Deep set eyes glittered in the candlelight, surveying Luc just as closely. In all, Drugo gave the appearance of a man not to be trifled with. Not a man to make into an enemy.

"If it's important enough to tell me what Drugo is, then I presume there's a reason you asked for me particularly, your grace," he said to the king. "How can I serve you?"

"Drugo," Stephen said, "give him the details of what you've learned."

The spymaster drummed his fingers on the table once.

"What I will tell you, my lord Luc, is in the strictest confidence."

"He's not an idiot, Drugo," the king muttered. "Would I have asked for an idiot to carry out such a mission?"

"I will say nothing," Luc promised quickly.

Drugo nodded. "I have received several reports from certain informants that, taken together, now point to a matter of great concern. In practice, the king relies upon the loyalty of the barons who have declared for him. Without that ring of defense, the army itself could never respond to every sally the empress dares to make. We need the barons and their vassals to hold their castles and other strongpoints. A gap could spell disaster."

Luc nodded. Nothing so far counted as a secret. It was common knowledge.

"The matter is this," Drugo continued. "There is a conspiracy among a small number of lords in the west, near the Welsh border. According to my sources, a few lords who publicly support the king have privately switched allegiance to the empress. They will *not* defend their castles when the empress's forces march through their lands. Indeed, they will lend her support and allow her to march unimpeded into the center of England, even to London where she can potentially claim the crown."

"If you know the names, then simply arrest these lords," Luc said.

"We need solid proof of their treachery," said Drugo. "Consider the situation. King Stephen must not appear to be anything less than scrupulous in his reaction. We cannot afford to lose the support of the nobles, and if they see what appears to be an arbitrary arrest, they may withhold their full support. If we arrest one of those we suspect, the others will hear of it and hide their tracks."

"So I am to find the proof," Luc guessed.

"Precisely," Drugo replied. He was about to go on, but at a gesture from the king, he fell silent.

Stephen looked at Luc. "Tell me, what did you think of the lady Domina?"

The change in subject startled Luc, but he answered all the same. "Well spoken. Obviously quick witted, though out of her depth at court. Beautiful," he added, though he was quite sure the king would see that for himself. "Should I have seen more than that?"

"Perhaps not," the king muttered. "I did see that Domina does not want to be your bride!"

"She was furious," Luc said, "but she covered it well."

"And she thought fast! The role of the dutiful daughter...how could I have thwarted such a move, if I'd been serious and not in jest?"

Luc agreed. "She did not oppose you, she merely diverted you. Excellent defense."

Stephen mused, "Imagine what a woman like that could do with an army during a war."

"You asked about the defenses of her father's castle," said Luc. "You think she has war on her mind?"

"After meeting her, I'm not sure what to think."

"Your grace," Luc said, "there is obviously something that bothers you about her. What is it?"

"Her? Perhaps only the fact that she appeared at all. It was Godfrey I summoned, and for a very specific reason."

"And that is?"

Here Drugo interrupted, clearly out of patience with the king's aside. "Godfrey de Warewic is the likely ringleader of the conspiracy."

Luc's mouth dropped open. "The lady's father? If he's the de Warewic I heard about growing up, he took the cross and fought in the Holy Land!" He wasn't naive, and he knew that not all crusaders were paragons, but something in Luc found it difficult to picture the glorious defenders of Jerusalem as the sort of men to engage in treason.

"So he did," said Stephen, "and he's sworn fealty to me, and my father before me. But he's been very quiet of late…too quiet for my liking. The evidence of Drugo's informants points directly to him."

"What is the evidence?"

Drugo pulled out a silver coin, flipping it over his knuckles. The silver caught the light, mesmerizing Luc. "The family of de Warewic has long used the swan as their symbol. It even appears on Godfrey's seal."

Drugo tossed the coin toward Luc. He caught it easily. He looked at the coin's face in surprise. It showed no king's head, but instead the image of a swan.

"When Godfrey came back from the Holy Land, he bore with him spoils of war—the family is known to be wealthy, not in land, but in coin. He had silver and gold struck with the symbol of the swan. But he didn't use his coins for usual trade, for he prided himself on not needing to do so. He kept them in his treasury in Trumwell Castle."

"So why am I holding one?" Luc asked.

"No fewer than three of the empress's agents in the west were captured while possessing some of these coins," said Drugo. "I recognized the sign, and realized the significance of finding them in the field, you might say. Godfrey de Warewic would not spend this part of his wealth on petty purchases. However, he would use these coins as his way of sealing a pact—and if the empress's people have these coins now, what else are we to assume…"

"But that he's made a pact with them." Luc frowned, flipping the coin over and over in his fingers. "Could it have been something more innocent?"

"Then he'd use ordinary coin," Drugo said.

Luc countered, "Perhaps he's gone through his ordinary coin."

"That gets to the heart of the matter," King Stephen said. "We do not know enough without speaking to Godfrey himself. Since he has not answered my summons, but sent his daughter instead, he must be playing some game."

He looked hard at Luc. "This is my order. I command you to go to Trumwell Castle under the guise of looking at the strength of the castle and garrison. Visit the de Warewic family's holdings as my emissary. Report what you find."

"If Godfrey is a traitor…" said Luc.

"He'll be executed."

"And the lady?"

"If she is involved, so will she." Stephen looked grim. He plainly didn't like the idea of Domina's head on a block. "For her sake, I pray she is not involved in her father's plans."

"Men have often used pretty faces to distract their enemies," Drugo said. He sounded as if he'd never been swayed by such tricks.

"As well that you were not serious about the marriage, sire." Luc shook his head. "I don't know the extent of her family's holdings…"

"Godfrey was given charge of Trumwell Castle as a reward for his military prowess," Stephen said. "I admit that the castle has never been taken, and the lands around it have been peaceful for years. But all it takes is one bargain with the empress or her generals, and those castle gates may open."

Luc thought about it. "I fear that my supposed mission will not allow me enough time to truly learn what's going on. How long does it take to assess the castle's preparedness? A few days at most."

"True," Drugo said. "We must not risk Godfrey discovering Luc's real purpose."

"Then have a marriage contract drawn up," said Stephen. "Luc of Braecon and Domina de Warewic."

Luc waited a moment for Stephen to laugh, then said in a low voice, "You cannot be serious."

"A potential marriage will give you plenty of reason to linger," said Drugo. "You will not carry it through, of course. It's the threat that matters. Think of the facts. Godfrey has a daughter, yet she is so old and not wedded—perhaps he's holding her as a promise to someone."

"Or he's not, and I'll be married off with no way out of the contract," Luc objected.

"In which case, you'll have even more power there. Yes, a single night of marriage may be more effective than a year-long siege."

"But the marriage isn't for a single night," said Luc. "If I recall, it's until death."

"Chances are you'll never need to carry it out," Stephen said. "If you do, well, enjoy her while you can. I'll see the marriage is annulled later. You won't be shackled to her. I'll personally guarantee a suitable bride for you, Luc. An earl's daughter. Expose a nest of vipers, and you'll be rewarded for your act. I will not forget."

"Thank you, sire." Luc paused. "I will go to Trumwell Castle and discover the truth. Your grace can decide on a course of action once I find out about this woman's true heart."

"Well spoken, Luc."

"Sire, I'll need a man I can trust with me. I may need to send word that I can't commit to paper. Or simply have someone to watch my back."

"Who do you have in mind?"

"Sir Octavian."

"The Levantine?" Drugo asked, his brows drawing together.

"We've fought together before. He is reliable."

"Then it shall be done," Stephen said. "Take him with you, and may God keep you both."

Stephen bid Luc good night, and left, leaving the two men alone.

Drugo drummed his fingers on the table once again. The spymaster's eyes held Luc's. "You said earlier that she was beautiful."

"The king asked my impression, and I gave it," said Luc. "Domina's certainly not ugly."

"No." The spy paused, then said, "As I said before, beauty can be a weapon. The devil has made use of it in the past. Be wary of the lady Domina. Don't fall prey to beauty, and don't trust anyone."

"I'm not in the habit of trusting traitors, sir."

"Good. Don't make it a habit, for the king has no use for men whose loyalty is in question."

"If the king doubted my loyalty, he wouldn't have asked for me to carry out the mission." Luc said nothing more as he turned and left. He didn't care for the threat in the spymaster's tone.

As he walked through the castle, Luc turned the conversation over in his mind. He knew what his father would say about it. This was an opportunity of a lifetime, and he recognized that the king was testing him, judging him.

So Luc would rise to the challenge. He'd go to Trumwell Castle, where he would discover every last secret within its walls. Then he'd return to the king and take his just reward. Marriage to an earl's daughter, the king had said. That was tantalizingly close to the possibility of being named earl himself.

The memory of Domina's face surfaced, disrupting his musing. Was she innocent of her father's manipulations? Would she be destroyed, an unintended victim of this shadow war? Luc shook his head once. Drugo offered his warning for a good reason. However beautiful the lady was, she couldn't stop him from carrying out his mission. He fought back a nasty feeling. Would he really sacrifice an innocent woman for his ambitions?

Or she wasn't so innocent. Those cool eyes held such intelligence...perhaps Domina knew far more than she was telling.

He sought out Octavian and told him of the developments. He related nearly all he'd been told, only concealing the fact that he possessed a marriage contract. The pious Octavian would never approve of the idea of suggesting a marriage simply as a means to gain information. Luc needed a trustworthy companion at his side, and he couldn't risk losing Tav. So he'd just keep the more unsavory tools of his mission to himself. In all likelihood, he wouldn't even need to mention the contract, let alone use it. He didn't want to be shackled to any woman who couldn't help him advance. Even if she was more intriguing than any other woman he could think of.

He told Octavian that they'd leave within the week.

"And be warned, I don't know how long we'll stay at Trumwell," he said.

"As long as necessary to learn the truth," Octavian returned, with the easy confidence of the innocent.

"God help us."

Tav smiled. "I'm sure He will."

Chapter 5

TRUMWELL CASTLE FARED WELL DURING Domina's short absence. Beatrice, the grey-haired maidservant who was most often at Godfrey's side, reported that he was as comfortable as could be expected.

"He asked after you a few times, my lady," she added. "I told him you'd be home soon."

Mina smiled, pleased that her father remembered her without her face being right there to remind him. Perhaps there was hope after all, as Joscelin promised.

The countryside had been quiet, Haldan reported when Domina returned. He'd surely enjoyed the fortnight when he could pretend the castle was his to command, though he also sounded relieved that nothing actually caused him to leave the warmth of the fireside. He fancied himself a commander, but he had the temperament of a lackey. He never thought for himself, at least not beyond his next mug of ale.

She stopped in her father's room, but found him sleeping, so she slipped out again. She'd have to warn all the servants to keep guests away from the building. In fact, they'd have to avoid all mention of it, or her father.

* * * *

A few days later, Domina walked down a spiraling staircase to a tiny chamber in the base of the massive stone structure. She unlocked a wooden door on the back wall. She pulled it open and sighed when she saw the emptiness inside.

Somehow, she always hoped the next time she opened this door, the treasury would be full again. But it was always empty. The few shelves were bare, when they'd once held boxes of coin and valuable goods. The floor in the center of the closet was bare stone. Mina wished that the heavy wooden chest she remembered from her childhood would reappear, but all her wishes were for naught. The chest was gone.

How was it possible that the greatest part of the de Warewic fortune vanished in the night, without a clue as to who spirited it away? The castle had never been taken by force, and if it had been such an enemy, they surely would have known! Domina found it difficult to believe that a thief could have infiltrated the grounds, but what other possibility was there?

Only one. Her father must have done something with the treasure—those gold ingots and silver coins all struck with the symbol of the swan. Had he moved the chest somewhere else? Had he concealed it for a reason only he knew? Perhaps he'd done it just before his illness struck. Unfortunately, the location of the chest was now locked away in his own mind, a better lock than any iron device a blacksmith could forge.

Several months ago, Godfrey had rallied for a time,

and Mina actually asked him where the money was. He'd answered in an indignant way —of course the money was safe in the treasury, where else would it be? Mina didn't press the matter, fearing that any excitement would hurt him. Indeed, she blamed herself for his subsequent relapse, even though Joscelin, who was at Trumwell at the time, told her that it wasn't her fault.

Now, Mina withdrew the tiny pouch of silver coins that Joscelin had given her, and placed it on a shelf. It looked so pathetic, sitting there. It was hardly worth keeping in the treasury, but it represented most of what she had. She'd sold nearly all her jewelry to pay the wages of the garrison. She'd sold some of the more valuable objects owned by the family to pay for grain and meat that could not be grown or hunted. Yet, every quarter the money dwindled further.

What can I do? she asked silently. What else could she do, other than keep a tight rein on expenses, and pray for her father's recovery?

She turned away before the tears clouding her eyes could fall. She would *not* cry.

Mina locked the door, and took a few deep breaths to steady herself.

When she walked into the great hall, a servant dashed over to her. "My lady, a runner has just come. The guests you mentioned will be here by this afternoon."

None of her prayers would be heard, it seemed. She had prayed most fervently for the irritating Luc of Braecon to be diverted to another path. "Tell the kitchens to cook a meal suitable for a noble guest. The chambers are prepared?"

"Yes, my lady. All is as you instructed."

She nodded. She'd be damned if her poverty would be

revealed to visitors. She'd show every courtesy to her guests, no matter what the expense. "Very well. I'll be in my chamber. Alert me when the lord's retinue is sighted."

All too soon, news of her visitor came.

Domina patted down the skirts of her gown. The gown was not nearly as fancy as what she wore to court. This was only a plain woolen dress, the blue color somewhat faded as the dyes ran out with each washing. Constance had redone the trim with new ribbon purchased in London, and Mina felt the dress would pass, especially among men who would not notice a thing like the tiny patches at the hem. She wryly surveyed her reflection in a hammered mirror. They would notice the neckline, not the fabric.

She walked to the front entrance of the keep, waiting patiently for the retinue to enter the castle gates. The cold air bit at her exposed skin.

"Do you not want your cloak, my lady?" Constance whispered.

Mina gave one short shake of her head.

The sound of hooves echoed, and then the retinue rode in, not unlike an invading army. It was smaller than Mina feared. She'd assumed the lord Luc would have a string of servants with him, not to mention numerous horses and mules who would all require room and board.

Fewer than ten people rode in. Luc was the most visible, riding at the front, the hood of his cloak down so he could look about. He was followed by another man whose face was concealed because his cowl was up, though the heavy cloak couldn't hide the broad shoulders of a knight. Three more men followed, probably men-at-arms. Behind them, four squires rode, each managing a few pack animals.

Luc rode all the way up to the steps of the keep before reining in his horse and dismounting. Something in Mina hoped he'd show discomfort after a day of riding, but he looked quite comfortable, almost as if he were returning home after a short jaunt.

"My lord, you are welcome to Trumwell Castle," she said formally.

"I thank you, my lady Domina." Luc bowed, very properly, then turned to where he'd been joined by the cowled rider, who pulled off his hood at the last moment.

Mina blinked in surprise, seeing a man with sepia brown skin, a shade she'd never seen before.

"My companion is also a knight in the king's service," said Luc.

The stranger bowed. "Octavian de Levant, at your service."

Domina offered him a curtsey, which she belatedly realized she'd neglected to do for Luc. She smiled, not wishing to blame this knight for the annoyance Luc brought to her life. "You are most welcome, Sir Octavian. I trust your visit will be a pleasant one." *And a short one*, she added silently. The sooner these men left her castle, the happier she'd be.

"Please come within. My people will care for the animals." Domina made a gesture, and her servants leapt to obey.

She then turned back toward the entrance to the hall, with the two knights on her heels.

The warmth inside made her cheeks sting, and she heard Octavian mutter in French to the effect that he was happy to be indoors again.

Luc was looking around very curiously. "I hope your father has recovered from his illness. Where is he?"

Domina was ready for this question with a little lie. "Thank you, yes. He is tending to a matter at one of our northern holdings, Sir Luc. I do not know precisely when he will return."

"Unfortunate. I wanted to speak to him in particular."

"Until you can, please direct your questions to me," she said, hoping to discourage him from speaking to her servants at all.

Turning to the other man, she said, "Were you not also Luc's companion that night in London? When my party was set upon?"

Sir Octavian nodded. "Yes. Apologies for not introducing myself at that time."

She laughed, unexpectedly delighted at the man's serious demeanor. "You were otherwise occupied, sir, and I found no fault with your behavior that evening."

Octavian broke into a smile. "How reassuring."

"You said de Levant?" she asked. "Are you from the Holy Land, then?"

"I was born in the city of Edessa."

"Ah, how I wish my father could speak to you. He spent some years in the Levant when he was young. He would enjoy hearing more recent news of the place."

"When he returns here, I shall be most pleased to speak with him," Octavian said.

Mina froze for a second, realizing her mistake. Then she pasted on a smile. "I look forward to the time when I can introduce you to him," she said. "For the moment, my servants will show you to your chambers. We will dine in one hour."

Chapter 6

IN THE GUEST CHAMBER HE'D been shown into, Luc found a small fire blazing away in the fireplace. He went to it immediately, stretching his hands toward the flames. The heat seeped into him. If only the lady of the castle was half as warm as this! Domina might have been carved from ice, the way she'd stood on the steps in nothing but a blue gown. Not even a cloak, though she'd surely been waiting for them for some time. Her cheeks glowed pink, but that was the only hint that she even felt the cold wind and the bite of the oncoming winter in the air.

Poor Octavian had been complaining of the cold all day. He was not made for the climate in Britain, he often pointed out. Well, he'd got a smile out of the icy Domina, so that ought to have warmed him sufficiently. Luc suppressed a spike of jealousy. Just the thought of Domina laughing sent a coil of heat into his belly. He could imagine her, her head thrown back and those red curls. He pictured her long neck exposed for a kiss, and her body twined with his…that idea took care of any lingering cold he felt.

He shook his head, trying to banish the admittedly delicious image. It was dangerous to think of Domina as anything other than the unwilling hostess she was. For all he knew, she was part of the conspiracy that so troubled the spymaster Drugo. He'd keep her at arm's length. Not that she seemed the slightest bit inclined to seduce him with her charms.

Luc found Octavian, and they went down to the hall together. In honor of her guests, Domina had arranged what must be a far more festive meal than usual. Still, it was no great celebration, and the mood was almost somber when Luc and Octavian entered the great hall.

The lady herself stood near the high table, and she gestured for the men to join her there. Luc noted her posture and her movement—so proper, so controlled. She was outwardly graceful—like a swan, he thought darkly—but that grace concealed a stiffness in her attitude. Because Luc was sent by the king? Or merely because she had to host two strange men when she had no one to support her? Perhaps that was reason enough. She'd let her guard down soon. Luc would charm her into pliancy. He'd never met a woman he couldn't coax a smile out of eventually.

The lady introduced the castle's steward, Ancel, and then a few others. The big man who called himself Sir Haldan introduced himself, and when Domina rather pointedly did not use the man's title, Luc got curious. Who exactly was this giant of a man, and what was his relationship to the lady of the castle?

Domina did thaw a bit over supper. She answered most of his questions with no hesitation, and in some cases grew positively voluble. Luc never thought the change in wool prices could be interesting, but when discussed in

Domina's gorgeous, contralto voice, they were fascinating.

At one point, Tav threw him an amused look. Luc shook his head, warning his friend not to make him laugh. Although he should be laughing at himself. How could a woman's voice be that seductive?

"If I remember correctly, my lady," Tav said then, "your father went on crusade."

"Yes," said Domina. "He took the cross at a young age. He was eager to see the Holy Land."

Tav nodded. "I heard the name of de Warewic when I lived in Edessa, and later Jerusalem. People there remember the deeds of the Franks—both good and bad. Godfrey de Warewic was a name people used with reverence. He once stopped a company of Frankish soldiers from slaughtering a group of people in a marketplace. He said that any soldier who would strike down unarmed folk was not worthy of the cross. He escorted the residents to a nearby mosque and stood guard till the Frankish company left. One man against twenty! They say he didn't need to draw his sword. His gaze kept the would-be attackers at bay."

Domina's eyes widened as Tav spoke. "I don't remember him telling me that. I always pestered him for stories."

"He was perhaps too modest," Tav said.

"Likely," she agreed. "But I'm glad I could hear it from you."

The talk turned to Luc's past, and he gave Domina a brief account of his family and upbringing.

"I took the martial path," he concluded, "knowing that I may well need to defend my lands once I come into them. Though my father is likely to live for many years yet, and I wish him health."

"So you became a soldier to occupy your time," she said, resting her chin on her hand as she looked at him.

"It was either that or the church." Luc flashed a grin. "I've not got the disposition for the religious life."

That earned him a genuine smile, which felt like a much larger victory. Luc was about to venture into slightly more dangerous territory with his interrogation, but Domina interrupted with a new topic.

"Who is that man?" she asked, lifting one finger toward the tables where the servants were dining. "The one sitting by my maid Constance?"

Luc glanced over and saw the man in question. He was indeed paying rather close attention to the maid. "That's Ban," he said. "He's served my family for years."

Domina's eyes narrowed, and Luc instantly caught her concern. "He's a good man."

"So all men say of other men," she responded skeptically.

"Do you wish me to order all my men to stay away from your people? They'll obey if I tell them so."

She said nothing for a moment, still gazing at the scene. Then she took a deeper breath, saying, "It's no great matter. Constance has leave to enjoy the company of a guest. After all, it will only be a short time until your retinue has to leave again."

Perhaps, Luc thought.

After supper, Domina excused herself.

"What do you think?" Luc asked Octavian, once they were alone at the table.

"Of the lady? Or her castle?"

"Everything."

"It all looks quite normal."

"Her people are looking at us in a strange way," Luc insisted.

"Everyone always looks at me that way," Tav said simply, "so I hadn't noticed. If you think it's strange, you may be right. On the other hand, maybe you're determined to see a problem where there is none."

"The king would not pursue the matter if he wasn't concerned."

"He's not infallible. The evidence against the lord Godfrey is not strong enough for the king to issue any proclamation. That's why we're here, isn't it? He needs more evidence than he has now."

"You're right," Luc admitted.

"Remember that story of Godfrey on crusade. It's not in character with a man who would become a traitor."

"Stories are often exaggerated," Luc said.

"Perhaps," said Tav. "But is that the action of a man who would betray the king he swore fealty to?"

Luc knew exactly what Octavian meant, though he remembered Drugo's damning accusations as well. "Here's another reading of your story," he said. "Godfrey's action in Jerusalem showed he was a man who wanted peace. Perhaps he thinks the empress will bring peace, and that's why he's switching sides."

"We won't know until we ask."

"You can't ask that outright!" Luc warned. "We must be circumspect."

"This is your mission," Tav said. "I won't say a word, for I want no part in your politics. I'm only here to lend you aid."

"Thank you."

"But for what it's worth, I think you've been given a task far more difficult than you deserve. And for what?"

For an earldom, Luc thought. But of course he could not say that. So all he said was, "Because I owe the king my loyalty."

* * * *

The very next day, Luc began to work on his ostensible reason for being at Trumwell Castle. He walked along the castle's walls and parapets. He consulted the man in charge of the garrison in Godfrey's absence.

Haldan had an open countenance and broad smile, but there was something in his eyes—a calculating look—that made Luc wary. Yet, just as with Domina, perhaps Haldan's concern was nothing more than suspicion of a stranger.

Luc thus kept his questions mild as he probed for information.

"You think Godfrey a good master?" he asked Haldan.

"I could not ask for better!" Haldan said. "Trumwell is a good place for me. I plan to stay here for a long while," he added, with an outsized confidence that struck Luc as boastful.

"And the lady Domina? Does she concern herself with the castle's defense?" Of course, Luc remembered her clear voice reciting Trumwell's strengths back when she'd stood before the king. But he wanted to hear Haldan's thoughts.

"She does," Haldan noted, his tone souring. "Too much, for a woman. She forgets her place."

"What's her place?" Luc asked.

The big man smirked. "Oh, I can think of a few places for her, like that big fancy bed she's got in her chamber."

Luc felt a strong desire to challenge Haldan to single

combat. "You say that about the lady of the castle?" He spoke very quietly, because that was the only way he wouldn't start yelling.

Haldan noticed Luc's lack of amusement, but he forced a chuckle out. "Just a joke, sir knight."

But it wasn't just a joke—Luc recognized lust as well as anyone else, and that's what had been in Haldan's voice. A true knight would immediately leap to Domina's defense, just for the insult to her virtue.

Instead, he contained his rage and asked Haldan about his combat experience. Luc listened with half an ear to Haldan's list of accomplishments, annoyed at himself for needing to ferret out information instead of following his instincts and challenging Haldan to a duel.

Eventually, he calmed enough to listen to the end of the speech. The man, it seemed, knew a bit too well how bandits in the area liked to operate. "They'll not trouble us here, though," Haldan said in conclusion.

Luc then asked for a short demonstration of the garrison's readiness for battle.

"Now, sir knight?" Haldan asked, nonplussed.

"You rarely get much warning when a battle is about to begin," Luc noted. "So yes, now."

Haldan looked about to argue, but then, remembering Luc was acting as the arm of the king himself, gave a short nod. "Indeed, sir. If you'll stand at the side of the courtyard…"

Luc moved to the suggested spot, and watched impassively as Haldan sounded a mock-alarm and directed the men who appeared in the courtyard, popping up like rabbits from all corners of the castle.

Haldan kept glancing at Luc as he directed the garrison through several drills. Luc gave no hint to his thoughts, though he was forming a rapid impression of what he saw.

Soon after, Luc raised a hand, indicating that he'd seen enough. "Thank you for indulging me with a demonstration," he told the group at large. "Return to your normal tasks now. I've no wish to disturb the order of the day more than I already have. God keep you all."

Without speaking to Haldan further, Luc asked for his horse to be saddled. He rode out of the gates, taking his horse around the perimeter of the castle, surveying the stone walls, the ditches, and the few redoubts set further out.

He then faced outward, just as he would need to if he expected the enemy to ride up. His gaze went to the lake not far from the castle itself. Spying a figure standing at the shore, he nudged his horse and rode down the slope to the water.

Domina heard him, and turned. She'd been tossing bread crusts to a flock of white swans who'd gathered near the shore.

"I should have guessed that the de Warewics would have swans," Luc said in greeting.

Domina nodded. "There have always been swans here, ever since my family first took charge of this castle."

"You feed them through the winter?"

"Always. I would hate for them to have to leave," Domina said. "They belong here. This is their home."

She tossed the last of the crumbs onto the water, then brushed her hands on her cloak. At least she wore a cloak today, Luc thought. She was human after all.

Domina took a few steps back from the water's edge, just as Luc dismounted from his horse. He found himself unexpectedly close to her. The idea of slipping one hand beneath the cloak to skim the curve of her lower back came to him, and he actually put his hand halfway out before he recalled himself. Domina would slap him for such a familiarity, and she'd be right to do so.

"You rode out of the castle to find me. Did you have need of me?" she asked.

He could think of a few things he wanted of her, but none he could say out loud. He merely said, "I wanted to see the castle in daylight. The walls themselves."

"And?" she prompted, curiosity replacing the coolness in her tone.

"An impressive structure," he said. "Though even I could see a few weaknesses."

"The north wall," she said.

He looked at her more closely. "So you are aware?"

"I can see the cracks myself," she replied. "It does not take a military genius to know that a cracked wall is a weak wall."

"Does your father intend to repair it?"

"Of course...just as soon as the weather turns fair again. Early spring, perhaps."

"Winter is not a bad time to do repairs. There's far less risk of a surprise attack—armies don't march in winter, as a rule."

"I'll bring your opinions to my father," she said dryly.

"Oh, I'll tell him myself when he returns." Luc watched her face, and he saw again what he'd noted the previous day. She froze completely when he mentioned speaking to her father directly. It was just a second's hesitation, but it was there. Why? What possible reason could Domina have to be scared of such a meeting, unless Godfrey had something to hide from an agent of the king?

She glanced up toward the castle gate. "If you'll excuse me, I must return to my work. There are plenty of tasks to complete before dark."

He fell into step beside her. "I've seen what I need to see for the moment. I'll walk you back."

She offered a tight smile. "How kind."

Once they returned to the castle, Luc kept an eye on Domina for the reminder of the day. It was difficult, because the woman seemed to be everywhere at once. She appeared in the kitchens, speaking to everyone from the cooks down to the scullery boys. She vanished into the stables, only to emerge with a flock of boys at her heels as she ordered them to move a fresh load of hay into the building to accommodate the guests' animals.

She dashed into storage buildings, she strode through the great hall. Ancel the steward hailed her, and they had a brief conversation Luc couldn't hear, though he could see that the steward didn't look happy. The man's lined face pulled into a frown, his high forehead wrinkled. Domina soothed him with a few words, and moved on.

Luc watched as she consulted a clutch of ladies spinning and weaving in a small room clearly devoted to women's tasks. She ran her long, slender fingers over a bolt of cloth, a smile briefly illuminating her face.

Then she was off again. Luc trailed her back outside. He was briefly distracted by the sight of a kitchen maid scurrying away from a building in the corner of the courtyard, one of the few places Domina hadn't gone that day.

He switched his path to cross that of the maid, who was returning to the kitchen in the main keep.

"What is over there?" he asked. "In that building in the corner?"

The maid had stopped short on being addressed, and two bright spots of color bloomed on her cheeks. "That…

that building, my lord?"

"Yes," Luc said patiently. "The one you just came out of. What's in there?"

"Storage, my...my lord." The maid offered a clumsy curtsey with her stuttered explanation. Was she so provincial that the mere presence of a stranger tongue-tied her? From the way she was staring at him, wide-eyed, it seemed possible.

"Storage for what?"

She opened her mouth twice before an answer finally came. "Wine and foodstuffs, my lord. The cats like it there, for they kill the mice."

"Very well," he said. "Go on with you." He watched as the maid dashed off to the keep, her shoulders hunched over as if she expected a reprimand.

Luc glanced back at the building, intending to go over and investigate it, for it seemed rather fine for mere food storage. It stood two stories tall, with shuttered windows on the upper floor.

Just then, a black shape slunk from around the corner of the building, one of the cats the maid spoke of. This one was a long but lithe creature, all black save for a patch of white on its chest. It fixed Luc with a contemptuous stare, as if to warn him from invading its hunting grounds.

"Not today, then," he muttered. "I know where I'm not wanted." The cat's gaze reminded him of Domina's look when he first arrived at her castle. She kept her claws sheathed thus far, but Luc knew she was capable of scratching.

Recalling his determination to keep watch on her—not that she'd done anything suspicious yet—Luc retraced his steps, hoping to pick up her trail.

He heard her before he saw her, so Luc stopped to hear the conversation. He'd recognized the deep voice of Haldan from this morning.

"There must be no further delay," she was saying, her normally calm voice now rather strained.

"Why not wait till your guests are gone?" Haldan asked.

"Because I do not know how long they intend to linger," she snapped back. "To wait any longer on this matter invites disaster."

"You worry overmuch, my lady." Something in Haldan's response raised Luc's hackles. Not just the man's dismissal of his mistress's statement, but also the familiar way he said it, as if he often soothed Domina's concerns.

"Trumwell is worth my worry," Domina retorted, in no way soothed. "The trees, Haldan. Tomorrow morning. Don't forget."

"Aye, my lady."

Heavy footsteps signaled Haldan's departure, and a moment later, Domina appeared on silent feet. Luc didn't try to catch her attention. He waited until she was halfway across the courtyard to the keep's doorway before he followed.

The lady of the castle was no mere ornament, content to embroider while the servants worked around her. She seemed to use every key that dangled from the chain at her waist, from the pantry to the cellar to the mews that housed the birds of prey used for hunting.

Through it all, she maintained a gracious calm and an air of confidence, as if this was how she lived every single day. Which, Luc realized, must be the case. Everyone seemed to rely on her, everyone asked her permission and her advice. This was no show for her guests.

That evening, she again presided over a generous meal, wearing the same gown as the evening before. Luc had no complaints. The gown hugged every curve from her shoulders to her hips, before flaring out to a wide skirt. He was a little surprised that she didn't show off her finery, though. Didn't all women look forward to opportunities to do so? Guests could not be that common at Trumwell Castle.

Perhaps wearing the same gown was Domina's way of telling her guests just how little she wanted them there. She wasn't rude, of course. Something told Luc that Domina would rather die than behave in a manner beneath her station. She didn't offer meager meals or stock the firewood too scantily in the chambers—he'd been in other places where the hosts did exactly that—but she wanted them gone.

Not till I speak to Godfrey, Luc thought. *So you'd better get used to me, Domina.*

Once again, she excused herself after the meal, telling Luc and Octavian to amuse themselves as they wished.

However, Luc saw her through the doorway of the hall, staring at something outside. Curious, he rose and moved to join her.

She was looking out the open doorway of the keep to the courtyard, where snow fell in fat flakes, the first snowfall of the season. They turned the ground white, a blanket covering every roof, every barrel, every windowsill.

"Beautiful," said Luc.

She jumped at the sound of his voice. Apparently she hadn't even noticed his approach.

He reached out to touch her forearm. "I didn't mean to startle you," he said. Without thinking about it, he curled his hand around the slender limb, feeling the warmth beneath the woolen sleeve.

Domina shook her head. "I was not paying attention, with the snow…" Her voice sounded almost completely different than what he presumed to be her usual tone. This voice was soft, musing, and dreamy. "I love winter," she said. "At least, when it first comes, and looks like this."

He moved beside her, still holding her by the arm. "It's hard to resist," he admitted. "Even knowing it won't last."

She nodded, her gaze still locked on the scene outside. "Seeing that purity and perfection…" she said. "We want to live in a world like this outside, but as soon as we step out into it, we ruin it with our presence."

Luc imagined the courtyard as a little world of its own. It would be rather peaceful to have a world to himself. Well, with the addition of one lovely woman to share it. He recognized the novelty of the idea—he'd always wanted to be in the thick of things, in the world of the court and the battlefield. But now, seeing the snow, and hearing Domina's sigh…

"I can't tell if the snow makes you delighted or melancholy," Luc said then.

"Both," Domina said, her expression momentarily unguarded. Her mouth was slightly open. Luc experienced a sudden, strong desire to pull her close and kiss that mouth.

She blinked, then looked to where he held her by the arm. "Excuse me," she said, taking one step away. "I must retire."

"You must be exhausted," he said, "if today was typical for you."

"The only thing unusual about today is that you're a

guest here."

"You should not overwork yourself," he said.

She gave a short laugh, one he couldn't read. "Women must not be idle. But don't think I endure days of endless drudgery. Tomorrow I will go hunting, a task that is all pleasure for me."

Luc smiled. "I'm glad to hear it." He wished her good night and let her go. He stared after her, though, thinking of the words she'd spoken to Haldan. *The trees, tomorrow morning.* Was the lady Domina truly going hunting? Or did she have other plans?

Chapter 7

DOMINA ROSE BEFORE DAWN. THE presence of her unwelcome guests was already straining the larder of the choicest meat. Ancel warned her the previous day, saying it
would look ill if the knights had to dine on everyday
meats.

"They might ask questions, my lady," the older man
said. "Game birds are expected, or venison, which we've
none fresh. The cooks can offer mutton, or fish…"

"Not fish," Domina said quickly. "I'll go hawking
tomorrow, and when the fowler comes around next, I do
have a little coin to pay for what he's caught in the
forest."

Domina would hunt for game herself today, in order to
keep the table supplied with the sort of food her knightly
guests would expect. If only she had venison or boar to
offer, but she lacked the means to organize that sort of
hunt. Hawking was far less extravagant.

She dressed warmly and ate a hasty meal of bread and
cheese, then strode out to the mews. The snow of the previous evening only dusted the ground, and though it was

cold, the air hinted of a warmer day to come. Good hunting weather, she thought.

The mews of Trumwell now held only three hawks, and none of the falcons both Domina and her parents once loved to hunt with. But her hawks were quick and clever, and worked well for her.

A couple of grooms had got her horse ready. A slender hound named Goldfoot sat nearby. He'd help retrieve any game the hawks might not be able to manage on their own.

"I think the river will be good ground today," she announced.

"Yes, my lady," one of the grooms said. "Two boys can go ahead of you to flush the game for the hawks."

"That will be quite sufficient," she said in approval. Domina disliked crowds for hunting, and in any case, hawking was often a rather solitary pursuit. If she couldn't visit her father while her irritating guests remained at the castle, she might as well be far away from the temptation.

"I'll begin with Brilliant," she said, referring to the female sparrowhawk who was her best hunter.

Domina rode out of the castle gate with Brilliant on her left arm. The sleek hound ran at her horse's side, and she took a deep breath of crystalline winter air. The freedom she felt while hunting was all too rare a feeling for her. A full day of solitude would restore her.

Then, the sound of hoofbeats behind her spoiled everything. Goldfoot barked once in warning.

Domina looked back to see Luc riding to catch up with her. He arrived in the space of a few breaths, not giving her much chance to summon a polite mask.

"You don't waste time," he said on reaching her. He

reined in to match her horse's pace. Domina could already tell that he was a master rider. He probably heard her say "hunting" and pictured falconry.

"My apologies," she said, hoping to dissuade him from joining her. "I am only hawking today. It will not be a spectacle."

"I need no spectacle," he said easily. "It's always a pleasure to watch a clever and well-trained creature at work."

She bit her lip. There'd be no turning him away. So much for solitude! "Today I ride to the river," she said. "There's always game there."

"Excellent," Luc said. "Then I can see more of the countryside."

"Is that your aim, to see the countryside?" she asked.

"Among other things," he replied.

A quarter hour's ride brought them to the banks of the river. Ice rimed the edges, but the water ran swiftly. Domina looked about, and listened for the sounds of wildlife. The shuffling and low talk of the grooms got in the way. Luc asked a question of one of them, earning a laugh and a quick response.

"There are too many people about," she told Luc pointedly. "My bird performs much better when there are fewer numbers."

He willfully misinterpreted her meaning. He turned to the grooms, saying, "My lady suggests that fewer people about will improve the hunt. You may return to the castle. I'll remain to attend your mistress."

Before she could object, the grooms accepted Luc's words and wheeled around to ride back to the castle gates, leaving only the boys to flush out game ahead. She'd be virtually alone with Luc.

"That was not my meaning!" she said. "Nor is it your place to give orders to my men!"

"They understood the order to be yours, my lady," Luc said, with no trace of contrition. "I'll serve as well as any groom when it comes to fetching and carrying. Believe me, you'll be well protected. No one will be allowed to even say a word to you as long as I'm here."

Domina looked heavenward, seeking strength. "If I must endure your company, then at least heed my instructions when it comes to my Brilliant, and don't get too close. She doesn't care for strangers."

"Where did she learned that trait?" Luc commented.

"She had a wonderful trainer," Domina said as she dismounted. "Me."

Domina sent Brilliant on flight after flight. The sparrowhawk was eager for the kill on this day, and succeeded at least half the time. On failed flights, Domina called her back in by casting the meat-baited lure in a circle. When Brilliant fell on the lure, Domina quickly caught her by the jesses tied to her legs.

"Better luck next time, my beauty," she murmured, feeding the hawk a bit of cold liver.

Luc remained fairly quiet at first, but he eventually asked a question, and then another and another. It started out innocuously enough, with questions about her birds. Domina was rather surprised at his interest, but she was pleased to talk about them.

"You don't have falcons in your mews," he noted.

"I used to," she replied. "But since my last merlin died, I have not had time to select a new falcon." Nor did she have the wealth to purchase the more expensive specimens. Hawks were far cheaper. "I shall remedy that someday, of course. My parents taught me how to hunt with falcons. There is nothing like it."

"You have a gift for hawking as well," Luc said. "I've heard only one flight in ten may bring back a prize." He nudged the basket at his feet, already half full of partridges and ducks.

"Brilliant is a clever hunter," Mina said proudly.

"And well-behaved for a sparrowhawk. What could you do with a peregrine, I wonder?"

"I shall likely never know," Domina said. "That's a bird far beyond my purse."

"Even with the fabled wealth of the de Warewics?" he asked. "I've heard your father has a cache of gold ingots, stamped with the sign of the swan."

Domina cursed herself for forgetting to maintain her facade. "Do I look as if I am the child of a man who encourages frivolous spending? That I would ask for a peregrine?"

"I don't know you, Domina," he said. "So how would I know what you'd ask for?"

"I ask for nothing," she muttered.

"You're his only daughter, though. Surely he dotes on you."

"No one dotes on me. Not my father, nor Joscelin."

"Who's Joscelin?" Luc asked, his eyes suddenly narrow.

"My cousin. Though he may as well be a brother to me, for he lived here many years, before he traveled to London to continue his career in the church."

"Ah," Luc said, relaxing. "I see."

Was he jealous? Was that possible? The idea of Luc being jealous of another man in her life gave her a little jolt of pleasure. Not that she necessarily wanted Luc's attention—certainly not now! If only she'd met him a few years ago, when all was well. Then she could enjoy being with him, enjoy his quips and his conversation, even enjoy the way he looked at her sometimes, with admiration in his eyes.

No. She must not get distracted by Luc's admittedly charming ways. The sooner he was gone, the better.

"Is your hawk loyal to you alone?" Luc asked.

Mina had seen how interested he was in the hunting, so she said, "So far, she's flown only for me, but if you'd like to try a flight, you may."

"I'd hate to lose her," Luc admitted.

"If you risk nothing, you'll see no reward."

"Is that so?" Luc's answering look was serious.

"A sparrowhawk is not nearly as expensive to replace as a falcon, and besides, I think you won't lose her. You seem a good hunter."

"How do you know that, when you've never seen me hunt?"

"It's mostly about paying attention, and knowing when to act. The worst hunters are the men who blunder around in the woods shouting about what fine hunters they are. I've seen enough of those sorts when I was growing up. My father often led hunting parties for guests. I know for a fact that it takes a very skilled gamekeeper to ensure a kill, even when the so-called hunters do nothing to deserve it."

Luc noted, "You're obviously a hunter yourself."

"Only with birds," she said. "I never wanted to go after hare or deer—the experience is entirely different."

By that point, Luc had pulled on a spare glove from Mina's supplies. She leaned forward to put her arm next to his, encouraging Brilliant to step over.

The position put her very close to him, enough that

she could feel the strength in his sword arm and the natural tension in his body. She kept her eyes on Brilliant, but she suspected that Luc was enjoying their proximity. Certainly, his smile seemed to be more than simple appreciation of the sparrowhawk stepping onto his arm.

"She's warming right up to me," he said in a low voice. "Just as I hoped she would."

Mina countered, "She's merely tolerating you, for she'll do anything to have another flight. She lives for the kill."

"Then I'll indulge her," Luc promised.

Luc sent the hawk up, watching as the bird's wings carried it up into the clear sky. Then it hovered above the tree tops for a moment, before diving down among the branches.

"Not as spectacular to watch as a falcon," Mina admitted.

"The goal isn't to be spectacular," Luc said, his voice remote. "It's to bring back what's sought."

"Yes, precisely," said Mina. "Though it would be a delight to fly a falcon again. I do like a little spectacle."

Luc was about to answer, but then the hawk appeared again, and he had to shift all his focus to swinging the lure to get the bird back within catching distance.

Mina watched as he worked. He moved well, not wasting motion or creating more fuss than necessary. As soon as Brilliant pounced on the lure's bait—a morsel of liver—Luc secured the bird's jesses and drew her in until she was perched on his arm.

"Well," he said, speaking to Brilliant, "You brought me no prize, but at least you didn't escape me entirely. That's probably the greatest outcome I can hope for today." With his bare hand, he ran a finger down the bird's back, smoothing down the slightly ruffled feathers.

For no reason she could name, Mina imagined him doing exactly the same thing to her, running a finger down her back, from her shoulder all the way down… Mina fought off a little shiver of anticipation.

Luc had noticed her staring. "Shall I give her back?"

"No." Mina shook her head, hoping to shake the odd thoughts. "That is, you don't need to. I can see you know how to treat animals well. Not everyone does," she added, her mood darkening.

"I've seen that sometimes," he agreed, with a frown. "I've no use for anyone who mistreats a creature, no matter what it is."

"Would you like to send Brilliant on another flight?" she asked.

"Perhaps next time, when she's more familiar with me."

Luc lifted his arm to give the bird back to Mina. When their forearms touched, he gave her a wink. "I hope there will be a next time."

Mina should have rolled her eyes at the comment, but the truth was, she actually enjoyed his company that day. "Perhaps," she said, "if the king's business allows you."

He gave her a half-smile. "Yes, that," he said non-committally. "We'll see."

Domina called the boys back from their posts, and soon the little party was traveling back to the castle. Luc and Mina rode their horses, Mina bearing her hawk on her arm. The pages ran along behind, one pulling a small cart.

"Has Haldan settled the matter of the trees?" Luc asked suddenly.

Mina blinked. "What?"

"I happened to overhear you say something to the effect of he had business in the trees this morning."

Luc's tone was far too casual, and he couldn't hide some spark of intense interest. But the remembrance of her order to Haldan made Mina so angry that she ignored Luc's expression for the moment.

"Mercy, he better have listened," she muttered. "I must ride round to the other side of the castle. Excuse me."

"I'll join you," he said, expertly matching his steed's pace to hers. Domina didn't bother to protest. She rode at as quick a pace as she could with Brilliant on her arm.

The view of the woods brought her up short. "I should have known! He didn't do it after all."

Luc pulled up next to her. "What was he supposed to have done?"

She pointed to a particular part of the woods, with visibly encroaching trees. "See there? The forest edge is much too close to the castle walls. I've been telling Haldan to take men to chop it back at least two hundred paces, though three would be better. He always finds excuses."

Luc surveyed the woods for a moment. "It could be a liability," he agreed.

"One easily solved, *if* I could find someone reliable to carry out the simplest order." She forgot to pretend she wasn't the person giving orders to Haldan. "I'm sick to death of his laziness."

"On that matter, I spoke with Haldan yesterday," Luc said.

Domina wrinkled her nose at the very thought of Haldan speaking to a better. "He wasn't churlish, I hope."

"Not to me, but tell me more about him."

She shrugged. "He's been here for just over two years,

I think. Before that he served another lord in the shire. I can't remember the name, but surely he'd tell you. Why?"

"I wondered about his qualifications. He calls himself Sir Haldan."

"Another thing I've warned him against. He's no knight, for all that he pretends to be something more than a soldier."

"Yet he's in charge of the castle," Luc said.

"He is *not* in charge of the castle," she said. "I am. That is, until my father returns, when he shall resume the duty," she added hastily. "Haldan is in charge of the garrison."

"Yes, about that. I saw a demonstration yesterday. The garrison is…soft," Luc said.

"How so?" Anger flared up in Domina. "You tell me they are inadequate?"

"Not lazy. But poor to respond to commands, as if they've forgotten what they once knew."

Her cheeks burned. "Truly?"

"I got the impression that it was not always so."

"Indeed it was not!"

"It also seems like something your father would have noticed," Luc added.

She closed her eyes, trying to think her way through all these inconvenient observations. "He's been…distracted…of late."

"By what?"

Mina bit her lip. "I can't say."

"Because you don't know, or you won't tell?" he pressed.

"Will you interrogate me now?" she snapped. "I am not on trial!"

"Who said anything about a trial?" he asked, one eyebrow rising.

"I'll send him on his way," she muttered. But even as she said it, Mina knew sacking Haldan would not be easily accomplished. He'd have to be bought off, at a price Mina couldn't afford. Or else he would loosen his tongue about Godfrey's true condition, and Mina would be in a worse position than before. "God help me," she muttered.

"What is the matter?" Luc asked, his voice conciliatory now. "Domina?"

"Never mind," she said. "It doesn't concern you."

She announced it was high time to return her bird to the mews. Luc rode beside her, without speaking, perhaps in an effort to assuage her anger.

In the courtyard, he leapt down and helped her dismount without a word. The bird ascended in a short flight, but since she was leashed, Mina easily recalled her. "Back to your home, my lady," she told the bird.

Luc trailed her to the mews, where the few hawks roosted, watched over by a young groom.

She allowed the hawk to settle on her arm for a moment, then slipped the hood over the bird's head. "Very well done today, my beauty," she murmured. "You make me proud."

She guided the bird to its perch and shut the door. The bird squawked very quietly, in acknowledgment that its job was done. Domina watched to see that the bird was calm, then turned away, intending to take the basket of kills to the kitchen.

Luc already had the large basket in his grip. "Show me the way," he said.

"It should not fall to a guest to carry the meat to the kitchens."

"The weight is too much for you on your own," he

retorted.

She walked him across the courtyard, carefully avoiding looking at the building where her father resided.

"Supper will be a rich one," Luc commented cheerfully.

"If you like duckling."

"Or partridge," he added.

"If you prefer venison, my lord, you can hunt in the forest yourself. The deer have been plentiful in recent years."

Luc offered her a smile. "A generous suggestion, my lady. As your guest, I ought to fill the larders you have been feeding me from."

"A gift of venison would be much appreciated," she said, her eyes downcast. Secretly, she was elated. If she could be sure of Luc's absence, she could spend some time with her father. The constant attendance of her so-called "guest" was making it nearly impossible for her to see him at all.

"What a humble lady, to ask only venison as a gift."

"I have all else I need."

"Except your father by your side," he needled her.

She looked up, alarmed, before she smoothed out her features. "I would be much happier then."

"You would smile more," he guessed. "And laugh more."

"Unquestionably."

"Then I hope he returns quickly. In case everyone else has neglected to tell you, your laugh is enchanting."

Despite her every intention to be unmoved by Luc and his courtly manners, his compliment warmed her from the inside out.

Chapter 8

As HE PROMISED, LUC TOOK steps to arrange for a hunt, though he did so for reasons of his own. Lord Bertram of Acton, a known ally of the king, lived nearby, and Drugo had given Luc the name as a man he could trust.

While Luc attended Domina, Octavian used the time to call on the local lord, using his own missive from the king to gain entrance. His appearance, that of a foreign and rather splendid knight bearing the king's seal on a letter, was impressive enough that he was granted an immediate audience. Bertram greeted the idea of a hunt with enthusiasm and, once the idea had been mentioned, he handled the rest of the details himself.

All Luc and Octavian had to do was be there on the morning of the hunt, which would begin in the forest of Lord Bertram's lands.

Bertram was a garrulous, rotund man with a perpetual sneeze. What remained of his hair was all white, and he refused to wear a hat, announcing that his head was already perfectly camouflaged for a winter day. Luc liked him right off, and wished that his sole reason for being here was simply to enjoy a day with good companions and good hunting. Unfortunately, he had to hunt for more than deer today.

Bertram gave the order to release the hounds, who soon surged among the trees, baying wildly. The riders followed, and it didn't take long for Luc to secure a place alongside his host.

"Does Godfrey often join you?" Luc asked after a decent interval of casual talk. "Domina said he loves to hunt."

"Oh, he adores it," the baron confirmed. "Though of late, he's been consumed with other matters."

"How so?"

"Well, I know not the details, but he seems to be traveling much. I've not seen him in many months. Can't say when exactly. Of late, whenever I extend an invitation, he's gone from the castle."

Interesting. If Godfrey was gone so much, where did he go? Plotting a conspiracy might well take him to other estates, or even abroad.

"Who in the area supports the empress?" Luc asked in a lower voice.

"I could give you names," Bertram said. "But first tell me why you ask."

"Perhaps Godfrey de Warewic hunts with them now," Luc said.

Bertram sneezed, and gave one firm shake of his head. "You're wrong, sir! Godfrey is a good neighbor, and Heaven knows that many of us are saddened to see friends take opposite sides in this conflict. But if you're suggesting that Godfrey has changed his mind, you don't know Godfrey! He keeps his oaths."

"You're quite certain."

"I knew Godfrey before you were born, young man." Bertram gave him a long look. "You'd be hard pressed to find a better man when it comes to such matters."

"I'll pass your words on to the king."

"See that you do! I know King Stephen suffered those months in prison—he surely questioned the loyalty of everyone but his own dear queen while he was in chains there. But he must not confuse inaction with dishonor. We all must protect ourselves and our lands, or what is left for us to offer the king? These are trying times. God grant that peace comes soon."

At that moment, a cry from the hounds signaled the hunters to get ready for the kill. In the ensuing chaos and excitement, Luc put aside his mission for the more immediate task. He enjoyed hunting, and this particular instance made him grateful that he could use his martial skills with no doubts about whether the outcome would be a political benefit. This time, it was just him against an animal.

The deer lost. It had been a clever creature, and a strong one, giving the hounds and hunters an exhausting run through the frozen woods. Luc was given credit for the killing shot, and Bertram's hearty congratulations on the feat.

"What a magnificent specimen!" the lord cried, surveying the buck on the ground.

"My hostess should be pleased," Luc noted. "I do owe her for the feasts she's been providing."

Bertram laughed. "A kind thought, though the de Warewics have never lacked for wealth. Still, the lady will appreciate the gesture. I remember her as a child, so solemn even then. Of course, with her mother sick and dying, she took on more responsibility than a girl child should have to, and at a far younger age. Godfrey was grateful for her—perhaps that's why he never married her off!"

"He wanted to keep her as chatelaine?" Or was that Domina's choice, to remain at home, operating as lady and housekeeper? The position conferred more power than being a wife, and Domina seemed to thrive on responsibility.

"Finest in the shire," Bertram said, with an approving nod. "She'll make a good wife someday."

"Someday," Luc echoed.

He left Bertram to direct the clean up of the kill, and rejoined Octavian.

"Good shot," Tav said, in laconic approval. "At least you'll come away with something from this day."

"I also got some information," Luc confided. "The good neighbor Lord Bertram, who knows the de Warewics better than anyone at court, is adamant that they are loyal to the king."

"Perhaps you were given bad intelligence," Tav said. "No one can be accurate all the time. The king's agent made a mistake."

"She's hiding something," Luc insisted. "I thought it from the moment I met her. There is something that Domina doesn't want us to know. You've seen it. Remember that building in the corner? Not a single man in our retinue has been able to look inside. You don't find that odd?"

"Not much more odd than your obsession with peeking inside a storehouse," Tav said with a snort. "Perhaps she keeps the wine there, and wants to keep it safe from greedy guests."

"Be serious."

"I'm always serious," Tav said. "You're the one determined to see problems where there are none."

"She's keeping a secret," Luc repeated.

"So? Many people keep secrets—just because there is a secret doesn't mean it's for *you* to discover it."

"If it doesn't affect the king's rule, then I'll let her keep it," Luc said. "But I have to know at least that much about it."

Tav shook his head. "You're going to regret taking this mission on."

"I had no choice. The king himself ordered it."

"And you came all the way here, as ordered. But you can also return to the king and tell him there's nothing to find."

"I can't do that." Luc wouldn't receive any gratitude for returning empty-handed. Who knew if the king would pass him over the next time such an opportunity arose? Luc could sense the reward of an earldom slipping away.

Octavian was looking at him with narrowed eyes. "Why is it so important for you to do this?"

Luc shrugged it off. "I like to finish what I start. That's all."

"Well, in that case, let's finish this hunt. The day isn't even half over."

The woods were frosted over with winter, and the light snow cover meant it was easy to see the tracks of all sorts of creatures. Luc wished he could have enjoyed it more, but his mind was on Domina, wondering what she was doing and thinking. As the sun sank in the western sky, the party called an end to the festivities and turned back to Bertram's manor.

Once inside the grounds, Luc pulled Octavian aside. "I've learned a little, but it's still speculation. The day was wasted."

"How can you say that? You have a buck and doe to show for your efforts." Octavian didn't even smile. His sense of humor was too dry for it.

Luc shook his head. He had learned too little thus far. Then he got an idea.

"Listen. Our hostess isn't expecting us to return until tomorrow. I wonder what she might be up to, when she's not entertaining unwelcome guests."

"Say what's on your mind," Tav said.

"I want to ride back alone, with no fanfare. Perhaps I'll see nothing, but it might be worthwhile to surprise her."

Tav nodded. "In that case, I'll remain here with Lord Bertram, until I can see the spoils of the hunt brought home."

Luc returned to Trumwell alone. He allowed a stable boy to take his horse. Before he could even reach the main keep, one of his retinue sauntered over to him.

"Good hunting, sir?" Ban asked casually, his voice loud enough for others to hear, in case they were listening.

"Satisfying. You might alert the kitchens that a cart will arrive, bearing two deer."

Ban nodded, then leaned in more confidentially. "I watched the lady, as you instructed."

"What happened?"

"Nothing." The servant shrugged. "Nothing besides the usual tasks, that is. She never left the castle grounds, nor did anyone enter with a message. She spent most of the afternoon there." Ban nodded toward the corner building. "Her people sent me off whenever I came close to it though, and I didn't want to press the matter."

"That's good work," Luc said. "Consider your task

done."

He sent Ban off and aimed for the mysterious building. What the hell was Domina doing there all day? Something she could not do while guests were around...

Luc stopped short on hearing a melody float out over the air. The words were simple, the tune an old French song, but the voice rendered the notes magical.

Who was singing in this supposedly neglected corner of the grounds? Luc instantly pictured Domina, though she'd never hinted she possessed a talent for singing.

He had to get inside the place without being noticed. He deliberately circled around the other way, in case someone was watching from a window.

Working slowly, he slipped among the growing shadows in the courtyard. The failing light helped him, as did the fact that he'd arrived alone, so no one of the castle was expecting to see a guest in the grounds.

Luc watched a servant leave the building, bearing a basket in his hands. The singing continued though, so Luc waited a moment to slip in the door and up the nearly dark staircase inside. His sword rattled in its scabbard, and he put a hand on the hilt to keep it silenced.

Luc found a narrow passage at the top, following the back wall of the building. There was a doorway about twenty paces ahead to his left. Luc moved silently ahead.

The door was barely cracked and he didn't dare push it open, not knowing how many people were inside. Pausing, he peered into the gap.

The voice was closer now, and he saw Domina sitting with her back to him. She perched on the side of a great bed, singing to someone Luc couldn't see, for her body blocked his line of sight.

He strained his ears but heard nothing more. Was she

alone in the room with whoever lay on the bed?

Luc felt an almost overpowering urge to sweep in, demanding answers. Who earned the right to Domina's voice, especially in such an intimate setting?

However, he was there to gather information, and he couldn't show his own hand too soon. He slid to the right. The planks below him sighed, and the song broke off.

He moved as fast as he could further down the hall. He ducked into the shadows of a second doorway, this one leading to a small room that looked like a servant's quarters, with a small stool and table in one corner, and a tidy, straw-stuffed pallet covered with a worn wool blanket in another. He held as still as possible, just inside the room, so he could hear. As long as she didn't walk this way, he'd remain hidden. His mind was far too muddled to face Domina at the moment.

Her footsteps sounded as she walked to the doorway of the bedchamber. There was an agonizing pause while Luc worked to not breathe overloud.

Then a long sigh from Domina snaked its way down the corridor. Everything about her voice now sounded sensual to him, the product of all this secrecy.

"No more," she said, evidently to her companion in the room. "I've stayed too long already."

She paced back and forth for a moment. More murmured words were spoken, far too low for Luc to overhear.

Her footsteps hesitated in the hall, then faded down the stairs. Luc breathed a sigh of relief, then sidled towards the closed door. He might have only minutes before she or someone else returned. Luc fully intended to track Domina down to question her. But first, he needed to see what secret was so important that Domina didn't even want him to know what was in this building.

The door to the mysterious room opened easily, for it had no lock. Luc peeked in, finding the same scene as he'd glimpsed before. He wasn't mistaken. This was a well-appointed bedchamber, fit for a lord. The man sleeping on the bed was of the right age and appearance to be a lord, though some illness sapped his strength, leaving a body that looked much diminished from the warrior he must have been once.

Luc crept closer to the bed, his gaze caught by a glimmer on the man's hand, resting on the bed clothes. In the light of the single candle, Luc bent to examine the gold signet ring on the man's finger.

The ring was well-wrought, with Latin words deeply inscribed in an oval all around the raised image on the face of the ring, which doubtless doubled as a seal.

Luc stared at the image in the center. A swan, graceful and proud. This was unmistakably the symbol of the de Warewic house, and only one person would be wearing such a ring. The silver-haired man lying unconscious on the bed was Godfrey de Warewic.

Chapter 9

AFTER MINA SANG HER FATHER to sleep, she had remained at the side of his bed, simply holding his hand. She bowed her head, wishing she could crawl into a corner and nurse her own sorrow, like a cat that hides from the world when it gets wounded.

"What can I do, Father?" she asked out loud, her voice breaking on the last word. What more could she do, other than wait helplessly for some change in fate?

She gripped her father's hand tighter, and prayed silently. She appealed to her mother first. Surely the late Emma de Warewic would want her husband and the father of her child to be well. Mina begged her mother to intercede for her. She could no longer suffer on her own.

After several minutes, a sense of calm returned to Mina. She fought back her tears and steadied her breathing. She must remember that she was the lady of the castle. She'd find a way out of this bramble.

She moved silently about the room, extinguishing all the candles but one. Beatrice would be back soon from her supper to watch the rest of the night. Mina's stomach growled—she had scarcely eaten a thing that day.

"Good night, Father," she said, kissing the cool forehead. "I'll visit again as soon as I can, I promise."

Mina carefully shut the door to her father's room, then hurried down the stairs. She had to get back to the keep before her guests returned from the hunt they'd attended today.

In the courtyard, however, she glimpsed the big figure of Haldan walking into one of the outbuildings near the stables. She changed her course to follow him. It was time she enforced the order he persisted in ignoring.

She entered the building, momentarily confused due to the dimness inside. "Haldan?"

A light flared up as Haldan emerged from a corner, bearing a guttering candle. "Here."

"Haldan," she said, ignoring his disrespectful greeting. "I want to discuss the matter of the overgrown trees."

"That again?" he asked. "I'll tell the steward to send some villeins to cut the wood."

"I'm not requesting mere firewood, you dolt! This relates to the defense of the castle, and that rests on your shoulders...unless you choose to leave Trumwell."

Haldan stared at her, eyes narrowing. "Don't think you want that, my lady."

"I've told you for the last time about the trees," Mina said. "Get it done. You could have done it today, while the guests are off on the hunt, so they wouldn't be bothered by the noise."

"Your guests are annoying, always asking questions and poking around," he said. "Send them away."

"One doesn't send away anyone on the business of the king," Mina said. "How dare you presume to tell me what to do!"

"Just like he said," Haldan muttered. "You're far too high and mighty. Women aren't meant to rule. They're meant to be ruled." He grabbed her arm roughly to make his point.

"Get your hand off me," Domina warned.

"Or what? If I wish to touch you, who will save you? Your invalid father? The aging steward? Your pious cousin?" He laughed at the list. "Or the strangers eating out your larder? Be honest. You have no champion."

"Then I'll fight for myself!" she said. She pulled her small knife, such that ladies always carried about them. A weapon of war it was not, but it could still draw blood.

He released his hold. "That much spirit is not becoming in a lady."

"As if you would know," she snapped. Underneath her bravado, she was scared. She knew how a fight between her and Haldan would end. Escaping the building was her only option.

He grinned when he saw her look to the doorway.

"Don't think about it," he hissed, just as he stepped forward.

Mina screamed and lashed out wildly with her knife, not even seeing how she struck him. Her knife dragged against something, and he howled, stumbling back.

She gasped when she saw him clutch a hand to his face, red dripping between his fingers.

"You wicked little whore," he snarled.

"Watch your tongue," she snapped back, "or I'll cut that too."

"You won't have a chance." Haldan recovered enough to lunge at her. Mina screamed out in alarm, ducking beneath his arms as he grabbed for her.

"Get away from me!" she warned, holding the knife

out again.

Haldan hit her outstretched arm. Mina stumbled back, the knife flying from her hand. Her elbow smarted terribly. Part of her couldn't even believe that the man had the temerity to touch her at all, and the other part realized he was just beginning his assault.

"This castle needs a master," he said, stepping forward again. "I'm as good as a knight, so why not me? After all, I've been the man putting up with you for all this time."

Mina edged back, only to hit the wall. He'd backed her into a corner. "Get back," she said.

"You can't do a thing, woman. I'll take you, and then you can't say no to a marriage, can you? Over and done in a night…and tomorrow I'll take Trumwell for myself. I'm sick of waiting."

"Waiting for what?" she gasped.

He didn't answer. He reached out again, seizing Mina by the shoulders. She pushed back with all her might, clawing at his injured face with her nails. But he weighed twice as much as she did, and he was a trained soldier. Mina winced when one meaty hand closed around her throat.

A few seconds later, she could no longer breathe, and strange colors pulsed in her fading vision. Mina's hands dropped, and her head rolled forward as darkness threatened to take her.

Dimly, she heard, "Get away from her!"

Out of nowhere, Luc appeared, rushing at the larger man from the side.

Haldan threw Mina to the ground in an effort to regain a fighting stance. She took huge gulping breaths, too focused on inhaling sweet, sweet air to see much of what happened next.

Whatever Haldan did to get ready for Luc's attack, he was too late. Within moments, Luc twisted the other man's arm behind his back, then shoved him hard up against the wall. Haldan growled, but the sound turned into a undignified whimper.

Haldan lurched, pushing Luc off him. However, the knight recovered his stance instantly, drawing his sword, the sound soft but ominous.

At the moment, Haldan had no weapon larger than the dagger he drew. He plainly didn't like his odds in this new round of the fight.

The sound of metal striking metal made her ears ring. Haldan and Luc circled, the hits following one another.

Haldan snarled. "You should stay out of this."

Luc only flicked his blade toward Haldan. The movement was so swift, Mina didn't see the hit, but Haldan gave a hiss of pain.

Mina struggled to sit up, choking with the effort.

Luc looked at her, and Haldan seized the moment to bolt past Luc and out the door. Mina expected Luc to give chase, but he instead moved toward her, laying his sword down and reaching for her shoulders to help pull her upright.

She tried to speak once, twice, before sound came out at all.

"What are you doing here?" she gasped out. It was the first thing that came to her mind.

"I came back from the hunt a bit earlier than the others," Luc said. "Good thing, too."

She agreed, though saying so was beyond her ability at the moment.

"What happened?" he asked.

"You know what happened," she whispered, her voice

rough. "You know what he was going to do to me."

Luc scanned her for injuries, his blue eyes dark with anger. "He was choking you to death."

"Poor way to secure a bride," she said, the grim humor surfacing unexpectedly. Then the full import of what Haldan intended to do settled in her mind. She felt sick. "No one has *ever* dared to touch me like that."

"No one will again," Luc said. "I'll go after him. He won't get far."

She shook her head, saying, "You're wrong. He knows the countryside here better than you do. He'll flee to Wales. Our laws mean nothing across the border."

"You can't let him go. He assaulted you! You're a lady. What he did…"

"Was despicable," she hissed. "I don't want to think of it again, let alone speak of it. If you care at all, you'll respect that!"

"I also respect the need to stop Haldan. I think you do too."

Mina knew he was right. "Very well, we'll organize a search."

"Let's get you back to the keep first." He slid one arm around her back, helping her to stand. "You can walk?"

She nodded, though her legs felt wobbly. Luc didn't release her until she'd taken a few deep breaths. Mina tried not to think about how near he was to her, but even in her state, she realized that Luc's nearness was entirely different from Haldan's. Still, he was a man, and she wanted nothing to do with men. She swallowed hard and took a step away. "I am well enough now."

He walked her across the courtyard, after looking about very carefully for any sign of Haldan, who seemed to have vanished.

She ought to call for Ancel, to relate the whole incident and set up a search for Haldan. But at the moment, it felt far too overwhelming to relive the details.

"Would you let me speak to the steward?" Luc asked, as if sensing her thoughts. "No need to bother you further tonight."

She nodded. Her arm ached, her neck was starting to burn with pain, and she'd be covered in bruises tomorrow.

They reached the door of the keep.

"Domina," Luc said.

She turned, her pain making her temper short. "What else?"

He handed her the knife she had dropped, offering it to her hilt first.

"Oh," she said, reaching out to take it. "Thank you."

"A fighter always takes care of his weapons," he said.

"It's obvious then that I'm no fighter, for I left this in the dirt."

"You drew blood," he pointed out. "I think you'd make a worthy ally…or a formidable enemy."

"Which is it?"

"That, my lady, remains to be decided. How is your throat?" he asked suddenly.

"It hurts," she said, "but I'll recover soon enough."

"That's a relief. If your voice is permanently harmed, Haldan should hang for it. I wonder if it will affect your ability to sing."

A chill ran down her spine. "I don't sing."

"Ah, too bad," he said, carelessly. "I've always had a soft spot for a woman with a beautiful voice."

Domina shot him a dark glance. "Then be glad you're not staying here long, Sir Luc. When you return to London, you will doubtless find a woman to your liking."

"Speaking of which, I do think I'll be leaving…"

"When?" She could hardly keep the intensity from her voice, she was so eager for him to be gone.

"Just as soon as your father returns. I can't consider my errand complete until I speak to him."

Domina swallowed painfully. "You are quite certain? I hate to keep you here with no end to your waiting. You could come back another time. In the spring, perhaps."

"But I'm here now," Luc said, "and it seems fate might want me here."

Domina said nothing to that, and she didn't dare meet his eyes. Despite what he'd just done for her, she would give anything for Luc to be gone.

Anything.

Chapter 10

AFTER MAKING SURE THAT DOMINA went into the keep and up to her own chambers, Luc found the steward and told him the bare facts. Haldan committed a crime by assaulting a noblewoman, and he was not to be allowed in the castle again. Anyone who saw him should hold him.

The word went out among the castle residents. Several men-at-arms gathered to begin a search. One man who'd been on watch had seen Haldan heading east after riding out of the gate, so they began on that road. However, Haldan's lead and the darkness were against them. An hour after they rode out of the castle, Luc called a halt, telling the men to return to Trumwell.

"Someone can ride to the sheriff tomorrow to tell him about the incident. He can sound the news more broadly," Luc added.

Once back at the castle, Luc went in search of a good place to brood. He was unwilling to be seen by anyone until he could think over all the revelations of the day.

It was foolish to have mentioned Domina's singing. Luc might well have announced that he'd discovered her secret. Yet, he couldn't stop himself. His blood was up after the encounter with Haldan, especially since he'd got away, depriving Luc of the chance to finish the fight.

Perhaps naturally, his attention shifted to Haldan's intended victim. Luc couldn't forget that Domina had lied to him. He wanted to see her face when she thought her secret was threatened.

Domina lied about her father. She'd lied again and again and again. To him, to her allies, to the *king*. If she could lie about one thing, why not a dozen? A woman who could lie so well would make the perfect traitor.

As soon as he thought that, he grimaced. He didn't want Domina to be a traitor. Perhaps she lied for a better reason.

He pictured the way she tended to the man on the bed. She treated her father with such care and spoke so gently to him. Dear lord, she *sang* to him. Was that what a traitor would do? No. A woman hellbent on betrayal wouldn't nurse her father back to health. She'd hurry him along to death, and invite the conspirators in.

But how could he reconcile that with the news of the spymaster Drugo? He'd been adamant that the de Warewics were involved in a conspiracy. Luc remembered Lord Bertram's comment that he hadn't seen Godfrey in months. Perhaps Godfrey's sickness was fairly recent, and Domina was innocently nursing a traitor back to health.

So what did that leave him with? Now that he'd met Domina, Luc could believe that she was intelligent enough to devise a conspiracy if she wanted to. Domina understood the principles of war, and how to attack and defend. Furthermore, she clearly kept her own council and had a mind of iron. If she wanted something, she had the force of will to attain it.

But was she really capable of treason? Was that in her heart? He went through every conversation, every scrap of her speech, every gesture and reaction she'd made to his own words. Nearly all she'd said or done was in line with a loyal servant of the king. Domina said she came to London to fulfill the king's order when Godfrey could not —was that the act of a traitor? But then again, wouldn't a traitor appear loyal until the very last moment?

Luc sighed in frustration. This was the conundrum. Once you doubted someone's motives, everything they said or did could be used to support those doubts. She was either lying or she wasn't. She was either loyal or she wasn't.

Then he had an idea. What if he could persuade her to share her true thoughts by pretending to share the same ideas? If he could trick her into speaking the truth, then he'd have the evidence he needed to take to the king. Domina kept her true emotions safe behind a facade of icy calm. All he had to do was melt that facade.

He couldn't speak to her about it until the next day at the earliest. The attack from Haldan had been no act, and Domina was visibly shaken. The thought of the man touching Domina sent Luc's blood boiling. He told himself that it was merely the man's audacity in hurting a lady, any lady. Luc would have intervened no matter what woman was being attacked.

What if he hadn't ridden back early? What would have happened if Haldan succeeded? He could have forced a marriage, then declared himself the castellan and shut the gates to everyone. Domina would be a prisoner in her own home.

Luc couldn't deny that some of his fury was because it was Domina in particular who was in danger. He barely knew her, and by all accounts, she would rather have Luc out of her life, but something in her personality had already snared him. Luc didn't like the idea of any other man touching her. Ever.

He shook his head, trying to laugh off the madness. He was letting the intensity of the moment get to him. The strange excitement after a physical fight always left him feeling restless. He'd feel like himself after a good night's sleep.

No sleep came to him. That night, Luc stared at the canopy of his bed. He couldn't close his eyes without seeing what transpired earlier that day: the secret room, Haldan's attack, Domina's ashen face when Luc mentioned her singing.

He couldn't sleep because he had too much in his brain, too much unresolved. He got up and lit a candle from the embers of the fire.

Luc sat for some time, contemplating his options. He reached for the folded parchment he'd kept hidden since arriving here.

An idea came to him. Luc dressed swiftly and left his chamber, moving through the dark corridors without aid of a candle.

He left the keep from a small door through the kitchen, and crossed the freezing courtyard, moving like a shadow. There was a chance that someone stood guard the whole night through, but it was equally likely that the household servants who were charged with the duty weren't able to stay awake.

In fact, Luc saw no one at all. He remembered the little room he'd hidden in earlier. Doubtless if someone was to stay near the old man, they were sleeping in the next room on the pallet.

Luc would have to be quiet, but he wasn't deterred. He opened the door to Godfrey's chamber. The dying fire offered some light. Luc lit a candle using the embers, and brought it to the old man's bedside.

"Godfrey," he said quietly, putting a hand to the man's shoulder. "Are you awake?"

After a moment, the man stirred from his sleep.

"Who calls?" he asked in a thin voice. "Joscelin? Is that you, my boy? Have you come back for good this time?"

Luc didn't correct the misapprehension. He was merely glad the old man didn't recognize him as a stranger and yell for help.

"Sir, how long have you been here?"

"On this earth? More years than you, stripling!" Godfrey blinked several times, and stared harder at Luc. "You look different, boy. What have you been up to?"

"Don't mind me," Luc said. "How long have you been ill?"

"Am I ill? Send for Mina, then. She'll know what to do."

Mina. Luc had never heard anyone call her by such a pet name, and the way Godfrey said it, with such affection, made him pause, considering again what he was about to do.

"Mina has been tending to you," Luc said finally. "She sang to you not long ago."

"Ah, yes." Godfrey closed his eyes. "I remember. A voice as sweet as her mother's. She taught her, you know. No...you were not here then..." Godfrey opened his eyes, troubled and confused again. "What's happening?"

"I need you to sign something, sir."

"Take it to Mina."

"This must be your hand, sir. Mina cannot sign it."

"Why not?"

"It's for her marriage."

"You always argued against marriage. You said she ought to take the veil."

What? Who did Godfrey think he was? The idea of Mina as a nun almost made Luc laugh out loud. "The veil?"

"You opposed every offer. You prayed for her, you said, and both offers failed. God's will, you said…"

"I will give you pen and ink, sir." Luc unfolded the parchment. "This is what you must sign."

"Who is the man? Why does he not come to me first?"

"The name is Luc of Braecon," Luc said. The enormity of what he was doing suddenly struck him. *It's just preparation*, he told himself. *Just in case. I can still walk back from this edge.*

"Braecon. King's man?"

"Yes, sir. King Stephen himself suggested the match."

"Ah." Godfrey relaxed. "The pen, then."

Luc handed him a pen from the nearby desk, with ink dripping off the nib. "The line here," he said, guiding the frail hand to the page.

Godfrey tightened his grip on the pen, but then paused. "What is Mina's thought on this? I should ask her first…"

"She knows the man," Luc said. "Remember, this is the king's wish."

Godfrey's hand trembled. "Mina is a little headstrong. She needs someone who is the match of her in mind. Is he? And is he honorable? She is my only child. I must speak with her. And her mother…" Godfrey stared past Luc, into nothing. "What has happened? What is this room?"

Luc could tell he was losing the old man. "Please, sir. Sign your name."

Godfrey obeyed that time, as if he'd forgotten the whole previous conversation, which was entirely possible.

He looked at the pen in surprise when he was done. "I can't eat my stew with this."

"No, you can't." Luc took the pen away from him. "I'll make sure you have a spoon."

"Thank you, my boy." He blinked. "Joscelin?" He frowned, lucidity returning for a moment. "You're not Joscelin."

"No, I'm not," Luc said, sick of pretending. "My name is Luc."

"Have we met?"

"No, sir."

"Why am I not dressed for company. Fetch Mina. Fetch Emma. Emma will know…"

He closed his eyes, exhausted.

I did that to him, Luc thought. The man was so weak that signing a document was too much for him. He was incapable of serving as lord of the castle. No wonder Domina strove to hide his condition. If this news became public, she might as well open the gate and invite invaders inside.

But she hadn't. Instead, she did everything she could to keep control of the castle and lands, and never turned to another force. If Mina was loyal, then she was also alone. No one was helping her as she tried to keep the castle and her lands secure. Or she was playing a more subtle game, something she was definitely capable of.

Luc went back to the keep as silently as he'd come. He'd taken a great risk, telling Godfrey his name. If the man told Mina, the situation might change quickly. Yet he thought the outcome worth the risk, for now he had real leverage if he had to challenge Domina in any way.

He hid the parchment again and returned to his bed. This time he drifted right off to sleep. He woke only once before dawn, from a strange but pleasant dream in which a swan lay beside him, singing sweetly in her sleep.

Chapter 11

THE NEXT DAY, MINA ROSE rather late, for Constance had made her drink wine blended with poppy syrup the previous night.

The maid was horrified to hear what had occurred, and swore that Haldan must be part devil to do such a thing.

"I'd rather not ever think of it again," Mina had said, while Constance helped her out of her gown and looked over the damage, which was thankfully limited to a few ugly bruises.

"Praise Him that someone came to your rescue," Constance said, ignoring the spirit of Mina's comment. "It might have been much worse."

"Yes, I know," Mina said, "but we're not going to discuss it again, Constance. Do you understand?"

"Oh! Yes, my lady," the maid replied, abashed. She'd then prepared the poppy wine, and very soon after drinking it, Domina was lost to the world.

Thus, her head was groggy despite the sunshine, and

she barely spoke when Constance appeared to dress her and fix her hair.

Domina went down to the great hall, where the steward greeted her with such a wide smile that she thought the war must be over.

"Come see, my lady," Ancel said, drawing her along to the kitchens. They proceeded to the courtyard just outside, and Domina stopped short on seeing a cart bearing the carcasses of two deer.

"What is this?"

"The spoils from the hunt yesterday," he said. "Sir Luc ordered his kills brought to his hostess."

"He never said," Domina murmured. Then again, the first time she saw him after the hunt, they were both rather preoccupied.

"This will stretch the larder," the steward went on. "Certainly until the guests depart."

"I ought to congratulate him," she said.

Hearing that he was in the solar, she went there, and found both Luc and Octavian near the fire. "Good day," she said.

Both men rose from their seats.

"How are you feeling?" Luc asked, looking her over.

Mina had tried to conceal the worst of her bruising by wearing her hair loose, but she knew it was partly evident. "I feel more restored than I may look." She spoke obliquely, not sure if Luc had mentioned the attack.

"I told Octavian what occurred," Luc said.

"I see." Mina blushed in embarrassment, as if she was somehow responsible. Well, in a way, she was. She ought to have sent Haldan away long before.

Octavian's eyes narrowed. "You blame yourself," he said, half guess, half statement. "You should not."

"It doesn't matter," she said. "It's over."

"We were talking," Luc said. "Octavian agrees with me. The matter should be taken to the sheriff."

She bit her lip. "But there's nothing to be done. I'm sure Haldan has fled as far from here as he can."

"What if he comes back?" Octavian asked. "What if he seeks to join another garrison, or another family's estate? What of those daughters?"

Mina closed her eyes, afraid to picture it.

"If his crime is made public, there's much less chance of further damage," Luc said. "Secrets won't help anyone now, my lady."

She nodded. "Very well. I'll write up an account of what happened and have it sent to the sheriff."

Luc exchanged a glance with Octavian, and Mina guessed they expected more resistance from her.

She recalled the real reason she came into the room. "What a demoralizing subject to speak on," she said, trying to get back into the role of hostess. "I meant to thank you for the gift of venison. It is most impressive."

"Little enough to pay for your hospitality," Luc said.

"Well, Luc has paid," Octavian added. "Both kills belong to him."

"You aided, Tav."

"So did the hounds," Octavian countered, deadpan.

Luc grinned, sending a tremor down Mina's body. She was acting foolish. Yes, he'd saved her...again, she thought, recalling the night in London. However, she shouldn't feel giddy whenever she looked at him. He was just like any other man.

Well, handsomer than many, she admitted. His eyes she noticed the first night, being an unusual shade of blue she'd never seen before. His smile could shift from gentle to sardonic in a moment, showing more awareness of the mood of a room than she would have expected of a knight. But Luc seemed to live for much more than battle. He loved to hunt, he flirted incorrigibly, and he certainly knew his politics. No matter what he was doing, those blue eyes took in everything.

Including, apparently, Domina gaping at him like an idiot.

Her blush deepened. "I'll…I'll write something for the sheriff's use. Please excuse me," she muttered. Thankfully, no one followed her from the solar. In her chamber, she called for parchment and ink. A short while later, she had written all she felt comfortable saying. She sealed the letter by dripping wax onto the edge, then waiting for it to harden.

She presented it to Octavian, who was still with Luc in the solar.

"No special seal?" Luc asked, peeking at the letter. "Not a swan?"

"My father wears the only seal we have, so of course I cannot use it."

"Of course," Luc murmured, "because he's not here."

"He always calls it his cygnet ring," she added, earning a half-smile from Luc when he heard the terrible pun.

"I'll ride to the sheriff as soon as I can," Octavian promised. "Only he will read this letter, my lady."

"I thank you, Sir Octavian," she said. "You're doing far more than your due."

"Whatever a lady asks, a knight is pleased to carry out," Octavian said simply.

"In that case, I ask you to deliver this and return safely."

He bowed. "Yes, my lady."

* * * *

Later that same evening, Domina was sitting in a small parlour, going over some accounts. She should have done it during the day, instead of at night, but she didn't want to neglect her work any longer.

At a knock, she looked up to see Luc in the doorway. "Did you need something, my lord?" she asked, striving to sound more polite than she felt. Would he always find her just as she thought she'd have a moment alone?

"I do." He entered the room, closing the door quietly behind him.

Mina noted the action but said nothing. Perhaps he was only concerned about a draft. The winter air was biting, even inside the walls. This little room boasted a merrily burning fire, and the walls being hung with woven cloth helped keep the room even more snug.

"Please sit and warm yourself if you have need," she said, indicating the seat opposite her.

He instead knelt in front of the fire itself, soaking in the heat of the flame as if he were a cat. The image of Luc as a panther suddenly came to her head. He was built as she imagined such a creature to be: narrow but strong, well-muscled, elegant and deadly, always ready to pounce. When he turned to face her, his eyes caught the gleam of fire, and the image was reinforced. She let out a tiny gasp, she was so caught by the notion.

He smiled then, a smile that belonged to a predator. "Am I stealing your fire, my lady?"

She shook her head mutely. The papers she'd been going through now rested in her lap. Luc reached out and plucked them away. "What task are you at now?"

"Reviewing household accounts, no more," Mina said,

recovering her normal demeanor. "Please give those back."

But Luc didn't, instead looking them over with an interested eye. "Tidily done," he noted.

"I employ a skilled clerk," she replied, putting acid in her tone. "Though such business is no business of yours."

"I'm curious," he admitted. "Everything about you and your life makes me curious."

Those words, delivered in his soft, suggestive voice, made the room a little warmer.

"I can't see why," she said. "The everyday minutiae of country life can only be dull for a knight such as yourself."

"You're different, though," he said. He returned the papers to her, sliding them back onto her lap. His hand lingered on her knee for a moment. "You don't think like most people, do you?"

"What do you mean?" She intended those words to be clipped, dismissive. Why did she instead sound so interested in his answer?

Luc shifted so he knelt in front of her, not the fire. Seeing him gaze up at her was most disconcerting.

"You don't simply think of everyday minutiae," he said. "You think past the next season. You plan. You prepare. You develop ideas for how to react if the world changes."

"Everyone does that."

"They do not," he said, flatly contradicting her. "They assume nothing will change, even when they should know better. You're smarter than that. You see the world around you, and you know how fragile it all is. The alliances, the battles, who holds what. It can all change in a day."

She'd never heard Luc speak quite like this before. "I

suppose you're right. I'd be a fool to ignore the possibilities that wait."

"Exactly." He put his hands on the bench, one on either side of her, and leaned forward. "You understand how important it is to be ready."

"Ready for what?"

He seemed to notice how close he'd got to her, but he didn't pull back. "Ready for an opportunity."

"Such as?" She couldn't take her eyes off him.

"What if you heard that fortune was falling away from the king?" Luc asked, his voice no louder than breath. "That the empress's own star was rising, that everything was about to change?"

"I…haven't heard that." She could barely breathe with Luc so close, let alone think clearly.

"I could tell you things most people don't know, things I've learned in my position, being so close to the king." He lifted one hand and touched the edge of her jaw, running his finger down to her chin. The frisson set up a whole new heat in her body, centered in her belly and running down to her hips and legs.

"For some reason," he said, "I feel compelled to share a few secrets with you."

"You…" she began to say, though his fingers on her skin was so distracting she had to stop and try again. "You should not betray a confidence."

"I'd be starting a new confidence. With you."

"It's not right." His touch felt right, though. No one ever touched her like that. She didn't want it to stop. "Please don't tell me anything you should not."

"We could both benefit," he murmured. "I know what the king plans, and you control a castle that could be the start of a new stronghold in the west."

She blinked, shaking off the pleasant haze his touch had put her into. "How can you say that?"

"What's wrong with making plans?"

"It's wrong when such plans lead to ruin." She stood up abruptly, forcing Luc to step back and rise as well. "I will not hear a word more. You say Stephen trusts you. Perhaps his trust is misplaced."

"That's not what I meant."

"That's exactly what you meant." Domina raised her chin. "I want you to leave Trumwell. Tomorrow morning. With your retinue."

"I'm not done here," Luc objected, his voice still quite calm.

"Carrying out your orders for King Stephen? What else can you possibly discover? You're aware of the castle's strength, the numbers in the garrison, how well stocked the armory is. You don't need to wait around for my father to know all that. Take your report back to Stephen, if that's who you truly serve."

Now Luc's eyes narrowed to slits. "Be careful in your words, Domina."

"Advice you should take for yourself, Luc of Braecon. I don't like the words you've spoken. I had doubts about you before, but they are tenfold now."

"If you don't like my words, then at least trust your eyes." Without warning, Luc lifted his shirt, revealing bare skin.

Luc's bare torso was all hard muscle, from riding and fighting and training. But, his skin was marked with a long, wicked scar that ran for several inches, parallel to his waist. The new flesh was still pink, and the surface of the scar was raised, not like the rest of his skin.

"I earned this in a battle in which I fought for

Stephen," he said. "I got it in the morning, and watched the blood slowly seep out of me for hours until my friends could get me off the field. I didn't have a bandage. Just my hand, so I stayed there, tying to hold my guts in while my company fought and died around me. Not glorious. Not pleasant. But I did it without question, and I would again. Because that's what my oath means."

Mina's eyes were locked on the scar. "You could have died," she whispered.

"A few hours more without aid, and I likely would have. I couldn't sit up by the end. I was carried off the field on a plank."

"How long did it take to recover?"

"Months. I was given leave, sent home to rest. But there's not a lot of rest when you know that the world is spinning on without you. Then you want to serve, but can do nothing but lie there. As soon as I could walk again, I sent word to the king."

"He sent you here, though," she said. "Far away from the battles."

"There are battles everywhere, Domina. Not all of them are fought in the open."

"Why are you here?" she asked, dragging her gaze from the scar to Luc's deceptively calm face. "*Why* has he sent you here?"

Luc let the hem of his shirt drop, and she breathed a little sigh of relief. "My orders are my business, and I'm not leaving here until my business is done."

Mina nodded absently, her mind in turmoil. She backed out of the room, not aware she was doing it and not sure where she was going.

Her instinct was to go to her father's room, but of course she couldn't dare do that now. Instead, she fled to the chapel, deserted now except for her. The space was cold, and only a pair of candles burned on the side altar. She walked to the light, then stood in front of the small iron-wrought cross, her mind full of Luc's words.

She didn't understand Luc at all. It was bad enough that he was here, disrupting her life and her peace of mind. It was far worse that she reacted to him so strongly. Every time she saw him, her heart raced more. Not just because she was nervous, needing to watch her words and her demeanor lest he suspect the truth. No, it was purely a reaction to him. The few times he'd touched her, she felt it like a burn. If he ever kissed her, she might catch fire.

When he'd driven off Haldan, she wondered for half a moment if her prayers had been answered in the form of a knightly protector. He certainly looked the part, and he seemed to say all the right things…until that disturbing conversation they'd just had. Did Mina misunderstand something? She reviewed the words in her head, striving to find a different meaning in them. Luc could not have seriously suggested treason, and yet no matter how she tried to change her mind, that was still how it sounded.

She had to get him away from Trumwell Castle as soon as possible, along with his whole retinue. If he was false, she couldn't trust anyone with him, from the quiet Sir Octavian to the lowliest page.

She decided that she'd simply tell Luc that she'd write to the king himself of her suspicions. If he was loyal, then he'd argue his case. If he wasn't, well, she was doing the king a good service. Regardless, Luc couldn't stay here.

* * * *

After Domina fled from him, Luc remained in the

room, thinking over what just happened. She certainly hadn't liked the suggestion of supporting the empress in any way. Her reaction gratified Luc, even if it meant she looked at him as untrustworthy for the moment. He'd weather that storm. His loyalty wasn't in question, not to those who mattered.

Luc picked up the papers Domina had left behind, scanning them. Household accounts, as she'd said. The amounts were rather small to his eye. Was a castle like Trumwell able to survive on such frugal spending? Perhaps not. He noted a few entries—the purchase of grain, the sale of some equipment a few weeks prior to that. They matched almost exactly. Did someone have to sell an asset to simply feed the castle's residents? Luc remembered an offhand comment from one of the garrison's men, who'd said that it had been a long time since the last real feast.

He knew little about stewarding a castle, but it seemed Trumwell wasn't faring particularly well. That didn't match with Drugo's picture of Godfrey de Warewic spreading wealth around in the form of swan-marked coins. Godfrey would consider himself first. Any noble would, if only because a financially poor ally was, well, a politically poor ally.

Then again, Godfrey wasn't directing life at Trumwell now—he was laying insensate in a corner building, while Domina pretended he was traveling. Luc frowned. The whole castle had to know the truth, and they all conspired to hide it from the guests. Everyone lied to Luc and Octavian. Everyone tried to keep them away from the building where Godfrey rested, to distract them in one way or another.

What was Domina's game, then? Why would she conceal the truth, if she was indeed following whatever her father's original intentions were? All she had to do was inform the king...

And there was the answer. If Domina told the king that her father could no longer defend Trumwell Castle, the property would be given to someone else—a knight or a lord whose favor the king wanted to keep. Domina and her family would be forced out, with no concern for where they might go. Domina might be married off to a man who needed a noble wife to boost his own standing.

Luc's fingers itched as he thought of the marriage contract he possessed. The king never intended him to actually marry Domina, but he had it all the same. Luc could use the contract for a more noble cause, such as protecting Domina from the political ambitions of some lord's son...

...some lord's son like him.

Luc heard his father's voice in his head. His father always counseled the need to view every situation as an opportunity. He should weigh the political advantages and disadvantages of this new situation. Was there some use he could get out of the paper?

Well, he could gain a castle. And a wife.

He'd already been promised a good marriage, though. An earl's daughter, a woman who would do far more than Domina to help him politically.

But she wouldn't be Domina, and Luc now realized that he didn't want just any wife. He wanted a very particular one. He wanted Domina, with her uncommonly sharp wit, and her clear concern for her people and her name. Was that worth throwing his ambitions to the wind?

Luc sighed, staring at the fire. The flames licked at the fuel, casting heat out into the room, denying the winter winds outside.

He wished Octavian hadn't left on his errand to the sheriff. Tav would view the whole mess from his outsider's view. He'd be honest with Luc. He wouldn't be thinking irrationally, seeing Domina's face every few moments, worrying about what would happen after Luc left the castle.

No, he didn't have to wait. In fact, he already knew what Octavian would say. The other man would tell him that it was natural for a *true* knight to want to be a champion, and that there was nothing more important than upholding one's oath. Luc swore an oath to the king, but he also swore an oath on the day he became a knight.

That oath said nothing about worldly goals or maneuvering for the most advantageous alliance. It said, very plainly, that the strong should protect the weak. That if a knight saw someone in trouble, he had a duty to assist.

True, the last thing a woman like Domina would want was to be rescued. Indeed, every time Luc rescued her before, he got nothing but the cold shoulder.

But she was acting in defense of her home and her people. Once she had Luc as a protector, that brittle exterior would soften. She'd be grateful, though she might not say so immediately.

Luc nodded to himself. Yes, marriage was the right choice, if he was thinking as a knight. Of course, he couldn't tell Domina the whole truth—at least not until he found Haldan and whoever he might be working for. She was loyal, but a traitor remained somewhere in the center of this web.

He certainly couldn't tell her that the marriage contract was initially intended to be a smokescreen. So he'd have to explain the matter as one of politics, rather than ideals. At some point in the future, he'd tell her the whole story, once she'd come to accept him and after the real traitor had been captured.

Besides, she *had* lied to him about her father. Luc was still annoyed that she tried to trick him in order to maintain her standing as the de facto castellan of Trumwell. Perhaps confronting her with a marriage contract would remind her just how dangerous such a game could be.

Chapter 12

THE NEXT MORNING DAWNED COLD and bright. Domina did her best to avoid Luc that day. Thankfully, whatever he was up to seemed to be a solitary pursuit. She was able to conduct all her usual tasks—with the notable exception of visiting her father—without interruption from her guest.

At one point in the early afternoon, a very young man rode into the courtyard on a raw-boned but sturdy country horse. He looked like a messenger, but since no message came to Domina, she decided it must have been intended for Luc. Perhaps Luc would be called back to glorious battle, where he could prove himself again, and earn favors from all the ladies of the court who were swayed by his charm.

Domina went to the solar to deal with some small tasks, taking advantage of the bright sunlight coming in the western windows. She didn't mind the work, especially because she was drinking her favorite tisane, a blend of sage and mint that always invigorated her.

While she was working, Luc entered the room, carrying a folded parchment in his hand. Orders to return to the king, she hoped. Or news that the war was over. Or anything that would take him away from here.

"You bear tidings?" she asked, in a tone of cool politeness.

He made a noncommittal noise. "I got a strange message from Octavian. He delivered your news to the sheriff, but he'll be delayed in his return due to a personal matter."

That wasn't what she expected to hear. "Forgive me, but has Sir Octavian connections in this area? He said he was only recently come to Britain."

Luc nodded absently. "A few years ago. However, we have mutual friends at the manor of Cleobury, near Bournham—you might not have heard of it."

"I've heard of Cleobury," she said. "It's to the north."

"Yes. I suppose his news must have something to do with the de Vere family…though I can't see how…" He trailed off. "I had hoped he'd be back by now."

She watched as he raised the folded parchment up. He looked at her, his expression changing to resolute. "My lady Domina, I have something important to show you."

"What is it?" She put down her cup and walked over to the table where he'd spread out the parchment.

"A document. It relates to you."

Her back stiffened instantly, and ice ran down her spine.

She picked up the document. She read it silently, her eyes running down and then jumping to the top again. After a long moment, she swallowed, her throat dry, so dry.

"I don't understand. He was joking," she said dully. "He said it was a joke."

"He changed his mind. Kings can do that."

Domina read the document over and over, but the words didn't change. The heavy black ink and the seal of the king stated in undeniable terms that Luc of Braecon was to be given the hand of Domina de Warewic, and with it all her goods and property.

But most horrifying of all was the scrawled mark on the bottom of the page. Though shaky, she recognized it as well as her own hand.

"What is this?" she asked in a low voice.

"Godfrey's signature."

"That's impossible."

"Why?" Luc stared at her, daring her to call him a liar.

"He is....not here."

"So you told me when I arrived."

"This cannot be," she whispered. She closed her eyes. Perhaps if she concentrated, she could wake herself from this nightmare. It had to be a nightmare. Everywhere, Luc outmaneuvered her, until she had nowhere to turn and nowhere to go.

"Say it, Domina," he challenged. "Say what's on your mind."

She couldn't. The possibility was too dreadful to say out loud. Instead, she picked up her skirts and ran.

She made it as far as the hall when Luc caught up to her. He put one hand on her shoulder and stopped her cold.

"You can't run from this, Domina," he said.

"Let me go." It sounded like begging. She hated the sound of her own voice, but couldn't stop herself. "Let me go, please."

"Go where? To the building where your father is sleeping?"

Mina never knew what it meant to swoon until now. Her skin went cold and she wavered on her feet.

Luc grabbed her by the waist to keep her from falling, but there was no gentleness in the gesture. "I know he's here, Domina. I've been inside the room. I saw him. And yes, I had him sign."

Her father might as well have signed her death warrant. Domina clenched her fists. "You cannot do this. He's not in his right mind. He can't sign a contract. If you try to hold me to it, I'll—"

"You'll what, exactly?" Luc asked coolly.

Mina took a breath, trying to think of a single way out of this corner. But Luc was right, and he *knew* he was right. Mina couldn't object to Luc's move without exposing herself to a much worse outcome. All her strength relied on keeping her father's condition secret.

"Why?" she asked. "Why are you here? Why are you so intent on ruining me?"

Luc put a hand on her face, forcing her to look at him. "Why are you so intent on lying to me?"

She choked up. No words would come, because she had no defense. She was in Luc's power. He knew all her weaknesses, and he could destroy her in a dozen different ways if he wanted to.

"You lied to me," Luc repeated. His blue eyes were clear, cold.

Domina bit her lip, unable to argue with that simple statement.

"Well?" he pressed.

"What would you have me say?" she whispered.

"The truth!"

She gulped in a breath. She would start crying at any moment. "You've seen the truth. Why make me say it!"

"I need to hear it from you," he said. "Tell me, and don't you dare try any trick. Not now."

She kept her eyes closed, too afraid to see the hate on Luc's face.

"The truth is…" she began to explain, "the truth is that my father took ill very suddenly. One evening, he was healthy and lively, a man in his prime, the lord of his world. In the morning, I found him unconscious at the foot of the stairs. It took four men to haul him to his bed, and despite all I did, he would not wake."

"Go on," Luc said quietly.

"I called for a physician, and then another and another. None could wake him, or even say what ailed him. I prayed for him to wake, but the day he did, it was as if…" She shuddered at the memory. "It was worse than I could imagine. He didn't know my name for a month. I told him everything he already knew, but nothing stays… He speaks, but it's nearly all nonsense, as if his body is here but his mind is gone, or lost in the past… I've tried everything I can *think* of. And nothing I do can *help* him…"

Domina inhaled raggedly, and then she was in Luc's arms. Even as she tried to ask what he meant to do with her, the touch of him around her felt so divinely comforting that she leaned against him, just for a moment. When was the last time she had leaned on anyone?

Luc held her without speaking, without telling her not to cry, which she was horrified to discover she was doing, loudly and without grace. So much for strength! Was that all it took? One gentle touch from a man, and she went to pieces in his arms.

"How long?" he asked after a little while. "Domina? How long ago did this happen?"

"Two years last spring," Domina whispered.

"Over two years?" he repeated incredulously. His hands went to her shoulders again and he held her a little distance away so he could look her over. "You've been concealing this from everyone, and running everything for *years*?"

"What choice did I have? If I told anyone, I'd lose any right to command my own castle, my own lands! Either the king would have given all to a lord he favored and packed me off to a nunnery, or he'd give me in marriage to whoever he chose and I would not even have my father to speak for me and bargain for a better match if he could!"

"Which is just what happened in the end," said Luc. His lip twitched, though he didn't seem amused.

"I never should have gone to London," she railed. "Such a petty matter. The king asked for the numbers of the garrison? The supplies? I could have sent that by letter! Instead I did what I thought was right, what my father would have wanted. I presented myself at court, I endured all those courtiers laughing at me, the naive girl from the hinterland…"

"And now you have me here," he concluded, releasing her at last.

Domina took a step back, swiping at her eyes. "It wasn't you in particular that I didn't want," she said.

"How heartening."

"Please listen to me. I have run this estate for years. I will continue to do so."

"No, you won't, not if you have no allies," Luc said. "Can't you see how it looks? I'm a knight. It's my duty to protect this castle. Marrying you will further that aim."

"No," she pleaded.

"Yes," he told her, relentless. "Yes, Domina. The king

himself decrees it. Would you oppose him?"

"I can't," she said, her heart breaking. Was this to be her life now? She would lose her name and her lands and her freedom and her spirit, all because a man far away wrote her name on a piece of paper. At that moment, Domina *hated* the king. But she could not oppose him. "I can't say no, can I?"

Luc stared at her for a long moment, his expression unreadable. "Then prepare for a wedding."

Chapter 13

IN THE END, LUC GAVE Domina and her people three whole days to get ready for a titanic shift in their lives. She'd protested, but he'd countered every objection, pointing out that the sooner it was done, the safer Trumwell would be. Once wedded, Domina couldn't be used as a pawn in the way that Haldan tried to do. Luc was helping her, he explained.

How generous, Mina thought bitterly.

With little choice otherwise, Domina oversaw the preparations for the wedding. Considering the circumstances, one might have thought she saw it as a funeral. In fact, Mina felt nothing about it. Nothing at all.

It was as if everything was happening very far away, and she was scarcely involved. Ever since Luc handed her that document, the game was over. She had no moves left, and therefore she lost.

Having lost the game at last, it should be no surprise that she also lost her appetite, her sense of humor, and her spirit. The plans for the wedding went ahead, and she made no objections.

Outwardly, she pretended a bit more enthusiasm. She

hated the idea of her people worrying over her fate or the fate of Trumwell. So she wore a smile when she could and retreated to her room when she was allowed to.

At the moment, she looked over at Constance, who was carrying her newest gown. "What is that?"

"I'm going to air out and freshen up the gown to see that it's made ready for the day."

"Why should I not wear an older gown?" Mina said. "I'd not want that one marred."

"But my lady, your wedding day…"

"Oh, very well then." She constantly had to remind herself that as far as everyone knew, this event was her choice!

Domina sighed, and stared at the table again. "What of your family?" she asked Luc, who had come to the room on some other matter related to the wedding. She hoped to find reason for some delay. "Or friends? You don't want to wait for Sir Octavian?"

"I don't know when he'll return. As for my family, there's time enough for that later. I'll write to let them know what's occurred, and we'll arrange for a visit in the spring."

Domina frowned. Luc wasn't budging on the date of the wedding. It made her sour, and she disliked his assumption that she'd be a biddable wife.

"Are you inviting them into my home," she asked pointedly, "or will you be dragging me out of my home to go to theirs?"

Luc looked at her steadily. "Which would you prefer?"

"I'd prefer not to be married."

"That's not one of the options. Both you and Trumwell need a protector."

"You're not my master yet," she warned him. Despite

his noble-sounding intentions, she suspected that he nominated himself as protector because he'd heard rumors of the de Warewic wealth. Well, he'd be bitterly disappointed when he learned the truth about *that*. The thought actually gave her an idea.

"Luc, may I speak to you?"

"You are speaking to me."

"Alone."

He nodded, curiosity in his eyes.

Domina sent the two maids away, then turned to him. "Listen to me. This marriage—you'll regret it."

"What makes you say that? Do you plan to poison me in my sleep?" he asked jokingly.

"No!" Mina went cold at the mere idea. "I've nothing against you!"

"That's a relief."

"But I think you misunderstand my value."

He looked puzzled. "How so?"

"I'm not rich."

"I know that."

She blinked in surprise. "You do?"

"All the wealth of the de Warewics still officially belongs to your father. He's the head of the family," Luc said, quite sensibly.

"It's worse…" Mina began to spill the whole truth, but something stopped her. Perhaps giving up that information would be foolish. After all, the assumption that she was an heiress was one of her last advantages. Who would listen to her if Luc revealed to the world that she was penniless? "Ah, I mean…you would not know when… things might change…"

"Domina," Luc said, stepping up to her. "You seem to think the worst of me. I have no intention of robbing you the morning after the wedding. I intend to stay here, in order to hold the castle in the king's name. It's part of my oath to the king."

"But you'll drag me off to your family's home for a visit?" Mina seized upon his earlier statement. "Wouldn't that violate your oath to protect?"

"We can wait to discuss the visiting," he said blandly.

She rolled her eyes and stalked off. Luc's refusal to engage in a proper argument made her almost as angry as the fact that she had to marry him at all. She never thought of herself as a dreamer, but perhaps a tiny part of her yearned for love. If Luc had courted her, she likely would have happily accepted him. But his proposal was nothing more than a piece of the king's defense strategy. Not exactly the stuff of a woman's desires!

On her way out of the room, she ran smack into the steward.

"Apologies, my lady," Ancel said. "It's chaos within these walls."

She nodded. At least someone agreed with her. "He's ruined everything."

"Who?"

"Luc of Braecon! Who else?"

"You ought not speak of your future husband in those terms," Ancel told her. "It's not seemly."

"Neither is a wedding with three days' notice!"

"My lady, have you written to your cousin? Do you not wish him here with you?"

Domina had nearly forgotten Joscelin still existed. Everything outside the walls seemed like a mere dream. "I'll inform him, but he'll not be able to travel soon enough for the ceremony, because it's only *days* away. "

"Well, times are troubled," the steward said. "Sir Luc

was most courteous when he explained the necessity of the speed of the marriage to me. It will be a great relief to have a knight directing the defenses of the castle."

"I do not recall the castle falling to an enemy under my tenure," Domina said hotly. *Not counting Luc himself*, a sly voice inside her whispered.

"My lady, you did the best you could under the circumstances. But surely this is preferable. What a weight off everyone's shoulders. We no longer have to hide the fact of your father's illness."

Domina bit her lip, turning away. She never wanted to hide the truth, but it was the best course of action, and one Ancel himself had agreed to when she first put the matter to him. Now he was acting as if she'd performed some dire deed, when all she wanted was to protect the de Warewic name, her father's fragile state, and her own destiny. Was that a crime?

What had she just told Ancel she'd do? She couldn't remember. Ah well, nothing mattered anymore.

Domina gambled everything and lost. She'd be a prisoner, with the pretty title of wife. What joy could she find in that, however charming her captor?

* * * *

On the day of the wedding, Constance and Margery dressed Mina in her best gown, and she reflected on the fact that she'd been so proud of it when she wore it to the king's court. Perhaps it was cursed, for that was the very day the king first mentioned his whim of marrying her off to the nearest knight to hand.

"He's very handsome," Constance said, to cheer her up. "You'll be grateful for that come tonight."

The chambermaid Margery laughed knowingly. "If you ever tire of your duty, my lady, send him to me."

Constance swatted the maid. "None of that talk."

"Why wait till I tire?" Mina said dully. "Margery, you can wear my gown after the ceremony. He'll be drunk, no doubt, satisfied with his conquest. He won't care who he beds."

"My lady, I couldn't feign to be a noble!" Margery gasped. "That's a crime, and a sin, I'm sure."

"It doesn't matter anyway," Mina said. "The man will do what he wants, and there's nothing we women can do about it."

"He'll heed you, for you'll be his lady," Constance said.

"He has never heeded me before, why should he begin after the wedding? He'll have what he wants. Trumwell will be in his control."

Margery gave a glance at Constance, who was now rummaging around in a little case at the other side of the room. She whispered, "If you fear the wedding night because you're virgin, my lady, you can do one thing."

"What?"

"Enough wine will carry your mind away, and he won't notice. Men never notice."

Mina shook her head once in refusal of the notion. "I want a clear head if I'm to deal with him."

"Yes, my lady." Margery continued to fix Mina's hair, and said no more.

However, once the idea was there, Mina didn't forget it.

All too soon, she stood at the door of the chapel. It was completely packed with people, nearly all of them residents of Trumwell Castle itself or the village nearby.

No one else had enough warning to have traveled there in time.

Mina walked unescorted down the center aisle, for there was no one to escort her. She was alone.

Luc waited at the side of the altar, also alone.

Well, there was a certain symmetry, she thought. Both of them were separate from their families on the day their families were supposedly joined.

The priest began the ceremony, but when he read out the words, "Who gives this woman…" he trailed off, confused, for Domina's father lay unconscious elsewhere in the castle.

"Oh, just tell me what to say," Mina muttered to him. "I have spoken for my father for the past two and half years. Why stop at this?"

The priest swallowed nervously, then in a low voice prompted with the words that her father should have been there to speak. "You would say, *I give thee my daughter…*"

When he finished, Mina turned to Luc and echoed, "I give thee my*self*, to be thy honor and thy wife, to keep thy keeps and to share with thee bed and goods." She finished the recitation in a flat tone, not looking him in the eye.

Luc repeated his lines as well, and then it was over. According to the church and the law, she was a wife.

People who didn't know the extent of Luc's coup came forward to congratulate the happy couple.

Beautiful. Beautiful. Beautiful. Mina heard the word like a buzz around her. Was that what they saw? A beautiful bride? Well, let them. Someone should enjoy the day.

The wedding feast was lavish, and the local villagers and those living near the castle had all come, eager for a festival in these cold days of the year. Mina couldn't remember the last time the hall had been filled with so much food and wine, or so many people. Certainly not since her father fell ill, and perhaps not for years before that.

Somehow, somebody had enticed traveling musicians to Trumwell in time, and now music filled the air. The tunes were lively and cheerful, in sharp contrast to Mina's inner turmoil.

Through the whole evening, Margery's words never left Mina's brain. When the toasts were offered at supper, she drank to every single one. She had never been drunk in her life, and had no intention of starting, but she hoped a little wine would calm her. That's all she needed, to calm her nerves so that she wouldn't go to pieces in front of him.

He'd bed her. She scarcely knew him and he was going to bed her. She should have asked Margery what that meant, exactly, for Margery would certainly know the details. Too late. Mina took another sip. Had she forgotten to water this wine? Oh, well, it was just a sip.

Luc looked like the true lord of the castle. He sat at the center of the high table, in the elaborately carved chair with the high back. It was her father's seat, but this stranger now sat in it.

She took another sip. The air in the great hall was hot now. So many fires and candles and revelers, it chased away even the winter chill.

The feast seemed to go on for ages. Mina sat and listened to toasts, to songs, to poems, and smiled through it all. *Be the lady of the castle*, she told herself. Show no weakness. Your people need to know all will be well. Even if Mina's life crashed down around her, she swore to God she'd never let Luc hurt her people.

A course of roast swan was served, in an explicit celebration of a de Warewic marriage. Mina didn't even want to think of the expense. She'd ceased to care over the past few days. Her years of careful spending were undone, her illusion of control shattered with a few words from her so-called suitor. It was all Mina could do not to sneer into her cup.

The wine went down smoothly now. She rather liked the flavor of this one, which might be a different vintage than what she began with.

Luc laughed at something and she rolled her eyes, taking another sip. He was comely, she admitted—a conclusion she'd arrived at many times before. She stared at him sidelong, watching how he acted.

As if he'd been there forever. Talking and laughing and exchanging jests with Ancel and Giles as if he'd grown up with them. Had he made friends with everyone during his brief, inquisitive visit? All but her?

Oh, but he didn't need her friendship, did he? Not when he had that parchment tucked away, the one granting him Mina with the stroke of a pen. Why get to know one's wife? It was easier to sneak up on her and announce the marriage when she had no defenses, when he was already inside the walls.

Traitor.

Then Luc looked over at her. His smile faded, to be replaced with a look she couldn't name.

He stood up, and reached for Mina's hand.

The cheering that went up made her cheeks hot, and she was already hot from the fire and the wine.

He pulled her to him. "Enough of this," he said, though only she could hear him, what with the din all around. "It's time that my wife shows me to our bed."

Chapter 14

LUC FIRST TOOK HER BY the hand, but the crowd of well-wishers followed them all the way up the flight of steps to the bedchambers, stepping on her skirts and slowing their progress. So Luc paused, turned, and picked her up in his arms.

Surprised, Mina let out a laugh, feeling suddenly weightless as Luc swung her around.

The distance to the door of the bedchamber was far too short, though. When he carried her through the door and cheerfully ordered someone to shut it tight behind them, Mina was no longer laughing.

"Put me down, please," she said breathlessly.

He walked her to the bed first, then put her on her feet right at the side of it. He turned away, saying he needed something to drink.

"I might be sleepy," she said, sliding onto the bed. She lay back, and the room spun slowly about her. She giggled at the sensation. She wasn't sleepy. She was something else, something she wasn't used to being.

"Do you want anything?" he asked, from where he stood.

"Rather late to ask what I want," she said, though she

wasn't sure she spoke the words or whispered them to the smoke-scented air.

She closed her eyes, feeling the strange spinning sensation continue. It was not at all unpleasant, and she sighed, momentarily forgetting why she'd been so upset all day. It could be sorted in the morning, she was sure.

The spinning slowly settled, to be replaced with a sense of warmth floating over her skin. Mina intended to ask Luc something, but when she opened her mouth, all that emerged was a little contented moan.

"So you like that?" Luc asked, startlingly close.

He was kissing her. The spreading heat was a path marked by his mouth, scoring her skin as he peeled her gown off.

"Yes," she said. "Yes, I like that."

Mina opened her eyes to see Luc bending over her. In the dim light cast by the fire, she was entranced by him. He'd cast off his shirt, and the sight of his body made her all the warmer.

"Luc…" she whispered hesitantly. "Is it time? You're going to bed me?"

"First I'm going to kiss you, Mina."

"Oh. Yes." She closed her eyes, again surrendering to the feel of his lips on her skin. He'd called her Mina. It sounded incredibly sweet to hear him say the name.

He'd been tasting her shoulders and arms. Now he moved to kiss her directly on the mouth.

This was the very first time he'd ever kissed her like this. Mina nearly cried out when his lips touched hers. She opened her mouth by instinct, and gasped at the touch of his tongue. No one warned her about this, about how she'd want more and more of it. Was it supposed to feel like falling into a fever?

Breathing seemed incidental, but eventually Luc pulled back enough to take a breath, sounding like he'd just run a mile.

"How do I taste to you?" he asked.

She didn't have enough of her mind left to describe all she tasted. He tasted like heat, like summer, like daring, like secrets, like danger. He left her dizzy, dreaming of summer skies and endless peace, just her lying next to him, feeding off his incredible warmth. She felt a sudden desire to make him close his eyes while she sang to him, making every rest a kiss. But she couldn't say all that, not now.

"You taste of wine," she whispered. Oh, that wasn't what she meant at all. Why had she drunk so much? The wine took away her ability to think, and she suddenly wanted to think, to remember everything.

"You taste of wine and honey," he replied. He kissed her over and over and over, until she lost count and couldn't even think of a number that matched the heat of his body.

She blinked once, it seemed, but when she opened her eyes again, she discovered she was naked. So was he. She closed her eyes again, alarmed at what the firelight revealed.

He was still touching her, and she wondered when she'd feel pain. She should have asked Margery for more information. She only knew that women were supposed to feel pain. She felt no pain, only this strange ache that made her moan every time Luc kissed her or touched her. Why did she want more of this?

"Luc," she whispered, fear lacing through her veins at last, despite all the wine.

"Yes, Mina?"

"I…" But she forgot what she was going to ask. She forgot what she was afraid of.

"Mina," he said. "Do you want me to keep going?"

"Yes," she sighed. Why would she ever want to stop feeling like this? "Please, yes. I wish I…" She trailed off, the words getting tangled up in her mouth, possibly because Luc kissed her then, drawing all the words off her lips. Her mind drifted, lost in a haze of pleasure, then lost in dreams too deep to recall.

* * * *

Mina woke up suddenly, as if thunder clapped above her. She sat up in bed, only to hide her pounding head in her hands.

"Oh, mercy," she moaned. She'd never felt so terrible.

She lay back down carefully. She'd call for water in a moment. She just needed to rest a little while.

That was the moment Domina realized she wasn't alone in her bed. Luc lay sleeping beside her.

"Oh, mercy," she repeated, with a different meaning. She'd married him yesterday. Which meant…last night's strange dreams must have been real.

She recognized the ache between her legs as the consequence of the wedding night. He'd taken her virginity and she couldn't even remember how it felt. What had happened?

She drank wine. She drank too much. Domina curled up on her side, desperate to either recall everything or forget everything about last night. Why could she summon only the vaguest images of what happened?

He kissed her. She remembered that. He kissed her everywhere, unless she dreamed some of it.

"God help me," she muttered, hitting the mattress with a fist. She'd be damned if she made a fool of herself on her wedding night, considering the marriage already robbed her of her freedom and her happiness.

She froze when she felt a hand on her shoulder.

"Mina? Are you awake?"

Luc's voice rolled over her. She'd never known how shocking it would sound to have a man speak next to her in bed.

After a moment, she nodded.

"Mina," he said. "Look at me."

She refused to turn. "I don't feel well," she said. "I'm thirsty."

"I'll call for a maid."

"Don't call," she warned. She didn't want to be seen. Not by anyone.

She tried to sit up again, but the dizziness surged, forcing her back on the pillow. She lay back, putting a hand over her eyes. "How hideous."

"I wouldn't say that." Luc laughed, the sound both familiar and strange, for she'd heard him laugh before, but never in a bed. "In fact, nothing about last night could be called hideous. Certainly not you."

"Last night." She swallowed painfully, mortified at what she had to confess. "I...I don't remember."

"No?" His voice sharpened a little, as if he didn't believe it.

"I drank rather more wine than I should have," she said, still skirting around the truth, which was that she'd drunk exactly as much wine as she intended to.

"How *much* more?" Luc sounded even sharper now. "You're telling me you don't recall anything?"

"I remember you were kissing me," she whispered,

wishing she remembered more. "Our marriage is, ah…."

"Consummated." He paused, then added, "Just as you asked me to do."

"Oh."

Oh. That was all she had of her wedding night. A lost memory and a puzzle of a husband.

Then the bed shifted as Luc got up, moving away from her. Perhaps she didn't even have a husband, after all.

Chapter 15

LUC DRESSED HIMSELF, AND TOLD Domina to remain in bed. "At least until your temper has recovered," he added, with a certain amount of unfairness. Still, his own temper was up, and he couldn't help himself.

He thought to hear a snappish remark back. Domina excelled at cutting comments, and with a little more practice, she'd actually fit in very well at court, where wit counted for much.

She said nothing, however, and when he glanced back, he saw that she had curled up on her side, her face buried in the pillow and her mass of red curls a protective cloak against the light of the morning.

Or against Luc. Whatever she might have thought of him last night, it was clear she was a miserable bride this morning.

Should he have guessed something was off? Domina never lacked for a quick tongue, yet in bed last night, she'd been unusually quiet. She'd simply offered herself and those maddening little moans every time he kissed her, and she had told him to go on. How the hell could he know she'd secretly drunk herself to near oblivion? He'd never seen Domina in any state where she wasn't completely in control of herself.

Yet now Mina had no memory of their first night together. Or at least that's what she claimed. Still, Luc was furious that she felt the need to take a single sip of wine on his account. He'd told her before the wedding that he wasn't her enemy, that the marriage would keep her safe. Didn't she understand that meant he'd never mistreat her? Evidently not.

When Luc left the chamber, he saw the maid Constance almost immediately.

"Let Domina sleep awhile," he warned her in a low voice. "But she'll be thirsty when she wakes."

Constance frowned in confusion.

"She had a little too much to drink last night."

"My lady never drinks more than a glass of watered wine," the maid objected.

"She did not account for the toasts, then," Luc said, unwilling to reveal the true reason for Domina's overindulgence. "Let her sleep."

"Yes, my lord." Constance curtseyed. "If you go to the great hall, Ancel would like a word."

Luc nodded, already intending to go there. Anything to take his mind off the revelation that Mina had apparently decided she couldn't face her wedding night with Luc when she was sober.

The steward approached while Luc was breaking his fast at the table. He bowed and asked if Luc had leisure to hear of the household accounts.

Luc could tell Ancel was delighted a master was in residence again, but he couldn't bear to listen to a litany of problems stemming from two years of hardship.

"I'll hear it all later," he said. "While the sun is bright, I have another task that can wait no longer."

"What's that, my lord?"

"Domina spoke of some trees encroaching on the castle's grounds. It's been bothering her for some time, so I intend to fix that." At least he could fix something this morning.

"Haldan was going to..." The steward stopped, remembering Haldan's undignified exit from the castle. "I suppose no one is in charge of the task now."

"Now I am," Luc said grimly. He ordered that any man who could be spared should join Luc at the woods. His own retinue volunteered immediately, of course, for they truly had few obligations. Several castle servants and most of the small garrison also appeared. Anyone who could find an axe or a saw brought one along.

So the people of the castle weren't lazy. Perhaps Haldan never even tried to organize a group.

Luc led a small number of workers to mark out a line where the cutting should stop. Then he declared that any tree growing closer to the castle walls was doomed. Ban marked each doomed tree with an x.

The din from the chopping and sawing was immense, made louder by the shouts of the workers and the baying of dogs who'd somehow joined the crowd. Everyone seemed to put full effort into it, and soon enough, wagons and carts were pulling loads of chopped logs to the castle, where they would meet their eventual destiny as firewood.

Luc smiled in satisfaction as the edge of the woods slowly shrank back to an acceptable line. Domina had been quite correct in her assessment. A force of enemy fighters could have used the trees for cover, getting far too close to the castle before being sighted.

As the sun marched quickly across the winter sky, Luc was conscious of aches and pains in his body. He was used to the pains of training with his sword. Chopping at trees used other muscles, and he'd hurt tomorrow. Yet the labor saved him from thinking too hard about the situation he'd put himself into, specifically whether he'd made an error in judgement about Domina.

One of the workers hailed Luc, offering a cup of warm spiced ale from a bucket brought down from the castle kitchens. Luc drank it gratefully, wondering if Mina was recovered from her headache.

* * * *

Mina slid into an uneasy sleep after Luc left her, but she was woken again when her headache sharpened into something far worse.

The pounding in her ears was so horrible that she moaned aloud. Unknowingly imitating a lioness, she called out for Constance. Mina buried her head in the pillows to try to drown out the awful noise, and only stirred when Constance put a hand to her shoulder.

"My lady?" the maid asked anxiously. "Are you well?"

"No, I've the worst headache of my life," she replied. "The pounding is so loud in my ears. As if a dozen axes are striking over and over."

"Ah, my lady, axes *are* striking."

Mina opened her eyes. "What?"

"The master has taken a group of men outside, and they're cutting back the trees even now."

"The master..." Luc. Of course. He was master here now. "He's down there? With them?"

"Yes, he led the whole group."

"Oh." Mina paused, reassessing. Now that she knew the sound came from without, rather than within, she realized her head in fact felt much better. "Well, at least I'm not going mad," she said aloud.

"Do you wish to dress, my lady? It's nearly midday."

Mina never slept so late. She rose immediately and let Constance dress her and style her hair. As the maid tamed the unruly red tresses, Mina sat quietly, still not feeling like herself. In fact, she would never feel like herself again. Not with Luc permanently part of her world.

I'm a wife, she thought to herself. The idea was still so new and foreign.

"Is it only your head that aches?" Constance asked, very hesitantly. "He was...kind last night?"

Mina blushed when she realized what Constance meant. She'd never admit she couldn't remember a thing. "I have no complaint," she said shortly.

"Yes, my lady." Constance understood that tone, which meant the subject would never be under discussion again. As the maid was settling a fine veil over Mina's hair, securing it with a pretty ribbon around her head, she added, "I am very glad for you, my lady."

"Glad?"

"He is both handsome and generous, and seems determined to be a good master here. Ban says only good things about Luc as a master. The king chose well. Everyone thinks you're very lucky."

Mina said nothing to that. So that was the talk of the castle, was it? Domina worked for years to keep Trumwell safe and in the hands of the de Warewics, but in one night, everyone forgot all that effort. Instead, they called her lucky for getting married off to a knight chosen simply because he happened to be in the king's line of sight.

She stood up, smoothing her skirts. "I'll go to visit my father," she announced. "At least I no longer need to hide that."

Mina marched through the great hall, striving to look as though nothing was different from the days before. It was difficult, considering the aftermath of the wedding feast. Despite all the maids' and scullions' efforts, remnants of the feast lay scattered about the hall. There were baskets of uneaten bread, boughs of winter greenery brought in to decorate the tables, and the occasional drunkard still slouched in a corner.

"I want all this cleaned up by suppertime," Domina told Ancel, who was approaching. "Send the excess food to the village church, if need be. And wake those fools up! Surely they all have work to do."

"My lady, yesterday was hardly typical…"

"I am aware of that," she said. "Do you think I get married off every month?"

"No, my lady."

"I'm going to spend the afternoon with my father," she said. "Unless you have business to discuss?"

"No, my lady," said Ancel. "I don't wish to prevent you from your filial duties. I'll speak to my lord Luc when he returns."

"Ah. So now that I'm a mere wife, my opinion is no longer needed?"

"That's not what I meant," the steward mumbled. "I only wanted to inform the lord of things he ought to know."

"Well, if you have need of me, you'll know where I

am. No more need to conceal it."

"No, praise the Lord."

She glared at him. "You agreed to the plan."

"Because I saw no other option. But no one liked keeping things hidden, and surely you see how much easier life is now that the lord knows."

"I would not say that my life has got any easier," she said, turning away.

Her fury kept her warm during the short walk across the courtyard. She went into her father's apartment, where Beatrice was warming something for Godfrey to drink. One of the castle cats lounged by the fire, stretching its claws whenever a spark snapped.

"How is he?" she asked the maid. "Has the noise disturbed him?"

"He's well enough," Beatrice replied. "He asked about the sound, which I took for a good sign."

"You told him what was happening?"

"I said the men were cutting back the woods, and he told me he'd done that only last fall. He doesn't know what year it is."

"Well, at least he remembers where he is."

"That's true. Tomorrow will be quieter. Bless the new lord—he's done more in a day than Haldan did in two years."

Mina said nothing to that, but told Beatrice she could leave. "I'll sit with him till sundown."

Beatrice nodded and left. Mina took up the embroidery that she kept in the room. The work kept her busy while she spent time with her father. She always tried to talk with him, but so often he slept, or mumbled incoherently. It was good to have her hands busy.

Today, though, no handwork could calm her mind.

Beatrice's comments seemed to be like everyone else's. They were all glad of Luc's arrival. They were all relieved to have a man in authority again.

She had to admit that in many ways, Luc seemed to be far better than what she might have got in a husband. He took the defense of the castle seriously, which was important. Haldan treated it like it was a game.

She shivered, thinking of her last encounter with the soldier. She couldn't deny that Luc's arrival helped her there, too.

Mina was glad Haldan was gone, though she hated that it was Luc who finally resolved the matter. She felt the tenuous threads of power slipping from her hands every hour. From the moment Luc set foot in her home, he'd begun to strip all her defenses away, leaving her helpless and weak. She hated herself for not standing up to him with more force, and she hated how everyone but herself seemed ready to bow to him, to accept him as lord and master with virtually no knowledge about him.

Mina frowned, recalling the oddness of the marriage announcement. He'd never quite explained why he was given notice of the arrangement while she was not—and the king's jest back in court certainly didn't qualify as an announcement!

He'd come to Trumwell Castle with some goal in mind, and it couldn't just be the marriage or he'd have told her about it immediately. Instead, he'd done so only after seeing her father's true state.

Mina reached out to her father and held his hand, thinking hard. What was Luc's game? He accused her of lying to him, of keeping secrets. Yet he was keeping secrets of his own, and until he revealed them, she'd be a fool to trust her new husband.

"Mina, my child?" her father asked, startling her out of her reverie. "Is that you?"

"Yes, Father," she said. "How are you? Thirsty? I have some warmed wine here."

He nodded. "Yes, that will do. The chopping has stopped."

She listened to the silence from the outside. She'd been so lost in thought she hadn't noticed. "So it has. We won't lack for firewood next season!" She smiled. At least there was one thing everyone could agree on.

"I didn't think it needed doing," he said, his voice growing a bit stronger. "How does Trumwell fare? Have I forgot something?"

"Trumwell is in good hands," she said soothingly. "You must not worry."

"I worry, Mina," he said, casting his gaze over her. "I have strange dreams. Where is my Emma? Where is little Joscelin?"

"Joscelin is in London, studying. Remember? And your wife has been taken to God, many years ago now."

He sighed. "Oh, yes. Sometimes I think I hear her. Perhaps it's your voice. You sound like her."

"That's what Ancel says," Mina told him.

"That old dog," Godfrey said fondly. "He said Emma was too pretty for me. Shows what he knows! I must find a husband for you, little Mina. You'll be old enough to marry soon."

"We can talk about that another time," Mina said, sadness washing over her. Her father seemed lost, thinking they were in the past. She didn't dare tell him the ugly truth, for fear he'd have a fit and lose the meager progress he'd been making.

"Not too long," he said. "I'll find you a good man.

One worthy of a de Warewic woman."

"I know you will, Father," she said. "Rest now. I'll come back tomorrow."

Her eyes brimming with tears, she fled the room as quickly as she could.

* * * *

Domina endured a supper in the great hall, sitting next to Luc at the high table, with everyone as jovial as they'd been at the wedding feast. They were all pleased with their day's work, and pleased with their new lord.

Luc himself looked sleekly content, like a cat full of meat after a fresh kill. Like a cat, too, he was clean and well-groomed. He'd bathed after all the hard work that day, so she couldn't even complain of a stench. In fact, he smelled of the herb-laced soap the castle's servants made, a smell Mina always adored…until now. Now the smell created a nerve-jangling tension, for it would follow her to bed. And tonight, she hadn't had a drop of wine to dull her senses.

She excused herself early and went to the bedchamber. Constance attended her, brushing out her thick hair and then tucking her into the bed, clad only in her shift.

Luc came into the bedchamber a few minutes after that. He shed his clothes without a glance in her direction. She peeked anyway, seeing the candlelight reflect off his bare skin, illuminating the muscles in his back and arms. His shoulders alone made her feel a little weak, and she recalled with an uncomfortable heat one image from her wedding night: Luc over her, the shape of his shoulder one bold curve in the candlelight as he…

She pulled the curtain shut, angry at her body's reaction.

Naturally, however she felt, she couldn't very well stop Luc from joining her in the bed. The candle snuffed out, and then Luc parted the curtain and slid into bed as if he had every right to be there...which he did.

In the darkness, he reached out to touch her. "You're still wearing your shift."

"It's winter, and I'm cold."

"Take it off."

"No."

"Take it off or I will," he said. His voice wasn't threatening. Indeed, there was humor in it. It was almost alluring. But she would have none of it.

"Do not think I'm going to happily obey every order you give," she said.

"It's not an order, Domina."

"It most certainly was an order. *Take it off or I will*," she mimicked.

"What if I make it a request? Would you please re-move your shift, wife, or let me do it?"

She wanted to snap *no* at him, but he'd gentled his voice so much that she felt mean.

"I'll take it off," she said finally. "Don't watch."

"It's dark," Luc noted, again with something close to a laugh in his voice.

"Nonetheless."

"Very well. My eyes are closed."

She sat up and gathered up the fabric of her shift. She barely pulled it over her head when she felt Luc's eager hands on her body, starting at her hips and moving up to her breasts.

"I said don't watch!" she gasped.

"I'm not watching. I'm touching. Or will you tell me

not to do that too?"

"I'm not sure I like it."

He said, "You liked it last night."

"I don't remember a thing about last night," she said, which wasn't *entirely* true.

"You must remember something, for at least you didn't feel the need to drink yourself into insensibility again." He paused. "You were that afraid of me?"

"Not *you*," she admitted. "Just...the act itself. I didn't know what to do, before or during, or even now. I should have told you no, that I didn't want it."

"But you did want it. You said *yes*, sweetheart," he told her. "Last night, I asked you if you wanted me to go on, and you—"

"I said yes?" she asked skeptically.

"You said *please yes*," he told her, adding an emphasis that made heat rise in her cheeks. She remembered, suddenly, saying exactly *please yes*.

With those words, he began to touch her again, growing bolder.

She lay silently beneath him, willing herself to not react at all. If Luc thought she was won after a single night, he was wrong.

It was difficult to remain unmoved, because the sensations he created in her were anything but mild. His hands seemed to scorch her skin. She grew hot, her breath quickened, and she found herself leaning into him, rising to meet him. But she refused to speak, to give any verbal hint of how she felt. It seemed important to show him that she didn't always go to pieces when he touched her so very, very, "*Oh*," she gasped, unable to completely hide her response.

He could probably guess exactly what moved her,

because he lingered over her breasts, playing with her until the buds hardened. Then he slid his hands down to her hips, telling her how perfectly shaped she was, how he wanted to see her in the light.

"No light," she whispered.

"As you like," he said. Obviously the darkness wouldn't stop him.

He settled over her, parting her legs with one hand. She obeyed, hating how easily he managed her, even as she loved the feelings he stirred in her.

Then he touched her right between her legs, and she thought she'd scream with delight.

Why was she so sensitive to his touch? Was it some trick of his? Why did she crave more of his attention?

She stifled a moan, instead inhaling deeply.

"Mina, I need you." The words surprised her, especially the way he said them. There was no more humor, no more confidence. "Please, Mina."

What could she say? He was her husband. "You can go on," she said.

Without another word, Luc entered her, and she couldn't stop a little gasp. She hadn't recalled *this* sensation at all. She felt filled up, pushed aside, penetrated.

Quite without meaning to, she gave a little cry of pain.

He stilled immediately. "Does it hurt?" Luc asked.

"Why, do you want it to?" she returned, fear making her voice harsh.

He sighed, his breath hot on the side of her face. "No. Never."

She swallowed, feeling ashamed. He'd treated her kindly in bed, and she was being so unfair in response. "Just…finish," she whispered.

He did that quickly enough, and Mina felt every stroke

as an assault, not so much against her body—he was obviously holding back—but against herself.

At last he gave a sound of...she supposed completion. He withdrew from her almost in the next breath.

She tried not to think of the heat he left her with, the ache between her legs. She rolled onto her side, facing away from him.

He put a hand on her shoulder a moment later. "Mina..."

"Don't touch me," she hissed. "Have you not touched me enough already tonight?"

"Nowhere near," he responded.

Shocked, she turned her head to look at him. "What does that mean? You're not finished?"

"Finished, yes. Satisfied, no."

"What's the difference?"

He slid his hand from her shoulder to her breast. "If you'd let down your guard for one moment, I'd show you."

His touch was gentle, incredibly so. Mina barely felt his fingers stroke the contour of her breast, lingering along the bottom curve. Once again, it stirred a response she didn't want to face.

"I'd prefer not to be shown whatever tricks you learned so far."

"No tricks, Mina," he said. "I only want to learn what you like."

"I'd like to be left alone."

"That's not what I usually hear."

Anger and something else—jealousy? Dear God, please no—flared up in her. "Perhaps the women you've lain with before knew what you wanted to hear," Domina said coldly. "Or they had their own reasons for flattering the son of a baron."

She turned her head away, huddled up to keep herself warm. Luc didn't try to touch her again, or speak, or persuade her of anything. How was it possible to feel so alone when another person lay so close?

Mina couldn't wait for sunrise.

Chapter 16

Luc rose early. He didn't wake Domina, having already learned to be wary of his new wife's ability to sting with a well-chosen word.

She'd proved it again last night, with her comment about how the women he'd known before had only been flattering him. She might as well have flicked a dagger at him. Luc had enough experience and presence of mind to know her accusation wasn't true…but the idea that he hadn't pleased Mina at *all* disturbed him far more than he'd let on.

He wanted to please her. He only had to look at her to want to touch her, and then touch her to want to be with her and in her. He wanted desperately to hear her ask for him that way, or to say she liked what he did.

It was early, he told himself. Mina had no experience, and plenty of prejudice. He'd break down her defenses soon enough, so he could show her she needed no defenses from him.

Luc sighed. It would take more than a few kisses to break Domina's icy exterior. She was unlike any other woman he'd ever met. She spent years running her castle and hiding her father's condition from the world—that shaped her whole demeanor. How could she change in a matter of days?

He ought to report everything he'd discovered at Trumwell to the king and his spymaster. The news of Godfrey's illness put a very different light on the events Drugo told him about. But Luc didn't want to offer such shocking news without also providing a few more details, and hopefully a few new clues leading to the real conspirator, whoever he was.

But first, there were other things to take care of. As promised, Luc sat down with the steward to learn more of the de Warewic estate. Trumwell Castle and its grounds was the principal holding of the family, but there were several other properties as well, some scattered quite a distance from Trumwell.

Luc made a careful note of all the names, thinking Haldan might have gone to them while employed by the de Warewic family. Perhaps he was at one of these places now, relying on the slow speed of news to ensure his welcome, for they wouldn't yet know he'd been sacked.

It took a few hours for Ancel to discuss everything with Luc, and by the end, Luc understood just how shaky Domina's hold on things had been. She apparently had no allies or relations in positions of power. Her father knew many people, but since he was incapacitated, she was unable to make use of any of those connections without also revealing her vulnerability.

Soon after that depressing conversation, a servant found Luc in the solar he'd more or less settled into.

"My lord, the knight Sir Octavian has returned. You asked to be alerted."

"So I did. Will you tell him to come here as soon as he's able?"

A quarter hour later, Tav strode into the solar. He'd changed from his riding gear into a clean outfit suitable for company.

"Good to see you," Tav said, "Sorry I was delayed. What have I missed while I was gone?"

"*Delayed*? Where the hell were you? You were going to ride to the sheriff to make a report and then come back. What business could you possibly have had that's more important than helping me uncover a conspiracy against the king?"

Tav looked rather taken aback at Luc's uncharacteristic crankiness. "Well, to be honest, I can't tell you."

"Why not?"

"It's not my story to tell."

"You're going to have to do slightly better than that, Tav."

"I encountered, let's say, an acquaintance who needed some...well, she wasn't where she was supposed to be..."

"She?" Luc asked, suddenly alert. "Who is this mysterious woman?"

"I promised I wouldn't speak of it. Let's just say she'd wandered away from home and I helped return her to where she was supposed to be. But since she's a lady—or she will be one—it's probably best that..."

"...that no one knows you were alone with her for a few days?"

"She's practically a child still, anyway." Tav sounded defensive. "I swore an oath to protect the innocent. She needed my protection."

"I'm not accusing you of anything," Luc said. "It sounds as if she was lucky she ran into you instead of someone else. All right, I won't ask more about it. But I do wish you'd been here earlier."

"What's happened?"

"Domina and I are married."

Octavian blinked. "Excuse me," he said in what was likely complete sincerity. "It sounded as if you said you and the lady Domina are married."

"I did say that. The wedding was two days ago."

"Ah...*why*?"

So Luc explained. Godfrey de Warewic was not absent; he was ill. Domina hid his condition from the world in order to maintain control of her lands. When Luc saw the tenuousness of her situation, he married her to prevent anyone else from doing so. And then, naturally, he had to reveal to Tav that the king's spymaster was the one who had arranged for a marriage contract to be drafted, and secretly given to Luc in case he might need it for leverage. But in any case, he chose to marry her to protect her, a decision Octavian should understand, considering he'd also gone out of his way to protect another, unnamed lady.

Octavian listened to the whole explanation without uttering a word. He crossed his arms, his gaze never leaving Luc's face. Tav's regard grew uncomfortable—Octavian could read people better than anyone else he knew—but Luc continued on. "And so we married. I didn't want to wait, in case something should go wrong," he concluded.

"*That*'s why you didn't want to wait?" Tav asked, one eyebrow raised.

"What other reason would I have for doing it this way?"

"Oh, I don't know. Perhaps because from the very first night we ran across her in London, you couldn't take your eyes off her."

"That's…" Luc was about to say that wasn't true, but Tav would call him out if he did. "That may be part of it."

"You waited till I left before announcing your marriage," Tav added.

"That was not intentional. I only made the decision after seeing what Haldan attempted to do to her, and then after I saw her father incapacitated. Domina needs protection."

Tav's voice dropped to a mutter. "Are you forgetting that you were sent here to find a traitor?"

"Godfrey de Warewic has been out of his mind and confined to a room for over two years. He can't be the ringleader of any conspiracy."

"But the lady could," Tav pointed out. "If what you say is true, she's had unusual freedom to pursue whatever plans she likes."

"I…tested…her," Luc said. "She didn't take the bait."

"Perhaps because she knew it was a test. Or because she didn't need to show her colors. She may well have enough allies in whatever plans she's already created."

"I don't believe she's involved."

"Because she's a lady?"

"Because…" Yes, because she was a true lady, and witty, and utterly bewitching. Had Luc stumbled directly into a trap? "I just can't believe it."

"Well, you'd best be able to prove it, then," Tav said. "Or your bright future at court will turn to ashes before you can blink."

"Then I need your help more than ever. I want to find Haldan—he was obviously up to something."

"Is it possible that you think Haldan is guilty simply because you're angry he touched the woman you married?"

Luc frowned. "That's not the reason. Granted, I want him to suffer for that offense as well. I shouldn't have let him get away, but I was worried about Mina at the time."

"What, then, is the evidence against him?"

"Nothing I would be pleased to hold up in a court," Luc admitted. "He made some remarks that could be construed as suspicious—Domina will confirm them, for he was speaking to her. She thought he wanted to take the castle for himself. But more than his words, it's his actions that are suspect. He stalled on carrying out a very simple order from Domina to cut back a fringe of trees that grew too close to the castle. Why would he do that? Even if he was lazy, it's not as if he needed to cut them down himself! I directed a group of men, and the work was done in a day."

Tav nodded thoughtfully. "Something could be made of that," he conceded, "though it's not much."

"When I find him, I'll learn more. He's guilty of something, and he's not working alone. He lacks the standing or the wit to be a leader."

"So we find Haldan, and learn the name of his employer," Octavian said. "All right. Where do we begin?"

"I have a list of properties belonging to the family. It's possible he's at one of them, pretending he's still in the good graces of Domina."

"We can ride to each one," Tav said. "But we can't send word ahead. That will only drive him off."

"Precisely."

They planned to ride to the smaller properties owned by the de Warewic family. All of them were within the shire, or in one case just over the border into another. When asked, Domina suggested the largest outlying manor, though she was of the opinion that Haldan would have fled immediately into Wales.

"It's the largest of the properties," she had said, "as well as the furthest from Trumwell. If he wanted to risk it, he'd go there, for it would take the longest to bring news of his disgrace."

So Luc rode out, Octavian with him. They were accompanied by a few long-standing men-at-arms who could affirm Luc's status, for the wedding was so recent as to be unknown to the world.

At the first three places, which were small manors not much larger than home farms, no one had seen Haldan in months. Luc introduced himself, explained that Haldan was now a fugitive, and told them to send word to Trumwell if he was found.

Then they rode on. When they reached the larger manor, Luc's hopes rose. He eyed the sturdy fence around the pale and noted that some men actually looked as if they'd had some martial training.

But Haldan was not there.

"He hasn't been here since, oh, early autumn," the steward of the manor explained. "Is something amiss?"

Luc explained the situation. The steward was appalled. "He'll not cross the threshold again, my lord. I'll have word sent out so everyone in the area will be alerted. He often acted above his station, and no one will weep to hear of his fate. Called himself Sir Haldan whenever he stayed here, and behaved as if he was a lord."

"Did he use any room in the house regularly?" Luc asked. "Did he leave anything here?"

"He used the same bedchamber every time."

"Take me there."

So the steward led Luc and Octavian to the room. "He

only stayed here a few nights each time."

"But he came here often?"

"It was one of his duties, to see to the defenses of the manor, such as they are. Not that he did much other than to look over the gate and tell the men to keep a keen eye out for trouble." The man snorted. "His advice was no different from what one could tell a shepherd…and no more useful."

"Things will change," Luc promised.

"I was surprised when he first arrived. Not a man I'd have expected Godfrey to have taken on. But it's not for me to question," the steward added hurriedly.

Luc said nothing, but the comment made him think. The steward obviously knew nothing of Godfrey's condition, which was probably for the best. But it also made him wonder who did hire Haldan. He was certain it wasn't Domina.

Octavian had already begun poking though the items in the bedchamber. There wasn't much there, for the manor had no permanent lord who would use this space. But Octavian found a wooden box tucked away under a pile of other items. He pulled it out.

"There's a lock," he noted.

"Did Haldan use that box?" Luc asked the steward.

"I don't know, my lord. I can tell you it's not mine, nor one I have a key for."

"I have a key that will work," Luc said with a smile. He ordered for a hatchet to be brought. A few strikes later, the box lid was little more than splinters.

Octavian swept the detritus away, and Luc examined the contents.

There wasn't much, but he could see why it had been concealed. He pulled out a small pouch, heavy with coin.

"See if any of these coins look like the ones we're seeking," he said to Octavian.

The other knight took the pouch. "By the weight alone, this wasn't merely Haldan's pay. Or else I'm in the wrong line of work."

Luc grunted in response, for he was already looking through a few folded and sealed parchments. He stared hard at the seal of the top one. It was the familiar de Warewic swan, and yet…

Luc called for one of the pages to bring in his saddle-bag. When the boy did so, Luc found a letter of his own that he'd brought along, which he knew for a fact bore the de Warewic seal, since he'd seen Domina use her father's ring to make the impression.

He compared the two seals closely.

"What are you looking at?" Tav asked.

Luc held up his own letter. "This announces my marriage to Domina. It bears Godfrey's seal, and I can attest it is authentic." Then he held up the other parchment. "This here was in Haldan's box. The seal looks very similar, but see…" He held up both for Tav to examine.

Tav scanned both, his dark eyes darting back and forth. He was never one to rush to conclusions, and Luc was happy to wait.

"I see," Tav said finally.

"I do not!" the steward said.

Tav handed the two document to the man. "You'll notice that the two wax impressions are different. It's subtle, but one is rougher in appearance, and the words around the edge are barely readable, they've been carved in so shallowly."

"What does it mean?"

"It means that someone has made a copy of the de

Warewic seal." Tav tapped the folded parchment. "This is almost certainly a forgery."

"A forgery?" the steward gasped. "But what could be so important as to require such an effort?"

"Excellent question," Luc said, holding his hand out. "I feel quite justified in breaking the seal now."

"Indeed," the steward said, handing him the parchment. "Also, there's no name on the outside, so who knows who it's meant for?"

"If it was sent to Haldan, he'd have opened it," Tav agreed.

Luc worked a finger under the flap and managed to open the letter without breaking the seal in half. He wanted to save it for evidence.

He read the letter over slowly. It was not very long, but it was damning. The writer promised to support the empress and to work with the recipient to do whatever was necessary to bring the empress to the English throne. At the end, the writer offered gold to pay for soldiers, supplies, or bribes.

It was signed "The Swan."

"So this is how the conspirator earned the name," Luc said.

"There's no indication of who it's to be sent to." Tav took the letter and read it over himself.

Luc nodded. "I think Swan—whoever he is—wrote up a few of these for Haldan's use. Haldan would make the overture, and this letter would serve as a guarantee."

"In as much as a letter signed with a false name can do," Tav muttered. "I suppose that explains why Haldan had these."

He pulled a coin out of the pouch, showing it to Luc.

The silver face bore the swan. "From the de Warewic

treasure," Luc said. "So Drugo was right. The silver coins sealed the pact."

Tav agreed. "It showed the Swan was serious, and allowed his allies to pay for whatever they might need to advance their cause."

At that moment, the steward was called away, being needed elsewhere. He looked pained at having to leave during such revelations.

After he left, Tav said, "Forgive me for pointing it out, but this evidence does little to clear the lady Domina's name."

"I know," Luc said grimly.

"She was perfectly capable of writing this letter, and of giving the silver to Haldan."

"She hates Haldan."

"That doesn't mean she didn't work with him earlier, before he decided to turn on her. Or," Tav added, more deliberately, "the attack was staged."

"No," said Luc. "That was real. Trust me. Domina sliced his face open with her dagger, and he had every intention of harming her."

"Still, this letter doesn't exonerate her." Tav pulled an identical parchment out, staring at it. "The Swan was looking for allies, and used Haldan to secure the agreements."

"Can we use this somehow?" Luc asked, pointing to the parchment. "Perhaps we can draw Haldan out."

"How?" Tav shook his head. "You can't walk about seeking the empress's supporters. Everyone knows your family name. As for me, I'm rather obviously outside the whole situation—though I suppose I could use another name and present myself as a mercenary."

"You know how to fight," Luc agreed. "Well, for now

let's bring these things back to Trumwell. I'll decide what to do after I can think this over."

They went through the remainder of the box, but found nothing else of great use. Haldan was nearly illiterate. He made no notes for himself, and the only letters were the ones written by the mysterious Swan.

They found no more clues, other than the comment of one guard who mentioned that Haldan once told him he was born in the town of Chepstow. "Said he had a brother there. But that's all I know of him."

As Tav pointed out, the new evidence didn't help Domina's cause. Luc still didn't believe she was guilty of conspiracy. As far as Luc had seen, she showed complete loyalty to Stephen, and Domina believed strongly in keeping her word.

The other reason Luc thought Domina was innocent didn't have much to do with reason at all. If the woman was a cold-hearted conspirator, she would have disposed of Haldan much sooner. The man was obviously not under her power—he made that clear enough. Domina had hinted of it beforehand, when she revealed that she wanted Haldan to leave Trumwell, but couldn't send him away because she lacked the authority to do so. A less scrupulous person would not have been so concerned. She would have simply had him killed. But Mina, he was sure, could never order such a thing. In some ways, she was politically adept, but in other ways, she was as innocent as...well, a sheltered lady.

On the road back, Tav brought up something else. "It all comes down to those coins stamped with the swan," he said. "We must trace them. Find who has them now, before they can act against the king."

Luc nodded.

"Will you ask Domina for the remainder of the treasure?" Tav asked. "That seems just as important, for you need to stop such coins from being used any longer."

Luc hesitated. He'd learned a lot from the steward about the finances of the de Warewic family, but Ancel said it was only Domina who held the key to the treasury itself. She always gave him what money was needed for purchases. Speaking directly to Domina about the topic would require more fortitude, and delicacy. If she ever suspected Luc came to the castle thinking her family were traitors, she'd never help him. He might as well speak to a block of ice.

"I'll bring it up when the time is right," he said to Tav. "But you've reminded me of something else. I will ask her who hired Haldan."

When they returned to Trumwell, Luc found Domina and gave her a slightly truncated account of what they'd discovered, leaving out all mention of the coins or the letters.

"As long as the steward there knows to keep Haldan out, I'll be content," she said at the conclusion of his report. "I don't want him on my lands again."

"How did he get the position in the first place?" Luc asked. "You never said, and as the steward noted, it seems unlikely Godfrey would have taken someone like Haldan on."

Domina frowned, thinking. "I always assumed my father had...wait. Now I remember. Haldan came here a few weeks after my father collapsed. He had a letter with our family seal, stating that he was to be the garrison leader, and naming the wages. So it must have been legitimate..." she trailed off. "Or..."

"Yes?" Luc was curious to hear how Domina thought,

given such facts.

"Could his mind have been failing even before the night he collapsed? That would explain why he thought he needed a new garrison leader, and why Haldan might have been able to trick him into thinking he was worthy of the position."

"I don't suppose you still have the letter?" Luc asked.

She shook her head. "No, Haldan kept it, and I've no idea what he might have done with it."

"Well, that's enough for now. When your father recovers, he may be able to tell us more."

"*When* he recovers?" Mina's expression shifted from troubled to hopeful.

Luc wished he could offer her more hope, but all he could do was keep optimistic. "When. After all, you must have got your stubbornness from somebody."

He left Mina before she could retaliate with a backhanded compliment of her own. Luc was actually smiling as he walked away. He liked sparring with Mina, especially when he could leave with the upper hand, and she just stood there with her face flushed and her red curls looking like a fire waiting to happen.

After locating Octavian, he reported what he'd learned. "Domina never even considered the notion of a forged seal, but I wonder if that first letter Haldan brought to Trumwell was actually the Swan's initial test. Mina would have been terribly distracted—her father was very ill, and she would have been thinking only of that. Based on what she said, I'll bet she barely looked at Haldan or his letter. She saw the seal, assumed it legitimate, and told Haldan to begin work."

"So the Swan had eyes and ears in the castle," said Tav, "in order to know that Godfrey was sick and couldn't confirm or deny whether that letter was to be trusted."

"Yes, and we'll have to discover who that might be. In the meantime, there are other paths to pursue."

"What's the first?"

"I want to learn more of the barons in this part of the country. The neighbor, Bertram, mentioned a few who seemed quite obviously on the side of the empress."

"We go visiting, then," Tav said. "We'll have to frame our questions carefully, or we'll leave some of these manor houses with knifes in our backs."

"That's what the armor is for," Luc quipped. "That reminds me. Another task for us is to strengthen the garrison here. Haldan was all but asking for the defenses to fail. The garrison's training is appalling."

"That's easily fixed," Tav said, showing more enthusiasm than before. "Together, we can get them into proper fighting shape."

* * * *

Over the next several days, that was exactly what they did. Luc directed the men of the garrison in new drills, and Octavian assisted him in training them all, which meant the men learned very quickly indeed. Though Luc was their de facto lord now, Octavian was more intimidating. He was taller and broader than Luc, and the sepia cast of his skin meant he was instantly noticeable on the training field. Added to that, Octavian was a natural fighter who made the work look easy. He'd already acquired something of a following among the youngest members of the garrison.

Every day brought measurable progress, and Luc was quite confident that should any attack occur, Trumwell

Castle stood a far better chance of holding out than when he'd arrived. But while the days showed promise, the nights were another story.

Domina clearly despised him for assuming control of her castle and her lands. She was civil enough when others were present, since she cared very much about maintaining appearances. Once they were alone in their bedchamber, however, he might as well be alone for all the response he got from her. She scarcely spoke to him, and never smiled at him. She behaved in a way that obeyed the letter of her marriage vows, while withholding all the spirit. Luc first assumed she'd warm up to him within a few nights. If anything, she grew more distant. She never refused, but she never kissed back, or touched him, or showed the slightest indication that she either enjoyed his attention or wanted more of it.

He hated it. Every moment felt like he was hurting her somehow, despite the fact that he treated her like spun glass—the devil knew that he wanted so much more. But even the gentlest touch seemed repellent to her. Now it repelled him too.

So one night, he decided he'd endure it no longer.

Domina sat on the edge of the bed, clad in her shift, watching him as he prepared for bed. Most nights, he kissed her before blowing out the last candle and climbing into bed, out of an insane hope that she'd respond and ask him to leave the candle burning. This time he didn't even want to kiss her, not when he could feel her stiffen up and shrink back.

So he merely blew out the candle and walked to the side of the bed. He lay down. Next to him, Domina hesitated, then also lay down. As always, she smelled faintly like...actually, he couldn't name the smell. He forced himself to ignore the teasing scent.

She shifted, and he could picture her on her side facing him, her body tense. "Well?" she asked.

"Well, what?"

"Here I am, your wife. Do you not intend to use me as such?"

He shook his head, not that she could see the gesture in the dark. "Go to sleep," he said shortly. "I won't touch you."

"You won't?"

"Trust me, there's no pleasure in it."

Domina hadn't expected to hear that, and in the dark, her silence stretched an unconscionably long time. Then she said, "Have I—"

"Let's not discuss it," he snapped. "You've made your opinion plain enough. Now I'll do the same. We share the bed, but I won't touch you again."

"Oh," she said. That was it. She didn't add a single word, or reveal a hint of her thoughts. Once again, he had to revise his opinion of Domina de Warewic. She'd excel in the royal court. She'd be a viper.

Luc kept his word. Over the next week and a half, they continued to sleep in the same bed, for the sake of appearances. He never laid a hand on her. Night after night, he thought about the beautiful creature lying next to him, and wondered how he'd made such a mistake as to think that marrying her was a good idea.

Worse, his desire for her hadn't slackened one bit. He wanted her, or rather he wanted the woman he dreamed of her being. He wanted to soak up her heat, curl her body right into his, and hear her voice in the dark. Anything. He'd listen to her complain about the grazing in the north pastures. He'd listen to her complain about him.

Instead, she kept herself locked up tight, her thoughts hidden, her secrets sealed. Short of begging, he could do nothing but wait for her to reach out and touch him, or ask for him, or smile at him. Luc wasn't going to beg. He had his pride too.

And all the while, the days grew colder and the nights grew longer.

Why did he decide to get married in winter?

Chapter 17

IN THOSE HARSHEST DAYS OF winter, Domina drifted like a ghost in her own home. Luc's refusal of her stunned her in ways she never expected. She told herself she never wanted him to touch her, and that their marriage was a sham anyway. However, to actually be told aloud that she disappointed him… She was afraid she'd cry in her sleep and accidentally reveal how much his words hurt.

The subsequent nights were no different. Luc virtually ignored her. She wondered if it was some trick, the way some falconers would withhold food from new birds until hunger forced them to obey their master's commands. Was Luc denying her his attention to show her exactly how in control he was? Or to make her beg for some affection?

Or perhaps she so profoundly failed to please him that he was done with her before their marriage was a month old. Mina didn't know, and she'd never find out, for she'd have to ask him, and that would mean exposing her own ignorance, opening herself up for his contempt. She'd rather live like a nun, shut up in Trumwell for the rest of her days, alone.

In reality, she was not permitted even that. With no warning, Luc announced his sister was coming to visit.

"You never told me you had sisters!" she said.

"Three of them. It's a burden." He looked up at her. "Besides, you never asked."

"I...I never thought to." She'd been distracted. Still, how terrible of her, to not even inquire about his family. So now Mina had to prepare to receive a female guest and her expected entourage, which kept her busy until the day the sister rode up.

It was a bright, sunny day, and a recent snowfall turned the world white. Mina surveyed her home with a critical eye. How would the daughter of a wealthy man such as the lord of Braecon react to Mina's less regal home? She would soon find out.

The face of the young lady who peered out of the side of the covered cart was as bright as the sky itself. Luc's answering smile made it clear that he truly looked forward to seeing her—they were family in spirit as well as blood.

He helped her out and turned to Mina, who followed him only a few steps behind.

"My lady Domina," he said. "This is my younger sister, Eva."

The woman made a pretty curtsey, then said, "So you are Domina! I must say I had no idea what to expect, but now I'm considerably less puzzled at Luc's sudden announcement!"

"Is that so?" Mina asked. Luc's sister shared so many of his physical qualities that their relationship was obvious. Eva had the same coloring—the brown hair and vivid blue eyes—and the same general frame, though in a much more feminine version.

"He said the king arranged the marriage, but now I wonder!" Eva clapped her hands together once. "Oh, I must meet everyone in your family, you know. I am expected to bring back all the news and report on what I've seen."

"Meet my family?" Mina said, glancing involuntarily at Luc. "What has Luc told you of my family?"

Eva's smile faltered. "Have I said something wrong?"

"No, Eva," Luc interjected. "Mina's family is small, and scattered. Not like ours...and I have to tell you that's sometimes a relief."

"Let us go inside," Mina said quickly. "Eva, you must be weary."

"The cart does rattle so!" Eva agreed. "I feel as if my bones are all misplaced. But I saw the lake with the swans, and they looked so regal and serene it restored me just to see them."

Mina shot Luc a querying look, trying to assess whether Eva was being sarcastic. In return, Luc gave her a very slight shake of the head, indicating that Eva was in fact always this way. The wordless communication was so brief, so mundane. Yet it sent an odd little shiver through Mina, like she'd learned a few words in a secret language.

It lasted only a moment, and Luc soon turned his attention to his sister, leaving Mina a spectator.

"The journey was uneventful?" he asked.

"Worse, it was dull."

"Good," he said.

Eva rolled her eyes. "Do you never wish me to have adventures?"

"No," he said flatly. "At least, not the sort of misadventures liable to happen to a woman on the road."

"Well, you're in luck, for the only thing I risked on the road is dying of boredom. The money is quite safe."

He looked alarmed. "You mean to say you brought it *with* you? Dear God, Eva, I didn't intend to have my little sister accompany the shipment. What if you were robbed along the way? The silver can be spared. You can not be."

"Oh, I had a dozen men-at-arms with me, and anyway, no one knew what I was bringing…other than Father and Mother, of course. What are you using it for?"

"What money?" Domina interrupted. Luc never mentioned money to her, which was a relief, for she could put off the inevitable moment where she had to reveal her poverty.

Luc looked at Mina, his blue eyes guileless. "This castle needs a few more defenders, and a few repairs. It's my duty to pay for that, since the king was particularly concerned about the security of this castle."

Mina frowned, about to ask for details. She hadn't known he intended to spend his own family's wealth on Trumwell. Once again, he had told her nothing of his plans.

"Trumwell was given to the de Warewics," she objected. "The responsibility falls to me, for despite our marriage, I will always be a de Warewic."

Luc's mouth tightened into a thin line, but he said nothing before Eva burst into another sunny comment.

"Marriage! Speaking of that, you must tell me everything," Eva said to Luc. "You never said she was so beautiful! My goodness, Luc! Did you fall in love with her the moment you saw her?"

Luc's mouth dropped open, and Mina quailed at the thought of how he'd answer.

"How did you meet?" Eva went on, not waiting for

any reply. "When? Was it raining or fair? I wish to know all the details."

Mina said quickly, "We met in London."

"Ah! At court, no doubt."

"No, on the street. Late at night. You see, I had been set on by footpads—"

"No!" Eva gasped, lifting a hand to her open mouth.

"—when Luc appeared. He'd heard the commotion."

"Oh, my, and you saved her!" Eva beamed at Luc. "Of course you did! Luc always wanted to be a knight. He's so chivalrous. To be rescued by a knight…" She sighed.

Luc laughed and shook his head. "It was nothing. Octavian was with me, and did half the work. He hauled the scoundrels off, and I saw Domina to her lodging…where she made it clear that she'd be just as happy to never see my face again."

Mina's cheeks reddened until they probably matched her hair.

Eva pouted. "Oh, I'm sure she couldn't have meant that, for you are married now."

"That's the result of the king's wishes," Luc said, his eyes darkening. Mina didn't know what to make of the sudden shift in his demeanor.

"Naturally," Mina said, "what the king commands, we must carry out. So we married. I'm sure the king had his reasons."

"Oh," Eva said, her eyes widening. "There is some strategy at work, then?"

"I can't say," Mina admitted, quite honestly. But Eva would no doubt create a dozen scenarios in her overactive mind, each one less accurate and more romantic than the previous.

"I won't ask, then," Eva said. "But tell me that you're

both happy!"

"It's...complicated," Luc said, immediately drawing Eva's attention.

"What's wrong? How could she not adore you?" Eva sucked in a breath, then turned back to Domina. "Oh, no! Do you love another?" she asked in a whisper.

"What?" Mina asked. She was suddenly aware of Luc's gaze locked on her as well. "No!"

Luc exhaled, his shoulders relaxing slightly. Domina frowned. Even if she did, why would he *care*? After all, he'd been quite clear that he only married her as a way to protect the castle. And, by extension, Mina herself.

Eva was still looking quite put out, and Mina didn't want to disappoint the girl. "Marriage is...well, it's a very different type of life."

"So you'll be content in time," Eva said, in evident relief. "I know you will be happy with Luc. You must, for he's really one of the finest men ever born." Eva said it with blind, sisterly pride.

Luc laughed, looking almost bashful. "I didn't tell her to say that."

"You don't have to!" Eva added. "Luc once saved me from drowning! I can tell you all about it—I remember every detail of that day. I woke up so excited to swim that morning. The sun was bright. It was in May—"

"June," Luc corrected.

"I think it's time to show you to your room," Mina said. So much cheerfulness was frankly disconcerting. "You'll want to wash and change before the evening meal."

Even with the addition of the lively Eva, supper was not exactly a festive affair. Luc didn't speak much to Mina, instead asking his sister of family news, and then speaking of more political topics. From the way the sib-lings spoke, Mina realized exactly how close to King Stephen their family must be. They mentioned the names of great barons and powerful lords very casually. Eva was quite pragmatic in her discussion of the various men she'd consider as a husband...although she did seem to value comeliness among the virtues of her future spouse.

Domina thought of how little she'd considered a hus-band until one had been chosen for her, and she wondered how Eva could be so romantic one moment and so cynical the next. Perhaps it was simply easier to be romantic about other people's marriages, where the illusion could be maintained.

As if the other lady could read her thoughts, Eva's gaze lingered on Domina while she spoke of the benefits of this or that alliance.

"The name of de Warewic is not well known to me," she said at one point. "Yet the king must think highly of it, to personally select a husband for you."

"I...I am not sure," Mina said, flustered.

"Did he tell you his reasons when you spoke to him?"

"The king?" Mina's only discussion with the king about her marriage had been when he made a joke about it. "He did not...precisely..." She stopped when she saw Luc's face, which was anything but amused.

"My marriage is not your concern, Eva," he said. "Speak of something else."

"But..."

"Speak of something else," he repeated, his tone flat and angry.

There was a moment of silence, and a wave of morti-fication came over Mina. She was a failure as a wife, in every way. Personally. Politically.

Clearly wishing to steer the conversation in a safer direction, Octavian said, "The scaffolding on the north wall was completed today. The repairs will be done within days, I think. The wall is far stronger than it seemed from the ground. Do you wish to see it tomorrow, my lady?"

Mina smiled at him, grateful he'd brought up something that didn't reflect badly on her. She responded, and the awkward moment passed.

At the end of the meal, Eva asked for Domina to walk her to her bedchamber. "I could get lost in a rowboat, you see," she said with a pretty laugh.

Mina agreed, and the two ladies excused themselves. Mina bore a candlestick in one hand.

As they left the great hall, Eva slid her hand around Mina's arm. "We are as good as sisters now," she said.

"I must have been a surprise to you," Mina said dryly.

"Yes, but a lovely one. Our family will be charmed by you."

"More than Luc is, I hope."

Eva looked over at her. "Do you not think he loves you?"

"We hardly know each other," Mina admitted. "I don't even know the names of your sisters. Or their ages."

Eva told her, but didn't lose focus. "Marriage agrees with Luc. These past few years, he's lived only for the court."

"He spoke nothing but politics this whole evening."

"Yes, but because I made him do so. His heart wasn't in it. He and Octavian were going on about defensive drills. He's never cared about such things before."

"Well, he's been working to improve the garrison. The castle's routine was not ideal before."

"Every castle needs a castellan," Eva said. "Quite understandable."

But was it? How could the king have known that the castle required a knight?

Eva was still speaking. "My dear, since you have Luc now, why do you not let him help you?"

"He has helped, as I said. He's getting the garrison into shape, with his own coin, no less."

"Not the castle," Eva said. "Why not let him help *you*?"

"I am well enough," Mina said. "I don't need anything from him."

"Nothing? Not support? Not comfort? Luc wants to be needed by you."

"Has he said so?"

"Well, no. He wouldn't, would he? Men don't say such things. But I can see it every time he looks at you, when he thinks you're not paying attention. He wants to be near you, to have you ask him for something."

"He has everything of mine," Domina said. "That's what he gained as my husband."

"He doesn't have your heart."

"He doesn't want it. He only wanted my hand."

"Luc does not want only part of *anything*. For him, it's all…or he walks away."

Mina thought about it—she presumed Eva would know. "It's complicated."

"So you both say. Why must it be so?"

"Neither of us chose this marriage."

"But it happened. Can you not be allies?"

"Allies are equals," Mina said. "We're not allies. We're husband and wife…which means I am expected to agree with him, give in to him, appease him all the time. Besides, I disappoint him."

"I'm sure that's not true."

"How could you possibly know?" she asked, growing tired of Eva's prying. "You have not seen us together for more than a day."

"No, but I've known him my whole life. He would never have consented to the idea of a marriage to you if he didn't truly want to marry you. He's clever at politics—but he's never been one for compromise, not when it comes to his own life. Our father was always a little worried about Luc's streak of idealism."

Mina couldn't get Eva's words out of her head, and she spent a more restless night than usual. Luc lay beside her, close yet worlds away. He didn't have trouble sleeping. He seemed to be perfectly content with one half of the bed, one half of a marriage. The romantic Eva had to be wrong about her brother's priorities.

* * * *

Eva made herself very much at home, just as Luc had when he arrived. She put her pert little nose into every corner of the castle. She inspired the garrison's soldiers to new heights in their training, for she promised that the solider who was declared the fittest and the most ready for combat by the end of a sennight would receive a pencel from Eva herself—a token he could wear for all the world to see, as the visible esteem of a lady. Octavian said he'd never seen such devotion to drills before.

She also pried her way into more private matters, such as when she appeared on the threshold of Godfrey's room while Domina was singing to him.

Mina felt the presence of a person, and turned, breaking off her song.

"What are you doing here?" she asked.

"I heard the music." Eva took a step into the room.

Mina watched in dismay as Luc appeared behind her. "You brought her here," she accused.

"It's no longer a secret, Domina," he answered in a low voice.

"So this is Godfrey de Warewic," Eva said, approaching the bed in some awe. "How like a saint he looks, so peaceful. How blessed he is to be in your care."

"My care can't restore him to full health," Mina said bitterly.

Eva's hand closed around hers. "How do you know what your care will accomplish? If I were an angel, I'd listen to your prayers, especially if you say them in as pretty a voice as you sing your lullabies."

"You're not an angel," Mina said. She deeply resented that Luc revealed her secret to Eva and brought her into Godfrey's presence without warning. He wouldn't ask for leave, naturally. He was lord here now. But he could have given Mina a hint!

Eva's face was full of wonder and worry. She had no idea of the tangle she'd wandered into. Domina tried hard not to include the girl in her fury. "Luc, please take your sister back to the keep. I'll join you shortly. I'm sure Eva of Braecon will have questions."

She left no room for protest, and Luc seemed to realize exactly how angry Domina was. "We'll wait for you there," he said, taking Eva by the hand.

Domina kept her eyes on her father while the two left. She overheard Eva whisper, "Have you not revealed it yet? You ought to soon, for she seems in want of such a thing."

Luc hushed her, and they hurried out.

Mina took a few deep breaths. What did Luc have left to reveal? Everything he'd revealed so far meant more trouble for Mina.

Domina did explain the story of her father's ailment to Eva, who showed far more sympathy than Luc. However, she also was of the opinion that Luc's presence represented a solution to Domina's woes, rather than a compounding of them. Mina didn't try to correct her. Let the girl keep her innocence a while longer. Mina hoped that when Eva married, it would be to a man who would want her for herself.

* * * *

So the world spun on. The hard frosts of deep winter receded, and the days started to lengthen infinitesimally.

Most mornings, Domina was at work as usual. Despite Eva's presence, despite everything, she was still needed as the lady of the house. In the middle of the day, a servant came up to her, telling her Luc wanted to see her.

"He's in the great hall, my lady."

Mina entered the room. "You asked for me?"

"I did." Luc stood near a large box covered with a heavy cloth. "I have something for you to see."

"What is it?" Mina asked suspiciously.

"That is for you to find out," he said, gesturing for her to uncover the object.

She took hold of one corner of the cloth. It was even heavier than it looked, a rich brocade that blocked both light and sound. She lifted the cloth a bit and peered behind it.

A squawk greeted her, and she gasped. With a little tug, she slowly pulled the whole covering aside, revealing what was underneath.

In a large wooden cage, a magnificent peregrine falcon stood on a perch. It stretched blue-tinged wings as wide as it could, showing a feathered breast as it gave a squawk of warning.

"Oh, how beautiful!" Mina gasped.

"Eva brought her along when she came. But I waited for the weather to improve a bit, and also, I wanted the bird to rest after the journey."

"You must be so pleased to have her here," Mina said. "Do you intend to go hunting with her soon?"

"I don't."

"What?" she asked, confused.

Luc smiled. "She's yours. My wedding present to you."

"Oh." Mina put a hand to her mouth. "You don't have to give me anything."

"I know that," he said. "Is it so difficult to believe that I'm giving you something just because you'll like it?"

"It's far too grand, Luc. This is a falcon for princes."

"It is a falcon for the lady Domina."

"I can't accept such a gift," she said, though she couldn't take her eyes off the bird, which was perfect in every way. "I never thought I'd get to hunt with a peregrine!"

"Now you can." He handed her a brand new glove, the leather tooled into a dense floral pattern. "Try it on, Mina. You ought to get to know your new hunter."

She slid the glove onto her wrist, and then opened the cage door very carefully.

The falcon shied away at first, but Domina spoke to it in a low, steady voice and it soon calmed.

"There you go," she said. "Come step up." The bird

obeyed, stepping from the perch to her arm, flexing its sharp talons into the heavy leather that protected Mina's skin.

"I'll get some meat from the kitchens, my beauty, to feed you."

"Our falconer councils against that," Luc told her. "Birds hunt better when they're hungry."

"Nonsense," Domina said. "I feed my hawks the choicest meat I can. They need to know I care for them. Then they will fly their best, to please me."

"Is that your method?" he asked.

"So I was taught. If you treat a creature ill, it will not trust you, and there is no bond between you. With a falcon, you risk losing her, for she'll choose the sky and fly away forever. She has no reason to want to come back."

"No one ever explained it to me quite so simply."

Domina was still looking at the peregrine with delight. "Oh, you're so gorgeous," she breathed.

"Are you speaking to me or the bird?" Luc asked.

Domina blushed, looking over at him. "The bird!"

"Too bad," Luc said with an exaggerated frown. "But I'm glad you like her. I bought her this past summer, when she was very young."

"What's her name?" Mina asked

"She has none yet. Our falconer trained her, but I had no chance to use her myself, for I've had no leisure."

"Are you certain?"

"You'll be a better mistress than I was master."

"Oh, who could not love her? She's wonderful. I can hardly wait to see how she flies."

"You'll have no trouble, I'm sure," Luc noted, now more openly surveying her. "I've already seen you hunt with your hawks. You can master any creature if you choose to."

Mina quickly returned her attention to the bird. "You must have a name," she mused. "Guinevere would suit you—it's a queenly name." She put the falcon back in the cage, knowing it would take some time for the bird to get used to her.

After she closed the cage door, she realized something else. "Now I'm ashamed, for you've given me Guinevere, and I have given you nothing to match."

"It's a gift, Mina," Luc said. He stepped up to her, reaching for the glove. He removed it, taking his time. Mina was terribly aware of how close he was, and how much he was enjoying stripping the glove from her, even though it revealed only her wrist. "It doesn't need to be reciprocated, for then it wouldn't be a gift, would it?"

"I must give you something," she protested.

"Then give me a kiss."

"That's hardly on the same level."

"Let me decide that." Luc dropped the glove to the floor, and slipped his hand around her waist, drawing her closer.

She tipped her head up, and kissed him, just a light touch of her lips to his.

It didn't stay light. Luc pulled her right next to his body, and when she gasped, he ran his tongue over her parted lips.

Mina reacted instantly, and she heard herself give a little moan before she even knew she was doing it.

Luc heard it and slipped one hand up into her curls, keeping her from pulling away.

Not that she was pulling away. Instead, she found herself leaning into him, tasting him, curious about every new sensation. Whatever reserve kept her silent in bed did nothing for her now. Why was she behaving like this? Had he just bought her affection? Was she so easily swayed? No matter how expensive the gift, she didn't like to think it inspired her kiss.

She broke off with a ragged breath.

"I asked for a kiss and you gave me all that?" He smiled at her.

"Was it too much?" she asked, already deciding that her behavior was wretched.

"More than I asked for, but not nearly enough." He kept her body close to his, and there was no mistaking his reaction.

She felt how hard he'd grown, and bit her lip. "This is not seemly...here in the hall."

Mina pushed herself away, and took a deep breath. She felt so shaky, so on edge. Blood seemed to sing through her body. "I must ask you not to do this again."

"Not here," he said. "But you're a fool if you think I won't ask for that again."

"Please don't talk like that," Mina said staring at the floor.

"You're my wife. I'll talk to you like that because it's the truth," he said in a low voice. "You might be made of stone, but I'm not."

"I'm not made of stone!" she snapped.

"Ice, then. You freeze up every time I try to please you."

"I...I'm sorry."

He sighed. "No. Ignore me. I should not have said that."

"Then why did you? You must believe it. You know about women. If you say I'm made of ice, it's true."

"Mina, that's not what I meant." He reached for her in

appeal, and she let him put his arms around her, as if that could make a difference.

"I know I'm not the woman you want me to be," she said miserably.

Before Luc could respond, one of the members of the castle's garrison burst into the room. Mina instinctively took a step back, as though there was something improper about her being in the arms of her own husband.

"What the hell are you doing in here?" Luc growled at the man.

"My lord, we just got word," he said, too flustered to bow or apologize for the interruption. "There's something wrong down at the village. We think it's being attacked!"

Chapter 18

LUC WISHED HE COULD SAY a sense of foreboding warned him of the attack, but the truth was that he was unpleasantly surprised. No, that was putting it mildly. Some idiot thought to take advantage of a presumably weak castle during the winter lull, raiding the village under the assumption that they'd face no resistance. However, now it was Luc's castle, and both his wife and his sister were in it.

He'd kill whoever was stupid enough to have instigated this.

Luc had every confidence that Mina would take care of Eva, so he could put his mind entirely toward the fight. After exchanging a few words with Mina, he ran to the courtyard, where the garrison was already preparing to march out. The men-at-arms seemed remarkably calm—perhaps they thought it another drill.

Octavian stood near the stables, along with their squires, who knew how to ready each of their war horses. Another pair of squires rushed out of a building, each carrying chain mail.

Luc nodded gratefully to Ban as he helped put the heavy layer on. "My sword," he said urgently.

"Right away, sir."

Octavian barked orders at various people, and despite his apparent displeasure, Luc could see that the garrison was responding well and quickly to the orders.

At last both knights were mounted, ready to lead the group out.

"Want to inspire them?" Octavian asked in a low voice.

Luc nodded once. He turned to the assembled soldiers. "Listen, men! I don't know exactly what we face, but remember that Trumwell Castle is yours. The village is yours. Stay calm if you can, and remember to defend yourselves as well. Our purpose is to defend what we have, not pursue. Above all, obey me. Does every man understand that?"

The answering shout was firm, though a little scattered.

"Are you ready to protect Trumwell Castle?"

The next shout was louder.

"Are you ready to protect your families and your homes?"

Now they sounded like an army.

Luc nodded in satisfaction. "Then we go!"

The knights and a few others were mounted—most of the garrison consisted of foot soldiers. So their progress was not quite as speedy as it might be, but not one man lagged behind. Octavian's much-despised running drills proved their worth.

The village lay at the base of the hill, beyond a fringe of woodland past the lake. The plumes of smoke curling up into the grey sky were probably what first indicated an attack was underway, and as the group got closer, Luc heard shouts and screams.

He halted just outside the village, scanning the scene. The castle garrison had been noticed. Villagers shouted in mixed warning and relief. The attackers jeered.

Luc turned halfway in his saddle to give the orders. "Trumwell men! The red company will sweep the streets and homes. Gather the villagers and keep them safe. The blue company goes after the hedge-born dullards foolish enough to attack us. Don't hold back. Sweep through west to east. Push the attacking force to the eastern green. Pin them by the brook."

Octavian repeated the orders sharply, then called, "Red, go!"

Half the men plunged forward, seeking to save the residents.

"Blue!" Luc shouted. "The knights ride through first. Follow us and clean up!"

Octavian drew his sword. "*Deus la volt.*"

Luc nodded and drew his own sword. "Let's show them how to fight."

The knights signaled their horses, who were tense with battle-readiness. The horses sprang forward, eager to be moving.

Both knights had conducted similar maneuvers many times, and they'd fought together enough to be able to call one word signals and warnings to each other that kept them in sync and their attackers off balance.

The attackers were obviously little more than hoodlums, men who were tough enough to scare travelers or take on a farmstead. They were not prepared to fight trained warriors on horseback. Luc incapacitated a few, and sent the rest running.

He glance toward Tav, and saw that the other knight was having an equally easy time of it. Behind them, the garrison's men found very few attackers to haul away.

"Something's wrong," Luc said.

Tav reined in. "What do you mean?"

"There are barely enough men here to cause more than a ruckus, and certainly not enough to actually raid the village."

"Just a few thieves, then?"

"Thieves don't start fires to get attention." Luc looked back toward the castle. "This is a diversion."

"From what? The castle?"

Luc understood his skepticism. It would take a large force to attack a castle with any hope of success. On the other hand, even a small number of men could potentially do some damage, if they had the right equipment and information.

"Round up every man with a horse," Luc said. "The foot soldiers can follow. Have a few remain here and hold the prisoners—if they don't all run off. But I'm sure the real attack is back at Trumwell."

Luckily, it was only a short distance to ride back, since the village only existed because Trumwell stood guard over the whole valley.

The castle looked serene, but Luc wasn't fooled. Something was about to happen, now that the main group of defenders had ridden out, leaving only a few men on the walls. The gates were shut tight, as they should be.

Only a complete fool would attack the front, so any force would be gathering in the woods, hoping to get as close as possible...

Then Luc knew where he needed to go. He called out to Octavian, explaining his whole plan in a few words.

Tav nodded in comprehension.

The group of defenders split up, each half taking a long ride around the castle to meet at the north side, exactly where the old wood had been chopped down so recently.

Luc smiled in satisfaction when he saw a small force of men huddling near the edge of the existing trees. Everything in their movements suggested hesitation. Their plan relied on the old wood still growing close to the castle, and now they were uncertain what to do. Luc's eyes narrowed as he surveyed the scene. Someone had been expecting that stand of trees to still be there…because he'd last seen the land look like that.

"Gesu," Luc muttered. He knew without a doubt who was behind this attack, even if he never laid eyes on him today. Haldan.

The attackers' hesitation turned into alarm when Luc's little squad bore down on them. Then another cry told him that Octavian's force was visible too.

Anger drove Luc forward faster than was wise, but still, his side had the advantage now. He slammed into the little group with all the power a war horse at full speed could provide. The first man to encounter Luc's sword didn't even have a chance to scream.

Chapter 19

ATTACK. MINA'S HEART DROPPED INTO her stomach. This was what she'd always feared, ever since her father fell ill.

As soon as Luc heard the word *attack* from the messenger, his demeanor changed completely. He took a long breath, then turned to Mina and put his hands on her shoulders.

"Will you find my sister and keep her safe till I return?" he asked, as if he were requesting a particular dish for supper.

"Yes, of course," Mina said.

"Go to the upper floor of the keep. The west facing chamber. Keep Eva and the rest of the women safe."

She nodded. He stared hard at her for a moment, his own expression unreadable. Then he left.

He left.

Mina stood there for a moment, gazing at the door he'd gone through. *Keep Eva safe.* That was his concern?

Well, she'd spent enough time telling him not to be concerned with her, Mina admitted to herself. But still…a little concern would have been nice.

Eva. It was Mina's duty to protect the young woman, who was a guest in her home. She sent word with a footman to find Eva and then ordered Constance and Margery to meet her in the highest room of the keep.

It was fortunate that the servants all understood the urgency of the situation. Footmen bolted doors and windows, and everyone moved through their tasks with relative calm. Luc's insistence on training the garrison also meant the household servants relearned their tasks.

Only a short while after the first alarm, Mina and the other women were all in the specified room. On the other side of the door, two of the younger soldiers stood guard. Though if the attackers ever got as far as the top floor of the keep itself, it meant all was lost. Mina might as well have placed two yearling lambs as guards.

Inside the room, the mood was calm, but it would get worse the longer they were stuck here.

The steward entered, and cast his eye over them all. "You're all here. Good. My lady, I trust you have the key?"

Mina nodded.

"You know what to do, then."

She reached for his arm as Ancel was about to leave. "My father," she began to say.

Ancel held up a hand. "Guards are with him. If there's any hint that the walls could be breached, he'll be moved to the keep. Not that the walls will be breached," he added confidently.

"Tell the kitchen workers to begin heating water." Any fight would bring injuries, and she wanted to be ready.

He nodded gravely. "I'll return when any news comes," the steward said. "You must protect yourself and the other ladies. My lord made it clear that if you were harmed, he'd take it badly."

"Badly?" Mina echoed.

"His exact words were, 'If my wife is scratched, I'll behead everyone bearing a weapon.'"

"Oh." Had he really said that?

"That sounds like Luc," Eva said, from where she sat by the fire. "He's always been possessive."

Mina was nonplussed, but she didn't dare pursue the matter, not with all the other people around to overhear.

Time passed, crawling moment by moment.

In the beginning, they all worked to pull clean rags into strips, anticipating the need for bandages. It was grim work, and in any case Mina knew that the castle already had a healthy supply, because it had been so long since there'd been any violence.

Soon, the women pretended to focus on needlework or knitting. Margery played with the chess pieces on the board, though she knew nothing of the game. Instead, she seemed to be turning the pieces into characters of some dramatic presentation. Then she cast them all aside with a heavy sigh.

"How long does a battle *take*?" she asked the air. She looked as distressed as Mina felt.

The women took turns looking out the windows every few minutes. The room had three windows, and its height meant that much of the castle's grounds could be seen.

Mina hovered at the windows most often, though she could see nothing of the village or the land where the fight was taking place. Then she caught sight of two groups of soldiers moving swiftly from the village back toward the castle.

"Something's changed," she announced.

"It is over?" Eva asked.

"I don't think so," Mina said. "It's our men, in two groups, but they're going fast, as if they're in a hurry to get somewhere el—"

A huge crash sounded. The women shrieked in alarm as the very stones of the castle seemed to shudder.

"What was that?" Constance asked anxiously.

Mina ran from one window to the next, looking outside to see what was happening. "If I didn't know better..." she muttered. "Oh, no."

"What?" asked Eva.

"Brace yourselves," Mina ordered.

Another huge crash came, followed by another quaking of the castle floor.

"Someone's made a catapult," Domina announced.

"What?" gasped Eva. "*How?*"

"Good question." Mina pulled the key to the room from her ring, crossing to the door.

"Where are you going, my lady?" Constance asked. "My lord ordered us all to remain here!"

"And so you shall," Mina said, turning the key in the lock. "I'll send more guards up to protect you."

"But you..."

"Trumwell belongs to me," Mina said, firmly casting her gaze at everyone in the room. "Now it needs someone to direct defenses from the wall, for the lord is outside on the field." She pulled the door open and slipped through, locking it again on the other side.

She glared at the guards before they dared to raise any objection. "I'm sending more men up, if I can spare them," she said. "Until then, remain here. People are depending on you."

Both straightened their posture even more. "Yes, my

lady," one said.

Mina nodded and rushed down the staircase.

She emerged on the northern parapet, seeing Ancel huddled with a group of men in a sheltered spot at one corner of the walls.

She strode across the parapet walk to join them, too annoyed to bother ducking or concealing herself in any way. She knew her hair would serve as a beacon if someone was looking for it. Judging by a few surprised shouts from the ground, someone had indeed noticed her presence.

"My lady!" Ancel cried in dismay. "What are you thinking?"

"I'm thinking that archers are needed," she said sharply. "How many men have we got within the walls?

"About twenty, my lady," a young guard replied.

"I want to see ten archers on this wall within two minutes," she said, "and five more on the western wall. Aim for wherever that catapult seems to be hidden—try just behind the cut down wood. If you have a chance to shoot at an enemy solider on the field below, do it."

"My lady, you can't be seen," Ancel begged.

"A little late for that," Mina said. She continued to move along the walk and through the various guard towers. After their initial shock, the soldiers at each point followed her orders without hesitation.

She kept an eye on the developing skirmish below, and noted where the heavy rocks seemed to be originating. Thankfully, it seemed there was but one catapult, and it had been assembled a little farther away from the walls than planned. The field below showed several rocks that hadn't made it as far as the outer walls, let alone the keep. Only a few hits occurred, limiting the danger to the castle itself.

Yet there was plenty of danger for the men on the field below. Domina leaned over the wall, searching for one figure in particular. She spotted Luc riding his horse in large circles, choosing to engage opponents who seemed the most dangerous.

Her breath caught in her throat every time he raised his sword, and every time someone attacked him, Domina experienced a thin, vicious stab in her heart. The thought of Luc dead brought no joy, no relief...only pain. *I'm too young to be a widow. I'm barely a wife yet.*

She took an unsteady breath, and almost pitched forward, except that Ancel was suddenly beside her, pulling her back.

"Hold on, my lady," he warned.

"No!" she shouted, her voice carrying across the field. She pointed at the archer nearest her. "You! Aim for the one in the red cloak down there! The one coming after Luc from behind!"

* * * *

Luc heard a voice float over the wind and he instinctively turned his head to find the source. Up on the northern wall, he saw the unmistakable red-haired figure of Domina, looking like a fury as she directed the soldiers to carry out some order.

"Gesu," he swore. Did the woman not understand the meaning of staying safe behind locked walls?

Then the archer closest to Domina seemed to take aim right at Luc. An arrow flew toward him—no, behind him. Luc spun his horse about just in time to see the real target of the shot, a man in a red cloak. He wore a helmet with a heavy face guard, which concealed the details of his identity.

The man barely dodged the arrow, but he swore in frustration; he'd clearly been going for Luc and now the element of surprise was lost.

He and Luc stared at each other for a long moment. Then the man in the red cloak wheeled his own horse around and fled through the various groups of fighting men.

That was all Luc needed to know.

"Tav!" he shouted. "I'm for the man in red. That's the leader!"

Octavian looked over, and nodded. "I'll clear the way."

Tav let out a yell and charged forward. The sight of a brown-skinned knight on a warhorse, howling a crusader's war cry in Latin and bearing a sword was enough to make most soldiers think that either God or the Devil was coming for them. Tav scattered most of the infantry in his path. Those who stood their ground regretted it. Tav's momentum and the edge of his blade made quick work of them. Luc followed him, dispatching the few remaining soldiers in the way.

The leader in the red cloak didn't rise to the occasion. Instead he howled for his group to retreat and then spurred his own horse into the woods.

Luc directed his horse to follow. There was no way he'd let some idiot attack and then run away.

Luc's focus on the leader made him less alert to the surrounding chaos than he should have been. One of the remaining mounted soldiers rushed him from the side. Luc barely deflected the blow the other man leveled at him.

"You go for the back as well?" Luc snarled in contempt.

His comment seemed to surprise his attacker, for he didn't quite parry the thrust Luc aimed at him. Luc's sword slashed into the man's unprotected neck.

He gurgled in shock and then slid off his horse.

Luc didn't stay to admire his handiwork. He nudged his own horse and continued after the fleeing leader.

"Haldan!" he yelled.

An old trick, but still useful.

Instinctively, the man in red turned back on hearing his name. Luc caught sight of his face, which was familiar, including the long, angry looking scar that slashed across it, the result of Mina's furious defense when he attacked her.

The scar fit his expression well. He was angry at being tricked, and angry that the day wasn't going as planned.

Luc rode faster, dodging the few trees between them. "Stand and fight me, you coward," he called.

Haldan hesitated, as if truly considering Luc's challenge. But when Luc pressed forward again, closing the gap between them, Haldan made his choice.

He gave a shout of frustration and turned, putting all his effort into making his horse flee.

Luc prepared to give chase, but a voice calling him from behind drew him up short.

Octavian hailed him from where he'd stopped, and Luc wheeled his horse about. Haldan could wait.

"They were starting a fire," Octavian said, pointing to the evidence. "Looks like the catapult didn't work as well as they hoped. They were going to shoot flaming arrows over the walls. It might have caused quite a difficulty inside if anything caught fire."

"Our opponent seems to have a predilection for burning things," Luc said. "I'll have to keep that in mind when I get my hands on him."

"One of these men might be able to tell you more about that," Tav said, using French this time. He pointed to three soldiers who were lying on the ground, very still, with their hands visible. A few men from the garrison then bound them.

"Walk them up to the castle," said Octavian. "Lock them up. We'll question them later. If they resist, kill them," he added matter-of-factly.

Octavian lowered his sword, looking toward Luc. "What would we have done if the wood hadn't been cut down?"

Luc shook his head. "No sense wondering. It's clear they expected the concealment to still be there. I'm glad we thwarted the attack."

The ache in his back began to worsen, and he felt a sense of vertigo. Lord, he was out of shape if a little sally like this could tire him out. "I think it's time to return to the castle." He swung his horse around, momentarily facing away from Tav.

"Wait," Tav said in a low voice.

"What now?"

Tav rode up next to him and put a hand on his back. Luc winced. "That's right where I ache!"

"No wonder." Tav lift his hand up—his fingers were red. "The mail's been severed. You're bleeding."

"That explains it," Luc muttered, then slumped forward onto the horse's neck.

Chapter 20

THE INJURED MEN HAD ALL been gathered in the great hall. Most managed to walk there under their own power, but six of them lay near the largest fireplace in varying degrees of pain, all covered with a mix of blood, smoke, and dirt.

Ban, one of the men in Luc's entourage, was on his feet, and as soon as he saw Constance, he rushed over to her, speaking to her in a low voice. Constance nodded several times, a blush spreading over her face.

Mina was glad something good came out of the horrible day. Then she caught sight of something that made all other thoughts fly out of her head.

Luc had been laid out on his stomach, because of the horrible wound in his back.

"Oh, my God," Mina gasped. She stumbled toward him, sinking to her knees beside him.

Eva stood frozen a few feet away, her hands over her mouth, her eyes wide.

"My lady." The voice was Octavian's. He knelt by

Mina. "It's not as dire as it looks, but he needs attention now."

"Yes." Mina nodded, but didn't move, too overwhelmed to think.

Octavian put one hand on her shoulder, shaking her gently. "*Now*," he repeated. "Tell us what to do."

That snapped her to attention. She looked around the hall, at the most gravely injured and the crowd of others.

She rose to her feet, with Octavian's hand now at her elbow.

Domina pointed to the men with minor wounds. "Margery, Constance. Tend to anyone whose injuries you know how to dress. Use hot water. Clean each wound and use clean bandages, as I've shown you. Come to me with questions."

The women nodded.

"Eva, can you help them?"

The woman nodded, her eyes still locked on her brother's form.

Mina looked to Beatrice, the older maid who'd seen more blood than any of them. "Beatrice, the five men lying here are under your care. Octavian, will you assist her? Some of the men will be too heavy for her to shift alone."

"Yes, my lady."

Mina nodded. "Very good. As for Luc, I want him carried to his bedchamber immediately. I will tend to him there. Bring water and bandages up, along with ointment."

She clapped her hands loudly. "Move!"

Everyone started to obey, going about the tasks she assigned. Mina turned to Giles. "I know not what Luc has ordered regarding the castle's defenses, but I now ask you to carry it out. Keep watch from the walls. Use whoever you need—men, women, children. I don't care. But use as many eyes as you can. I want no more surprises today."

"Yes, my lady."

A short while later, Domina led a few men who carried a groaning Luc up the stairs to the bedchamber. She pointed to the space in front of the fire. "There, on the rug. Set him down gently."

Two maids entered. One bore a basin of steaming water, and the other carried a basket full of cloth for bandages.

"Put them down by the fire," Domina directed them. "Tell the footmen to bring up more hot water as soon as enough has been boiled."

"Yes, my lady."

The men hovered uncertainly. "Do you have orders now, my lady?"

"Yes. Go to the great hall and make yourselves useful, or find Octavian and ask for further instruction."

"We could send for a doctor."

"I am his wife," Domina said firmly. "It is my duty to care for my lord and husband. Leave us."

They left.

Domina turned to Luc, who was actually attempting to sit up.

"Stop that," she ordered. "You'll move when I tell you." Yelling at him felt good. It felt normal.

Luc gave up his efforts to rise. "How bad is it?"

"That is what I am going to find out. Lay still, my lord."

"Don't call me that when I'm bleeding to death, Mina."

"You're not bleeding to death. It looks as if the blood

flow has already slowed. What you need is to have your wound cleaned and bandaged."

"Domina, you should not have to see this."

"You have little choice in the matter, my lord."

The cut was not nearly as bad as she feared. It was shallow, and most of the ugliness was due to the clotted blood and angry bruising around the cut itself. Apparently, Luc's mail armor had done its job, taking most of the impact before breaking.

She wet a cloth in hot water and began to clean the wound, starting at the shoulder. He flinched when the hot cloth touched flesh.

"I am sorry," she said, putting one hand to his unharmed shoulder to steady him. "But it is imperative to clean the cut well, or it may fester and give you a fever… or worse."

He only nodded. Domina continued to clean the wound, working as quickly as she dared. Soon, the basin water was dark and filthy, but the cut looked clean.

The door opened. A footman bore another basin, this one with steaming fresh water. Domina nodded gratefully. "Please put it right down here. Take the old water and dump it somewhere far from the kitchens."

"Yes, my lady." The man picked up the old bowl and hurried out.

"The cut is a long but narrow one, fortunately," she said to Luc. "Once bandaged, it should knit well."

"Then bandage it," he said shortly.

"Not quite yet." Domina opened a jar of ointment.

He was watching as best he could. "What's that?" he asked suspiciously.

"Something to help the skin heal. It's not poison!"

"I didn't say it was." But his expression was doubtful.

"Ugh! Such a baby!" Domina took a bit on her finger and licked it off. "See? If it were poisoned, I wouldn't dare eat it."

"I trust you, Mina," he said. He reached out to take her wrist. He brought her hand closer and inhaled the scent of the ointment. Domina held very still, all too aware of the strength in his arm. He took his time in studying the greenish ointment on her finger.

"Certainly, the stuff has not harmed your skin."

Domina tried to pretend that she didn't enjoy the compliment, or the stroke of his finger on her pulse. He inhaled again, slowly. "It smells good. What's in it?"

"Comfrey and yarrow, macerated in honey. They are all quite beneficial."

"Sounds delicious." With no warning, he drew her finger to his mouth and sucked the ointment off.

Mina gasped in shock. Why did that feel so good? His tongue teased the pad of her finger, and he looked quite content to simply stay there, suckling.

"Give me my hand back, my lord."

"Luc," he said softly.

She used the single word to snatch her finger back from his open mouth. "You must have hit your head as well. You're acting mad."

"Not acting," he said, the words a little slurred. He had the audacity to smile.

Domina applied the ointment to Luc's cut, then helped him to sit up. She wrapped thin strips of cloth over his left shoulder and underneath his right arm. She tied the two ends of the cloth at his chest, kneeling in front of him to do so. "After a day or two, this won't be necessary. But you shouldn't tax yourself until the edges of the cut knit together."

"You are a very good nurse, Domina." His face was close to her, his eyes disconcertingly bright. He was not incoherent nor unaware of what was happening. She knew what that looked like.

"As you know, I've had much practice," she muttered, looking at the floor.

He caught her chin and made her look at him, their faces on a level. "I am grateful, Domina."

She stood up, looking away from him. "It is my duty," she said, ignoring the little voice in her heart, the one that reminded her how terrified she'd been when she thought he might be killed.

Mina tried to make him lie down on the bed to rest for a while, but he insisted on being dressed so he could go down to the hall and see what was happening.

"You're not dressing till you bathe," she told him.

"I can't bathe with half of me bandaged," he argued. "All your work would be wasted."

Domina glanced at the last bowl of clean, hot water. "Very well. Sit down. I'll wash you as best I can."

She added a few shavings of a bar of her favorite soap, and dipped a sponge in the water.

Luc needed the wash. The smell of battle—sweat and blood—clung to him. "Is this how it felt before?" she asked. "When you got the scar you showed me?"

"That was worse," he said. "Far worse. I had no caring wife attending me after that battle."

"Don't make light of this!" she snapped, plunging her hands into the water again.

"Mina, I'm serious." Luc reached down to put his hands over hers. "I don't know what I'd do without you."

She shook off his hands, then wrung out the sponge. He was clean enough, she decided. Being too close to Luc was making her addled. "All I did was wash and bandage a wound."

"You did more than that. You always do more than you have to."

"You should rest now," Mina said. "You need to sleep."

"The castle needs to see me walk," Luc argued. "There's already one lord here who is confined to a bed. They can't see another like that."

Mina closed her eyes. His words cut her.

"I don't mean to hurt you," he said. "I'm thinking of Trumwell. Put yourself in the shoes of one of the servants here. They need to see someone in control."

"I'm in control." Dear God, she was not.

"So you are, but when another decides to test the strength of this castle, it won't be you who rides out. Am I right?"

"You won't let this go, will you?"

"No," he said. "Now. Help me get ready."

Chapter 21

LUC COULD BARELY STAND UP, but if this was what it took to have Domina close to him, he would ride into battle every day. The scent of her intoxicated him.

At his order, they dined in the hall. The kitchen servants managed to produce something resembling a feast —the food was plain but abundant, and the wine flowed in celebration of Trumwell's stalwart defenders. The mood was jubilant

Luc was determined to shrug off the effects of the wound. He wanted every man in the castle to know he was as strong and as capable as ever. Domina, without speaking a word, supported him invisibly as he made his way to the high table. She pretended nonchalance, but her body leaned against his, subtly lending him strength. Domina might not like him, but she understood the importance of presenting a strong front. She demonstrated again and again her mastery of battle.

Before he could sit, Eva entered and rushed up to him. Damn, she'd kill him with her embrace. Mina suddenly put herself in front of Luc just before Eva reached them. To anyone watching, it looked as if the two women were embracing out of relief.

Luc heard Mina whisper, "Smile, dear. And don't crush him. We are putting on a play."

Luc was so proud of his wife at that moment, it almost hurt more than the wound itself.

Eva smiled, her eyes scanning Luc, who smiled back.

"You're not rid of me yet, sister," he said.

"Praise God," Eva murmured, giving him a very gentle embrace. Then she turned and took her seat next to Luc, with Octavian on her other side.

Luc sat down in the chair set at the very center of the high table. Domina moved away to take her own seat next to him, and he missed her closeness. If only she truly wanted to be close to him.

As a play, the meal went perfectly. There were toasts, naturally. Domina lifted her glass high each time, but drank barely a drop. The toasts went on. Toasts to Luc, and toasts to the garrison, and for the Welsh to go to hell.

"Was it the Welsh?" Eva asked in a low voice.

"No," Luc said, "but if that's the conclusion they've reached for the moment, let them be content with it."

"If not the Welsh, who was it?" Mina asked.

"I'll explain later," he told her. "Believe me, a few hours won't matter."

Mina studied him, but said nothing.

He felt much better after eating and drinking, so that he could walk back up to the bedroom perfectly well on his own. He didn't tell Mina that, enjoying her pressed against him as she provided support he didn't strictly need.

She helped him remove his clothes and helped him into bed.

"I'm not an invalid," he groused. He disliked heartily

that she was treating him like a child...and not like a man.

"Of course you're not, Luc. Trust me, I know well the difference."

Naturally, Domina blew out the candle before she stripped down to her shift, denying Luc even the small, torturous pleasure of seeing her half dressed.

She slid into the bed next to him. "Are you comfortable?" she asked in low voice.

"As comfortable as I can be with a slice out of my back."

"Lay with me," Domina urged him.

"What?" He didn't quite believe the words uttered by his wife.

"You'll never be able to sleep lying on your back. So use me as a bolster. Please."

Ah, she wasn't asking what he wanted her to ask. Luc sighed, but she took it for a sound of pain.

"Now, Luc." She put a hand on his arm, encouraging him to roll halfway onto her. Luc was all too aware of the softness of her body, even with the hateful fabric of her shift between them. He tried desperately to ignore her closeness, the scent of her skin. Domina was offering comfort, not desire.

"There's something I should tell you, about the fight today," he said.

"What is that?"

"The leader of the group was Haldan." Luc said it as simply as he could, but he could feel Domina tense up.

"He was? How dare he... Well, I suppose I know exactly why he dared."

"Which is why?"

"Because he knew the strength of the garrison, or he thought he did. He had intelligence from his time here, and he put it to use as soon as he could gather enough men."

"I'm not sure that was the whole reason."

"What other motive could he have?"

"You forced him away from here."

"That was you," she objected. "I remember the encounter." She shivered as she spoke.

Luc cupped her head in his hand, hoping to soothe her. "My point is that he was embarrassed by how he was forced out, and sought to restore his reputation as a fighter."

"That didn't go so well for him, did it? Not when he fought you."

"I was lucky today. But if Haldan had been more clever—attacked at a different time, had a few more men…it might have gone very differently."

"You would have won," she said. "I know it."

She shifted slightly, pulling his hand from her head and resting it on her chest, tantalizingly close to her breast. She entwined his fingers with her own. Luc felt as if a rare bird chose to alight near him. He hardly dared to breathe.

He waited a few interminable moments, feeling her heartbeat beneath his hand.

He wanted her so badly he couldn't speak. Not just out of lust, though there was a healthy dose of that, but to have her next to him, touching him, a body as warm as his own. Every night.

Luc slowly drifted to sleep, lost in a pleasant haze of dream and desire. He blamed Mina's scent, an unnameable aroma—partly her and partly an herbal blend, sharp and clean and cool. Not a single flower in it, he was sure. Domina was not a woman for roses. She would insist on being different.

He loved her scent. This night, with him in the wonderful position that he was, with his head on her shoulder and his body half over hers, the smell enveloped him, making him dream of her with more vividness than ever before.

In his dream, she touched him. He could almost feel the strokes as she explored him. Domina moved one hand to his arm, trailing a finger up and down slowly, feeling the muscles under the skin. Then she boldly moved to his chest, and explored the flesh not hidden by the gauze. She let her touch linger there, curious to feel the curling hair under the pads of her fingers.

She followed the contours on his body down to his torso. Luc could hear her breathing, even the tiny catch in her breath when she ran one finger along his old, ugly scar.

With a jolt, Luc realized it wasn't a dream at all. Dear God, Mina actually was touching him.

He kept his eyes shut, lest the slightest flick of his lashes against her skin warn her. He struggled to keep his breathing even, as if he slumbered on.

Every passing moment made that more difficult. He wanted to touch her back, to beg her to let him try again to please her as she was pleasing him now.

Every brush of her fingers made him want to moan. Since he was lying as he was, she could surely feel him harden against her soft skin. Yet she continued with those lovely, maddening strokes that woke his whole body. If this went on, even if she touched no more than his *arm*, he'd spill.

That would horrify her. He had to stop her. Domina was so intent on her explorations that she was taken by surprise when Luc suddenly grabbed her hand.

"What are you doing, my Mina?" he whispered, his voice hoarse with need.

"Oh! I didn't mean to wake you." She inhaled sharply, causing her breast to rise, to press into him, a move he warmly welcomed.

"Did you think I could sleep through that torture?"

"Torture? Did I hurt you?" she asked, concerned.

"Hurt me?" He laughed. "You've been tantalizing me for what feels like an hour with your sweet hands, and yet I'm not permitted to touch you. Yes, that hurts."

He guided her hand downward, until Domina's fingers brushed against his shaft, hard as rock. "Just so you know," he growled.

He let her hand go, and she immediately pulled it back. "I...my touch did that?" she whispered.

"Just thinking about you can do that, Mina. Imagine how I feel when you are actually here, next to me, and touching me like I dream of you doing."

"You don't dream of me."

"How would you know?"

"I suppose...I do not," she admitted.

He rolled onto his back, sighing.

"Don't!" she hissed. "It must hurt to lie like that."

"Believe me, it's a welcome distraction," he said, his breath nevertheless coming out in a hiss of pain. "It's certain I couldn't have endured much more of your curiosity without breaking my word."

"I didn't think," she said. "I'm so sorry."

"So am I," he said, though with a different implication.

"Does it hurt your back now? To lie like that?" She rolled on her side to watch him better, though the embers gave little light in the room.

"Yes," he said unwillingly.

Domina said nothing, and he closed his eyes. God, why had he ruined it by letting her know he was awake? He would have happily endured another hour, or minute, or instant of her touch.

Taking a long breath, she laid her hand on his chest.

"Domina, do you hate me?" he asked, his voice choked. Did she really intend to torture him now?

"No," she whispered. "If I hated you, I wouldn't care how you felt. But I do. Let me touch you," she said.

Dear God, yes. "Please. Please touch me, Mina."

She resumed her explorations, now fully aware of his reactions to every shift and stroke. He no longer had to hide his reactions—not that he could at this point—and he let her know exactly how much he loved her touch.

Domina seemed to enjoy touching him as well. She asked, in a whisper, "Does this distract you from your pain?"

"What pain?" he asked, with a low laugh.

Amazingly, she laughed too, shyly and charmingly. He didn't think she could do anything to make him want her more, and then she did it.

Then her laughter stopped. She asked, in a hesitant way, "Luc…would you like it if I…"

She touched the tip of his shaft with one finger. He went completely still, desperate not to scare her off.

"Don't stop," he said finally. "Don't stop."

"What should I do, though?"

He put his hand over hers, and he showed her what to do. Mina was a devastatingly quick learner. A stroke of her finger wreaked havoc in him. He loved it. He adored having her this close to him, this interested in him.

He was going to spill any moment. He couldn't let that happen yet.

He grabbed her hand, probably too roughly.

"Did I do wrong?"

"Mina, one more touch and I'll be done. I don't want to end yet. Let me recover."

"Did you like it?"

He laughed. "You know I did. I just want to enjoy you as long as I can. I know you won't let me enter you."

Mina paused, then whispered, "I would."

"You hated it. You said you never wanted me like that again."

She took a breath, then said, in a low voice. "I told you that because I was angry. At how you told me of the marriage. How you…took over. My life. Everything."

"I haven't been fair to you." Even now, he kept the full truth from her. God, he didn't deserve what he truly wanted from her.

"If you would accept me," she said, "I would begin again. Laying with you, I mean."

"Mina, is that true?" he asked desperately. "You're not just humoring me now."

"I…I…thought you were…from the first."

"Thought I was what?"

"You don't need me to tell you you're handsome. As you made clear, you had plenty of other women to tell you that."

"Who were just flattering me."

"No. Not flattery. Or at least, not dishonest flattery. You're so gorgeous, in face and body. You stir me. You know that."

"I didn't know that. You hide your thoughts so well."

"I'm telling you now," she whispered.

Chapter 22

DOMINA FELT MORE EXPOSED TELLING Luc she desired him than she had the night he'd first stripped her bare and taken her virginity.

He didn't laugh, he didn't hold it over her. He only shifted his body very slightly, tipping his head to kiss her right where her shoulder met her neck. His mouth felt divine.

"Let's begin now," he said, the words vibrating against her skin. "Tonight."

"But you're hurt."

"You've healed me."

"You're lying."

"Mina, will you light a candle?" he asked.

"You want light?" she nearly squeaked. It was difficult enough to be bold in the dark.

"Please. As a gift."

Again, he had to ask for something so unassuming she couldn't refuse him. And after he'd nearly died defending her home.

Mina said, "I'll have to get out of bed."

It took her a moment to walk to the fireplace and light the candle with an ember. When she came back to the bed, the candlelight illuminated Luc lying on his side, propped up on one elbow. She saw every contour of every muscle in sharp relief. He was in superb condition—the scars and bruises didn't detract at all from his allure. He was a warrior. Her warrior.

Who was now very much at attention.

Mina looked away, feeling her cheeks burn. She put the candle in its holder by the bed.

"Come back here, beautiful," Luc said, his voice low.

She slid back onto the bed, reaching for the cover.

Luc stopped her. "Not yet. I need to see you."

"You can see me very well."

"I see your shift. Take it off, or I will."

She bit her lip, remembering the last time he said that to her. Then she grabbed hold of the fabric and pulled it up and over her head.

Luc didn't reach for her this time. Instead, he surveyed her from top to bottom, a slow smile growing as he did. "Beautiful," he pronounced. "The light makes you glow."

She looked at him. "What should I do?"

He pulled her closer. She lay on her back with him alongside her once again.

"Kiss me," he ordered.

She kissed him, reveling in the heat of him. He ran his free hand up and down her side, from her shoulder to her hip and back again.

The kiss deepened, and when his tongue touched hers, she moaned into his mouth, finally allowing herself to reveal how much his touch devastated her.

"Mina," he said, pulling away from the kiss so he

could look at her, "you're so beautiful. I love seeing you like this."

"Naked?"

"Yes. Not just your body, but your thoughts. Hearing you react. Seeing your true emotions…no one else sees you like this." He ran his fingers along the outline of her face. "I'm the only one who's seen you like this."

"Of course." She looked away, shy again. "You don't think I've ever…"

"Not that," he said quickly. "I never doubted your virtue, Mina. I'm just thinking how precious you are. How hidden you keep yourself."

"Not to you," she whispered. He saw more of her than anyone in the world.

"Promise me that, Mina. Promise me you'll never hide yourself from me."

"How can I? You're my husband."

"That means nothing. I've been your husband for weeks. It's only tonight that I feel I've got to glimpse you." His hand slid down to cup her breast. "God," he groaned. "I need to see your face when you come for me."

"What do you mean?" She didn't understand him, but her body reacted to his words. She ached a little, and she was restless.

"I'll show you." He gave her breast a gentle squeeze then reluctantly released her. With one finger, he traced the outline of her mouth as if he'd never seen it before. "I'm going to learn you," he said. "I'm going to learn what you need from me."

He nuzzled her. "Mina, what's that scent you wear?"

"My soap is made with rosemary."

"I love it," he growled. "It suits you."

"Then…then I'll keep using it," she promised with a

laugh. How easy Luc was to please, after all.

"Forever," he insisted. "I love the smell of you, too. Your body's own scent. I'm going to taste all of you when I'm fully recovered." He bit her neck lightly, then added, "And you're most welcome to taste me too."

The way he pressed his shaft against her made his meaning very clear. "Not unless you want to," he added, laying a kiss on her chest. "But know that *I* want you to."

Mina felt a jolt of excitement at the idea, though she'd have to work up considerable courage to actually do it. "Someday."

He gave a satisfied sound. "Then I await my lady's pleasure," he said, twisting the meaning of the polite phrase.

Mina flushed. "You're trying to shock me."

"I'm being honest," he said.

"Then be honest. What do you want from me?"

"At this moment? I want to please you. I want to show you more pleasure than you've ever felt before, and *I* want to be the man who gives it to you," he said fiercely, showing his possessiveness and pride.

"How do you intend to do that?"

"Where to begin," he mused.

"You've already begun," she retorted.

"So you like what I've done so far?" Luc smiled. "You like my mouth?"

He lowered his head and laid a kiss on her chest, right over her heart. Then he kissed a trail to her breast, and took one bud in his mouth, swirling his tongue around it till it hardened. Mina gasped, feeling a thrum of pleasure jolt down into her belly, then lower. Every kiss, every lick quickened her breath. Her breasts seemed exquisitely sensitive, and she closed her eyes, giving herself up to the feelings he created in her.

"Mina," he said softly, between kisses. "I'm going to touch you, and you must be honest with me. If I cause you any pain at all, tell me."

"How could you..." She broke off, for his hand rested between her legs, and his meaning was clear. "Oh."

He slid a finger gently between the folds of flesh, stroking her most intimate places, drawing out damp heat. If his tongue on her breast summoned one type of enjoyment, this was even more intense.

"Luc..." she whispered.

He paused. "How is it?"

"It's...wonderful."

"Ah. Good."

He resumed, and it was wonderful. Mina hummed with pleasure, her body striving to meet his touch. He kissed her breasts again, and the combined sensations drove her to a series of little gasps that had her moaning for more without knowing how to form the right words. Luc never stopped, so intent on her reactions that his own breathing became harsh and uneven.

Mina would have told him to stop, fearful of his injuries, but by then her body was overwhelmed and she tensed up, just before emitting a cry of release as something happened deep within her, like a vessel breaking.

She cried out again, only to be caught in his arms as she shook with a feeling she'd never known. "Oh," she whispered. "Oh."

How lovely. How strange and wonderful, to lose herself in his touch like that. Was that his intent? To shatter her like glass and then let her drift on the waves of pleasure, free of any tension at all?

"Mina," he said. "My Mina."

She blinked, lazily coming back to the world from wherever she'd just been. If he hadn't used her name, she wasn't sure she would recall what it even *was*. "Luc?"

He'd wrapped one arm about her, tucking her head into his shoulder. His wounded shoulder, she realized belatedly.

"What did you do?" she asked, her voice soft and astonished even to her own ears.

"What I wanted to do to you since our first night together. How do you feel, my beauty?"

"Beautiful," she admitted shyly.

"You look beautiful," he said, his eyes raking over her. "So soft."

She smiled, still feeling dazed. "Do you ever feel like this?" she asked.

"When I'm with you," he said.

He looked intense, desiring. She understood now why he sometimes seemed so eager for her before. Lord, if the marriage act always resulted in such a feeling for a man... well, no wonder some didn't wait for marriage to indulge in it.

"You need me now," she said.

"Yes," he admitted, his voice rough. "I've been at the brink since the moment you touched me tonight."

"Then please use me," she said. "Please."

He closed his eyes, clearly delighted with her invitation.

Luc moved so he was kneeling back on his heels. Mina watched him, her shyness at last fading as their new intimacy took hold.

He surveyed her as well. "I want you like this," he said. "This position." He slid his hands to her hips and pulled her right up his thighs so her center brushed against the side of his shaft. He groaned at the contact.

"I can't…" She began to protest.

"Yes, you can," he said. "But you should be more comfortable." He leaned forward to seize a pillow, using the moment to kiss her. "Trust me?" he asked softly.

"Yes," she replied, almost soundlessly.

"If you don't enjoy it, tell me," he said. He sat up again, and slid a hand around her back. He lifted her up while putting the pillow under her. When he let her down again, it was more comfortable, her hips settling into the pillow's softness.

"Like this?" she asked, gazing at his body.

"Like this," he said. He reached to touch between her legs.

He closed his eyes when he felt the wetness there. "Mina, you're exactly what I need."

Domina gasped as he slid her body over his shaft, sheathing himself in her slick warmth, the angle of him pushing against her in a way she'd never felt before. She sighed.

Luc made a sound of pure satisfaction, and held her still for a moment. Then he began to thrust within her, slowly at first, but then with increasing urgency. "You are heaven, Domina," he gasped. "Please tell me you like this."

Liked it? She never wanted it to end. "Yes," she promised.

"I'm not hurting you, am I?"

"No, you're not. I like it." She rocked her hips against him on the next thrust, and the sensation made her cry out.

"Oh," she moaned. "Oh, Luc." Could she feel that burst of pleasure again, so soon? She hoped so.

His hands tightened around her hips, slid to her rump and he lifted her a little. "More?" he asked. "Please say more."

"More," she confirmed with a breathless sigh.

"You're heaven, Mina. I won't last…long."

She didn't need him too, not when another ripple of pure pleasure cascaded down her body. Even Luc felt it, grinning savagely.

"Mina, I need you," he gasped.

One more thrust. He stiffened, holding her hips down on him as he spilled his seed into her. Domina watched in astonishment as an expression of bliss transformed his face. After a long moment, he opened his eyes and leaned down over her so he could kiss her, lips to lips.

It wasn't a hungry kiss this time, but one indescribably sweet, one of gratitude and perhaps even of love. "Mina." His voice against her skin made her shiver. "You are one of a kind."

She closed her eyes, reveling in the words. She felt too fragile, too unready to offer such words back, so she merely said, "Will you lie next to me? On me? As you did before?"

"You still want to be my bolster?" he asked, his voice hesitant.

Domina smiled at his tone. "Please." She liked Luc this way.

He rolled, half covering her body again, his bandaged wound in no danger of touching the bed. "You must behave yourself this time, sweet Mina," he murmured sleepily. "You must not press your advant…" Within seconds, he nodded off.

Domina did not. She lay on her back, her arms clasped lightly around her husband. *How strange*, she thought. A month ago she could not have dreamed of being married, let alone being in bed after exchanging such pleasures that it rendered Luc unconscious. And yet, she might be happier now than she'd ever been in her life.

Chapter 23

DOMINA EVENTUALLY SLEPT, AND WHEN she awoke with a sigh, it was to find that Luc was teasing her the same way she had inadvertently done to him last night. Except that he was fully aware of what he was doing. One hand roamed up and down her body. He trailed his fingers along her curves, making her gasp.

"I see you're finally awake," he said, laughing quietly. He didn't stop touching her.

"How long have you been..."

"Hours," he said.

"Liar. I would have known."

He bent his mouth to her ear. "You make such interesting sounds in your sleep, Mina. As if you were in the midst of a wonderful dream."

She blushed. "I do not!" Oh, what had he done to her?

He merely laughed again. Then he kissed her ear, drawing another gasp.

"Luc!"

"Hmm. You make interesting sounds when you're awake as well." He continued his kisses along her jawline and ended at her mouth, capturing her lower lip in his teeth. Domina gave herself up to the kiss, reveling in Luc's attention, his touch all over her skin, waking her passion.

"You're still hurt," she whispered, remembering the bandage.

"I barely feel it," he said, with a low laugh. "Not when I have you to feel instead."

"And what parts of me do you intend to feel?" she asked archly.

"I like your feet," he said, moving to grasp one. "Your toes are adorable." He kissed each one to make his point, and Mina giggled at the sensation.

He was so different this morning, so playful and open.

She barely heard the door creak open, but she heard the maid's startled squeak. "Oh, I'm sorry, my lord. My lady. I'll come back."

Luc broke off the kiss to say, "Bring some food when you do!" to the maid's retreating figure. He grinned at Domina, who was embarrassed, not by the maid knowing they shared a bed...of course everybody knew that...but at seeing them play like this together.

Luc could tell what she was thinking. "I fear it will be rumored that we are in love."

She bit her lip. "Everyone knows why we really married."

Suddenly, his expression closed, as if he recalled something dark. He pulled away from her. Without a word, he sat up and swung his feet to the floor.

"Wait!" she said, stopping him. "Don't leave me."

He turned back. "What?"

"Don't leave me in anger. I don't want to fight anymore."

"Were we fighting?"

"Aren't we always? Until last night, that is."

He gave her an odd half-smile. "One thing we can agree on, but only when it's dark, and there's no one else to see how weak we are."

"Why weak? Why should it be weakness to need someone?" Domina sighed. "We're married. We should be allies."

"Does that mean you think I should change sides?" he asked, a strange intensity in his voice.

"I don't know what you mean," she said, uncomfortable. "All I know is that every time we begin to understand each other, something pulls us apart."

Luc moved so he could hold her. "You noticed that," he said.

"How could I not?" she said, miserably. "All I want, all I ever wanted, is to live happily in my home, but nothing has gone as planned…"

Without warning, a tear rolled down her cheek. Luc saw it and brushed it away. Then his mouth was on hers and she was kissing him back hungrily. The physical awakening he brought about distracted her from her mental anguish, and she gave herself up to the bliss of not needing to think. She didn't have to when she could feel.

His hands were all over her body, and then in her body, and she was willing to do anything for him. She was crying into his chest as he wrapped their bodies together. She moaned in relief when he entered her, and she loved his weight on her. There was only heat and shared breath, and then they were lying in each other's arms, entangled in the bed linens, their bodies spent.

Luc's breath slowed, and he shifted so she could relax against him. Something within her had unhooked again, and she felt as if she might drift away if she didn't have him to hold onto.

Some time later, he nudged her. "Domina," he said softly, "Are you hungry?"

She stretched and yawned, feeling remarkably calm. "Mmmm. Yes. I suppose we should call for food."

"She's already come and gone," he said.

Domina sat up and blinked. "When?"

"Over a quarter of an hour ago," he said with a laugh. "You were adrift, weren't you?"

She blushed. "I fell asleep, that's all."

"Not all," he said, his voice warm. "God, I love hearing you when you come for me."

Desire ran down her bones, but one couldn't spend all day in bed. "Now that you mention it, I am hungry," she whispered, suddenly shy again.

"Good. Stay there."

Luc got out of bed, but only to retrieve some of the dishes brought in by the maid…who must be telling the whole castle what she saw that morning.

Domina shifted to sit up against the carved headboard. She realized Luc intended to feed them both in bed, a gesture that felt both incredibly sweet and very proprietary.

The smell of warm, honeyed apricots silenced any objection. The dried fruit was cooked in a spiced honey wine which was slowly rendered down into a thick sauce, and the resulting dish was sticky and sweet and delicious. The apricots were whole and could be eaten with the fingers. Luc fed her one, then ate one himself. Between them, they emptied the dish within a minute. He put the dish on the floor. "That took the edge off," he said, pleased, licking the stickiness from his fingers.

Inspired, Mina leaned forward to kiss Luc, getting a final taste of luscious honey.

His arms tightened around her. "Domina, I'll keep you in this bed all day. Don't think otherwise."

"I would like that," she murmured, kissing him again.

He smiled, but pushed her back against the pillows. "Tempting, but I'd be afraid of hurting you."

"Hurting me? How?"

"You don't feel sore?" he asked.

She hadn't, until he reached down and touched her between her legs. The pleasure mingled with traces of pain. Their bout of morning lovemaking was rougher than she realized. "Oh. You're right."

He took his hand away, then kissed her very gently. "So we must wait. I'm never going to hurt you, my Mina. I promise."

"How long will we need to wait?" she asked anxiously.

He laughed. "Not long. Until tonight. And I'll go slower. You surprised me this morning."

"I surprised myself this morning," she admitted. "I hadn't intended to…ah, well I just hadn't intended anything. I wasn't using my head."

Luc traced the length of her body with his fingers. "Neither was I," he said. "I saw you crying, and I only wanted to stop it." He looked at her. "Why were you crying?"

Domina thought back to their exchange. "Frustration, I suppose. It's not important."

"Of course it's important. You're my wife. If you're unhappy, I need to know why."

"I'm not unhappy. I'm just…"

"What?"

"Things have changed, so quickly," she said. "I've barely had time to think. You said I'm your wife. But sometimes I think I hardly know you and I don't want to disappoint you...and I don't want to disappoint my people, or my father..."

"Who could be disappointed in you, love?"

"You didn't want this marriage, did you? I saw you in the throne room that day. You hid it well, but you didn't like the idea any more than I did."

"I was surprised," he said. "But I have no regrets. Not now."

He looked like he was about to say something more.

"What is it?" Mina asked.

Luc sighed. "I...I need to tell you something. Something I should have told you before."

Chapter 24

THE EXPRESSION ON MINA'S FACE, the way she looked alarmed, then set her jaw, ready for the worst, made Luc wish he'd never said anything. Because whatever Mina thought would be the worst was nowhere near the truth.

He couldn't tell her the whole truth, not yet. But he had to say something.

"So," he started to explain, "I wasn't sent solely to assess the strength of the castle and the garrison."

"Well, no," Mina said tartly. "A marriage contract would hardly be required for that task."

Luc grinned, though he inwardly cursed Mina's sharp mind. He'd have to step very carefully to avoid giving her any hint that he was actually sent to investigate the de Warewics. If she learned that, whatever regard she had for him would be gone.

"Part of my task was to check on the castle, for it's true that even one or two strongholds falling to the empress would hurt the king's cause."

"I don't understand why the king thought Trumwell would be weak, though, for he couldn't have known about my father's incapacity."

"Trumwell isn't the only castle he's concerned about," Luc said. That part was true enough. The king naturally wanted to make sure about all the castles held in his name. "But this area of the country is particularly vulnerable. For not only is the empress quite likely to try to pick up territory in the west, the Welsh are a constant threat. Together…" he trailed off.

"Plus Haldan," she added. "A third front to this assault."

"Yes, and a reminder that it only takes one man to undermine the work of many others."

Mina was nodding slowly, accepting his explanation. Then her eyes narrowed. "But why the marriage contract?"

Now Luc had to lie. There was no way around it. "Well," he began, "the king did first say it as a joke."

"Yes, I remember." Mina's cheeks went a pretty shade of pink, distracting him.

He leaned forward to kiss one cheek, enjoying the warmth. "No need to be embarrassed, sweetheart. Nothing about it made you look bad."

"Other than being my age and yet unmarried."

"Well, you made an impression, even after you left the audience chamber. I spoke with the king later that day,"— Lord, he was making it sound like a casual conversation, not a clandestine meeting—"and the king mentioned you again. He suggested the possibility of a marriage, and had the contract drawn up just in case. Remember, everyone assumed I'd be speaking with Godfrey once I arrived here."

"That's true." Mina's expression softened a bit. "I suppose it would have been a normal enough negotiation, if my father was able to speak for me. Though in that case, he'd have gone to court, and you'd never have seen me."

"I'm glad to have seen you," Luc said, meaning it. "Once I saw the state of things here, how you had no…" he trailed off.

"Master?" Mina asked archly.

"I was going to say support. Ally."

"You thought that the marriage would better protect Trumwell," she concluded. "I see."

"Not just Trumwell. You too, Mina. Believe me, you're a force on your own. But still vulnerable. I wanted to protect you."

"You didn't phrase your proposal in quite that way," she noted frostily, though he detected a bit of laughter underneath.

He seized on that, kissing her again. "I beg your forgiveness."

"Why?" she asked, even as she turned her mouth to his.

One long kiss later he murmured, "That's why, Mina. I was angry when I first confronted you, but I don't want anger between us." *I want love.* The thought jolted Luc. He hadn't expected it, and he wasn't sure where it came from. He liked Mina, he respected her independence and her intelligence. He definitely enjoyed her on a completely carnal level. But love was something altogether different, something he actually knew nothing about.

Mina pulled away, her expression thoughtful. "You know, if Haldan was in the pay of someone else, he may well have gone to them after fleeing here yesterday."

Well. That comment put paid to any idea that Mina had love on *her* mind. Even in the middle of a kiss, she was still thinking of her castle, not of her marriage. Which was good, Luc told himself. It kept her focused and kept him free of potential entanglements…though part of him wanted to remain entangled with Domina forever.

"Haldan wasn't acting on his own," Luc agreed. "He's an agent of someone else, someone working against the king. I found some evidence to show it."

"You did?" she asked. "You never told me that!"

"The attack on the castle distracted me, along with a few other events."

Mina frowned. "But why would an attack against Trumwell be part of such a plan?"

Luc looked away, frustrated. "I can't say. That is, I don't know exactly. I do think Haldan truly wanted to take control of Trumwell, and not just lash out in anger against an employer who threw him out."

"He said something on the night…that he attacked me," Mina said slowly. "I didn't really consider his exact words at the time, but he did say that he wanted to be the castle's master. It was not mere rape in his mind. I was to be a means to an end."

Luc bit his tongue.

"He said he was sick of waiting," Mina went on. "Do you think…do you think he was promised Trumwell? Whoever hired him kept his loyalty by offering a castle as payment."

"A castle *and* its lady," Luc said, flatly. "You may be sure you were part of the bargain."

Mina's eyes unfocused slightly. "No," she whispered.

"I think so," he argued, reaching out to hold her. "Believe me, most men would do quite a lot if they thought their prize would be a beautiful woman under their thumb."

"You sound quite confident."

"I'm a man. I know how men think." Hadn't he come here with exactly the same thought? Mina was a means to an end—his political advancement. That would make him no better than Haldan...*except I saw that I was wrong*, he reminded himself. "That doesn't excuse what Haldan did, which I intend to make very clear to him."

"So what will you do?" she went on. "Do you mean to go after him again?"

"Of course. He was a criminal before, but now he has more to answer for after attacking Trumwell. Beside, even if his only crime was to touch you, that's enough to hang him."

Mina raised an eyebrow. "Hardly his greatest transgression."

"That depends on your perspective," Luc said, drawing her closer again.

She laughed softly. "Your sister did mention that you were possessive about everything."

"What I care about," he said. "Which, yes, includes my wife."

"I wasn't your wife when he attacked me."

"You are now," he said. "That's what matters."

Mina allowed herself to be held for a moment, and Luc relished the simple contact in a way he hadn't anticipated.

But then she said, "So what is your plan to find him?"

"I'll question the men we captured—they'll know something, and they probably won't show too much loyalty to a man who left them behind."

"Then you'll go after Haldan? Alone?" Mina asked, frowning.

"Not alone. I'll have Octavian, and my men."

"Against who knows how many Haldan—or his partner—has gathered. I don't like those odds, Luc."

"I'll be careful," he assured her. "Why, are you worried about me?"

"When I saw the blood, and your shoulder..." She shuddered. "I never want to feel like that again."

Luc kissed her forehead. "I'll do my best to ensure that you never have to, my Mina."

Chapter 25

LUC HAD BEEN LOOKING FORWARD to a lazy day of recovery, spent with his beautiful partner, whose newly awakened interest was the best medicine he could ask for. Besides, he'd driven off an army the day before. Surely a man deserved a little rest after such a feat.

Yet it was not to be. A knock sounded on the door, and after Domina gave permission to enter, Margery stepped into the room. She gave Luc a look of shameless appraisal, but quickly curtseyed to Domina.

"My lady," Margery announced, "your cousin Joscelin is below, in the parlor. He seems rather distraught."

Mina gasped. "Oh, no."

"What's wrong?" Luc asked. "I thought you got along with your cousin."

"I do! Or I did. But why would he leave his studies?"

Not long after, in the bright room below, Luc saw a lanky young man dressed in the plain, somber garb of a clergyman. When he turned to face them, what most struck Luc was the man's youth. Mina said he was younger than she, but this person was scarcely more than a boy. He wore his pale hair in the customary tonsure, like a monk. His eyes were a remarkably clear blue, and at the moment, his expression was troubled.

"Domina," he said, his eyes looking her over intently.

She stood close to Luc, a fact that Joscelin seemed to take exception to. She said, "You never sent word you were coming here! Joscelin, what caused you to leave London? What has happened?"

"That is what I must know from you, Mina! I came because I heard an absurd story about a marriage. It is being mentioned in the church as well as the court. Tell me it is not so."

Domina glanced at Luc, guilt on her features. Then she said to Joscelin, "It is true. Luc of Braecon is my lord and husband. We were married some weeks ago."

Joscelin's face paled slightly. "Cousin, why did you not tell me?"

"I meant to," she said, hesitantly. "It slipped my mind."

"Slipped your *mind*? To tell one of your only living relatives of your wedding day? Have I offended you somehow? Did you not want me here?"

"Oh, no!" She rushed to embrace Joscelin, who returned the gesture after a moment's hesitation. "Please don't be angry, Joscelin. It was…somewhat of a surprise. You would not have been able to travel here in time, and I was so distracted by everything that I didn't write to you when I ought to have. Forgive me."

He sighed. "Of course I forgive you, Mina. But I must know what is going on!"

"Yes, you shall." She looked to Luc, her expression rather frantic. "I must, ah, speak to Constance. It will not wait. Please speak to Joscelin and I will rejoin you both as soon as I am able."

It was a patently false errand, but Luc didn't try to stop her. She hurried off, and Luc and Joscelin merely stared at each other for a long moment, assessing.

Luc decided he'd better offer the first gesture—after all, it was his home. "So. You are Joscelin. Domina has spoken of you quite often."

"She's never told me a word about you, nor even of an impending marriage. How long has this been in the wind? How do you know her?"

"Our marriage was arranged by the king."

"Why?" Joscelin asked bluntly. "To what purpose? I've heard your family name, and much as I value my own and Domina's bloodline, I know that it's no match for yours. Why would the king seek to marry a powerful baron's son to a woman of little renown?"

"Domina has many excellent qualities."

"To be sure!" Joscelin said defensively. "As I well know, being close kin to her. But again, without casting a shadow on her, I say that of her qualities, political weight is not among them. She comes from a line of loyal but minor nobles, castellans of a quiet river valley far from the center of England."

"But it is an important point to defend," Luc said. "For the Welsh threaten from the west, and Maud's armies could easily sweep in from the southeast. In a matter of months, this whole part of the country could fall."

"I am aware of that," Joscelin said.

"King Stephen is keen to keep what he holds now."

"That does not explain a marriage. Would it not be just as sensible for the king to have sent more soldiers?"

"So he will, if I ask," Luc explained. "He wants a knight here, one who understands war."

Joscelin frowned. "It is all too hasty. I pray that no one

will look upon the speed of the marriage and think ill of my cousin."

"No one thinks ill of her. Her people continue to respect her, as they did before I arrived. Less has changed here than you fear."

Joscelin stared at him a moment longer, then sighed. "Well, there's nothing for it now. It's done, is it not?"

"It is," Luc confirmed, "and I intend to uphold all the vows I've made." Most particularly, his vow to Stephen to ferret out the traitor who seemed to be making Trumwell Castle and the de Warewic family part of his plot. Perhaps Joscelin could help with uncovering the name—he was kin to Domina and also stood to lose if the family name was stained. Even in the church, blood mattered. He was part of the family, but also an outsider, living in London as a clergyman. What if he'd noticed something no one else had?

Joscelin looked out the narrow windows. "Forgive me, my lord," he said, in a conciliatory tone. "Mina is all I have, and I feel it is my place to make sure no one takes advantage of her. I do try to visit when I can. It is difficult, considering the distance from London, but she would not hear of my postponing my studies in order to stay with her."

"You do not speak of Godfrey's wishes," Luc said mildly.

Joscelin started, plainly not prepared for that topic. "I...I..."

"I know the truth about him," Luc said. "And I see you do as well. Yet you've said nothing to anyone about it?"

"Mina begged me to keep silence," Joscelin said slowly. "Though I had misgivings, I could see sense in her decision. I will confess I never expected it to go on as long as it has. I prayed—I still pray—that the situation is temporary. It tears her apart, you know."

"I know."

"Not just his condition, but that she had to conceal it."

"She excels at it. Nearly three years, and no hint or rumor about it. Even the king did not suspect."

"You have not shared the truth with anyone, have you?" Joscelin asked nervously.

"Not yet. However, I serve the king. At some point, I am bound to tell him everything."

"Of course, of course. But I ask that you choose the time of your telling carefully. For Mina's sake."

"I'll do what I think best," Luc said bluntly.

"What is for Mina's sake is also for your own now, too. You are bound to her for life. Do you care for her at all?" Joscelin asked, his eyes seeming to pierce right through Luc. "Or is this to be a political alliance, done for worldly reasons alone?"

"That is between me and my wife," Luc said, keeping his tone cool.

"I see," said Joscelin. "Well, I shall pray for you both." The way he said it spoke volumes about Joscelin's opinion of the marriage and his expectations for its success.

Luc had no time for the young man's opinions on that topic. Before Mina returned, he wanted to ask about something else. "Now that you've returned to Trumwell," he said, "perhaps you could explain something to me. You know Mina far better than I."

"What do you wish to know?" Joscelin asked.

"It strikes me as curious that despite all the stories of de Warewic wealth, Domina is so modest about it. She never shows off by wearing fine clothes or jewels, yet no one could ever mistake her for someone less than a lady. Was that a trait of her mother, perhaps?"

"I never paid much attention," Joscelin said, after a moment of thought. "As far as I know, Godfrey never lacked for wealth. I never knew want while living here. As for Mina's choice to forgo the more extravagant trappings of nobility, it may well have been the lessons of her parents. Mina has always been a true lady, and she has never shown much interest in worldly distractions. Not that she's ever expressed interest in the holy life," he added. "That was for me."

"Yes, she mentioned your desire to become a priest."

Joscelin nodded. "It was Godfrey himself who made it possible for me to pursue my schooling and my career in the church. I owe him more than I can possibly repay, but as for the specifics of the family's finances, I can't help you much. If you wish to ask about the wealth of the de Warewics, you should ask Domina," Joscelin said. "She is the heiress, and she keeps the keys."

Luc had been avoiding that. Domina was intelligent, and she would know that he had reasons for asking about the treasury in general, and the swan-stamped coins in particular. One question would lead to others, and Luc had no excuses to distract her. Domina would see his face and know that he was keeping something from her.

"The de Warewics have always been close," Joscelin continued. "They welcomed me into this castle, and treated me like a son. But there may be a few secrets they shared only among themselves. If Godfrey had a secret of any kind, it's Domina he'd trust with it, and vice versa."

Joscelin's words were well-meant, no doubt, but they made Luc wince. Domina was far too good at keeping secrets.

* * * *

Not long after Joscelin arrived at the castle, Luc received a message from Somerby, one of Domina's outlying manors. The steward of Somerby said Haldan had arrived there expecting a warm welcome. The steward attempted to keep Haldan there in an effort to detain him, but Haldan grew suspicious and fled during the night. The message concluded with a plea for Luc to send a few more men-at-arms to the manor, for they feared an attack.

Luc read the message to Octavian, who said, "Haldan has shown he has a temper. He might well attack a small manor just to prove he can. We know he's still got a considerable force of men at his command."

"Then let's help re-fortify the place," said Luc. "While we're there, we can pick up his trail."

Octavian gave a little smile. "Indeed."

They gathered a small retinue of men-at-arms and rode out the next day. Somerby was nearly two days' ride, and Luc was growing sick of wintertime travel. Octavian didn't like it any better, though he hid his annoyance at the cold and the damp.

"Pray he's nearby," Tav said at one point. "How can a man like Haldan move like a ghost? He's not the most subtle of people."

"Not to mention that he has a small army with him at times," Luc agreed. "We'll find something to lead us. If nothing else, the manor will be better fortified by the time we leave." Luc decided ten more soldiers, trained by him and Octavian, would be sufficient to defend a small property, once added to those already there.

When they arrived at Somerby, they found a solidly constructed fence and a prosperous manor on the other side. No wonder Haldan wanted to enjoy the comfort of the place.

On giving his name, Luc was granted immediate entry, along with the rest of the group. The steward was delighted to hear ten new men would strengthen the manor, and he treated Luc with great deference. Octavian was a puzzle to him, but he accepted the appearance of the strange knight after Luc explained that Octavian was his companion.

"I want to hear everything about Haldan's visit," Luc said, over the evening meal. "Even if it doesn't seem important."

The steward dutifully recounted all that happened. Haldan had come with a group of forty or so rough-looking men. The steward said he could only grant entry to Haldan, because the manor could not offer food and shelter to so many on such short notice. In truth, he knew Haldan was no longer in the employ of the de Warewic family, and suspected that Haldan wanted to take over Somerby. The big solider argued for a time, but the steward stood firm, secure in his own authority and the weakness of Haldan's position.

"Eventually, though, he sent his men away, to find shelter in town or elsewhere," the steward explained. "I think Haldan told them that he'd open the gates from the inside…perhaps the next day."

"But you did let him in?" Luc asked.

"I was afraid to deny him completely. We weren't ready to fend off an immediate attack. Also, it was getting dark, and it began to snow. Haldan's never liked to be uncomfortable. The promise of a warm fire and a warm drink was enough to sway him."

"Even though his men would sleep in the cold," Luc said.

Octavian commented, "He isn't a very good general. That's the sort of thing soldiers remember."

"Good. Maybe they'll desert by the end of the winter." Luc turned back to the steward. "What happened after Haldan came in?"

"He demanded food and drink, and for a bedchamber to be prepared for him. Asked after one of the maids, as well. Lettie. Leticia."

"His favorite?"

The steward nodded dourly. "She went to him after dinner."

"I want to speak to her as well."

"I'll send for her," the steward promised.

Lettie proved to be a slip of a thing, just five feet tall, with long pale hair in a braid curled around her head. "My lord?" she asked as she curtsied. She had a pretty, if somewhat pouty, air.

"You're Haldan's woman?" Luc asked.

Lettie's expression went from polite to wary. "It wasn't my fault," she said.

"What wasn't your fault?"

"I wouldn't have said anything if I'd known it was a secret."

"You told Haldan the steward knew he'd been sacked?"

"I asked if he had a gift for me this time. He always gives me a gift when he leaves, but if he had no money, how could he give me a trinket?"

"What did he say to that?"

"He was angry. Not at me—he's never mean to me,

for I know how to speak to him. But he thought he'd have a few days' peace. He said he had to leave early now, to make sure he'd be able to keep his appointment."

"With who?"

Lettie made a face. "He called the person Swan. I asked if it was a woman, because he likes to think he can make me jealous of his other women."

"Did he say it was?"

"He only smiled when I pestered him. But later on, Haldan said '*He won't wait, so I have to be there first.*' That's how I know Swan's not a woman he's chasing."

"Useful. Did he mention anything else? Perhaps where he planned to go?"

Lettie shook her head. "Not this time."

"Not this time? So he's told you the names of other places in the past?"

"Well, a few times. Cinderford and Chepstow. But he didn't confide in me. I was just here to warm his bed."

"What sort of gifts did he give you for that, by the way?"

"Oh, ribbons for my hair. A chain to wear around my neck, and a pretty wooden bracelet. Only once he gave me coin, but I wasn't offended because it wasn't a real coin. It's more like a little jewel to look at."

"Not real?"

"Well, it hasn't got a king's head on it. It's a swan swimming. I keep it by my bed."

"May I buy it from you?" Luc asked.

"How much?" she asked, her eyes narrowing.

"Enough that you won't mourn its loss," he assured her.

So Lettie brought him another of the silver coins that seemed to appear wherever he sought Haldan. Luc pocketed it, and paid her well.

Octavian compared the new coin to its brethren. "Undoubtably from the same cache," he said. "I bet Haldan wasn't supposed to give it to her, if it was to be a signal for the conspirators to recognize each other."

"Haldan rarely follows instructions," Luc said. "His sloppiness will be what lets us catch him. On to Cinderford."

* * * *

The next day the two men reached the town of Cinderford. Octavian said he'd watch over their horses and their things while Luc went in search of Haldan or someone who knew him.

Luc inquired after Haldan in the few shopfronts, describing the big blond man as an acquaintance. A shopkeeper's wife directed him to the inn, saying she noticed a man of Haldan's description staying there not long ago.

The inn was quiet during the early afternoon, and the keeper offered Luc a friendly, hopeful look. "Food or drink, sir? Room? All three?"

"News, actually. Of a man who stayed here. Name of Haldan."

"Don't know the name," innkeeper said too quickly.

"I'm willing to pay for it." He slid the coin over the table toward the other man.

The man picked it up, and saw the image stamped on it. He swallowed nervously. "Ah. Him. I...know who you can talk to about him. If you'll wait?"

Luc nodded once. The barkeeper disappeared into the back part of the building. He was gone for such a long time Luc started to wonder if he was summoning a gang to haul Luc off. Or perhaps he'd simply run away.

Eventually, the man emerged from behind the curtain. "This way, sir."

Luc followed him, making sure his dagger was loose in its sheath.

The barkeeper led him up a staircase and into a room that must sit exactly above the main dining hall. It was piled high with crates, barrels, and furniture in various states of disrepair. The few windows were shuttered, letting in only slivers of light that blinded Luc far more than they illuminated the room. At the far end, a candle burned on a desk, offering a bit more light.

The barkeeper was only a few steps ahead of Luc when a voice said, "Stop there."

Luc halted. The barkeeper offered a rough bow to the unseen figure and said, "Here's the man with the coin. I'll…I'll go back downstairs." He fled without waiting for approval.

Luc stayed where he was, searching the shadows. He avoided looking at the candle itself, hoping his eyes would adjust to the dimness.

"What brings you here, friend?" the shadowed figure asked.

"Are we friends?" Luc asked.

"Good question. You come bearing a coin that's not from the king's mint."

"It's more appropriate for an empress," Luc said.

The voice gave a snort of laughter. "Perhaps so. What's your name?"

Luc made something up on the spot. The man wouldn't expect a true name in any case.

"And what led you here?" the stranger asked.

"The lord I served was once a supporter of Henry. But

he flew to Stephen all too quickly. I left his service—
didn't exactly ask. Since then I've been looking for a new
situation. I can fight."

"Fighters are easy to find."

"But not always easy to keep, if they're not skilled
enough."

"You want glorious battle?"

"Not if I can help it," said Luc. "But if I fight, I want
it to be for the one who's going to win, and that will be
the empress. I've heard about the forces she's gathering.
Robert of Gloucester is a leader who will win battles."

"You heard this from who?"

"I was talking with a man named Haldan. He gave me
the coin."

"If Haldan gave you this, why did he not just hire
you?"

"He said he would. But I had to attend to a few matters, and I missed him. You know where he is now? I can
meet up with him there."

The man in shadow said nothing for a moment. Luc
waited him out. A nervous man would start chatting, and
risk saying too much. Luc wasn't nervous at all.

"Huh," the man said at last. "What's it matter to me?
If Haldan doesn't like seeing you, that's between you and
him."

"So it is."

"Mind you," the man said, sounding slightly hesitant,
"I don't wish him to know that we spoke."

"Then we didn't speak," Luc agreed easily.

"All right, then. Haldan has a brother who lives in
Chepstow. It lies about twenty miles southeast. Whenever
things go badly for Haldan—and in his life, that's happened plenty, from what I've heard—he flees to his broth-

er's home to lay low for a while."

"What's the brother's name?"

"Haldan's never said. But I know he's an innkeeper there. How many can there be in one village?"

Luc put his hand out, showing off two ordinary silver coins. "Two for one?"

The man leaned forward to slide the swan coin back across the wooden surface. The action put his face in the light. Two bright eyes peered out from a heavily bearded visage, but even all the growth couldn't hide the disfigurement from a nasty burn.

He put a finger to his face. "Looks bad, doesn't it?"

Luc nodded, not willing to lie.

"Truth is, this burn came courtesy of Haldan and his stupid schemes. Whatever your business with him is, remember that."

Luc picked up the swan coin. "I won't forget."

When Luc returned to Octavian, he related all the news.

"Do we continue on the trail, then?" Tav asked.

"Not just yet," Luc decided. "I want to return home first. We ought to rest, and plan for the next step. Also, it's time I examine the source of these coins that keep turning up."

"So you want to go home to Braecon?" Tav asked, puzzled.

"Not Braecon," Luc said, "I meant Trumwell." For he realized that he thought of Trumwell as his home, because that was where Mina was.

Chapter 26

ALMOST A WEEK HAD PASSED at Trumwell. Mina missed Luc keenly. The days were a little dreary without the extra commotion of Luc and his retinue in the castle. The nights were considerably colder, even though Constance shared her bed, just as she used to do before the marriage.

The two women spoke softly over those nights, the distinctions of class disappearing in the dark. Mina confided in her maid, who was likely the only person who would ever hear such whispers, as Mina asked how she might be sure to please Luc.

"Oh, my lady," said Constance. "I can't tell you much about that. It's Margery who knows how to please a man in bed."

"Not in bed," Mina said. "I meant…in life."

"You're a perfect lady," Constance said loyally. "He must know it. You're beautiful as well. I wish I was."

"Why do you wish that?" Mina asked, already knowing the answer. "Ban likes you just as you are."

Constance sighed. "He says so. But he's so…proper."

"Is that a failing?" Mina asked.

"Well, Margery has so many tales of men and their behavior, and none of those sound the least bit like how Ban acts."

"Margery seeks one thing from men," Mina said, with a bit of censure in her tone. "And it's not to be encouraged. If Ban treats you with more deference, it's because he wants more than a night's pleasure."

"Or he's not interested in me at all."

"In that case, he'd court another. Why are you so worried?" Mina asked.

"I only wish he'd try to kiss me," Constance said, miserably.

Mina put a hand out to comfort her maid. "Give him time."

Privately, she remembered an early comment she'd made to Luc. She'd warned him that if any of his men took advantage of any of the women in the castle, Domina would retaliate. Luc must have passed the warning on. Perhaps Ban took it to heart, and was being overly cautious. She'd have to discuss the matter with Luc when he returned. She hated to think Constance would be hurt by Domina's too-strict guidelines, especially if Ban truly cared for the maid. Constance deserved to find happiness.

* * * *

The next day, Luc did return. Mina looked up from the accounts when Luc entered the solar. She'd been working most of the afternoon, and she was more than ready for an excuse to put the troublesome papers aside.

"My goodness. Where have you been?" she asked, seeing Luc's travel-worn clothing. "Or has Somerby lost all its launderers?"

"I went to Somerby." He sat down in front of the small fire. "And a half-dozen more villages in the same area."

"Was he at Somerby?" she asked.

"Haldan was there, though he's not any more." Luc sighed, then said, "It's been difficult to track him."

"You could leave word at each town where's he's been!" she suggested eagerly. "Anyone may get a reward if they tell you Haldan's been there. Though I suppose that would also alert Haldan…"

Luc smiled. "We're starting to think alike, Mina. I sent one of my men to each place he'd been or was known to frequent. They all know what Haldan looks like, and they'll send word when he's spotted."

"But no one else will be alerted, unlike a publicly posted reward," Mina concluded. "Clever. You'll get him in no time."

"I hope so. I didn't expect him to have enough money and contacts to elude us for this long. Everywhere I chase him, there are clues that he's definitely still in the area. He raised that little army to march against Trumwell—they didn't march all the way from Wales. He's somewhere much closer than that, probably within the shire."

"Well, soon enough someone will catch his trail."

"It's not cheap to do what he's doing," Luc muttered. "Remaining hidden while paying fighters to take on a castle's garrison."

"Where is he getting that much money?" Mina asked.

Luc looked up from the fire, and his expression was serious. "That's something I must ask, Mina. You need to show me the treasury."

"I'd rather not," she said hastily.

"I'd rather not have to ask," he said. "I'd definitely prefer not to insist."

"But you will." Mina closed her eyes. It was amazing she'd been able to delay this long. It was proof of Luc's distraction that he'd not already demanded the key. He was lord here. She could do nothing to resist him.

"Mina," Luc said. "It's important. If he's stolen some of your wealth, or in some way cheated you…"

She shook her head, feeling a sickness in the pit of her stomach. "I'll show you. You'll hate me, but I'll show you."

Domina led Luc down to the base of the castle keep, down a series of spiraling, narrow staircases, designed to make it impossible for an attacking force to swarm the space in numbers. The air was cold, and the torches Domina lit along the way did little to dispel either the darkness or the chill.

Luc followed her silently. Mina sensed his presence behind her, and wondered exactly how he'd react once he saw the truth. The last time he'd discovered a secret— when he saw her father's sickbed—his next move had been devastating.

Yet now I'm glad he chose to marry me, she reminded herself. How fitting, she reflected. Just as soon as she wanted to keep Luc, she would lose him for good.

They reached the lowest level where the treasury room was located. Mina looked at it with a stranger's eyes. It was a small room in the very center of the castle base, surrounded by thick stone walls. The door was massive, constructed of heavy oak, covered with metal bosses that were as much defensive as decorative. A heavy iron lock completed the picture. This was a door nobody opened without the key.

She reached for the key, one she always kept on the ring hanging from the belt at her waist.

Luc took the torch from her and held it up, illuminating the lock. After a silent prayer for mercy, Domina turned the key and pushed the heavy door inward, stepping into the dark.

Torchlight flickered around her as Luc followed. The flare showed the reality of the small room: mostly empty, with only a few small wooden chests, and some carefully wrapped objects Mina hoped she'd not have to sell.

Mina stood in the little room, which was perhaps eight paces wide and deep. She stared at the near-empty shelves with despair. Though he'd claimed he married her in order to protect her, and Trumwell, she was certain that Luc also married her under the impression that the de Warewic family had moveable wealth—an asset that made her worth marrying even when she was politically powerless. What would he say now?

Luc slipped the torch into an iron ring on the wall. He scanned the room, then Domina, taking his time.

She bit her lip, waiting in agony. Whether due to the shadows cast by the guttering torch, or the strangeness of the situation, she couldn't guess at Luc's thoughts, though he must be furious.

When he spoke, though, his voice was calm. "Would you like to tell me what happened?"

She flinched at the words, for she'd been expecting to hear something loud and cruel. This reasonable request was somehow worse.

Then Luc stepped closer to her and took her hand. Domina clutched his fingers, desperate for the warmth in them.

"What happened..." she began to explain, picking her words as carefully as she could, "is that shortly after my father's accident, I came down here to get money to pay the doctors who'd come to examine him."

"And?"

"This room used to be full. There were chests brought all the way from the Holy Land, chests I had seen open, filled with coins my family had minted especially."

"The coins marked with the swans," Luc said intently.

"Yes. There was a smaller chest too, with gold. More gold even than we spoke of, for it's not always wise to let people know how much money you have."

"Go on."

"When I came down here that day, the chests were gone. Not hidden, not moved. Gone. My father would have told me if he had moved them—yet he had said nothing before. After he fell, I couldn't ask. He was unconscious, and then barely coherent. So I just...pretended. There was a little left, enough to pay expenses for a while. I worked with Ancel to reduce our spending, though I couldn't tell him of the money's disappearance, not when I was already asking him to keep the secret of my father's bad health."

"Mina, you're too apt to keep secrets," Luc said, reaching up to stroke her cheek.

"What could I say? I couldn't tell you that I was destitute when you were already threatening to expose my other secret to the king."

"In fact, you didn't have to tell me," Luc said.

"What do you mean?" she asked, startled. "You knew all this time?"

"Let's say I suspected," he clarified. "The steward praised your frugality, and I don't doubt the castle benefited from your administration. But there's frugality, and then there's wearing the same gown day after day while you're hosting somewhat important guests. There's appearing before the king himself wearing not a single jewel besides a plain silver cross."

"Did I offend the king?" she asked.

"Oh, no. You looked modest and pious—no one would have thought you poor. It wasn't any one thing you did. It was all of them together. When I learned the truth about your father, it became the obvious conclusion."

"What, that I managed to lose my family legacy?" she asked, sneering at herself.

"You said you discovered the treasury empty."

"You only have my word on that."

"I take you at your word."

"You do?" Mina was, frankly, astonished. She'd just revealed she was not the heiress she was thought to be. Where was his outrage at being cheated?

"Mina." He put a finger on her neck, just below her ear. He traced a line only he could see all the way to her shoulder, where the edge of the dress began.

"What is it?" she asked, rather nervously. "Is there something amiss with my gown?"

"No," he said, his gaze lingering on the neckline. "In fact, I believe this cut is the only one you should wear." He touched her neck again, just at her collarbone. "This place," he said, musingly, "is where I want to kiss you first and last. And your shoulders. I've never seen more beautiful shoulders. You're so well-made, Mina."

"If I please you, that is enough," she whispered.

"I can't decide whether I want to drape you in neck-laces to draw attention to your particular beauty, or if you should go unadorned so nothing mars what nature has given. What is your thought?"

"How can you ask me that, knowing I have sold all my jewelry?"

"If it's jewels you want, I'll cover you in them."

"That's not what I want."

"Then what?" he asked, his eyes on her.

"You," she whispered, "but this is not the time."

"We could make time."

"Nor is this the place."

"I'll take you anywhere you like," he said. "But in fact, this is as fine and private a place as you could ask for."

He kissed her collarbone, in a trail like a strand of precious stones. His single-mindedness was exciting, but also unnerving. "We must not, not here," she protested.

In response, Luc pulled her closer to him, and then pressed her hard against the wall. Mina gasped, and he lost no time in covering her with demanding, desperate kisses.

His hands cupped her breasts, pushing them up, dangerously close to the neckline of the gown.

"Luc, please…" she began to say in warning, but then his mouth found one hard bud just exposed, and she inhaled raggedly.

"Just like that, Mina," he growled. "Breathe."

She shuddered with desire, even as she realized that every breath pushed her breasts directly at him, as if she were begging for it, demanding his attention.

Maybe she was. Heat poured into her veins, and her body grew heavy. She felt a sudden wash of moisture between her legs. "Oh," she moaned.

"Tell me to go on," he hissed between kisses.

"Go on," she whispered.

"Why? Do you like it?"

"Yes. I need you."

He laughed once, a low sound that shook her to the

core. Then he ran his hands over her breasts and up to her shoulders and back again, looking like he intended to eat her. "Your body, Mina. You'll drive me insane. I've never wanted a woman the way I want you."

She took another breath, inadvertently giving him more of what he wanted. Then his mouth was on her breast again, giving her exactly what *she* wanted. She made a sound she never had before, one of pure lust.

He stopped, pulling away from her.

Mina gasped once in bitter disappointment. "No."

"Tell me what you want," he hissed.

"You," she gasped. "Now."

"Here?" he asked.

Anywhere. Just so she could feel that tantalizing shimmer when his tongue touched her skin.

Luc's eyes were dark with desire as he knelt in front of her, his head on a level with her waist.

"Lift your skirts for me," he said. "Hold them up, or I swear I'll rip this dress off if I have to."

"You won't have to," she whispered, gathering the thick fabric in her hands.

"No?" He smiled, a crooked grin that left her breath-less.

The hem of the dress crept higher, higher. "What will you do?" she asked, pausing when fabric barely covered her hips.

"Taste you," he promised.

He ran his hands up her legs, right to where they met. Mina leaned back against the wall when he slipped a finger into her center, parting the folds of her flesh. His breathing changed, became heavier. He leaned forward and flicked his tongue along the most sensitive part of her body.

Dear God. Mina's knees almost buckled. Luc's hands helped steady her, but his tongue...sinfully, indescribably wonderful. Mina gave a strangled sob, releasing her grip on the dress with one hand to tangle her fingers in Luc's hair.

He made a sound then too, and his voice reverberated against her in a way that made Mina shake.

He stopped only long enough to say, "Guide me," and then his mouth was on her again, his tongue against her flesh, but still.

He was waiting for instruction. Mina sighed in delight, then said, "Lick me like before. Except a little...faster. Oh."

Luc obeyed, and she gloried in it. She put her hand on the back of his head, encouraging him onward.

"Don't stop," she begged.

He didn't stop. He responded to every whispered command she gave, though soon her commands sounded more like pleas, until she cried out in release, the sound trapped by the solid walls of the treasury.

Mina sagged, only to be caught in Luc's arms as he rose to his feet. She leaned into him, burying her face in his chest.

"Mina," he asked, his voice more urgent.

She raised her head to look at him. "Tell me what you need."

"My belt," he ordered hoarsely. "Take it off."

She unbuckled the leather as quickly as she could, flinging the belt into a corner. Without being asked, she pushed his leggings down from his waist. She stroked him, marveling in the hardness of him.

Luc groaned, muffling the sound by sinking his teeth into her neck, a half-bite that nearly undid her. "I need you, Mina," he hissed. "Here, against the wall."

He slid his hands to cup her bottom, and lifted her up, pushing her back against the stone. He pushed up against her, sheathing himself inside, filling her completely.

She moaned as he pressed into her exquisitely sensitive flesh.

"Put your legs around me," he ordered.

Mina did, clinging to him desperately, wanting him as close as humanly possible.

He held her steady even as he thrust against her. It wasn't violent, but it was more base and carnal than ever before. She loved it.

"It's. Not. Your. Money. Mina," he managed to get out. "This is what I need. You're all I want, love. I love you. I need you. You're mine."

"I'm yours," she gasped in agreement. "I'm yours, Luc."

His grip tightened to near pain as he spent himself within her. "You're mine," he repeated. "I want no one else. No other woman. Not ever."

She put her arms around him. "Luc," she whispered.

"It's true, my Mina."

"I love you," she confessed. "Not just what you do to me. I love you."

He sighed, pressing against her for a moment, then reluctantly sliding out of her. He made sure her feet were firmly on the ground before he let her go.

"You drive me to distraction," he said, kissing her gently on the forehead. "My beautiful wife. I feared you'd never ask for me. Such a proud beauty I married."

"Pride has kept me safe," she admitted.

"You have me to keep you safe now, love," he said.

A glow suffused Mina's whole being. She almost

wanted to weep with joy.

Luc rearranged her gown and helped her restore her hair to something resembling proper. Mina smiled each time she caught his eye. He dressed himself again, and leaned in to kiss her afterward.

"Perhaps my new favorite room in the castle, love," he said.

"Not our bedroom?"

"I imagine that tonight, our bedchamber will once again be my favorite," he admitted.

She shook her head. "We have hours before nightfall. And I have work to do."

Luc watched as she shut and locked the door of the treasury room. "I must at least pretend the money is still there," she explained in a quiet tone.

"We'll find where it's gone," he said confidently. "Or build a new fortune."

Mina laughed. "If only it were so easy."

He walked her up the narrow, winding stairs, and they emerged in the great hall. They hadn't gone more than a few steps when a young boy of about twelve came skidding in from another door.

"My lady!" the servant nearly shouted. "We've been looking for you everywhere!"

"Why? What's happening? An attack again?"

"My lady, please come. It's your father. He may be dying."

At the word, Mina rocked forward. She grabbed the servant boy's arm. "We go now," she gasped out.

The boy helped her out of the hall. Everything behind her was forgotten: Luc, the treasury, the shocking act of pleasure, her confession of love, everything.

Chapter 27

LUC WATCHED MINA'S FACE WHEN the fool servant said the word *dying*. He saw the color drain so fast he was sure she'd faint, and he wanted to curse the boy for delivering the news so carelessly.

Mina didn't faint. Instead she leapt away like a fleeing deer, leaving Luc behind without even a backward glance.

He stood there helplessly for a long moment. A flutter at the corner of his eye caught his attention. Eva walked toward him.

"Godfrey has taken a turn for the worse," she said. "Apparently, it began less than an hour ago. I know Joscelin was with him in the morning, and he was doing quite well then, according to the maid Beatrice."

An hour ago, Luc thought. Right about the time Luc dragged Mina to the empty treasury and kept her there, greedy for her softness and her arms around him.

He swallowed, trying to focus. "She's an excellent nurse," he said. "She'll know if there's anything to be done."

"Has no doctor been summoned?" Eva asked.

Domina had long ago spent all the money she could spare on doctors' advice. Luc shook his head. "I'm not sure it would matter," he said. "Though I should summon one, just in case." He'd pay for it. He was done with Mina taking on so much and not allowing anyone to share the burden.

Eva herself took on the task of sending for a physician, asking for the best one in the area, who, it turned out, was a brother in a nearby monastery. A request for aid was dispatched, though it would be several hours before they could hope to see the physician.

When Luc went to Godfrey's room to tell Mina that help would arrive, he found a scene of controlled chaos. Mina directed a few servants to either heat water or fetch brandy or warm some soup. Mina hovered over her father's bed, watching for every sign of his body's distress. A change in breathing or a sudden sweat made her issue a new string of orders.

Joscelin was there as well, his face pale. He stood in a corner, out of the way, so Luc joined him there.

"How is he?" Luc asked.

Joscelin shook his head, as if it was all too much to think about. "He's still breathing."

Luc noticed how shaky Joscelin looked, and chalked it up to concern for his uncle's fate. The younger man was gripping the crucifix he wore, his fingers white.

"You should rest," Luc told him. "You look terrible."

"I feel…so powerless," Joscelin said, the words coming out in a hiss. He blinked rapidly, as if he'd been lost in a daze. "Excuse me. I must go pray." With a nod, Joscelin slipped out of the room.

Luc remained, his eyes fixed on Mina.

"Mina," Luc called, after observing the scene for several minutes. "Mina."

She looked over at him, blinking almost as if she didn't recognize him. "What?"

"We've sent for a doctor. He should be here this evening."

"Oh. Yes. Good." She nodded absently. "Thank you."

"Is there anything else I can do?" he asked.

She shook her head, the loose red curls spilling out around her face. "I must stay with him. That's all. This has happened before—he seems to improve for a while but then collapses again. I can't tell you how often I've written to Joscelin, telling him that our prayers have been answered, only to see my father fail again days after Joscelin has rushed home. Sometimes I wonder if hope is actually a curse."

"I'll tell them to bring you something to eat," Luc said, looking for something he could do to help. He already knew she'd never leave her father's side to attend supper.

So he left her, troubled by how ill and drawn *she* looked. If Mina got sick through tending her father, it wouldn't help anything.

After Luc ate supper in the hall, he returned to Mina, who'd not left her father's side. An untouched tray proved she'd not even taken the time to eat. She still hovered by her father, though now she was watching someone else. The monastic physician had arrived. He wore the dark brown robes of his order, and his grey hair was tonsured, leaving a bare circle at the top of his head.

He was administering to Godfrey while Mina asked what he was doing at every step.

"Patience, child," the physician admonished. "Let me work. I'll explain the methods once I'm done."

"But…"

"The lady needs to rest," Luc said from the doorway.

Both Domina and the monk turned to look at him.

"I need to be with my father," she objected.

"It's late," Luc said, "and he won't be alone. Let this man—"

"Brother Paul," the monk said helpfully.

"Let Brother Paul do his work."

"I can help," she said.

"Not if you fall asleep on your feet, child," Brother Paul warned her. "Go to bed. I'll stay the whole night through. I'm used to such a schedule. You are not."

Luc nodded gratefully to the sensible monk. He took Mina's arm. "He's right. No one can be strong forever, Mina. Not alone. You need to rest, love."

"I can't," she said desperately. "He needs me."

"Yes, he needs you, which means you must rest so you can continue to care for him, and the castle."

Luc held her by her shoulders, and despite her struggles, he didn't let her return to the bedside.

"Let me go!"

"No, Mina. You can't do anything more today. You can barely stand on your feet. Let me take you to your bed."

"But…"

"You're exhausted Mina," he said. "What if you gave him the wrong medicine by mistake?"

She went still.

"You're listening to me now? Good."

Luc very firmly kept hold of one shoulder, but then swept her up into his arms. "I'm taking you to the keep."

"I can walk."

"So can I," he said. "No more arguments, love."

She initially struggled a bit in Luc's arms, but then sighed and leaned her head against his shoulder, closing her eyes for a moment.

"Have I made a fool of myself?" she asked in a small voice.

"Not at all. You're a daughter concerned for her father. No one would expect less."

Even after he crossed the threshold of the keep, Luc wouldn't let Mina out of his arms. Joscelin saw them and stared openmouthed.

"What's going on?" he asked. "Is Mina ill, too?"

"Just tired," Luc told him. He ordered a servant to bring some food and mulled wine up to the bedchamber, then he carried Mina all the way up the stairs.

Constance hurried into the room just as Luc allowed Mina to sit on the bed.

"My lord, my lady," she said with a curtsey.

"Constance," Luc said. "Prepare your mistress for bed. She is to eat when the food arrives and then she will go directly to sleep."

It was a clue of how tired Mina was that she couldn't even summon a sharp remark back. Luc busied himself at one side of the room while the maid readied Domina for the night. Luc watched as Constance brushed out Domina's hair with the sort of care a sister might show. Mina inspired devotion in everyone who lived in the castle.

When the food was brought in, Luc dismissed everyone. He'd already discovered how much he liked feeding Mina.

After choosing a dish, he sat on the edge of the bed, offering her a piece of tender meat.

Mina dutifully chewed and swallowed, but her expression was troubled.

"What's wrong? Don't like it?"

"The food is delicious." She sighed. "I'm not hungry."

"Eat a little more. Then you can sleep."

"I can't sleep. My head is too full."

Luc made her eat several more bites, and then offered her the mulled wine. "It's not too strong, but it will help you sleep."

"So you say," she groused.

Luc took the cup from her and sat down next to her. "Come," he said, holding out an arm. Mina accepted the offer, tucking herself against his body like a sheltering bird. Luc relished the feel of her. He sought out one of her curls and twined it around his finger, loving how the red caught the glow of the candles.

"You can't blame yourself for what happened today," he said.

"They were looking for me the whole time we were…"

"Enjoying each other?" he asked. "True. But not your fault. It might as easily have been when you were out hawking. Or gone to the village."

"Both tasks I need to do."

"Ah. So the guilt stems from the fact that you were doing something you didn't need to be doing? Merely something you *wanted* to be doing?"

"You know what I mean," she said, hiding her face.

"No, I don't. You deserve joy in your life, Mina. You work as hard as anyone else here. You're usually up at dawn, and you don't rest until the night's halfway over. You're flying everywhere, counseling everyone. But you've been neglecting yourself."

"I am needed."

"Not to the point that you collapse," he said. "I'm

serious, Mina. You wouldn't work your hawks or falcons to exhaustion. You wouldn't ride a horse until you kill it. A human being is no different. Strain too hard, and you'll break. I don't want to see you break."

Mina said nothing, so he hoped he was getting though to her.

"You'll feel much better after you sleep," he said, "and then we'll see how your father fares. Would you like me to summon a doctor from London?"

"But then…" She stopped, looking confused.

"There's nothing left to hide," he said. "It's so in-grained in you that you must tell no one. But that's not a problem any longer. We're married. You won't lose your castle, you won't lose your father."

"The cost," she whispered, as if trying to find an ex-cuse.

"No longer your concern," he said. "If a doctor's fee is all that's needed to bring your father back to health, then I'll pay it happily."

"Why are you being so good to me?" she asked.

His face clouded for a moment, but then he chuckled. "Besides that you're my wife?"

"Yes."

"Well, you can repay me one day. Perhaps with a song. I've already heard you, you know. I heard you singing the first week I arrived. Sing to me now."

"I can't."

"Why not?"

"I've only been singing to my father. To help him re-member me. I feel as if…if I sang for anyone else, I'd be…"

"Betraying him? That's not how music works."

"How do you know?"

"I suppose I don't. Still, I'd love to hear your voice."

"I can't. Not yet."

"When he's well again."

Tears rolled down her cheeks. "Oh, God, Luc. Will that ever happen? Or am I grasping at shadows?"

Luc cradled her and kissed her until the tears slowed. He had no answers for her, and offering false hope seemed cruel. Eventually her crying subsided, and she merely clung to him, her hands bunched into fists, clutching at his clothing.

"I don't know what I would have done today if you hadn't been here," she said at last. "I've never had someone to turn to when this happened."

"You do now, love."

Chapter 28

DOMINA SLEPT LIKE THE DEAD. The castle could have fallen under siege and she wouldn't have even shifted in her sleep. When she finally awoke, the eastern window was already unshuttered, allowing a bright stream of sunlight in. Mina lay in bed, still drowsy, watching the dust motes float in the light for a while. She felt remarkably well rested, and admitted Luc had been correct when he insisted she needed rest.

Then she remembered what made her so frantic the day before and she sat up.

"Constance!" she called, even as she swung around to put her feet into the leather slippers on the floor.

The maid came in a moment later. "Good morning, my lady," she said cheerfully. "How are you faring today?"

Mina initially thought she was well, but as soon as she sat up a sense of dizziness settled over her. Still, she said, "I'm well. What is the news of my father, though?"

"He's sleeping, last I heard. The holy brother tended him most of the night, but he ate some food in the great hall this morning, and told my lord that Godfrey seemed to be past the worst of it. Shall I bring you something to break your fast, my lady? You barely ate yesterday."

The thought of food made Mina want to retch. "Later," she said, waving her hand. "I must dress and see my father now. It must be near noon!"

"My lord wished that you should sleep as long as you needed," Constance said.

"Where is he now?" Mina asked, as Constance helped her to dress. Mina stood quietly, hoping the dizziness and the churning in her stomach would subside.

"He's with his sister, I believe. Your cousin is in the chapel, praying."

Mina went to the chapel first, hoping to bring Joscelin along with her for support. However, the space was cold and empty, with no candles burning on the altar.

"Joscelin?" she called. "Are you here?"

There was no answer.

She waited for a moment, then decided that something must have called him away.

Mina continued on to her father's room. She found him sleeping peacefully, with Beatrice watching over him as she sat by the fire.

"Has my cousin been by?"

"No, my lady," Beatrice said.

"Hmm." Mina sat on the edge of the bed, putting Joscelin out of her mind for the moment. She sang several lullabies to her father, and then recounted some the recent events at the castle, including the arrival of Guinevere, the falcon.

"You'd love her, Father," Mina said. "When you're better, we can ride out to the meadow and watch her hunt. Luc gave her to me as a gift. You haven't really met Luc yet," she added, "but you will. He's...well, he's..." Mina trailed off, unable to put her ideas into words at the moment. Her feelings for Luc were too complicated.

After visiting Godfrey, she returned to the keep, and found Luc and Eva in the solar. The two were talking in low tones with the monk, Brother Paul.

"Ah, it's Mina!" Eva said, seeing her step into the room. "Come and sit, dear. You'll want to hear this."

"Shouldn't we wait for Joscelin?" she asked. "Where is he? I went to the chapel earlier, but he wasn't there."

Eva raised an eyebrow. "You know, I wanted a word with him several days ago, but when I was told he'd be at prayer, I couldn't find him either. That's poor practice for one who claims to want to be a priest." She gave a light laugh, but also looked a little annoyed, as if Joscelin was a disappointment. "Oh, well. Let's get on with it. We can tell your cousin the news later."

Both Luc and the monk had risen to their feet at Mina's entrance, but they resumed their seats when Mina sat next to Luc, who had chosen a padded, highbacked bench near the fire. He put a hand on hers. "How are you feeling?" he asked, concern in his eyes. "You still look a bit peaked."

"I'm well," she reassured him. "It's my father's health I wish to discuss."

"Yes," said the monk. "I can't tell you exactly what happened, my lady, but I can be sure it was not connected to what's been ailing him these past few years."

"No?"

Paul shook his tonsured head. "This was a sickness of the body, not the mind. His first symptoms were sweating and vomiting, followed by a rapid fever, and much discomfort in his belly. All of that is quite different from the usual problems described to me."

"I hadn't thought of that," Mina said. "I was just so worried he wouldn't last the night."

"I think the danger is past," Brother Paul said. "So long as whatever caused the sickness does not linger."

"But how can we know what caused it?"

"The signs are similar to the sickness caused by tainted food," Paul explained. "It's possible he ate something he should not."

"He eats what the kitchen prepares," Mina said. "But I'll have a word with the cooks. Perhaps a bad bit of meat got in a pot."

"See the kitchen is well cleaned," Paul advised. "Filth has no place where food is prepared. You're lucky no one else took ill." He paused then. "Has anyone else in the castle reported feeling sick?"

Mina herself had felt a twinge of nausea, but she dismissed it, for it passed already. "I don't think so," she said, "but I'll ask. Thank you for coming to tend to him."

The brother smiled at last, his face wrinkling up in pleasure. "What use are my skills if God gives me no opportunity to use them?"

He rose then, saying he wished to see Godfrey once more before he began the journey back to the monastery. "I'll leave instructions with the servants," he promised. "And you must send for me should the symptoms return."

"Yes, brother," Mina said. "Will you add his name to your prayers?"

"No fear, my lady, for I already have." With a little bow, he excused himself.

Mina sank to the seat again, thinking hard.

"Well, this is good news, isn't it?" Eva asked.

Luc nodded in agreement. "It is, though I will also

send to London for a physician my family knows there. He'll come when the weather improves. Perhaps he can offer some insight into Godfrey's other complaint."

"But the cost…" Mina murmured.

"Unimportant," Luc said, taking her hand in his again. "I already told you. Don't worry about it, Mina."

"Very well." She took a breath, letting it out slowly. It felt so strange to say that, to allow someone else to take her problem away and simply…deal with it. She felt oddly light, as if the burden of responsibility had somehow been physically punishing.

"There is another topic to discuss," Luc went on. "Eva must return to Braecon, and I think you should go with her."

Both women looked at him in surprise. "Leave so soon?" Eva protested, just as Mina said, "Leave my father?"

Luc said, "I have yet to resolve the matter of Haldan. I've put some of the men-at-arms at all the locations where we think he may show up, but who knows when I'll actually get word. Meanwhile, Haldan could be anywhere. There was an attack not so long ago. Braecon will be safer for you both."

They argued, predictably. Luc was at a disadvantage, considering both Eva and Mina objected. Mina used the opportunity to push for Eva's safety over hers, and Luc eventually seemed to concede that one victory was better than two losses. He got Eva to agree to return to their family home, where she could share the news of her adventure to Trumwell while remaining safe.

The packing would take a day or two, so Mina helped Eva prepare for the journey. Luc helped by instructing the visiting men-at-arms to guard Eva with their lives, or face

Luc later on.

"He's *so* possessive of what he considers his," Eva said with a roll of her eyes when she heard the news. "You must get used to it."

"I suppose I must," Mina agreed easily. In truth, she was learning to enjoy many aspects of Luc's possessiveness, not least what occurred in their bed, where Mina was growing to adore being possessed.

If only her mornings would improve as much as her nights had. Once again, she rose a bit late. Luc had woken earlier, and left the room after kissing her cheek softly enough that she barely woke.

But an hour later, she did wake up, and barely got to the chamber pot in time before she heaved the contents of her stomach into it. She crawled to the window and flung open the shutter, but quickly returned to the chamber pot, for she felt as bad as before.

What was *wrong* with her? This lingering tiredness and the daily nausea was unlike any illness she'd experienced before. Could she be falling ill with something serious? Or…

Mina sat still for a long moment, inhaling the cold winter air and willing her stomach to not rebel. After a little while, the worst of it passed, and she could relax a bit.

She'd heard the women around the castle speak often enough of this symptom that she knew exactly what was happening.

Dear God, I'm with child. Luc's child.

The idea both terrified and thrilled her. What would Luc say? Would he be pleased? Would he still want to touch her, to be near her at night? Would they fight over what to name the child?

"Of course we will. We fight over everything," she muttered. Yet the thought filled her with an absurd joy, and she burst out laughing a second later.

She was absolutely certain of what was happening. As soon as the truth dawned, she felt a bit better. She stood up, leaning against the wall, wondering what to do with this revelation.

She would wait to tell Luc. Just until the right moment, when the mood was right. And until then, she'd have her own secret. Luc had once said she always liked to have a secret, and she felt the power in hidden knowledge.

Mina couldn't wait to see the look on his face when she told him, and anticipating his reaction made her so giddy that she wanted to cherish the feeling for a while. Of course, she should wait to be certain. That was the wisest course of action. In her heart, though, she knew it. She and Luc were going to have a child.

* * * *

Eva left the castle early the next morning. A last minute protest did nothing to sway Luc.

"Who knows what next may happen here?" he asked Eva. "Our parents would disown me if anything happened to you while you're under my protection."

"I still think you should keep half the men-at-arms who escorted me here," Eva said. "They may be of use, and six will be more than enough to protect me."

"No," said Luc. "You'll take them all back with you. I'm not bringing this up again."

"Yet I expect you'll bring up *your* suggestion again," Eva said.

"It's no use. I am not leaving Trumwell," Domina said. She'd had quite enough of that discussion. Luc thought she'd be safer at Braecon, which might be true. But Mina had many reasons for staying at her home.

Eva reached out to pull Mina into an embrace. "No matter what, you must be careful," she said. "I have only just gained you as a sister—it would be cruel to lose you at this point."

Mina returned the gesture, feeling an unexpected warmth. She'd never had a sister, and never knew how much she wanted a sibling until Eva. "I'll mind your words, especially because I've yet to meet my other sisters."

"They'll love you just as much as I," Eva said. Then she added with a sly look, "Though not so much as Luc does!"

Mina smiled, a sense of shyness coming over her as she remembered the secret she held. "I hope to see you again soon, and the rest of your family."

"Indeed!" said Eva. "I'll be waiting!"

Luc gave Eva a kiss, along with several warnings she was sure to blithely ignore. Then her entourage headed out of the gate, the bright presence of Eva of Braecon now just a memory.

"Well," said Luc. "I suppose things will be quieter here."

"For now," Mina agreed, smiling at him.

Indeed, over the next days, they enjoyed the relative calm of the castle in winter. Joscelin was reclusive, often staying in his room to study his theological texts, except for the times he went to the chapel to pray. Mina asked if he needed to return to London, but Joscelin said he felt the Lord wanted him to remain at Trumwell for a while.

"The Lord spoke to you?" Mina asked.

Joscelin gave her a decidedly non-ecclesiastical grin. "In the form of a snowstorm that blocks the roads all through the south of England until some of it melts. Don't you listen to travelers' gossip, cos?"

"No, and you should not listen to any gossip," Mina teased. "How unlike a holy man!"

Joscelin shrugged. "The church isn't always holy, nor are all the men in it."

"Then I'm glad the church will soon have you," she said, looking at him proudly.

"Thank you, cos." Joscelin looked away. "Your faith in me is very heartening."

The pace of life at Trumwell was slow. They waited for roads to clear and for news to be brought. Until either of those things happened, not much could be done. Mina and Luc spent a fair amount of time together, doing nothing more than the usual chores and tasks that fell to them. Mina never knew that sitting by a fire mending clothes could be a pleasure, but it was when she could look across to see Luc nearby, especially when he caught her eye and gave her a half-smile in the flickering firelight. It occurred to her this was exactly what married couples did. *How dull*, she thought, *and how delightful.*

A servant entered the room just then. "Apologies, my lord, my lady. This is unexpected."

"What is it?" Luc asked, for the servant was eying him.

"You have a visitor, my lord. He gives his name as Drugo, and says he serves the king."

Chapter 29

ON HEARING THAT DRUGO WAS there, Luc's good mood vanished. "What's he doing here?" he muttered.

"Who is this?" Mina asked, instantly picking up on his discomfort.

"A messenger of the king," Luc said in explanation. "It may be a minor matter." He didn't want Mina to grow concerned, or in fact to even speak to Drugo—though as the lady of the castle, she naturally would greet him. Damn.

"Shall we go down?" she asked.

There was nothing to do but bull though it. With luck, he'd be able to send Mina away fairly quickly, then tell Drugo what he needed to know before getting him back on the road to London.

Luc knew that the chances of things going his way this time were next to nothing. Still, he didn't anticipate how bad it would actually get.

Drugo bowed politely upon greeting Domina, though the flat look in his eyes was anything but courteous.

Domina, of course, was always courteous to her guests, even unexpected ones, so she immediately welcomed Drugo and asked his purpose in coming to

Trumwell.

"I must speak with Luc of Braecon," he said, "on a matter of great import."

"So it must be, for you to ride all the way from London," she said, "instead of sending a letter."

Luc braced himself, recognizing Mina's early circling as she prepared to go in for the kill. Drugo had no idea how good Mina was at putting pieces of a picture together.

Drugo quickly made things worse for himself. "Nothing to worry you, my lady. I am falconer to the king and have some business in the area."

"Of great import," Mina said, nodding innocently. "What counts as great import to a falconer? Is Luc expected to bring tribute in the form of gyrfalcons from Wales?"

"Ah…"

"That's rather more west and northerly," she went on. "So a stop at Trumwell Castle doesn't make much sense."

"Well…"

"Once you do acquire the birds, how do you intend to transport them? Surely you will not manage all the cages yourself?"

Drugo opened his mouth but didn't say anything.

"Tell me, sir," Mina said in a deceptively sweet voice, "just how long have you been a falconer to the king? Your knowledge of the general subject seems somewhat lacking."

"Perhaps we should talk alone," Luc said. "I'll show Drugo to the solar."

"Excellent," Mina said. "I'll see that refreshment is brought to you."

Luc watched her go, dreading the return. Then he said,

"This way," to Drugo. In the solar, he turned and said, "*Why* did you call yourself a falconer?"

"It's a useful lie," Drugo said. "Falconers travel many places and serve many masters."

"Well, if you use the lie so often, you might learn a little of the profession to flesh out the story!" Luc gritted his teeth. "She saw right through you."

"Bad luck on my part. Most people know nothing of falconry." Drugo shrugged. "It matters little. She's only a woman, and may soon be silenced."

"I have written, and told you your suspicions are wrong."

"And I told you not to be seduced by a pretty face."

"She did not seduce me. Everything I've done has been by my own choice and for my own reasons."

"What are your reasons for actually marrying the lady? We were agreed that the contract was only meant to persuade Godfrey to act like a reasonable man."

"Godfrey is ill and has been ill for quite some time," Luc said. "He's unable to act in any way at all."

"So you married her to get control of the castle?" Drugo asked. "I suppose that is not without wisdom."

Luc bit his tongue to prevent himself from snapping at the spymaster. He'd married Domina because she needed a champion, and because he'd rapidly grown attracted to her, and then to respect and adore her. But those words would mean nothing to Drugo, who appeared to have no emotions at all.

"Well," Drugo went on. "Now that you hold Trumwell, what do you wish to do with the lady?"

"Do with?"

"The reward for your success was an earldom by way of marriage. Or are you content with a castle and the daughter of a lesser lord? It seems a shift from your earlier stance."

"What stance was that?" The voice came from the doorway. Domina stood there, bearing a tray with a wine bottle and horn cups.

Luc looked over in dismay. How long had she been standing there, listening? He quickly reviewed what Drugo and he had discussed—completely damning to anyone overhearing the conversation.

From the expression on Domina's face, he was already damned. Still, he took a step toward her.

"Domina," he began.

She glared at him from narrowed eyes. "I came to offer refreshment," she said. Her tone was icy, correct, and as distant as the moon. "I apologize for interrupting your conversion with this very curious falconer."

"He's not—"

"Of course he's not," she snapped. Then she turned her attention to Drugo, who actually looked slightly uncomfortable. "Which makes me wonder exactly what you do for our king, my lord Drugo."

The spymaster recovered quickly. "I protect the king from those who mean him harm."

"Then why, sir, did you come here?" Domina spoke each word cleanly, little stitches with a needle directly into Luc's flesh.

"I have reason to believe that Godfrey de Warewic is working with agents of the empress."

Domina's mouth dropped open. "What?"

"Luc was sent to discover the truth of it...yet he failed to offer a full report."

She turned her gaze back to Luc, and now he saw the pain beneath the outrage, and that hurt a hundred times more. "I don't understand," she whispered.

"There was...tenuous...evidence pointing at Godfrey," Luc began to explain.

"Not that tenuous," Drugo said.

But Domina asked, "What could my father possibly have done from his sickbed?"

"No one *knew* he was sick, Mina," Luc said. "You hid it very well! Too well!"

"If Godfrey was not the instigator," Drugo said, "we must look elsewhere." He leveled his own gaze pointedly at Domina.

Luc said, "No. Domina is as loyal to the king as any knight."

"So quick to defend your new wife, the one who it was never in your plans to marry. Is your union so satisfying then?"

Domina gasped indignantly, but Luc only said, staring coldly at Drugo, "I've told you that neither Domina nor Godfrey can possibly have anything to do with a conspiracy against the crown."

"Then what of the money?"

"What money?" Domina echoed.

"The de Warewic wealth appearing in the coffers of the empress's agents," Drugo said. "Coin and even ingots stamped with the swan."

"That's why you wanted to see the treasury," Domina breathed, staring at Luc in growing horror.

Luc shook his head, saying to Drugo, "The treasury is empty, and has been empty for over two years. I've seen it."

"She could have moved the money."

"Why move it from a secure location?" he protested, trying to employ logic in the face of Drugo's prejudice.

"Why pretend near poverty for two years? Why manage accounts like a miser for so long? The coins we've seen show up among the empress's agents hardly match the total wealth of the de Warewic gold."

"You are credulous," the spymaster told him.

Mina gave a laugh at that, and turned on her heel. Luc threw a dark look at Drugo and followed Mina out the door.

"Wait," he said, catching her by the arm.

She pulled herself free of his hand. "Were you laughing the whole time? Or just when you tricked me into thinking you cared about me?"

"Never. It was never a joke."

"It started as a joke, by the king himself. Lord, he must have been laughing when he suggested a marriage. I swore my fealty to him, and this is what happened! How could anyone even think such a thing is possible?"

He shook his head. "I should have told you long before."

"What? Told me what?" she asked desperately.

"When the King summoned Godfrey to his court, it was because he'd heard rumors about your family—specifically, that your father was lending secret support to Maud. But you arrived instead. The marriage contract...was an impulse."

"An impulse?"

"He directed me to come here to Trumwell Castle in order to find out if the rumors were true. The contract was to be used as…"

"Coercion?"

"Persuasion."

She began to back away. "So he did send you as a spy. You married me to find out if I was a traitor. I'm going to be sick."

She stumbled away from Luc, her face deathly pale.

"Mina," he said. "I know now that you are incapable of such an act."

"How do you know that? I lied to you, to the king about my father's condition. I could be the traitor you seek."

"You're not."

He tried to approach her, but Domina moved quickly. "Don't come near me! You married me under false pretense. You are no true husband."

"The marriage is legitimate. We are bound."

"Legitimate!" she echoed. Then she sneered. "The only thing we are bound by is lies."

"Mina—" He reached for her hand, clutching it.

She snatched it back. "Don't touch me. Don't ever touch me again."

"Let me explain."

"Your friend has already explained! You turn over someone to the king, and you are granted lands and wealth and title and a better wife. Did you plan on repudiating me? Having our marriage annulled? On what grounds?"

Luc didn't know what to say, and by her expression, she assumed the worst. "Oh, mercy. I'm to be killed, aren't I? I'm to be declared a traitor and killed. My father too? And Joscelin? Will you spare the garrison and the servants, or are they to be executed too?"

"Mina, no one will be executed."

She kept shaking her head, clearly not hearing anything he said any more. "I'm going to be sick," she repeated in a low voice. "I must find Constance."

She turned and walked away, not even looking back.

He let her go. He would explain it all, ask amends. But first he had to deal with Drugo, who so quickly destroyed the balance of power with a few choice words.

Luc, his mood utterly black, returned to the room where Drugo waited. "You could have sent a letter," he muttered.

"I needed to see this situation for myself." Drugo sighed. "You're obviously besotted with this woman, blinding you to her true designs. You've already admitted that she's lied to the king, and concealed much that she's had no right to keep hidden. You tell me she tried to take control of this castle by herself, as castellan in all but name. If Godfrey died, would she have continued the farce? Or would she then have entered directly into an alliance with the empress, offering the castle as a gift?"

"Domina keeps the castle in the name of the king."

"So she says. We have no proof she would have kept her word."

"Our word is all any of us have!" Luc snapped. "I've bled for the king more than once, yet I could switch sides tomorrow. Many barons did switch sides when Stephen claimed the throne for himself! Those who promised to recognize Maud pulled their support the moment Stephen asked for their fealty."

"Stephen is a man, and therefore a better leader."

"Maud is the granddaughter of the Conqueror, and whether you believe she would be a good leader or not, you cannot deny that barons swore oaths to her...which they then broke. Yet Stephen now trusts them."

"You say he should not trust them?"

"No! I'm saying that Domina has never broken her word, and you must let her defend herself before you pronounce judgement."

"She may have a trial, if the king desires it."

"I don't intend to let her go to a trial," Luc said. "I know who's behind much of the mischief laid at the de Warewics' door. It's the false knight Haldan. He's the one who should stand trial."

Drugo's nostrils flared as he huffed out a breath. "You have him in custody?"

"No, but I know where he is. I had several men put to the task of watching for him, and one of them reported back only two days ago. I hadn't time yet to muster a force to go after him. But yes, I do know where he is. Allow me four days to ride there, capture him, and bring him back here. You may question him, and you'll be convinced."

"And if I am not?"

"Then you'll proceed as you wish," said Luc. "But know that I will defend Domina's honor for as long as I have breath, and I'll use the Braecon name and standing to do so."

"If you wish to risk pulling your own family's name down into the mud along with the de Warewics, then so be it," Drugo said. "But I'll give you four days to produce a miracle."

"You will join me," Luc said. He was not going to ride off, leaving Domina and Trumwell at the whim of Drugo. "We ride out tomorrow."

"Very well."

A knock sounded at the door.

"What now?" Luc called irritably.

Octavian walked in. "You might want to look to the lawn outside the gates," he told Luc.

Luc didn't understand what Tav was talking about, but he crossed the room to the window that overlooked the courtyard in front of the keep.

Mina was standing in the very middle of the paved area, the peregrine Guinevere on her arm.

He leaned against the edge of the frame, staring at the scene below. Mina was surely not going hunting at this point. What was she doing?

She bore the peregrine on her forearm as she rode her horse, with a hound trailing behind. She looked, in fact, like the very image of a high-born lady, like the ideal woman he'd always assumed he'd marry as he climbed the rungs of the social ladder.

Domina stopped in the middle of the park, which was still somewhat green despite the winter. She turned her horse around to face the castle. She lifted her face toward the keep itself. Though Luc knew she couldn't see him in the window at that distance, he was certain she knew he was watching.

She extended her arm, called a command, and let Guinevere fly free. The bird shot upward, the powerful wings beating until they caught an unseen breeze. She circled once, high above her mistress. Then Guinevere flew toward the distant woods, growing smaller and smaller until she disappeared against the blue of the sky.

She wouldn't fly back.

Mina had done it deliberately. She understood how her birds thought, and she would know that the peregrine would seize its chance for freedom if she allowed it to. Luc swallowed, his throat gone dry. All the stinging remarks Domina flung at him couldn't match the harshness of her releasing Guinevere. It wasn't the cost. It was the fact that he'd given the falcon to her.

Now she'd flung the gift away, along with any hope he had of convincing her they still had a future together.

Chapter 30

DOMINA WATCHED AS GUINEVERE'S SILHOUETTE shrank to a speck. The urge to let the falcon fly had come to her as soon as she entered her bedchamber. She didn't think of the cost, or the months spent training, or even of the joy she felt every time she'd looked at the peregrine before.

Now it had become an instrument, part of a divine test. If she released the bird and it returned to her, it was a sign she had hope. If it flew off, then that too was a sign from above—a warning that she placed too much trust in something beyond her control. She'd trusted Luc, and all his words, and all his promises. She was foolish to do so.

So she rode out with the gorgeous bird on her arm, Luc's incredibly lavish gift that may well have been a bribe.

Guinevere was out of sorts, cawing and ruffling her feathers. Hunting commenced in the morning. Now it was nearly twilight.

Domina stopped in the middle of the wide parkland that spread out in front of the castle. Ahead of her, the lake lay still and cold. She turned to face the castle again.

"Oh, Guinevere," she whispered. "You must show me the truth."

The bird squawked softly as Mina removed the hood. "I will let you fly, beauty. Come back to me if God wills it, or fly onward if there's nothing to return to."

She gave the signal, and Guinevere launched herself into the air, flying ever higher. She watched as the bird rose and circled…and departed.

Part of her called silently for the bird to return, to serve as a sign that there was some hope for her life with Luc. But the falcon chose the sky—she knew it would.

Still, Mina waited there, the wind growing cold and sharp around her. Finally she admitted the truth. The bird was not coming back. She had the sign she asked for.

"Goodbye, my beauty," she whispered, heartbroken.

After returning to the castle, Mina didn't speak a word to Luc for the rest of the day. She half expected him to yell at her for releasing the bird, but he didn't confront her at all. Perhaps now that the truth of the marriage was out, nothing she did mattered.

She did have to run to her bedchamber, where another bout of sickness had her doubled over, retching into a pot. She prayed Luc wouldn't see any signs of her condition. She'd rather die than tell him she was carrying his child now.

After she recovered and assumed a modicum of control, she went to her father. There she cried, furious at fate and Luc and the king and herself.

"Why can you not wake now?" she begged her father. "Why am I alone *now*, when I need my family?

Then she spoke to him in low tones, and then she sang, her voice choked and unbeautiful.

Naturally, that was when Luc appeared, bringing Drugo in his wake. The king's agent looked surprised when he saw Godfrey, as if he thought it was all a fiction, or that Godfrey was acting a part.

It only took a few moments of Drugo speaking to Godfrey and seeing the latter's vacant, confused responses to convince him. "Lord, he's in his dotage."

"He may yet recover," Mina said, glaring at him. "Or are you as fine a doctor as you are a falconer?" she added.

Drugo's jaw tightened, but he said nothing.

"You've seen enough," Luc said quietly. He hadn't gone further than one step through the door. "Let's go and plan for tomorrow's journey. We'll need Sir Octavian to join us for it."

Mina didn't even look at him as he left. She considered praying for him to never return from the journey he mentioned, but then decided he wasn't worth the effort of such a prayer.

"If the Devil wants him, he'll take him," she muttered.

* * * *

Supper was miserable, though blessedly short. Octavian looked as uncomfortable as Domina felt. He plainly didn't approve of anything happening in Trumwell just at the moment, though his opinion was cold comfort to Mina. He must have known of Luc's mission, yet he'd said nothing. So he was like any other knight. Well, not quite like any other knight, she amended, glancing at his deeply brown skin. But under that unusual color, he was the same—and certainly not someone she could go to for aid.

Domina contemplated telling Luc to sleep elsewhere,

but to do so, she'd need to speak to him. And that she refused to do.

Besides, what if she did order him away and he sought another bed, such as Margery's? The maid sounded quite willing to take on the nighttime duties of a wife, when she'd cheekily offered so long ago on the wedding day. Of course, since then, she'd cast her eyes on a young man of Luc's retinue. Mina wondered if that young man would repudiate Margery as well, simply for serving the de Warewic family. And what of Constance, who felt such affection for the soldier Ban? Lord, how many people would be hurt by this debacle? Mina knew Constance would be heartbroken if her beau left...as seemed likely.

Unless Luc didn't intend to give up Trumwell Castle. Perhaps Domina would be the one forced out. It was the far more likely outcome. He father would be moved to some other place to die—assuming the journey there didn't kill him. Domina could expect arrest, then the humiliation of a trial, followed by execution or banishment. She held no hope of being found innocent of whatever charges would be brought against her. She was a woman with no money, no allies, and no champion...facing the king himself. There was only one way such a fight would end.

If the king was feeling merciful, perhaps she'd be allowed to live out her days in a nunnery somewhere, never to leave the pale after being forced to take vows. Her marriage would be annulled, leaving Luc free to take another, more useful bride.

Mina put a hand on her still flat belly. What would happen to her completely innocent child? Would Luc take it from her? Not likely—he'd want nothing to do with such issue, for it would be illegitimate and a reminder of how he'd once slept with a traitor.

"Mina?" Luc was there in the room, speaking to her. "Mina, please listen."

She hadn't heard a word he'd been saying.

"Mina, I'll be back in four days. Perhaps three. You have nothing to fear."

She laughed harshly.

Luc sighed. "Very well, I admit there may be some... difficult moments ahead. But I won't let any harm come to you."

She finally looked him in the eye. "You already have."

Luc looked as if she'd knifed him. Mina merely shook her head and turned away. "I'm going to sleep. Kindly don't say another word to me. And if it's not completely clear, you may never touch me again."

Luc said nothing, not even when Mina climbed into bed and pulled the cover tight around her body. Why did silencing him feel like a defeat instead of a victory?

* * * *

When Mina awoke in the morning, she was alone in the bed. She reached out and found the mattress cold. He'd got up some time ago, and left without a word to her. Without a touch. Just as she ordered.

A wave of nausea rose up. She barely made it to the chamber pot in time. She sank down to the floor as the worst of it subsided. Lord, how was she to endure this once her condition became known?

If only she could fly away as easily as the falcon had. Then the answer to her predicament came to her like summer lightning. Of course.

Mina sighed in relief, then summoned Constance. The

maid listened to Mina's proposal, her face slowly growing pinched and pale as she understood exactly what Mina intended to do.

"Oh, my lady," she said. "Is there any other way?"

Mina said, "This is the only solution I see for the moment. You have been with me for nearly my whole life, Constance. May I rely on you?"

The maid straightened her back and said resolutely, "Always, my lady."

"Then please prepare what's needed, and tell no one."

"Will *you* tell no one?"

"Who can I tell?"

"Your cousin!"

Mina paused. Unburdening herself to Joscelin held undeniable appeal. Yet by telling him her plans, she risked putting him in danger too. "What he doesn't know, he can't be accused of participating in. I don't dare tell him. Not yet."

Constance bowed her head. "As you wish, my lady."

"Help me dress, then carry out what I've ordered. And be careful. No one must suspect what we intend to do."

"Yes, my lady."

* * * *

Mina's plan proved slightly easier to enact than she'd feared. Luc took nearly all of his retinue with him to wherever he'd gone. Drugo and Octavian were also with him. Therefore, Mina had the luxury of not being watched as keenly as she'd been for the past several weeks. She worked closely with Constance and Giles, the man-at-arms she trusted the most. They spent two days getting everything prepared for the journey. Then, early the next morning, Mina dressed as if she intended to go hunting. She even took along Brilliant, her sparrowhawk.

She bid goodbye to Ancel, feeling a stab of remorse that she didn't dare confide in him. The steward served her father and her so faithfully over the years. Yet she knew that he'd try to talk her out of it, which she could not abide. Further, someone needed to watch over Godfrey. Joscelin would likely return to London soon enough. He could not neglect his studies forever. She hoped both men would be spared Luc's wrath when he discovered what Domina had done.

"My lady, it's time." The words came from Giles, who had ridden up to her in the courtyard.

She nodded, wishing she felt more triumphant about her next move. "Let's ride out," she said, as if nothing more than a day of hunting was planned.

When the small party rode out of the castle gates and past the pond, it was all Mina could do not to turn and look back. Her stomach churned with worry. For some reason, she feared she'd never see Trumwell again.

Which, indeed, might be the case. Her plan was audacious: a ride of four days' length through a countryside torn by war and the dubious loyalties of many people whose lands they'd be passing through. With great luck, Domina and her party would not be attacked. Giles and the two other men-at-arms would do their best, but Domina knew that such a small party was vulnerable.

Despite the dangers of travel, they rode north, toward a shelter only Domina knew of. There, she'd be as safe and hidden as it was possible to be.

Four long but blessedly uneventful days later, near noon, Giles pointed to something in the distance. "Praise God," he said. "I see the roof!"

They rode on, entering the pale of a small, secluded manor. Someone sighted the party and called out.

Giles almost sagged in his saddle, relieved that the journey was near an end.

Domina shared his relief. The decision to flee Trumwell was not one of her better ones—though it certainly didn't come close to marrying a man who merely wished to use her until he had her family declared traitors to the crown.

Poor Giles had aged four years over these four days, terrified that the little party would be set on by bandits or worse. He'd argued at first. But Domina was his liege lady, and he capitulated, agreeing to escort her and Constance to the manor of Pencombe.

Pencombe was modest, not much more than a house with a few farm buildings nearby, all surrounded by a rough wooden fence. The manor had been established decades ago by Domina's mother's family. The forest around Pencombe was lush and virgin. Tall trees were harvested for timber, and the rarer cherries and ash sold to the makers of fine furniture. Some of the wood from Pencombe's forest now rested in the great homes of the royals on the continent.

But over time, there was less profit to be made, and it no longer made sense to keep all the foresters and servants and villeins at the manor. It became the private retreat of the family, sometimes used as a hunting lodge, though it was underused even for that. In the end, Domina's mother came to hold it in her own name, and she decreed it be passed directly to Domina as well. Since the manor was entirely separate from any dowry, and because no one particularly valued it, Pencombe was not listed among Domina's bridal goods.

That was why she felt safe here. Luc would never know about it. She could stay here for years.

The house and property supported only three servants now. A family of father, mother, and daughter lived here and kept an eye on the forest for their lady. Domina's unannounced arrival startled them mightily, but she could see that the place was still managed well. Very soon after their arrival, the small manor house looked ready to host a lady. Domina and Constance helped air out the chambers and clean the long-neglected, empty hall. They swept floors, shook out bedding, and strewed sweet-smelling herbs over the stones. With a fire crackling in the massive fireplace of the hall, the last of the sleepiness was banished. Pencombe was awake again.

"My lady," said the housemaid. She was about twelve, with a smattering of freckles across her face. "I am to ask how long you expect to stay here? And will you have guests coming? Mother, that is, the cook wishes to know how much meat will be needed until spring."

Mina smiled at her kindly. "Tell your mother that I will be staying indefinitely, but there will be no guests. She need not prepare any feasts. If there is little meat left, we will eat more bread."

"You need meat, my lady," Constance interjected. "We can do with less, but in your condition…"

"Enough," Domina said, cutting her off. "I do not intend to starve myself, but I want no extravagance."

The little housemaid curtseyed and then hurried out of the hall.

"Speak not of my condition," Domina told Constance. "I do not want people to gossip."

"Who will they tell?" Constance asked. "Pencombe is a day's ride from the nearest neighbor, and two from the closest village of any size. No one will know you're here, let alone with child."

"Let us pray it remains so."

"My lady, you do not intend to stay here forever…"

"Why should I not? Pencombe is mine, is it not? My so-called husband has no claim on this property, and he should be content having stolen Trumwell from me."

"At the king's orders."

"Speak not to me of the king. My family served his since the Conqueror. My father fought to keep our land safe. And how does this king think of me? As a traitor, all because of some whispered rumor? What sort of king renders justice in this way? I am not even allowed to stand up to speak for myself or my father." Domina glared into the flames. "No, we'll stay here, well out of politics and the business of men."

"Yes, my lady." Constance bent her head to her sewing again, seeing the argument was useless.

Chapter 31

THE LATE WINTER AIR BIT. The only thing keeping Luc warm was the thought of finally getting his hands on the elusive Haldan. He was sick of riding through cold, muddy, and icy streams. He was sick of the road, sick of Drugo's insinuations about his motives, and sick of being away from Domina.

Luc thought a few days of separation would be beneficial. Mina would cool in his absence and he'd be able to decide what to say to her. It certainly wasn't the first time he'd fought with her. Once he brought Haldan to justice and sent Drugo on his way, everything would settle down.

But first they had to actually get Haldan.

"You're *sure* he's here?" Tav asked once again as they neared their destination.

"I'm sure," Luc said, confident in his knowledge. "I sent several of the men-at-arms from Mina's properties to all the places Haldan had been sighted. Once a man saw him, he sent word to Trumwell."

"Let's hope he hasn't moved on," Drugo muttered.

"He's still there," Luc said.

Soon they arrived at the town of Chepstow, where Haldan had been sighted. The three men halted just outside the village.

"Haldan's brother lives here, and he owns the inn by the east gate of the town," Luc said. "That's why Haldan stays here when he has no other options."

"If we march in as we are, he'll see us long before we see him," Octavian said. "I'm rather recognizable," he added wryly.

"He'll know my face too," said Luc. "He's surely memorized it, because he'll want to kill me when he sees me."

"Worse, Drugo doesn't know Haldan by sight," Tav said. "He can't scout ahead."

"Actually, that might work to our advantage," Luc said. "If Drugo plays the part of a mercenary better than a falconer, I have an idea."

"What is that?" Drugo looked interested despite himself.

"We'll bind my hands, and give my sword to Drugo," Luc explained. "I'll be his prisoner."

"What's your crime?" Drugo asked, eyes narrow.

"Being born noble," Luc told him. "You can simply be a mercenary intending to ransom me to my family. It will just be a coincidence that you've come into the same drinking establishment that Haldan happens to be living at."

"You want him to *buy* you from me?" Drugo asked, catching on. "He wouldn't be able to afford the price."

"Oh, I think you'll find he can. And that will be just the proof you need."

"Perhaps," said Drugo. "Either way, it will be enough to take him into custody. Very well. Let's try it."

They found an out of the way place to keep their horses and to complete the transition from nobles to a mercenary and his prisoner. Octavian would stay out of sight, but close enough that a loud yell could alert him if something went wrong.

"Keep a dagger in your boot," Tav muttered to Luc as they got ready. "Just in case you aren't able to retrieve your sword in time."

Luc nodded. "If we don't return in two hours, do as you think best."

"I'll do as I think best in one hour," Tav said. "Good luck."

Drugo made a most convincing mercenary with only a few subtle changes to his clothes and bearing. His wiry frame, bald head, and calculating eyes fit the part. The assortment of weapons he carried would do the rest of the convincing. Tav bound Luc's wrists with rope carefully arranged to look tight, but if Luc twisted his arms the right way, the rope would slide off.

"Clever," Luc noted.

"Learned it from a sailor in Constantinople," Tav told him.

Then it was time. Drugo, in the persona of a rough mercenary, dragged Luc into the common room of the inn. Considering that Luc's hands were bound and he was obviously dressed as a noble, all eyes fell to them.

A man wearing a long apron, the mark of a barkeeper, addressed Drugo. "Stopping for a meal?" From his tone, it was clear the man hoped Drugo and his guest would be leaving quickly.

Drugo nodded, but then shattered his hopes by adding, "And a room for the night. Private room."

"All the private rooms have only one bed."

"That's no matter. My cargo here will sleep on the floor." Drugo gave an evil looking smile, then steered Luc to a table close to the fireplace. Two men were sitting there, but when Drugo grunted at them to move, they did so with alacrity.

A serving girl emerged from the kitchen, bearing a bowl and a mug of ale, which she silently put down in front of Drugo.

"Go back and get some for my guest," Drugo told her. "He's got to eat."

She nodded and vanished as quickly as she came.

Drugo began to eat, and Luc glanced around the inn as well as he could with his head down.

Someone approached, and just from the weight of the footfalls, Luc knew who it was. A huge hand filled his vision as Haldan raised his chin so he could get a good look.

Luc surveyed him in turn. Haldan was outwardly the same—still hale and brash, still blond and bearded, with a toothy, smug grin. But he looked a bit haggard now, as if life wasn't quite agreeing with him. However, at the moment, he was in a good mood.

"Well, well, well." Haldan took his hand from Luc's face—fortunate, since Luc was about one instant away from dropping the act in order to rush at Haldan and punch him squarely in the jaw. He sat on a bench opposite the one Luc and Drugo occupied.

"Thought you looked familiar," he said to Luc. "Though last time, you were spouting a lot of nonsense about how you were better than me. Looks like the worm has turned." Haldan looked at Drugo. "What are you doing with him?"

Drugo took a sip of ale, then grunted, "I don't recall

asking you to join me for dinner."

Haldan grinned wider. "Ah, my family owns this inn, so I'm practically the host! Tell me, what's your business with the lordling?"

"My business is my own," Drugo said, not warming up in the slightest. Of course, from everything Luc had seen, Drugo wouldn't warm up if someone set him on fire.

Haldan didn't like the answer, for he leaned in with a hand laid meaningfully on the hilt of his dagger. "Come on, friend. I'm just curious."

"He's cargo," Drugo said then. "Going to sell him."

"Who would pay for him?"

"His family. Ransom for a lord pays better than a shipment of slaves. Especially when he's the only son. And if his family doesn't like him much, I'll sell him as a slave and take the loss."

Haldan nodded, impressed with Drugo's business acumen. "What's a lord worth, if I may ask?"

Drugo named his figure, an amount so high that most commoners wouldn't see that much over their whole lifetimes.

But Haldan merely nodded. "Well worth the effort."

"Hardly," Drugo said. "This one was a handful. Lost a few good men getting him. I'll be well rid of him."

"Perhaps I can help with that," Haldan said.

"Don't need an assistant to transport him."

"I meant that I'd buy him now. Today."

Drugo paused, staring at Haldan as if he were genuinely astonished. Then he laughed. "Don't imagine you can match the price."

"You might be surprised," Haldan said softly.

Drugo put his mug down. "I want the price in coin,

not promises."

"Then that's what you'll have. Follow me." Haldan rose.

Luc spoke for the first time. "Don't," he warned Drugo, just as he would if the situation wasn't an act.

"Shut up," Drugo hissed. "You don't tell me what to do."

He dragged Luc up by the arm, his manner rough, in keeping with his role. Luc stumbled along behind Haldan as he led the way out of the main room and up a flight of stairs. The lack of windows meant that the stairs and hallway were dark as night.

Haldan's room wasn't much better, even after he lit a candle.

Drugo kept hold of Luc's arm. "Well, let's see if you can put your money where your mouth is. I don't believe you've got a quarter of the amount I want for him."

Haldan laughed. "As it happens, I have a very generous employer."

"Doubt he'd want you to spend the money on me," Luc spat out, truthfully enough.

"You don't know the first thing about what he wants," Haldan said. "In any case, I may decide that it's worth the cost of buying you just so I can kill you myself. You got in the way of my own plan, and made my winter miserable when I should have been living high with my highborn wife."

Haldan sounded honestly put out about that, as if he'd been cheated. But Luc focused on the first part. "So it was your idea to try to marry Domina by force? Not your employer's?"

"I saw an opportunity," Haldan said. "I'd been taking his orders for two years—I was sick of waiting. But then you had to show up and ruin everything." He glared at Luc. "Now it's my turn."

"You say you want to buy him," said Drugo, in a tone that conveyed how little he cared about Haldan's motives. "But so far you've only offered words. Let's see the gold."

The blond man held up a hand for patience. He bent down to yank out a small, locked chest that he'd secreted in a corner. After a few moments of wresting with the lock, Haldan flung open the lid and pulled out an ingot, a slender bar of gold, which he offered to Drugo to inspect. "I admit it's not in coins, but I think you'll be satisfied with the quality."

Drugo took the ingot in one hand, his eyebrows shooting up when he felt the weight. He examined it closely, perhaps looking for signs that it was merely lead painted with gold. But Luc knew it was real enough.

"A swan," Drugo muttered, looking at the top of the bar. The symbol was distinct,the shape of the swan exactly like the silver coins both men had seen before.

"My employer's mark," Haldan said with a shrug. "It's pure gold. Take it and leave this lordling here. Then our business is concluded. Agreed?"

Drugo looked directly at Luc. "Well," he said, "if I were the type of man to place a wager, I'd have lost."

"What are you talking about?" Haldan asked, suspicion replacing his cheer.

Luc gave Drugo a short nod to indicate that he was ready for a fight. Drugo reacted by flinging the gold ingot directly at Haldan, who was so surprised that the bar hit him directly on the nose.

He howled a curse even as he drew his dagger. His nose was already bleeding.

Drugo lunged forward as Luc wriggled free of the ropes around his wrists.

Haldan was a huge man, but he was stunned and not prepared to fight both of them. The scuffle lasted only seconds. By the end, Haldan was on his knees, getting tied up with the very same rope Luc just discarded.

His chin and the shirt below were soaked in red from the bloody nose Drugo gave him. Haldan cursed without stopping, his words mostly aimed at Luc but some saved for Drugo. Apparently Haldan thought there should be some honor among thieves, and Drugo's turnaround hurt him mightily.

"You ought to know better than to trust strangers you've just met," Luc told him, as he hauled him up to stand. "Now walk. We're going back to Trumwell. You were eager to get in the walls the last time you were there. Now you'll get your wish."

"Go to hell." Haldan sneered at him.

Luc looked back to Drugo, who had gathered the chest of money and all the other items of interest.

At least some of Mina's fortune would return to her, Luc thought. He hoped that would soften her attitude a little bit, even if just enough to make her listen to the rest of what he wanted to tell her.

Haldan proved to be a reluctant guest. He struggled all the way from the room, and down the stairs. No one seemed inclined to fight Luc and Drugo for him, and they quickly proceeded to where Octavian waited with the horses.

"Do I need to find a fourth?" he asked, "or can the prisoner just walk behind?"

The prisoner's response to that was another string of invectives, this time questioning the manhood of his captors.

"Enough," Drugo said, cuffing the big blond man on the side of the head. "No more words unless it's an answer to a question we ask."

"Let's get back to Trumwell," Luc said, rubbing his wrists to make the rope marks fade. "A few days in confinement there may cause him to reconsider his position. He'll talk then."

Haldan grinned, showing blood between his teeth. "Send the lady of the castle to ask me. I'll tell her what's on my mind. She can—"

The words broke off as Octavian smashed the pommel of his sword against Haldan's thick skull, knocking him unconscious. The blond man collapsed face first into the ground.

"Apologies, Luc," Tav said as he resheathed the sword. "Did you want to do the honors?"

* * * *

They journeyed back to Trumwell in a better mood than they left it. The roads had improved, and the weather warmed slightly, which helped. With Haldan captured at last, Luc allowed himself some optimism. He could use the information from Haldan's eventual confession to convince Mina that someone was working against her family—and that Luc was working to help her family. It was fitting, he thought, that he fell in love with a woman who had exactly as much pride as he did. Neither of them was particularly good at admitting mistakes or asking forgiveness. But Luc would do both until he regained Mina's trust. She was proud, but she was also fair. He'd seen that in all her dealings with the people at Trumwell.

If he was honest with her, she'd listen. Eventually.

"Luc," Octavian said. He rode up beside Luc, looking at him in concern. "What's on your mind? I called your name three times just now, and you didn't even look up."

"I was thinking," Luc said.

"That much I was sure of." Tav rolled his eyes.

"I was wondering how long it will take for Mina to forgive me," he explained.

"Oh." Tav took a deep breath, considering. "Afraid I can't help you there. Understanding women's minds isn't in my experience."

"Wise decision," Luc muttered.

After glancing back to where Drugo rode, leading the prisoner on foot, Tav asked, "Do you wish you hadn't got married?"

"No," Luc said instantly. It was true. Despite the less than ideal beginning to the marriage, he didn't want to think of a life without Mina. "I just wish I'd hadn't tangled love and politics. They don't weave together well."

"Best to unravel yourself from one of those, then," Tav said.

Luc nodded. "Yes. Though it will be Mina's choice in the end. She could very well decide she never wants to see me again. In which case I might have to take the cross and ride to the Holy Land, because I'll be miserable if I have to live in the same country as my wife who doesn't want me. Want to join me? I hear it's warmer there."

Tav shook his head. "Let's not pack yet. She may be more forgiving than you think. Just give her a bit of time. Forgiveness can't be demanded. It must be offered."

Luc didn't feel particularly reassured by that.

Upon returning to Trumwell Castle, Luc saw Joscelin emerge from the keep, instantly recognizable in his somber black clothing.

"So you've found the man you've been seeking," Joscelin said, looking at Haldan curiously.

Luc nodded. "He was foolish enough to linger in one place for too long, so we were able to get him."

"Has he said anything of interest?"

"He refuses to say a word," said Luc. "Though in truth, we haven't begun to question him yet. That task will fall to Drugo, and I expect he's quite skilled at getting men to talk." Luc also suspected Drugo's methods wouldn't be something the gentle priest would be comfortable viewing. "Haldan will be confined in the cell by the east wall. A day or two of solitude may impress upon him how his circumstances have changed."

By that time, Octavian and Drugo hauled their prisoner toward the cell. As they passed by the steps, Haldan's eyes lit on Joscelin.

"A priest!" he said. "You can't deny me a priest! I wish to give confession in a church!"

Drugo cuffed him on the side of the head. "Do you think I'm stupid? You'd never respect the sanctity of a church for confession. I've never heard such an obvious attempt to escape. The only confession you'll give is to me, while you're in chains in a cell."

Haldan spat on the ground, but looked up at Joscelin. "Please! You've got to help me!"

Joscelin held up one hand. "I agree you need help, so I'll pray for the release of your soul from whatever torment it will surely give you when you are alone tonight. I counsel you to keep silence, think on your sins, and pray for our Lord to ransom your soul."

Luc expected Haldan to howl an insult against the church, but he merely stared at Joscelin, breathing hard after his struggles to get free of Drugo.

"Be at peace," Joscelin said, "and have faith."

Haldan shook his head, muttering. But he gave up his constant pulling at his ropes. Drugo and Octavian hauled him off to the cell.

"Perhaps you'd be more effective than Drugo at getting him to talk," Luc said.

"I wish it were so," Joscelin said, "but I would hardly know what to ask. This matter of power and politics is beyond me. In any case, I will not be here. I am called away to Gloucester to speak with the bishop there, and was in fact just about to leave when I saw you return. I expect to be away one or two nights."

"Take some men-at-arms with you," Luc said. "Even for such a short journey."

Joscelin smiled. "My cassock and cross are all the armor I need. I will place myself under the protection of God."

Luc had seen many men die while invoking the protection of God, but he didn't particularly want to raise the topic at the moment. He wanted to see Mina.

He asked Joscelin where she was.

"I believe she's gone hunting today. I heard her voice in the courtyard quite early this morning."

Luc sighed. Mina could be anywhere within several miles of the castle, and it would be useless to try to find her. He'd wait till supper to share the news that Haldan had been captured.

At the hour for supper, Luc entered the great hall, but didn't see Mina sitting at the table. That was odd. No matter how angry she was at him, she always observed the courtesies of being a hostess.

He turned to Ancel, who was sitting further down.

"When did my wife come back?" Lucy asked

The steward blinked owlishly, as if he'd been day-dreaming. "My lord?"

"My wife," he said with exaggerated patience. "The lady Domina. I heard she was going hunting today, but it is now dark, and therefore she can no longer be hunting. So she must be here."

"I...I don't know, my lord. I haven't seen her."

"Send someone to fetch her then."

"Yes, my lord." The steward bowed and left.

Luc waited. Drugo, being the terrible conversationalist that he was, said nothing.

"She's doing this deliberately," Luc growled. He remembered the first week he came to Trumwell, when Domina had been the proud, icy chatelaine of the castle, barely deigning to speak to her unwelcome guests any more than courtesy demanded. Was this his future? Domina once again cold and untouchable? Would she ever forgive him?

The door opened.

"Finally," Luc snapped.

But it was Ancel who stepped through. "My lord, I regret very much to report..."

"She'd going to make me come to her?" He stood. "Then I shall. If she thinks that she can hold court in her solar and I won't come up..."

"My lord, she's not in her solar," the steward said desperately.

"Where is she?"

"I don't know."

"What?" Luc paused at last, staring at the steward.

The older man looked more than nervous. He looked...distraught. "I was not privy to this, my lord. I knew nothing of her intentions."

"Where is she?" Luc repeated.

"Apparently, she left the castle this morning, and has not returned. She took her hawk, and three men-at-arms. But she also took Constance. Constance does not ever attend my lady while hunting."

"What are you saying?"

"My lady has left the castle." Ancel's voice dropped to a mumble. "I regret to say that she did not confide in me. I have no idea where she may have gone."

Chapter 32

LUC NEVER KNEW WHAT IT meant to lose one's mind until then. He couldn't hold any thought in his head long enough to do something useful with it. Every other second, he saw Mina's face and had to know where she was.

No one seemed to know.

Luc lost a day to the frantic search around the castle and village, just in case Domina and her group had been hunting. Though that was madness, because what could have possibly happened that would detain the whole party? Someone would have returned to Trumwell to ask for help.

So she really was gone.

Octavian's steady presence was the only thing keeping him remotely sane. Whatever Tav's opinion on the way Luc concealed the whole truth from Mina—and it was clear that Tav thought him an idiot for it—he never spoke a word of censure after Mina was discovered missing. He could see how truly distraught Luc was.

The other knight translated Luc's incoherent grunts into intelligible orders. He was the one who directed riders to the most likely places, and told them what to inquire after and how to report back. Every neighboring manor was visited, every local village with a market was ridden through.

Drugo suggested London, perhaps thinking Domina would attempt to approach the king himself to protest her innocence. A man from the garrison volunteered to be a rider and was dispatched to the city, though it would take a week to hear anything back, positive or negative.

In the chaos, Haldan was ignored by Luc and the others. A guard always stood outside of the cell, and meals were brought morning and evening. No one attempted to interrogate him—Domina's disappearance was far more urgent. Even Drugo offered his assistance, though his reasons for wanting her back diverged from Luc's rather seriously.

Luc woke the next morning in a more foul mood than ever. He met with Octavian and Drugo in the great hall, and from their expressions, he knew that nothing had changed in the search for Mina.

"I'm going to talk to Haldan," Luc announced after the men broke their fast. "We've let him stew for a day and a night, so let's see if the fight's gone out of him. I need a distraction."

Octavian stood. "I'll come with you."

Luc grinned without mirth. He knew exactly what Octavian was thinking—Haldan wasn't safe around Luc. He was right. That false knight deserved to die for what he tried to do to Mina, for what he tried to do to Trumwell. Every breath he took fouled the air of the world, and Luc wanted to purify the air.

However, Haldan was also the only man they knew of who could reveal the names of the real conspirators against the king. Since Haldan felt no loyalty to anyone but himself, it was very likely that he'd talk…given the right incentive.

"What do you plan to say?" Octavian asked curiously.

"He ought to leave the questioning to me." Drugo appeared in the hallway. "I know how to get answers."

Luc didn't doubt it, but he was loathe to give Haldan up to the king's spymaster. "You may ask the questions, but I want to be there in case violence breaks out."

"You plan on starting a fight?" Tav asked.

"Of course not. But if Haldan happens to start anything, I will finish it."

The trio proceeded to the building on the side of the courtyard where Haldan was imprisoned. Two members of the garrison stood guard, though the walls of the little building were thick enough to prevent even a sound from getting through it. The window was too small for Haldan to get through, even if there was no grate over it. The single door to the cell was so solid that the iron bosses studding its surface seemed entirely unnecessary.

Luc himself had kept the key for the door. Drugo had grumbled about it, but Luc was the lord of the castle, after all. Now he selected the proper key and slid it in the lock. "Haldan?" he called.

There was no answer. Luc glanced at Tav, who drew his sword. Drugo drew his own poniard. If Haldan thought to trick them by lurking in a corner or hoping to overpower the three of them, he was dumber than Luc thought.

He turned the key and pulled the heavy door toward him. The opening of the cell was dark and silent.

"Light," Luc called. One the guards pulled a torch off the wall and thrust it into Luc's hand.

Luc strode into the cell. "Haldan, what are you playing…" He stopped on seeing the sprawled out form of the soldier. "Tav! Drugo! Get in here!"

Tav was already there, falling to his knees to reach for the prone man's arm. "Flesh is cold," he pronounced. He felt for a pulse, watched for sign of breath, but then sighed. "Dead. And has been for a while. He must have killed himself sometime in the night."

Luc cursed in anger. "How? He was locked in, with no weapons!"

Drugo cursed as well, sheathing his poniard. "You kept the key, Luc. Are you sure you didn't stop by earlier to exact some revenge?"

"Not *before* getting the name I want to know," Luc burst out. "God's wounds! Even dead, this man manages to be insolent."

"If he killed himself, then how did he manage it?" Drugo asked. "Anything that could have served as a weapon was taken from him."

"Search the cell. He must have had a blade hidden on him somehow."

Drugo felt around the edges of the body. "Ah," he grunted. "Here." He pulled out a small but wickedly sharp blade.

Luc took it from Drugo's outstretched hand and examined it with a frown. "I barely knew the man, but I find it difficult to believe he would take his own life."

"It's a sin," Tav said.

"He sinned regularly," Luc argued. "But he wanted to live."

"What are you thinking?"

"He had some help. At minimum, he got this blade after he was imprisoned. He was searched thoroughly."

"An accomplice?" Tav suggested. "Someone who remained here in the castle after Haldan fled. Perhaps the garrison should be questioned."

"Am I to doubt every man who's fought for Trumwell since Haldan left?" Luc asked sourly.

Tav said, "There is also the possibility that it was not a friend to Haldan, but an enemy. Someone who wanted him dead badly enough that they would kill him even while he was under lock and key with little hope of release."

"Who? Someone else Haldan wronged?"

"He tried to force himself on the lady of the castle," Tav pointed out, "so it's quite possible he tried to do the same thing to another woman."

"Someone avenged her," Drugo said musingly.

"Or she took matters into her own hands. The women of Trumwell are most independent," Luc added in a bitter tone.

* * * *

All Luc's efforts to find out where Mina had gone were fruitless. He'd sent riders out along every major road to seek word of her. Nothing.

Joscelin rode into the courtyard that afternoon, returned from his short journey. Luc braced himself for what he had to tell the young man. In fact, it seemed impossible that so much had changed in the short time Joscelin was gone.

"Did you take care of your business?" Luc asked, noticing a rather satisfied look on the younger man's face. Luc reached to hold the reins of the horse.

"Indeed, though the road to Hereford is nothing but mud at the moment," Joscelin said as he dismounted.

Luc followed the movement with his eyes. "I thought you said you went to Gloucester? Isn't that where the bishop was?"

"Ah, yes," Joscelin said quickly. "I misspoke. I'm tired from travel. Forgive me." Then Joscelin asked, "How do you fare, my lord?"

"Not well," Luc said. "Come inside with me."

Joscelin's face went white when he heard Mina was missing. "Mother of God," he whispered. "Where can she have gone?"

"Believe me," Luc said. "That's exactly what we're trying to discover."

Joscelin sat down heavily on a bench, looking stunned. "This is not like Mina. Not at all."

"If she ever were to leave," Luc asked, "where do you think she'd go? You grew up with her. You may be able to think of something."

Joscelin was silent for a long minute, though his eyes flicked as he thought. He frowned, then sighed. "I would say she would come to me. But that makes no sense now, for I was already here."

"No other family? No friends she might visit?"

"She would not go to your family's estate?" Joscelin asked, doubt in his voice.

Luc shook his head. His family were still all strangers to her, with the exception of Eva. In any case, there was no reason she would seek refuge at Braecon.

"Trumwell is Mina's home," Luc said. "She's made that clear. So where can she have gone?"

"Is there not another question, sir?" Joscelin asked. "*Why* did she leave?"

"We had a...disagreement," Luc said.

"A disagreement?" Joscelin echoed. "A disagreement

results in raised voices, or a broken dish. What did you do that made Mina flee her own home?"

Luc shook his head. "It's a private matter."

"Your private matter is now causing the whole shire to search for a missing woman," Joscelin said, his voice going cold. "My own cousin is gone. I deserve an explanation."

Luc stared at the young man, so forceful despite his gentle demeanor. He was more like Domina than he seemed at first. He too would make a fine lord of Trumwell.

"Very well," Luc said. "I'll tell you what I can. But you must promise to keep it to yourself, on your oath."

"Consider it given."

So Luc gave the bare bones of the truth to Joscelin, who obviously was trying to conceal his offense and then horror. "So you came here to find a traitor among the de Warewics."

"Yes. At first."

"Poor Mina. To be caught up in this stratagem of marriage simply so you could prolong your stay here and increase your control."

"It was not just that."

"But it was partly that," Joscelin said, unrelenting in his disapproval. "Well, where does this leave us?"

"In the same situation. We need to find Mina and bring her home."

"Agreed." Joscelin sighed. "My mind is…frankly, overwhelmed. I must think on this revelation of yours. I'll be in the chapel should anyone need me. Perhaps if I pray, an answer will be given to me."

Octavian also returned late that night, after riding out along another road. "I went north as far as Cleobury," he said, referring to the large and prosperous manor both Luc and Octavian knew well.

"Any news of a woman traveling that way?" It would have made sense for Domina to have sought shelter there if she had taken that road, particularly because Luc never told her that he'd practically grown up there, having spent many years at Cleobury in training as a knight, along with his friends.

"No news of Domina, but they'll be able to send word further out for her, and either Sir Alric or the lady Cecily will send a message here, should they find any news at all." Tav paused, then added, "I didn't tell them much of the situation, but you can expect Alric to want more of an account after this is finished."

"After Mina is home again," Luc corrected. To him, it was the only acceptable outcome.

Over the next two days, other riders came back from whatever places they'd been sent. No one could offer better success.

Luc railed in frustration. "She cannot have simply vanished!"

Joscelin had remained at the castle while the others searched. Now he sat near Luc and listened to the same reports.

"Praise Him for one mercy," he said to Luc. "We've heard nothing of a woman dead, or taken. Such news would be hard to conceal, I think, if Mina were attacked on the road. She must be alive."

Luc looked at the younger man. "Of course she's alive! I'd know if she were not." He believed that. It was impossible that something could happen to Mina and he would not feel it. He loved her. There was a connection between them that transcended a mere contract. He'd find

Mina again.

She had to be alive. But was she safe? Was she happy? Luc didn't know if he wanted the answer to the last question to be yes or no. Did she not feel ripped in half, as he did? Would she accept him back, once he found her?

"My lord?"

"What?" Joscelin had been speaking, and he'd not heard a word. "What did you say?"

"I said, my lord, that an idea came to me while I was waiting here. If Mina did not flee to an ally or a town, perhaps she took refuge in a different sort of place. She is a woman, and therefore she might be among women—in a nunnery or an abbey."

"She's married!"

"A community of holy women would take in any lady seeking shelter, even if she is not there to take vows. Let me travel to the ones closest by, and I will inquire. I am of the church—they'll listen to me."

"I'm her husband, and they'll listen to me! I will go with you."

"My lord, the castle needs you here," Joscelin said, holding his hands up to calm Luc. "There are other things to think about besides Mina's whereabouts. Do not forget there was an attack on the walls not that long ago. If any other force appears, you need to lead the charge against them."

"Very well," Luc said, persuaded at last. "Go tomorrow morning then, and send word from each place she may be—even if the word is that they know nothing of her."

Joscelin left the next morning, saying that he would begin by traveling to the holy houses north of the castle. "The roads are well traveled that way. Mina would not make the journey more difficult than necessary."

Luc wished him luck, feeling angry that even the young cleric was being more active than he was when it came to finding Mina.

"Don't be an ass," Tav said, upon hearing Luc's self-accusation. "You've ridden miles of road yourself these past days, and you've written how many letters to how many people? Everyone here knows that you are doing all you can to locate her."

"I felt less hamstrung when I was laid up for months recovering from a damned sword in my gut! I'm supposed to just sit here, while she's out there somewhere?"

"Just until you know what your next move will be," Tav said patiently. "Lady Domina does nothing without reason. She'll explain herself in her own time."

"You presume she's safe and healthy and able to do what she likes," Luc said. "But the fact is that she left Trumwell with her maid and a few men-at-arms. These are dangerous times for anyone to travel, let alone a poorly defended group like hers."

"You don't give her enough credit," Tav said. "She is neither capricious nor a fool."

* * * *

"Oh, I am a fool," Domina moaned to herself, as another bout of morning sickness drove her to the chamber pot. "What was I thinking? I can't escape feeling miserable. The misery is inside me."

They'd been at Pencombe for a few days, and already Mina regretted the decision. It served her right for letting her emotions get the better of her. Worse, the physical symptoms of her delicate condition had intensified, perhaps due to the days of travel.

"Drink this," Constance said, offering a tisane steeped with raspberry leaf. "You'll feel much better."

Mina took the hot drink, wishing a sip alone could cure her. "It's not the baby," she said. "It's me. I'm miserable. I'm in despair."

"Despair is a sin, my lady," Constance said practically, "so you must not despair."

"You think it so easy?" Domina hit the side of the table next to her, causing the dishes on it to clatter. "Ah! Well, look at that! All the despair is gone! If it were spring, I'd go pick wildflowers."

Constance rolled her eyes. "You have never been so insufferable, my lady, if I may say."

"You may not." Domina glared at her. "Lord, why did he have to find us that night in London? Why did he have to be at court the next day? Why did he have to come to Trumwell? Why did he have to turn me inside out with his infernal…charm." Tears pricked at Mina's eyes. "I want to see him again," she confessed. "I want to hear him laugh. And hold me, and tell me he loves me."

"Oh, my lady." Constance took two steps and reached to take her mistress in her arms.

Mina clutched at her maid and sobbed, "I'm so sorry I've dragged you here. I thought I had to get away, but it's useless."

"My lady," Constance repeated. "I cannot advise you in this. But whatever you decide to do, I'll be next to you."

"I can't decide either. What can I possibly do, when I love him and hate him, and I'm carrying his child, and he's the kindest and cruelest person I've ever known." She wiped her eyes, only to find fresh tears. "Lord, he must despise me for running."

"My lady, no one could despise you."

"Will he look for me, do you think?"

"My lady," Constance said, holding her at arm's length. "One thing I am sure of is that he will look for you and never stop until he finds you."

At that moment, the little housemaid knocked timidly on the door. "Apologies, but there's a man in the parlor. He wishes to speak to the lady Domina."

Domina's heart soared. Just at the moment they'd been talking about him, Luc appeared!

She hurriedly made herself presentable, and took the stairs down to the main hall, which also served to receive any guests.

When she saw the figure standing by the fireplace, though, she halted, her heart crashing downward. It wasn't Luc who'd come for her. It was her cousin Joscelin.

"Joscelin?" she asked.

"Domina," he said turning toward her. "I thought you might be here."

"How did you find me?"

Joscelin gave her an odd smile. "Did you think I'd forget your secret manor, cos?"

"What are you doing here?"

"I heard about what happened," he said more soberly. "Why Luc came to Trumwell in the first place…a very ugly truth. I thought you would need aid of family. We are still family, are we not?"

"Of course we are." She stepped back. "Wait. Did you tell Luc about this place?"

Joscelin shook his head. "I thought it would be better to come for you by myself. I wasn't sure what you were thinking."

"Oh, Lord! *I'm* not sure what I was thinking!" Mina confessed. "After hearing Luc speak to that man Drugo... I was all turned around. All I knew was that I couldn't stay at Trumwell."

He nodded, putting a hand on her arm. "That's understandable. He's come in and invaded our home."

"I shouldn't have fled," Mina said. "It was cowardly, and now he has Trumwell completely under his control."

"Your father is still there," Joscelin pointed out.

"Yes," she said. "I can only pray that Ancel will be allowed to see to his health. Not that Luc ever showed rancor toward my father," she added. Even in her worst mood, she remembered Luc's actions toward Godfrey, which had all been above reproach.

Joscelin merely shook his head, unwilling to hear any good of Luc. "At least I found you before he did."

"I'm sorry to have been so difficult."

"You've had a difficult time," said Joscelin. "Luc's motives were hardly worthy of a knight, though he apparently only carried out the king's wishes. To think a king would use a lady so callously...but then, perhaps that king does not think as we do. Poor Domina, is there anything I can do? Anything at all? You must be feeling so betrayed."

Without warning, tears began to stream down her cheeks. "Oh, cousin!"

Joscelin offered her what comfort he could, and after a bout of tears, Mina recovered her usual equilibrium. She called for refreshments, and she and Joscelin sat together for much of the day, talking over the situation from every angle. At first, Mina hoped that Joscelin would have a solution, but as the hours passed, she realized that in the end, she'd have to come to terms with what happened on her own, and decide her own next steps.

Joscelin did try. He suggested several options, none of which appealed much to either of them.

"There is another possibility," said Joscelin in the afternoon. "I haven't mentioned it yet, but it would solve one difficulty. You could take holy vows. The church would protect you against the wrath of Luc, and even the king."

"In exchange for giving up my whole life!"

"Not your life. Just your worldly life. Granted, you'd not have Trumwell, though one could argue that you've already lost it. So what else would you forsake?"

"My freedom. I'd be just as imprisoned as ever, behind the walls of a nunnery."

"You'd *keep* your life, though it would be as a nun instead of a lady," he said. "Isn't that worth it?"

Mina couldn't answer. She wasn't at all sure it would be worth it. She'd tasted only a very little of life, since she lived most of it at Trumwell. But she loved her home, and she couldn't imagine leaving it forever. To take vows meant that she'd be sworn to celibacy, as if her marriage never happened. Though her marriage was tumultuous at best, the thought of never again being touched by Luc made her want to cry. Marriages could be repaired. Holy vows were irrevocable.

Then another thought rose up. "Oh, no," she murmured. "I can't enter a nunnery, even if I wanted to."

"Why not?"

"I am with child," she confessed to Joscelin. It didn't feel quite right to tell him this news before the father himself knew, but the burden of her secret was too heavy to bear.

Joscelin stopped what he was doing and stared at her. "With child?" he said. "Are you certain?"

"Yes. I know the signs well enough. I don't know what to do, and I don't know how Luc will react."

"He doesn't know yet?"

"I was going to tell him, but then I learned the truth of why he married me. I left as soon as I could, and how could I tell him such a thing now? I'm nothing to him. Our marriage was just a means for him to get the better favor of Stephen."

"This changes things," Joscelin said quietly, as if to himself. "Sweet Domina may now be carrying the heir of the de Warewics, or even of Braecon. What if your child should be a boy?"

"Then he inherits all that was mine and much of Luc's wealth too... Perhaps even more, depending on how his sisters are married. Unless Luc annuls our marriage. He has the ear of the king, and therefore clout enough to have it done. Then the child would be declared illegitimate."

The urge to cry against her fate made her gulp back tears. "Oh, Joscelin, I don't know what to do. I shouldn't have run away, but how can I go back, now that I know what he thinks of me?"

Joscelin pulled her into an embrace. "Oh, Domina. Just be calm, cousin. Let me consider what options are open, and then the answer will present itself."

"Are you sure?" she asked.

"I've lived my whole life by that principle," he said smoothly. "It's served me well."

Mina sighed. She'd never lived like that. She'd always strained against the options presented to her.

Perhaps Joscelin was right. He was her cousin, after all. She could trust him.

Chapter 33

AT TRUMWELL, LUC WAS GROWING increasingly frustrated at the lack of news. No one knew a thing, which seemed insane. How could a noblewoman and her escort simply vanish without anyone seeing them?

He wandered into the great hall. After ordering the nearest person to bring him some food, Luc sat and ate what appeared without tasting it at all. He glanced at the maid Margery, who was sitting at one of the lower tables, mending something. Her motions were steady as she stitched up some tear with a patient hand.

He refilled his cup of ale from the clay pitcher, but when he put it back down, he missed the edge of the table. The pitcher fell to the floor, shattering into a mess of broken clay and frothy ale.

Luc cursed at his own clumsiness even as Margery put aside her task and sprang to her feet.

"Never mind it, my lord," she said hastily. She sank her knees to pick up the broken pieces of pottery. "The handle must have been loose."

Luc sighed. "No, that was my fault. I can't keep my

mind on something as simple as eating or drinking."

The maid looked up at him, sympathy on her face.

"Fear not, my lord. If she's at Pencombe, Joscelin will surely bring her back. He can convince anyone of anything."

"Pencombe?" he asked, puzzled. "Is that a nunnery around here?"

"Oh, no, sir," said Margery. "It's her manor. My lady inherited it from her mother."

Luc frowned, looking more carefully at the woman. "What are you talking about? I've read over every property this family holds. I've been to most of them. Pencombe is not on that list."

The maid looked nervous now. "Well, it's not part of the de Warewic holdings. It was a private gift to Lady Domina from her mother. Godfrey never owned it and never shall. Did my lady never even mention it?"

"Never. Where is it?"

"About four days' ride to the north, toward the hills. I can give you directions. Joscelin asked for them before he left, so I remember them well."

"Joscelin asked how to get to Pencombe?"

"Why, yes, sir. He thought it likely she was there."

"He told me he intended to inquire at local nunneries."

An expression of disbelief crossed Margery's face. "Oh, Lady Domina would never beg shelter at a holy house, not when she had her own refuge available."

"Refuge, is it?"

"She loves Pencombe. That's why a family lives there to maintain it, even though she's not been able to go since her father took ill."

"Tell me where it is, and tell someone to saddle my horse. I'll ride out today."

He told Octavian he'd have charge of the castle for a few days, which inevitably brought up a few questions.

"You suspect Joscelin now?" Tav asked, astonished. "The priest?"

"He's not a priest yet, and he may never be, if he's responsible for anything that's been happening around here."

"Just because he's going to a manor instead of a nunnery doesn't mean he's up to something nefarious."

"Then why not tell me where he intended to go? It wasn't a whim. He had to ask how to get there before he left. No, Joscelin wants to reach Mina before I can, and not out of a sense of family pride."

"You're sure?"

"Think about it. It fits what we know. Until the marriage, Joscelin was next in line to inherit Trumwell if anything happened to Mina. He was not overjoyed by news of the wedding. I think it disturbed his own plans, whatever they were."

Drugo overheard what happened as well, and he insisted on accompanying Luc to Pencombe, much to Luc's surprise. Luc nodded curtly. "As long as you're ready to ride in an hour. I'm not waiting for you."

He waited until Drugo left to get ready, then said to Octavian, "Will you stay here and see to the castle's defenses? I don't know how long I'll be gone, and there's no one else I trust to do it. Though I'd rather have you accompany me instead of Drugo, there's no chance I'll leave him here."

Tav nodded. "You can count on me. Send word if you can, though. The people of Trumwell will want to know what's happening."

Luc agreed. "With luck, it won't be long. Margery

said the manor is four days' ride. I intend to go faster than that."

Indeed, Luc rode like the devil the moment he left the castle gates. Drugo, despite being twice Luc's age, kept pace. On the second day, they traded their horses for a fresh set, courtesy of a local lord who promised to keep Luc's horses in his stables until they returned.

They slept a few hours each night, but kept pushing onward, determined to make four days' ride into half that.

Joscelin had too much lead time, but perhaps he was too pleased with himself to rush. Luc would kill him when he found him. If Mina was safe, he would kill Joscelin quickly. If she was not...well, then Luc would have nothing left to live for other than vengeance. He could go very slowly indeed.

Why had Joscelin lied? What was his game? Why should he want to keep Mina hidden from Luc? The young man was bound for the priesthood, and in all likelihood a bishopric, or higher. Why meddle in such a mundane, worldly affair as this spat between husband and wife?

"If this young man is up to something nefarious," Drugo said at one point, "it seems likely that he is the one called the Swan, not Godfrey or Domina."

"Yes," Luc said. "He was a member of the family. He knew the family's secrets, and he would have known why Domina wanted to keep quiet about her father's condition. In fact, he probably encouraged her in it. It suited his plans, because neither Domina or Godfrey knew anything of what was happening, and neither of them could defend themselves."

"So does that mean Haldan was working for Joscelin?" Drugo asked. "They appeared not to know each other, but that may have been an act."

"I think so. I expect Joscelin is behind Haldan's death, though I'm not sure how. He was away from the castle at the time."

"He paid someone," Drugo guessed.

"Perhaps." Luc wasn't so sure. The Swan didn't reveal himself to many people. Who would he trust to kill another loyal associate?

They discussed a few other matters along the way, but for Luc, the only thing that mattered was reaching Domina in time.

On the morning of the third day, Luc spied the manor of Pencombe, the outer fence exactly as Margery described.

"Wait," said Drugo. "We can't just ride in. If Joscelin is here, he'll be alerted."

"The longer we wait," Luc said, "the more chance he'll hurt Mina. I won't risk that."

Chapter 34

DOMINA HAD SPENT MOST OF the morning inside the manor, alongside Joscelin, who showered her with attention as he tried to distract her from her misery and help her decide what to do next. He kept telling her to eat, pointing to a covered dish he said he requested especially for her. But Mina's stomach rebelled at the mere thought of eating. She might be able to keep something down after noon, but for now, she refused each time.

A breath of fresh, cold air would probably help settle her stomach and her nerves. She asked for Constance to fetch her cloak.

"Where are you going?" Joscelin asked, rising as if to accompany her.

"I need to walk outside. Don't get up. I'll only circle the garden a few times, then come back in."

She left Constance and Joscelin in the main hall. Constance worked at mending a gown, and Joscelin had an open bible on his lap.

Outside, the crisp air made Mina feel better immediately. In fact, she ranged further than the little herb garden just beyond the kitchen, walking along the inner side of the fence that marked the boundary of the main yard.

She almost felt like her old self when a shadow crossed her path.

"Mina."

She froze. Luc was less than an arm's length away. He was dressed for the road, in a heavy cloak lined with fur. His sword was strapped to his back rather than at his side, but he looked as if he was ready for battle anyway. He also looked more handsome than she wanted to remember. His vivid blue eyes watched her carefully, and it was all she could do not to reach out and touch his face, now partly covered in stubble from days of travel. Despite everything, she wanted to lose herself in the warmth beneath his cloak.

Instead, she forced herself to step back. "What are you doing here?"

"I came to find you," he said bluntly.

"How did you know I was here? I told no one. Joscelin was able to guess…"

"Joscelin. He's here now?" Luc broke in. He moved closer, reaching for Mina. "Where?"

"Why does it matter? You intend to punish him for not telling you where I was?"

"In fact," Luc said, "I intend to turn him over to the king."

"For *what*?"

"For conspiring with the empress's forces. For stealing your fortune. For murdering Haldan. For endangering you, and possibly for harming your father. I won't know about that until we can interrogate him."

Mina just stood there for a moment, unable to reconcile Luc's accusation with her gentle cousin.

"Joscelin? My cousin Joscelin? Joscelin who will soon be an ordained priest?" she asked. "Have you gone mad?"

"No. I finally have proof of the traitor I was seeking. It's not you, Mina. Nor your father. It was Joscelin."

"You're lying," she said. "I don't know why you're saying all this, but this can't be true."

"It is," Luc insisted. "I'll make Joscelin explain how he did it all, but I need to know you're safe first. Away from him."

"I won't listen to this." She tried to turn away, but Luc blocked her.

"Mina, you must listen. What you do afterward is up to you, but please listen to me for a little while. I know you don't trust me anymore—"

She tried to jerk away at that, but it was impossible to escape him.

"—but please. This isn't just about you. It's about Trumwell and your father and your family."

Mina stilled. "What of Trumwell?"

"Joscelin plans to claim it for himself, partly by discrediting both your father and you. Tell me where he is right now so I can question him."

"That's all you'll do to him?" she asked.

"For now." Luc's expression softened then, as he looked her over. "I'm glad to see you. I was worried."

"Why should you want to see me?" Mina asked.

"Because I love you. Did you think I'd not look for you?"

Her heart fluttered, but she tried to ignore it. "Yes. But it's my cousin you were chasing after, and that's what brought you here."

His eyes hardened again. "Where is he?"

"I left him in the house."

"Let's go then."

Luc kept hold of Mina's arm as he turned. She was annoyed to see Luc hadn't come alone. The horrible Drugo was there too, walking with two horses in tow.

"Oh, mercy," Mina said. "Did you not return to London yet?"

"Not without seeing this traitor first, so I can bring him back with me." Drugo gave her a perfunctory bow.

"You believe what Luc's saying?"

"Enough to ride nearly three days with almost no sleep."

Something in Drugo's face convinced her of the seriousness of Luc's announcement. "Is it possible that Joscelin is truly at fault for all you say?"

"That's what I want to be sure of," Luc said.

"Oh. Oh, no. He's with Constance right now."

"Take us there," Luc said.

She led Luc and Drugo into the small manor house, and down a short hall to where she'd left the others.

Constance was sitting in a chair by the fire, her back straight and her eyes on the doorway. She gasped when Mina came in, for good reason.

Joscelin stood behind her, holding a knife to Constance's throat. He looked so incongruous with a weapon. Mina couldn't remember ever seeing her frail cousin with a blade.

"Careful, cos," he said as Mina stopped short. "Don't startle me, or I might do something regrettable."

"Put the knife away," Luc ordered, coming in behind her.

"Ah, my lord," said Joscelin, his normally soothing voice now stronger, louder. "I heard horses enter the gate. Good thing I went to look, or you'd have got me by surprise."

"Let the maid go," Luc said. "You gain nothing by harming her. You wouldn't escape anyway. Not from both me and Drugo."

"Perhaps I'm willing to kill anyway."

"Joscelin," Mina begged. "Not Constance. She's done nothing! You can't truly intend to hurt her. This isn't like you!" But the fact that she saw him doing such a thing was the final confirmation that Luc's accusations had weight.

"You don't know me as well as you think, cousin," Joscelin said, in that same mild tone. "In fact, you know nothing at all."

"Tell us, then," Luc invited.

"Why?" Joscelin sneered at them. "Why should I?" Perhaps unconsciously, he pressed the knife into Constance's neck. She gasped and flinched back.

Mina almost screamed in fear. "Joscelin, don't do this. Please let her go."

"In exchange for what?" he asked.

"For me," she offered.

"No!" Luc said.

Mina was already taking a step toward Joscelin. "Let me take Constance's place. Surely that would be better for you. A lady instead of a mere maid. Your cousin instead of a stranger."

"*No*, Mina," Luc repeated.

Joscelin, however, smiled and gestured with his free hand. "Come then, cousin. Killing you would be more effective. In fact, I've been trying all morning."

Mina paused. "What?" She saw him glance toward the covered dish. She changed direction, reaching the table and pulling the lid off. It looked like ordinary gruel.

"What is this? Did you put something in it?"

His smile thinned. "Something just for you."

Rage replaced her fear. "You intended to poison me? Like some skulking coward?"

"I'm not a coward!" Joscelin snapped. "I'm noble. My blood is every bit as good as yours, and you're just a woman!"

Mina picked up the dish. "So I'm just a woman? Then you must expect me to fight like one." She hurled the dish toward Joscelin. He saw it coming right at his head and instinctively raised his arms to block it. Constance saw the moment when the knife pulled away from her. She threw herself forward, hurrying away on hands and knees.

A moment later Joscelin realized his mistake, and cursed his own inattention. By then Luc was charging toward him, covering the distance from the door to the fireplace in an instant. Domina knelt by Constance, pulling her into an embrace.

"Are you all right, dear?" she asked the maid.

Constance nodded. "Oh, my lady. I didn't know what to do."

"You did exactly right. You're safe now."

She looked up to where Luc had Joscelin in a hold that left Joscelin's eyes watering. The physical difference between the two had never been more stark.

"Don't hurt him," she told Luc. "He's barely more than a child!"

"That's not true," both Luc and Joscelin said simultaneously.

"He needs to explain!" Mina said.

"Yes, I need him to explain," Luc agreed.

Luc moved Joscelin to the same chair Constance had been in. Drugo shifted to stand in front of the now closed door, his sword drawn.

Joscelin struggled for a moment, but he soon calmed. "For God's sake, get your hand off me," he said. "I know I can't run."

"Seminary students shouldn't blaspheme," Luc said. "Though that's the least of your sins. Where would you like to begin?"

"I don't understand how you can say such things at all," Mina said, still reeling from seeing this new, ugly side of her cousin.

"I say what I have to!" Joscelin snapped. "That's what everyone does in this world. Some people just say it more elegantly."

"But you were different," she protested. "You had a calling. Even when you were a little boy, you had such strong faith."

He shook his head. "No, Mina. Never. I never felt anything but hollowness in church. I never felt that the saints listened to my prayers. You remember me as a little boy. You know what I remember from that time? My family dying! What need do I have for a god that took my parents, my sister? None. I would not trust any god who could do that."

Mina said helplessly, "But your whole life has been devoted to the church."

"Because I had a revelation, just not of the religious kind. After my family died, I went to the funeral," Joscelin said. "I felt dead, too. I wanted to rip the stones apart to get my parents back. But that would have done nothing.

"The priest who buried them asked me if I felt peace. Something inside me woke up. I looked right into his eyes and said yes...and he believed me! He not only believed me, he was delighted. A little boy mourning his parents, and the man believed that *peace* was possible for me." Joscelin recounted the incident in a stunned voice, as if it just happened a day ago.

"I realized I had a gift," he went on. "A gift for telling people exactly what they wanted to hear. If the church was filled with such idiots as that priest, then what might I accomplish there?"

"Your vocation was all a lie, from the very beginning?" she asked.

"You know, sometimes what I said *felt* true," he mused. "Sometimes, I wanted to believe the things I said, about the glory of heaven and the marvelous gift of grace. It would have been comforting to believe all that. But grace does nothing in this world, and this world is the one I live in. I was a poor relation, with few prospects for inheriting—unless those ahead of me in line died. So I focused on the church, where I had more advantages."

"Then what changed?" she asked.

He shrugged. "I suppose I did. I kept asking myself why I should have to carve my own fate, while you didn't simply because of who you were born to. And, to be honest, there's a limit to how much time I can tolerate in a church, especially because I know it's all lies. There is no god worth worshipping."

Constance gasped at the blasphemy, but Mina was too consumed by his confession.

"Did you hurt my father?" Mina asked. "Are you responsible for him falling ill?"

"Not the first time," Joscelin said. "When you found him at the bottom of the stairs—that was pure chance, and I won't take the blame for it."

"You said the first time. There were others?"

"I didn't think I had to do anything at first. Godfrey seemed to be on the edge of death, and surely he'd topple over into the grave quickly. But he didn't. You hovered over him, and he wouldn't die. Maddening. So I helped fate along, with a particular herbal concoction I brewed up myself. Every time I came to Trumwell, I gave him a bigger dose, and each time, he nearly died. The final time, I gave him a massive dose. Unfortunately, so much of the concoction taken at once made him vomit it up before the potency could manifest."

"But he didn't die!" Mina said triumphantly.

"No, he's tougher than I ever imagined," Joscelin admitted. "At least he was incapacitated since his collapse, though. That was almost as good, especially as it tied you to the castle. You were so terrified someone would find out and take your lands from you. Of course I kept your secret. I didn't want you married off to some lord! I intended to reveal myself at the proper time, to argue that it should be a man of de Warewic blood who kept the title, and to sorrowfully retire from the church to take up the duties of the family name. *Then* you'd be married off."

Domina paled as she heard him talk so calmly about her fate. "You would not! Do you hate me so?"

"I never hated you, cousin," said Joscelin. "You misunderstand. All I've done is simply to better my position. I don't seek revenge or to destroy anyone. That's a foolish path, and it leaves one open to weakness."

"Don't lie now. You tried to kill me today!"

"Oh, well, that was your fault. If you hadn't let that lord into your bed…"

"I was married to him, you dullard."

"You should have gone to a nunnery first." Joscelin's tone was petulant now, as if she'd denied him a sweet. "I tried to encourage it, but you were so resistant. Always wanted to be the lady of the castle."

"And so I was," Domina said. "While you were off in London, pretending to follow a righteous path, I was managing the estate. I made sure the harvests came in, that taxes were paid. I watched the walls and I obeyed the king's summons. If not for me, you'd have nothing to fight for at all."

Luc interjected, "Isn't it true you offered your allegiance to the empress?"

"I'd have offered it to anyone who was in a position of strength," Joscelin said. "The empress seemed to respect that even though the Swan was no great fighter, there were other benefits to an alliance, namely wealth. Alas, someone must have talked to the wrong person. My secret dealings as the Swan were less secret than I would have liked. I had to start moving more quickly."

"Through Haldan?" Luc asked. "You used a forged seal to get him the position at Trumwell after Godfrey collapsed, and Mina was too distracted to wonder at it."

"Yes, Haldan was my man. I met him in London, and saw how his simple mind worked. He did what I ordered him to—at first. He shouldn't have put a hand on Mina. I warned him about that, but he never listened well when it came to women. He lost that gamble. He was still useful from outside of the walls. I ordered him to attack Trumwell, using the information on the castle's weaknesses to secure a quick victory. Then I was going to approach the king and confess that Domina was ruling in her father's name. The king should have been grateful for the knowledge, and given the castle to me."

Joscelin looked at Luc. "But Haldan didn't account for what a couple of true knights could mean for a castle's defenses, and the failed attack, plus the marriage, made my previous strategy useless. It also made Haldan useless," he added.

"You couldn't have killed Haldan, though," Luc said. "You weren't even in the castle when it happened."

Mina said, "There's a passage from the lower level of the keep. It goes under the eastern wall and emerges near the forest. It was dug at the founding of the castle, in case of a siege. Only the family knows about it—Joscelin and I used to creep through it, as part of our childhood games."

Joscelin nodded, almost proudly, at Mina. "My cousin has the right of it. I left Trumwell on an excuse, then returned after dark to visit my faithful retainer Haldan."

"How did you manage to kill him? The guards didn't hear a scuffle."

"They were barely awake." Joscelin snorted. "Anyway, Haldan didn't even understand he'd become a liability. I spoke to him, told him I was working on a plan to sneak him out the next evening, and all he had to do was remain silent for a day. I passed a few items through the bars—the knife, a few small biscuits, a little dried meat. Then I had him hold up his cup to the bars, and I poured some wine for him…which contained poppy syrup. He fell asleep within a quarter hour. Then I used my copy of the key to enter the cell."

"You cut him after he fell unconscious," Luc said, enlightened.

"Yes, and arranged it all to look as if he took his own life. I wasn't sure you'd believe Haldan killed himself, but I knew no one would suspect young, skinny Joscelin! And anyway, I didn't wish someone to think that another copy of the cell key existed."

"When did you make a copy of that key?" Mina

asked, rather astonished at her cousin's foresight.

"Oh, I had duplicates of several keys forged, cousin. Including the treasury. Godfrey never noticed."

"*You* stole the money!" she gasped.

Joscelin laughed. "I broke into the treasury shortly after his fall. I spirited the money away through the secret passage over a series of nights. It was too heavy to do all at once." He shrugged. "I buried it in the woods. You want to talk about nerve-wracking! Any fool walking by might have stolen the gold for the pain of a few minutes digging. As soon as I could, I moved it to a much safer location." He looked over at Mina, adding, "It's in my rooms at the bishop's home in London, where you'll find the remainder of the treasure under the bed, wrapped in old canvas." He gave her a lopsided grin that made him look so much younger, more innocent. "I enjoyed sleeping over so much wealth! And once I had control of the money, I decided to simply wait."

"Wait for what?"

"Initially, for Godfrey to die. Then I would have presented myself as the next male heir. But as we know, the old man refused to die, even with a little nudging. But then by chance, I encountered a man who supported the empress. This was while Stephen was imprisoned last winter, and it seemed the empress would get the crown. So I decided to play a slightly more dangerous game, but one that would have a much better reward.

"But Mina proved rather too…capable when it came to keeping Trumwell going. I thought she'd come to me for help much sooner. But she didn't, not until the king himself decided she ought to be married. That was *not* in my plans."

Luc said, "So you returned to Trumwell when you

heard of the marriage."

Joscelin nodded. "I knew I'd see some opportunity. There has never been a problem I couldn't think my way out of. Of course, once Mina took it upon herself to flee, I had to track her down....all very messy." Joscelin sighed. "No wonder most men just use swords to solve their problems. Sometimes I wonder if God hated me from birth, and that's why I'm so weak."

"Your weakness has more to do with the Devil than God," Mina said. "Don't ask for pity. Everything you did was because of greed."

"Perhaps." Joscelin looked at her steadily. "So how does that make me different from you, cousin, so intent on keeping your castle to yourself? Or your husband, who married you for distinctly selfish reasons?"

"Shut your mouth," Luc said, his voice hot.

Joscelin grinned. "Soon enough. But first tell me, what are your plans for me now?"

Chapter 35

STUNNED BY JOSCELIN'S CRUEL WORDS, Mina was barely listening when Luc started discussing his plans for her cousin.

"You'll stand before the king and tell him all you know," Luc spat. "If you've knowledge of the enemy's plans, he may allow you to live."

"Then you'll waste the king's time. I assure you I'm not so high in the empress's regard."

"That's for Stephen to decide. My duty is to take you to him."

Joscelin shook his head. "As you wish. I am sick of all this talk. It dries me out." Then Joscelin looked up at his cousin. "Give me something to drink, Mina."

"After all this, you want me to serve you?"

"Even a prisoner can beg, can't he?" Joscelin looked so young and so pitiful that Mina sighed.

"Very well."

Luc kept a cold eye on Joscelin while Mina ordered a maid to fetch a jug of ale and some glasses. She was thirsty herself, and it would do no good to starve him.

She poured the ale into glasses, watching her cousin as she did. Joscelin was fiddling with his crucifix, turning the metal cross over and over on its black leather cord.

"You should be ashamed to wear that," she told him, "and ashamed to pretend such piety."

He took the glass she offered. "I'll soon wear other accoutrements entirely," he noted, with a dark laugh.

Drugo waved off her offer of a glass. She sighed and moved to Luc, handing him a glass as well. "Drink. You deserve it."

"You should too," Luc said. "You've been through a lot today, and you look pale."

Mina got a glass for herself and took a long sip of clear ale. It did help, and she felt better after. She refilled Luc's glass before he even asked.

"Joscelin? Would you like more?" The courtesy came naturally to her, even after all that happened.

"I have enough, cos," he said from where he sat.

She put down the pitcher again, then turned back to Luc. She couldn't bear to look upon Joscelin for more than a second or two.

"Luc, after you've taken him to the king—"

"He won't," Joscelin said.

Mina looked at her cousin. "Don't try to convince us otherwise, Joscelin! You think your clever words will work now?"

"No. They don't have to." Joscelin put down the glass, and then pulled off his crucifix. He held it out to her. "Take it, cos. I'm done with it. As you say, I should not wear it."

Mina took a step forward, but Luc stopped her. "I'll take it."

Joscelin laughed, coughing at the end of it. "So careful. I'm no threat to you now."

He coughed again, and then doubled over, his body convulsing.

"What is this trick?" Luc asked.

But Mina understood immediately. "He's taken something in his drink. Luc, he's poisoned himself!"

Luc rushed over to Joscelin, pulling him upright. "Did you? Tell me how to stop it!"

"You can't." Joscelin held the crucifix out again, his arm shaking now. "Always kept it handy, just in case. I'll not be dragged off to court like a whipped dog."

"Joscelin, this is wrong." Mina was at his feet a moment later, reaching for his hands. "I can save you. You can drink more to dilute the poison. Or throw it up. Something must—"

"Too late, Mina. It was too late when I took the first sip."

"Joscelin, how could you?"

"It was easy. I only had to picture my sister. And my parents. Now I'll see them agai—"

He coughed again, violently, and blood appeared on his lips.

"Oh, Lord. Luc, help me."

Luc put an arm around Joscelin's shoulders to keep him sitting, but nothing could be done to stop the progress of the poison. Joscelin coughed again and again, more weakly each time, but with more blood appearing.

He sagged, and Luc helped him lie on the floor.

Joscelin made a grabbing motion, and Mina caught his hand in her own.

He couldn't speak, but his eyes locked on her face. Such pain. Not just the pain of dying, but pain that he carried for years as misguided hate and resentment. His breath grew fast, shallow.

"Joscelin," she said. Perhaps she should tell him she forgave him, or that she loved him. But she couldn't say those words. Not now.

"Joscelin, be at peace," she whispered.

His mouth pulled into a grimace as a final convulsion ran through him. His hand tightened, then let go.

"Oh," Mina said. "Oh, Joscelin. What have you done?"

Luc pulled her up from the floor. "Come on, Mina. You shouldn't be near him."

"He killed himself!"

"I know, Mina. He killed *himself*. It wasn't your fault."

"But what can we do now?"

"About him? He can be buried in a potter's field. No church will have him."

"You needed his testimony. What will you tell the king?"

"I will tell the king what I heard," Drugo said. "He'll take my word."

"Good," Luc said. "I trust that the de Warewic name is clear in your mind."

Drugo nodded slowly, looking at Joscelin's body. "His work was more subtle than most, because he was working against his family as much as the king. But he's the only one to blame—he and his lackey Haldan, who is already disposed of." Drugo looked over to Mina. "You've nothing to fear in regards to your name. Though you understand that I'll tell the king of your deception around your father's health."

"I know," Mina said, her head high. "You may also

tell him that I regret doing so, and never intended to harm the king by concealing the truth."

"He'll likely be lenient, considering that Trumwell is still secure and there's no lasting harm done." Drugo shrugged. "I must go and write down all that's happened, so I remember the details when I speak to the king. Excuse me."

He walked out of the room, leaving Luc and Domina alone.

Mina swayed a bit on her feet, and Luc immediately announced he was taking her to the bedchamber. She led him there without another word, too tired and confused to argue.

The bedchamber was much smaller than the one they'd shared at Trumwell. Mina walked to the fireplace, putting her hand out to the flames.

"Did all that just happen?" she asked. "Or am I somehow having a nightmare?"

"It happened," Luc said. "I found you here. Joscelin confessed to his crimes. And he died by his own hand."

"Oh, Lord." She bent her head.

"I'm sorry you had to see him die, Mina," Luc said. "Despite what he ended up being, I know you loved him."

"I did. I still do, I think. He always acted like he should, even if that wasn't what was in his heart."

"If you like, we don't have to speak of it back home."

"Back home?" she echoed, still not entirely in command of herself.

"Trumwell. We must return to our home, Mina. You can't stay here."

"You call Trumwell our home."

"So it is."

"It's your home. You took it from me."

"It's ours, Mina. Yours and mine."

"But I heard what you told Drugo. You don't intend to keep me. You're going to have our marriage annulled. You want to become an earl. You are done with me."

"I am never done with you, Mina. Not until I die."

"Don't lie to me," she said. "I know why you married me."

"You don't know the half of it."

A tiny spark of hope kindled inside her. "Then perhaps it's time you tell me."

"May I hold you?"

"What?"

"Mina, more than anything, I need to hold you."

She stood stock still. Luc stepped to her, and reached for her. He moved slowly, as if she might fly away or vanish into a mist. But Mina couldn't move.

Then she was in Luc's arms, sobbing. Her emotions were so unpredictable of late, so intense and erratic. But she'd ached for Luc's embrace, and now that she was in it, she never wanted to be anywhere else.

After several minutes where neither spoke, Luc told her the whole story, in his own words. "The king heard of treachery, but not the specifics," he concluded. "The coin with the swan pointed to the de Warewic family. But beyond that, he wasn't sure. So he sent me to discover the truth."

"Then why the marriage, if you suspected treachery?"

Luc looked at Domina ruefully as he explained. "The king saw the marriage as a way to ensure control. I could marry you for the purpose of keeping control of the castle, for I'd be master. But that was not why I had your father sign the papers."

"Why, then?"

"After I saw the state your father was in, and I heard the story of how you acted as both lord and lady in an effort to maintain Trumwell in your family, I wanted to help you."

"By taking it all away from me," she said, though the words had no force behind them.

"By giving your rule my support. You're the lady of Trumwell, Mina. You always will be. I'll do everything to make sure that's true."

"You aimed to be an earl by marriage, and on the king's council before you died."

"I had many plans for my life and my family's future. Once I got to know you, those plans meant less and less, until I couldn't even remember why I dreamed them. I have married well, because I married you."

"Then why did you not *tell* me so?"

"I was afraid to reveal the truth, because if you knew how I came to Trumwell, you'd hate me for it, and I couldn't bear for you to hate me," he confessed. "You told me once how you trained your falcons, Mina. You said that if you kept your bird hungry, if you didn't show her love, you lose her. You said she would choose the sky. She'd fly from you and never return because you treated her ill.

"I've treated you ill, my Mina, and there's no excuse for it other than that I was afraid to lose you. If you had a chance to fly, you would. And you did…as soon as you learned the truth."

"I couldn't stand the thought of pretending all was well, especially when…" She broke off.

"When what?" he asked.

She couldn't tell him of the child, not yet. It was all too much, and one more revelation would drown her in tears. Having Luc so close also summoned another need.

"Enough talk," Mina said. She put her hands on him, drawing him down to her. He required no convincing, and seconds later he tumbled her to the bed.

Mina was gratified by his enthusiasm, but she gasped in shock when he merely grazed her breasts. "Gently," she hissed.

"That was too much?"

"I'm rather...tender." She was sure he'd notice how much her breasts had swelled already, or that she was as skittish as a cat.

But if he noticed anything, it was her hesitation. "Would you have me stop, love?"

"No! Just mind me."

"You've been through too much," he said, frowning. His touch gentled, becoming soothing rather than demanding.

Mina sighed. "I like that. Touch me like that."

He did, showering her with attention, until both of them were satisfied. Then they drifted off to sleep together almost in the same moment, Mina tucked in Luc's arms.

In the morning, Mina made it all the way to the breakfast tray brought up by Constance before the nausea seized her.

She lost the little breakfast she consumed in a chamber pot. "Dear Lord," she moaned. At some point this symptom had to end.

Luc, who she'd left slumbering in the bed, now heard her and rose.

"What's wrong?" he asked urgently. "Did you eat something? Drink something?"

"It's nothing."

"Nothing! When you watched your cursed cousin die from his favorite weapon? He might have arranged something before he was caught."

As he spoke, Luc was pulling her up from the floor, despite her moans.

"Stop it!" she cried. "I'll be sick again."

"We need a doctor."

"Luc."

"I'll send for—"

"Luc," she shouted. "Will you calm down! I'm not dying. The sickness will pass. It's quite common for women in my condition."

He stopped at last, as comprehension dawned. "Your…condition."

"I am with child," she confessed. "I only found out just before that irritating Drugo arrived…and we fought…"

Luc wrapped strong arms around her as if he intended to keep the whole world out. "Mina, Mina," he said, stunned. "Are you certain?"

"I am. Perhaps I shouldn't be, for I've no experience of it, but I know it's true. Every day, I feel my body change a little, and I know it's because of our child."

Luc took a breath, then another. "I don't know what to say."

"Just promise me that you'll look after us," she begged.

"Always." He kissed her once, then again and again. "I love you, my Mina."

"I love you. I've loved you for a while," she admitted. "Though I'm terrible at expressing it."

"I disagree. Many times you're wonderful at expressing it. But from this point, no more secrets. For both of us.

You trust me, and I trust you."

"To provide a good example for our child?" she asked.

"To be able to live together," he said. "For you're stuck with me, Mina. Forever."

"Oh," she said, with a little laugh. "I like that."

Chapter 36

THEY LINGERED A DAY MORE at Pencombe, then rode slowly back toward Trumwell Castle, a small entourage with horses and a few carts. The last cart bore a shrouded body in a wooden coffin. Mina wouldn't leave her cousin behind.

Luc showed intense concern for Domina's delicate condition—almost to the point of annoying her—though every time she might have grumbled or snapped at him, he leaned over to give her a kiss, and her pique dissolved in a wash of giddy joy.

Mina's reactions amused Constance, who hid her laughter poorly behind her hand.

"Oh, hush," Mina told her one time.

"I said nothing, my lady."

"I can hear you thinking, Constance. How one kiss from my husband tames me."

"One kiss?" Constance noted with an arch of her eyebrow. "Closer to one hundred, and that's just since sunrise."

"You think me foolish."

"I think you're in love."

"So I am, even if it makes me behave with all the brains of a newly-hatched chick."

"Well, some of that may have to do with the fact that you're breeding, my lady. But you need not fear. It's a delight to see you smile again. For so long, you've been burdened with a weight no one should have to bear alone. Now you have a lord who is pleased to carry it for you… you deserve the happiness you've found."

"Thank you, Constance." Mina felt tears spring to her eyes. "Oh, my. I can't stand how I laugh and cry in the same breath!"

"I think it will pass after a time. So will your morning sickness."

Mina gazed over at Luc. "Will he mind, do you think?" She put a hand on her belly, thinking of how her body would change so much.

Constance chuckled. "Ask him."

Domina didn't have a chance to ask on the road, and a few days later the walls of Trumwell Castle rose before her.

They passed into the main gate, riding alongside the pond, where the swans swam gracefully in the parts that weren't iced over.

Inside, everyone greeted her with relief and joy. Margery embraced both her and Constance like long lost sisters. Octavian bowed to Mina and told Luc that all was well in their absence. Even Ancel looked a bit teary. Ban actually ran to Constance, leaving no doubt about how he felt after all.

"Ah, it's good to see everyone here," Mina confided to Luc.

"That's what it means to be a good ruler. They love

you and know that you're the lady of the castle. They would have no other."

In the great hall, Mina stopped short on seeing Guinevere standing on her perch near the fire. "It's my falcon! How can she be here? Don't tell me she flew back on her own."

"No," Octavian said. "A young man came here two days ago. He found a falcon in the woods several miles away, and was able to capture it. He saw that it wore jesses, so he brought it here, the nearest place a noble lived, in hope of a reward. Wouldn't be the first time a falcon's escaped from its owner."

"Of course he shall have a reward," Mina said. "Oh, my lovely, you've come home after all."

Guinevere squawked softly, puffing her feathers as Mina spoke to her. Luc joined her.

"I'm glad to see her home," he murmured.

"It was a mistake to let her fly away," Mina said. "One I won't repeat."

"Nor I," Luc agreed, dipping his head to kiss Mina's cheek.

Over supper, Luc and Mina shared the news with Octavian and Ancel. However, no one else would know the extent of Joscelin's treachery. Even Drugo, who planned to return to London as soon as possible, swore it would remain secret.

"I'll tell only the king, and perhaps a few men who must know a detail or two," he said. "But to the world, the Swan will simply disappear. It will trouble our enemies and frighten those considering a similar path. That's all we can ask for."

"Well," said Octavian then. "Thank God he was never ordained. He would have been a terrible priest."

"I can never tell if you're joking or not," Mina said.

"There's no harm in finding humor in serious matters," Tav replied. "But I'm not really making light of it. Perhaps his end was brought about by Providence, for he would have disgraced the Church."

Luc took Mina up to their bedchamber as soon as it was reasonably polite to excuse themselves. That night they made love slowly, lazily. Mina never felt closer to him. "Enjoy me while you can, love," she murmured. "Soon enough I'll not be able to please you."

"You'll always please me, my Mina. You'll always be perfection, no matter what shape your body takes. You're going to be the most lovely mother. When will our child be born, do you think?"

"I'm not sure," she admitted. "I don't know enough to say when I conceived. He'll be born in late summer, perhaps."

"He?" Luc put a hand on her belly, giving her a quizzical smile. "What makes you so sure it's a he?"

"Or she. I don't know. The women all have guesses, but they keep contradicting each other!"

"I care not, so long as the child is healthy and you're healthy. I can't lose you."

"You will never lose me, darling."

* * * *

The next morning, Domina rose early, intending to visit her father. Now that she knew the true cause of his persistent malady, she had hope that he would survive…if it was not already too late.

Luc said, "I'll walk you there. I want to be there with you."

He escorted her to the chamber in the keep where her father now resided. Mina worried the whole way. If she lost her father after all that had happened…it wouldn't be fair.

"I wish to go first," she said.

"Of course." Luc released her.

When she arrived at the doorway of her father's room, she saw Beatrice smiling. "My lady!" the servant said. "How did you know? Your father has been asking after you."

"Mina," her father said. He was sitting up, though cushioned against a number of pillows. His gaze was clear and questioning. "Come here, child. I am quite concerned."

She sat on the edge of the bed. "Father, what's wrong?"

"Wrong? Well, I'm in bed in the middle of the day, to begin. They tell me I have been ill, and I think it must be true, for I've had strange dreams." His eyes flickered past her. "Who is this?"

Mina turned to see Luc in the doorway.

"I am Luc of Braecon," he said, striding forward. "We spoke once before, but you would not remember it."

"Father," Mina said hesitantly, "you have been ill…for a while. But I think that you will recover at last. I will tell you everything, but you must not strain yourself."

"What do you mean by a while?" Godfrey asked, watching Luc put one arm around Domina.

"Long enough for Domina to be married," Luc said.

"But not so long that you will miss meeting your first grandchild," Mina added with a smile.

Epilogue

THERE WERE MORE QUESTIONS, AND more explanations. Luc didn't mind any of it, because Mina was next to him every day. Octavian returned to London with Drugo, in case he'd be useful in providing details of what happened. Luc missed his friend's presence, but he knew without a doubt that he'd see Tav again.

Now that Joscelin was no longer able to feed him poison, Godfrey slowly recovered, though he seemed to have suffered some permanent damage and would never quite be the man he once was. Spring had arrived when Godfrey walked out of his chambers on his own feet, and by summer, life in Trumwell Castle was as lively as it had once been somber.

Domina, her belly now swelling gently under her breasts, still acted as chatelaine, and she was no less active as she moved through the castle, directing everyone from the steward to the scullions.

As spring advanced, Luc and Domina prepared to travel to Braecon. Luc wanted Mina to meet his whole family at last. He was sure they'd love her immediately—especially if Eva had anything to do with it—and they'd all be overjoyed to know that a child was already on the way.

Mina agreed to his proposal with a mild "Naturally, love." Her whole being seemed calmer now. She had her father and her fortune restored. The castle of Trumwell was in safe hands, and she smiled every time she put a hand on her belly. Luc loved to watch her, and he loved that she was his. He long ago gave up thinking that encountering her in a dark street in London was a coincidence. God did not send coincidences.

They left Trumwell on a fine spring morning. Along the road, they stopped at the manor of Cleobury, where Luc's good friend and brother in arms Alric now lived as the lord. He and his lady Cecily greeted them effusively.

Luc introduced Domina to them, and Cecily beamed at them both. "How content you both look," she said. Luc knew Cecily from when she was a little girl, and her primary goal in life seemed to be ensuring the happiness of others.

"You don't need to worry about me any longer," Luc assured her. "I have Mina."

Cecily smiled. "Mina, is it? Well, Mina. You must be tired from the road. Come for a walk in my garden. If that doesn't restore you, I have some mint tea that will do the trick." The two women walked off, Mina casting a glance over her shoulder at Luc as she went.

"Congratulations," Alric said. "I assume there's a story behind all this."

"More than you can guess," Luc told him. "I'll tell it all to you, but not till we're comfortable, for it's a long story."

"One filled with intrigue, I bet," Alric said. "You always had a nose for politics."

"I did," Luc admitted. "But less now than before."

"You don't intend to take your lady to live at the court, basking in the glory of the royal presence? That's what you always wanted growing up."

"I was an idiot."

Alric smiled wider. "I'm going to enjoy this story."

"Don't laugh too hard," Luc warned. "There's plenty of tragedy in it."

"It seems to have ended happily enough," his friend said, with a nod toward where the women had gone.

Luc shook his head. "It hasn't ended at all," he said. Indeed, he was looking forward to every moment of his life with Domina. That reminded him of something. "Alric, as the closest person I've got to a brother, I wish to ask you something."

"Anything."

"Will you come to Trumwell for the baptism? Will you be the child's godfather? And Cecily the godmother?"

"Gladly. If it's a boy, he'll need to be trained as a knight, and I'm better than you on the field," Alric teased his friend.

"Speaking of skill on the field, have you heard anything of Rafe?" Luc asked, referring to their mutual childhood friend, who'd disappeared from their lives in disturbing circumstances.

Alric sobered, then said, "I've been asking after him, but he seems to have vanished from all his old haunts. This past autumn, there were a few reports of a knight in black mail and black surcoat with a raven insignia. Rafe's symbol. This knight's been accepting challenges at tournaments and in other places. He fights so well he's not lost yet. At least, so the rumors say."

"Rafe simply gave up war and is earning his wealth by tourney?" Luc asked, incredulously.

"*If* it's him," Alric said. "It may not be him—this knight is reputed to give nearly all his spoils to the local churches."

"Certainly not Rafe, then." Rafe had never been known for his piety.

"He's also said to turn every woman's head," Alric added, with a knowing look.

"So it may be Rafe after all." Luc wasn't sure he could believe such a profound shift in behavior. But then he thought of Domina, and remembered how quickly he'd fallen for her, and how it upended all his expectations. "I suppose anything is possible."

"We won't know until we can find him and see for ourselves," Alric said. "I hope that day is sooner rather than later. Rafe was a friend to both of us for a much longer time than he spent as an enemy. I want to see him again, if only to tell him there's no need to run away."

"*If* that's what he's doing," Luc said. "Well, now that I've settled down, perhaps we'll both be able to look for him. Octavian will help too, I'm sure. He travels more than any of us—he may be the one to find Rafe."

Luc and Mina stayed a few days at Cleobury before pressing on toward Braecon. Just after they bid goodbye and were riding away, Mina said, "I feel as if I'm gaining family every time I meet someone you know. First Octavian. Then your sister Eva. Then your friends. I hadn't known what an isolated life I was living till I met you."

"You were happy growing up at Trumwell, though," Luc reminded her.

She looked thoughtful. "In a way, yes. But perhaps it was mostly because I didn't know any other life. I'll always love Trumwell, but it's not my life. I realize that a place can never hold my heart. Only another soul can."

"A soul?" he asked.

Mina smiled at him, and he fell in love with her all over again.

"Your soul, specifically," she said. "Wherever you are, that's my home."

He leaned over to kiss her. "I knew the moment I saw you that you were destined to play a role in my life, but I never guessed you'd become my life."

"Enjoy it," Mina breathed. "For we're bound. Forever."

ABOUT THE AUTHOR

Elizabeth Cole is a romance writer with a penchant for history. Her stories draw upon her deep affection for the British Isles, action movies, medieval fantasies, and even science fiction. She now lives in a small house in a big city with a cat, a snake, and a rather charming gentleman. When not writing, she is usually curled in a corner reading...or watching costume dramas or things that explode. And yes, she believes in love at first sight.